BLUE LEADER

BLUE LEADER

Walter Wager

ARBOR HOUSE NEW YORK

Library of Congress Catalog Card Number: 78-67778

ISBN: 0-87795-206-X

Manufactured in the United States of America

1. In accordance with NSC directive 7243 of 6 FEB 1979, BLUE LEADER (attached) is dedicated to James A. Bryans.
2. As per JCS 8411/2/b, all names and events in attached are fictitious to maintain security for personnel and operations associated with BLUE LEADER, Hacksaw Two and Clean Slate.
3. Special commendation will be placed in classified file of Edward Jablonski (M.O.S.: author), whose book titled FLYING FORTRESS (classification: Doubleday) provided valuable data for BLUE LEADER.
4. Contributions of current and former U. S. and foreign correspondents, narcotics and intelligence specialists in Washington, Hong Kong, Bangkok and Chiang Mai are to be acknowledged.
5. Personnel file of former Agency employee A. B. Gordon is to be sealed. Future access will be strictly limited on NEED TO KNOW basis.

by authority of:

Director of Central Intelligence

1

IT WAS COLD in the white-tiled room.

It always was in these grim places, she recalled.

She was a very attractive woman. The face looking down into the large metal drawer was tanned, beautiful, composed. The face looking up was pale, agonized and ready to decompose. The nineteen-year-old-boy had been dead for thirty-two hours, but it was still clear that he'd perished in awful animal pain. The horror was stark and tangible, and—though the chicly dressed woman was no stranger to terminal violence—she shivered.

"Stiffs bother you, lady?" the bulky detective beside her challenged.

Another macho moron.

"It's the temperature in here, lieutenant," she replied.

"If you can't stand the cold, get out of the morgue."

The woman with the almost perfect features of a model was beginning to find Lieutenant R. J. Fetler of the San Paloma P.D. irritating. She'd dealt with this type of oaf before. You had to run them over with a truck. There were a lot of men here in Southern California—and elsewhere—whom you had to run over with a truck or a Porsche. She drove these, and a dozen other motor vehicles, like a Grand Prix veteran, spoke five languages and was a crack shot with the .357 in her belly holster and other handguns. Skilled with automatic weapons and knives, she got $400 a day, and results. If she had to be pleasant, she could do that too.

"Lieutenant," she said nicely, *"please* tell me how he died so I can get out of your busy day."

"He died like a *dog*. Very pure heroin. Too pure—even for him.

Your boy was a junkie. Died in the gutter in his own filth, crawling like a mutt hit by a car."

"Where?" she asked, her voice as cool as the room.

"Patrol car found him on Castle Avenue. Nowadays we pick up the garbage the sanitation crews won't touch."

The idiot was trying to shock her.

"How long had he been an addict, lieutenant?"

"You a relative?"

"No, sir—I'm a private investigator. I showed you my license."

"You can *stick* your license, lady."

He slammed the metal drawer shut with a loud clang, strode to the nearby desk where he found matches. Standing in front of a NO SMOKING sign, he lit a dark Philippine cigar and blew the aroma right at her.

"Who's your client?"

"His uncle," she lied.

Fetler shrugged, started for the exit.

"Please, lieutenant, I really need your help."

"Balls."

He opened the door, turned to blow another blast of smoke that made her recoil.

"Lieutenant, I'm only trying to—"

"Do it somewhere else. You think I'm just a turkey, don't you? Well, I could tell you plenty. I could tell you the brand of smack this kid was shooting. Yeah, they sell it by brand names these days—like candy bars. I could even make a pretty fair guess about who sold him the stuff."

"Yes?"

"No. Screw off. Switch your fancy ass right out of here—now."

She could break his collarbone, or make the phone call. She chose, reminded herself that most California police were not like this animal and marched past Fetler down the corridor with the awareness that he was observing every curve and movement of her body.

It was warm in the street, and the sudden contrast of the seventy-six-degree temperature with the morgue's cold made her shiver again. She moved swiftly to the phone booth at the corner, scooped a handful of change from her purse and dialed the unlisted number in Sacramento—the private line. Three rings and eleven seconds later she heard the well-known voice.

"Jerry," she said, "its Alison. Can you talk?"

He joked about having told her never to call at the office, but then he listened and told her exactly what to do.

"In five minutes," she repeated. "Thanks, Jerry."

"Come on—I owe you one."

"No, you don't."

"You're right. I owe you *two*."

She glanced at her wristwatch, and slipped on sunglasses before stepping out into the midday glare. Quite automatically, she looked up and down the street as she'd been trained and she remembered a dead man who hadn't. She walked the half block back to her Porsche, fed the parking meter another quarter and plugged a gold-tipped Sobranie into an onyx cigarette holder. Seated on the right front fender, she smoked and ignored the scrutiny of men— and women—who passed by. The trick was to avoid eye contact. She studied shop windows, then looked skyward where a light plane circled slowly at 4,000 feet as the chief pilot of the San Paloma Flying School reassured the wife of an important—if often impotent —local banker that she was doing just fine.

The Apache flew into a cloud, and she checked her watch again. A man she'd been married to had given her this gold Omega, but now she was thinking about another man named Fetler. She slid off the fender, identified the sensation in her middle as one related to the lunch she hadn't had yet and walked slowly back to the police station. As she entered, she *knew* once more that there was something odd about this case and wondered what it was.

"You didn't have to do *that*," Fetler erupted after he'd carefully closed his office door.

Her half-smile reply was a work of high bitchery.

"Jesus Christ, lady, why didn't you tell me you were a friend of the governor? I thought you were just another pushy broad from Beverly Hills."

Maybe she *should* have broken his collarbone.

"Now . . . *right now*," she ordered, "tell me everything you know about the death of Timothy Hessey."

Opening the file folder on his desk, the beefy detective read and told her a great deal. The boy had been "doing" drugs since he was fifteen, concentrating on heroin for the past two years. It was Double Uoglobe brand that killed him; a narcotics cop named Galindez had found a piece of the red and blue label with the two lions in the dead boy's room. The dealer was very probably a bartender named

Marty Cooper, whom the police had known about for eight months but didn't have the manpower to get around to.

There was more—an addict girlfriend named Dolores and a mother who'd gone to a religious commune in the mountains three months earlier after recovering from her latest breakdown. The father had died nine years before in a fire, and must have left plenty of money, because the boy and his mother had lived well. Timothy Hessey had his own MG and a reputation as a lousy driver.

Alison listened, asked questions and took notes. It was almost two o'clock by the time she stood up to go. There was still something missing, though, and she was very hungry—and her other gut instincts were working too.

"Give me the cassette."

There was no doubt in her mind. This was the sort of creep who'd tape everything—covertly.

"What makes you think—"

"Give it to me."

He shrugged, faked a grin and handed her the cassette from the recorder in his desk drawer. Yes, she should have broken his collarbone.

"Don't get sore, just routine. Nothing personal. Hell, I'm not such a bad guy."

"I've killed better men," she replied truthfully, and slammed the door behind her.

2

THE HEAT and the glare oppressed her again as she walked to the phone booth on the corner. She checked Kaplan's number in her green suede address book, filled a hand with coins and reached forward to drop a quarter in the slot. Her hand stopped an inch away—just in time. In a town with cops such as Fetler, it was entirely possible that public phones near police headquarters were tapped. She could wait.

She climbed into the Porsche a minute later, drove four miles—very carefully—down the coastal highway to a neo-Tudor restaurant overlooking the Pacific. The beam-and-stucco front wasn't so bad, but the gilded domes and minarets added by a second owner pushing Indian food were an assault. A third management had tried fruits and nuts and barefoot waitresses who smiled a lot. The current proprietors were doing well with great burgers and fresh fruit salads, and the woman with the .357 ordered one of each before she made her way to the pay phone.

"Kaplan, Glass and Sherman," the switchboard operator sang with the cheerfulness that came from learning the problem was only a yeast infection and not a social disease.

"Mr. Kaplan, please. It's A. B. Gordon."

Paul Kaplan, who had (1) a Harvard law degree (2) a reputation as one of the best doubles and tax-shelter players in Bel Air and (3) a terrific British secretary whose shorthand was as impressive as her jugs, was on the line almost immediately.

"Hey, Babes, how'd it go?"

"Hey, Babes," she parodied, "it wasn't nice. The boy was a junkie and the local homicide cop was a son of a bitch."

"But you charmed him?"

5

"No, but it was very democratic. He didn't charm me either. Paul, did you know this kid was an addict?"

Kaplan took a few seconds to plan his strategy. He was known for his way with movie producers, network vice-presidents, rock stars, mad-dog agents and militant vegetarians. He could even deal with female novelists and IRS officials from broken homes.

"I didn't know anything, and I still don't," he replied. "Tell me what you found, please."

The "please" always got them . . . well, almost always.

"He died of an overdose. Very pure heroin and very messy—in the gutter."

"Jeezus Christ."

"Jeezus Christ," she agreed, and then she reported on the brand of dope and the pusher and the manpower problems of the San Paloma Police Department.

"Think it's true?"

"Probably. The town's so small that the cops, the court and the morgue are all in the same building. Paul, what the hell is this all about?"

"About $400 a day, from your end. Honest, I don't know much more than that, Babes. I got a call from a VIP lawyer in New York, and he asked me to get the best investigator in the state to dig into this. You're the best."

"Who is this kid?"

"I'll try to find out."

She could hear the lie in his voice.

"Give me your phone number," Kaplan said, "and I'll get back to you."

Maybe he was right.

Perhaps $400 a day was all it was about—just another case.

Not getting involved—*personally* involved—was one of her basic rules.

"Just mail the check," she answered abruptly and hung up before he could say anything more.

Six minutes later and some thirty-six hundred miles away, a tall thin man named Richardson shook his head and sighed.

"Düsseldorf again?" he complained.

"Please do what you're told," the black woman with the vaguely Caribbean accent urged.

"But we had it only ten days ago," the projectionist reminded.

"He's had it for thirty-four years."

It didn't pay to argue with Miss White. Richardson didn't know whether to believe the rumor she'd worked her way through the Columbia Business School by moonlighting as a topless dancer, but he was certain that she could get him fired from the best-paying job he'd ever had. One or two words to The Old Man would do it. Richardson opened the large metal cabinet, pulled the can of film from the rack.

"Miss White, I'd like to explain."

"Fast. He's on his way."

Richardson began stringing up the film on the machine, wondering how to tell her. He'd never been confident in dealing with this new breed of female executive, and he didn't want to make her any more irritated.

"Miss White, it's just . . . well . . . maybe it's none of my business . . . but every time I run Düsseldorf . . . well, dammit, he cries."

"I know."

Not another word was spoken in the screening room until The Old Man—who still swam forty pool lengths every morning—walked in two minutes later and dropped into one of the big chairs. She put out the lights, and Richardson started the film he knew too well. It was poor quality 16-millimeter and silent, standard U.S. Army Air Force combat footage.

The real stuff.

No pretty music.

No bombastic baritone narrator intoning about heroics or the marvels of air power.

No sound at all aside from the hum of the projector.

Four-engine bombers taxiing for takeoff, swooping off the runway in what seemed like an endless stream.

Armada airborne. Beautiful. Flying high in classic V formations, a whole skyful of once marvelous machines that now looked like primitive toys. In 1944 these were the heavies, Flying Fortresses to the public relations types but 17s to their crews.

The fighters arrived, P-51s. Long-range escort, but some times not long enough. This was one of those days. The little planes rode shotgun for almost four hundred fifty miles, then waggled their wings and peeled away. The bombers moved a little closer to each other like a wagon train bracing for a Sioux war party, as if men in the 17s sensed danger closing in around them.

The war was on five seconds later.

Puffs of smoke as the German antiaircraft batteries opened fire, and then a dizzying glimpse of three Messerschmitts coming in from the right.

"Bandits at two o'clock!"

The Old Man had called out suddenly in that tough, taut voice, and Richardson felt a tightness in his throat. He knew what was coming. In seconds more of Goering's ME-109s would flash down out of the sun. No one on earth—not even The Old Man—could stop it now.

The first wedge of fighters knifed through the bomber formation with machine guns and nose cannon blasting; the Americans hosed the attackers with .50-caliber bursts as they hurtled by. Smoke curled from the left wing of one of the 51s.

"Five o'clock high!"

Nine more Messerschmitts. Plummeting fast out of the solar glare.

It wasn't 1944 in that screening room anymore. It was now. Men were fighting for their lives. The war was right there. You could touch it. Richardson couldn't understand why or how, but it happened every time they reviewed and relived that raid on the armaments plants outside Düsseldorf. The battle raged, and The Old Man raged with it . . . "Tighten up the formation! Tighten up!"

The bombers drew together to build their walls of defensive fire, but the 109s attacked again and again as more Luftwaffe squadrons arrived. One damaged 17, then two more staggered out of the action. Two damaged Messerschmitts began to lose altitude, and a parachute blossomed as the pilot of another jumped for his life. Maimed men, and machines, tumbled now from the clear blue sky.

There were the targets, seventeen thousand feet below.

Blue Leader was flying the "point" plane as usual, and he took the armada in through the massed antiaircraft barrage and waves of fighters with the special cool that was his trademark. The bombs fell in near-perfect patterns. The blasts below and towering columns of black smoke signaled hits. Those bombardiers must have cheered and boasted—until the Messerschmitts came at them again in massed frenzy. Two dozen widows and some forty orphans were created in less than half a minute.

"Move 'em *out,*" The Old Man shouted.

Blue Leader seemed to have heard him as the whole American force swung sharply seventy degrees and raced off at top speed— 302 miles an hour, that was it then. The flak batteries clawed at the big Boeings as they moved away, and fire flickered abruptly at the tail of the bomber just behind Blue Leader.

Richardson sighed. He thought of closing his eyes, but he couldn't.

The Messerschmitts were joined by a squadron of the Focke-Wulfs, best of the Luftwaffe interceptors. The rear gunner in the B-17 with the burning tail was busy fighting the fire when two of the FWs charged the blind spot and killed him. Other German interceptors struck at the wounded plane, knocking out the left inboard engine.

The left wing was ablaze.

The woman had been able to control herself until now, but she began to swallow hard and blink to force back the tears. Richardson sat ten feet away, swearing silently in the blackness.

"Jump, Jeff . . . *jump,*" The Old Man was yelling at him.

No one parachuted from the burning Fortress.

No one ever had.

No one ever would.

The fire reached one of the wing tanks, and the wounded B-17 exploded. Chunks of metal and flesh, wires and pipes, radio tubes and bombsights and charred emergency rations and survival kits fell in a grisly rain. A ball of flame, an ugly smear of dark smoke, and they were all memories—it went that fast.

"Jeff! *Jeff.*"

There was no one to answer. The film ran on for another few minutes as the bomber formation smashed a path through the enemy fighters, shooting at least eight more out of the sky. But none of the three people in that screening room now paid any attention.

Richardson was crying.

Miss White was crying.

The Old Man was crying, just as he always did when they ran the film of that raid on Düsseldorf so many years ago. His grief tore at Richardson, and the projectionist wondered why he chose to relive this anguish.

Why couldn't The Old Man leave it alone?

3

THERE ARE—at least—3,005 odd and varied numbers people do in Beverly Hills and adjacent chunks of expensive real estate, and the private investigator with the model's face knew just about every damn one of them. Alison Gordon had coped with larcenous network accountants, gay blackmail rings, industrial spies, record pirates, pyromaniacs from good families, art forgers, stock swindlers, crooked computer experts, S-M clubs, fake gurus, nymphos, kleptos and all the other o's and most of the p's and q's. In her six years as a private investigator, she'd done just about everything except divorce cases and windows.

This, however, had never happened before.

No one had ever sent her $6,000 more than her bill, and the Hollywood-Beverly Hills-Malibu set never paid this swiftly. She should have suspected something when the messenger brought the check only two days after she had mailed the invoice to Kaplan. It wasn't a mistake or an accident. She looked at the check on her desk, swiveled to stare at the Saks store across Wilshire Boulevard and calculated.

Paul Kaplan was sending her a message.

What was it?

He expected her to telephone to ask. No way. Let him try his games on someone else. It was almost seven hours since the messenger left her office, and the lawyer would be getting itchy. Well, that was his problem. She didn't want to think about that dead boy anymore. Something about the Hessey case bothered her, and that was annoying because she didn't know why. She'd worked hard to build her defenses, so why should this foolish vulnerable addict have touched her? Just another junkie, she told herself again.

She lit a cigarette, ground it out after four puffs and glanced at the six-foot-tall grandfather clock in the corner. Mark's mother had given it to them as a wedding present. It was a family heirloom, eighty-three years old and still kept perfect time.

4:55 P.M.—the cocktail hour.

Time for drinks at the Polo Lounge, lovers' assignations slipped in before dinner, tennis matches with movers and shakers in Bel Air, phone calls to reserve tables at this year's "right" restaurant.

"Mr. Kaplan on two."

She picked up the red telephone.

"Hello, Paul," she said *very* casually.

"Hey, Babes, you free for a drink?"

He was still trying to maneuver her into raising the question of the check.

"I'm on my way out."

"Fast Tequila Sunrise at the Brown Derby? Just two blocks from you."

"I'm going to Brentano's."

"What for?" he asked with exaggerated good humor.

"To buy a *book.*"

Some people let out their tensions by purchasing shoes or shirts or the new LP of Joni Mitchell or Jean-Pierre Rampal. A. B. Gordon bought books, but she wasn't going to tell that to the lawyer.

"Great. Backbone of civilization. Man can't live on TV alone, right? Catch you there in fifteen minutes."

He hung up before she could refuse.

Good old Paul, still manipulating.

What the hell did he want?

She said "good-night" to her secretary, rode the elevator twelve floors down and crossed the street to scan the department store's windows. They offered little for her taste, and there wasn't anything exciting two blocks down at Bonwit's either. Pausing to let a pride of Mercedeses roll by, she crossed the street to the gracious old— and new—Beverly Wilshire Hotel. The senior section faces on Wilshire, but for those who need something flashier there's a more modern wing in the back with razzle-dazzle decor and furnishings contemporary enough for the trendiest British film director or Arab petrol pasha.

No rock stars.

The civilized gentleman who runs the place is so old-fashioned that he cannot abide destruction of the tasteful and costly furniture

11

—even by good-natured lads who'll pay for the damage. There may be more big deals made on the plug-in phones at the Beverly Hills Hotel or more conventions at the Hilton, but the Beverly Wilshire is—brazenly—more gracious. It even has a large and thriving bookstore—Brentano's.

A. B. Gordon walked in, ignored the glass cases of mediocre American Indian jewelry and turned left toward the hardcover books. The selection wasn't inclusive—not comparable perhaps to that at Hunter's a few blocks away up Rodeo—but a new Edna O'Brien novel she wanted was there. She reached between the stacks of *The Fig and Cashew Diet Cookbook* and *The Lord's Way to Better Skin and Teeth* to pluck out her choice. She wandered on past stacks of biographies of aged film stars who had total recall, no compunctions and lusty ghostwriters, paused to study a handsome book of John Marin prints.

"It's yours. Birthday present."

She turned to face Kaplan, an attractive curly-haired man of forty-three or forty-four who always wore the best blazers and loafers, button-down shirts to signal his Ivy League education, and discreetly cheerful ties.

"My birthday was four months ago."

"Better late than never."

He was determined to be charming. What else?

"Thank you, Paul."

"Babes, I'm one of your super-fans. You're *numero uno* in my book. Some job you did on that Hessey thing. *Very* fast."

"Do my best."

"You *are* the best, Babes. That's what I told the guy in New York."

Her eyes rambled back to the cashier near the door to the street, and she noticed the stiffness in the woman at the register and the brown-suited customer who faced her. They had trained A. B. Gordon to notice things.

"You know," Kaplan explained, "the fellow who wanted to find out about the Hessey kid."

"That's finished," she answered as she made up her mind.

Heist.

The man in brown must have a gun under the raincoat draped over his left arm.

"Not exactly, Babes. Let me put it this way. Six grand says it isn't."

She started strolling toward the cash register, and Kaplan walked with her.

"You got the check, right? That's a retainer. Down payment."

Her hand touched the revolver in her belly holster. No. The heavy slug from the .357 Magnum would cripple or kill, and that wasn't necessary. They'd taught her that too. She steered the lawyer around two plump women savoring the latest "definitive" text on the sexual practices of Atlantis, looked around for the stickup man's confederates and saw none.

"No thanks, Paul."

"Listen, it's no big deal. You've got the name of the pusher—that bartender. Just help the cops get the evidence to nail him. Think of that dead kid. Don't you want the bastard responsible to pay?"

"I'll send you the six."

They were almost at the cash register, and she saw the white-faced clerk shoving bills into a paper bag.

"*Wait* a minute," Kaplan protested.

"I haven't got time."

Without warning, she shoved the lawyer out of the way, drew the .357 as she stepped forward. The holdup man saw the movement, turned—too late. She hit him across the back of the skull with her weapon, then chopped his wrist twice. The man and his gun crashed to the floor. The cashier screamed once, fainted. A. B. Gordon kicked away the thief's tin-plated Saturday Night Special, returned her own gun to its holster as an assistant manager and two other employees ran up with a barrage of questions.

"Call the police," Alison Gordon instructed, "and get her some smelling salts. She isn't hurt, just fainted."

The holdup man moaned.

He had no idea how lucky he was.

Paul Kaplan stepped forward, quickly identified her as a licensed private investigator with a valid gun permit and suggested they call a security man from the hotel to guard the dazed man until the police arrived. It was at that point he noticed A. B. Gordon moving toward the exit to Wilshire Boulevard.

"*Hey.*"

She walked out, saw the leather-jacketed young brunette on the motorcycle. She wore the same tense look, and she flinched nervously as Alison approached her.

"They've grabbed your friend and the radio cars will be here in ninety seconds. Get lost."

The Honda roared away, and Kaplan joined Alison Gordon at the curb as she remembered another girl on a motorbike who'd tried to kill her with a bomb. Another time, another place—but she could still taste the coppery fear.

"That was some number."

"Jam it."

"What the hell are you sore about?"

"Games. Don't ever play games with me again."

The ice in her voice jolted him.

"What's wrong, Babes?"

"Don't send me cute messages or funny checks. I don't like wise guys. All clear?"

Coping with temperamental people of all sexes was one of Paul Kaplan's specialties. He knew just what to do.

"I'm sorry. I apologize. It was dumb. A real schmuck stunt. Please forgive."

The girl in the leather jacket couldn't have been more than two or three years older than Tim Hessey. They both still had their baby fat, she recalled.

Shit.

"Alison, I sort of . . . you might say I told him you'd . . . the hell with it. Here are your books. Enjoy."

The son of a bitch had paid for the O'Brien novel and the Marin prints too.

"That wasn't necessary, Paul . . . I'll do it."

She wasn't about to explain why.

She wasn't that clear about it herself.

"Terrific. You're sure?"

"Scout's honor, Paul. I'll nail your pusher," she said as the sirens sounded the imminent arrival of police cars.

"Thanks. Thanks a lot. You're a real pal, Babes."

"No, I'm not, but who cares?"

Kaplan laughed uneasily as she crossed the street, wondered why she'd changed her mind. He was too intelligent to think that his efforts had anything to do with it. Walking back toward the Bonwit's parking lot, where he'd left his convertible, he thought about what she'd said. She was a little crazy, but she was dead right about one thing. That man back East—the one who'd ordered the destruction of the pusher—wouldn't care a bit.

After all, he was only relaying orders.

4

THERE ARE MANY fine people of Mexican birth, including brain surgeons, novelists, archbishops, painters, educators, architects, political and social philosophers and Anthony Quinn. Dolores Camargo wasn't one of those distinguished contributors to contemporary civilization. There are also hard-working Mexican pharmacists, sea captains, irrigation experts, petroleum engineers, civil servants, farmers, bus drivers, mariachi players and taco testers. She wasn't one of those either.

She wasn't fine and she wasn't hard-working, and she was already half dead at the age of twenty. For classic reasons set forth in at least five Ph.D. and eleven masters dissertations on file at several progressive California universities, she was a drug addict and a whore —a victim of economic injustice, cultural disorientation and several generations of misery. Perhaps centuries of poor nutrition had something to do with it too, but in any case Dolores Camargo was a walking tragedy.

She had a pretty face, large lovely eyes, long black hair and enough street smarts to wear clothes that masked her thin heroin-ravaged body. Fortunately some men liked girls with boyish figures, and other such as Tim were attracted by her hunger for affection. He needed it, too, and they'd huddled together like kittens sharing body warmth for nearly a year. Everything had been all right as long as he'd given her himself and his heroin. Now he was dead and she'd used up the last of the white powder she'd stolen from his room, and she was out on the streets again these nights. She looked too worn to lure men in the daylight.

It was nearly half past four in the morning when she approached the cheap boardinghouse. She was tired. Only five johns—barely

15

enough to pay for tomorrow's dime bags. The room rent would have to wait. Everything would work out after she bought the smack from Marty, she told herself as she let herself into the shabbily furnished room that smelled of unwashed sheets and stale cigarette smoke.

They were waiting for her in the darkness.

Two men in suits—the kind cops wore.

She saw them as soon as she flicked on the light, and spun instantly to run. The third invader—the chunky one poised behind the door—stepped forward to block her exit. She opened her mouth to curse, and he hit her in the face.

Cops. They liked to punch-out hookers.

She staggered back halfway across the room, crashed into the plywood dresser. It didn't make sense. Three of them to bust a $15 hustler? She'd never seen them before, had no idea that they'd been following and photographing her for five days since they parked their trailer in the mobile home park just north of San Paloma. They'd put a bug in her room too, and she hadn't noticed that either. She'd never been very observant, and it was a full ten seconds before she saw her hypo and rubber tube on the bed table.

"We found your works, Dolores," the man who'd hit her announced in a hoarse voice. He'd been speaking this way since 1970, when somebody shot him through the throat in a suburb of Saigon.

She didn't know what to say.

The younger one seated on the edge of her bed suddenly raised his left foot, stamped hard.

"Cockroaches. Hookin' and shootin' up and keepin' your room like a goddam pigsty. You're a one-whore crime wave, honey."

"Three to five, easy—even if the judge is an old customer," the third detective with the mustache agreed.

"Unless you're nice," the puncher rasped.

She began to unbutton her blouse, but he shook his head.

"Nah, nah. We don't want your ass, Dolores. We want some co-op-er-ation. Play ball with us, and we'll forget the whole crime wave."

"I'll walk?"

"Any street you want. You can clap up the whole town, mu-cha-cha."

They didn't want sex and she had no cash, so what kind of co-op-er-ation could these cops have in mind?

"Can I sit down?"

The one with the mustache shook his head.

"We'll talk first." And his foot lashed out to kill another roach. There weren't many in San Paloma, except in this cheap section on the south side of town. She thought about telling them that the *cucarachas* weren't her fault, decided they wouldn't be interested. She was right.

"Talk about what?" she asked warily.

"Marty Cooper."

She winced as if she'd been struck again.

"Marty Cooper," the puncher echoed.

"Don' know no Marty Cooper. Can I sit down, man? My feets hurt." She tried her best schoolgirl-whore smile, failed.

"You're gonna hurt all over if you don't speak up about Marty."

"You can't knock me aroun', mistuh. I got rights. Yeah, I see TV. You gotta read me my rights."

"She's a hip chick." The one with the mustache shook his head. "Read her her rights, Bob."

"You got a right to keep your mouth shut because you're a dumbass junkie," the man whose name of course wasn't Bob said, "and you got a right to spend three days screaming on the floor in the slammer without a fix. You like cold turkey? It's yours."

"You also got a right to get so crazy with pain that you'll smash your head against the wall. It's in the Constitution," the third man volunteered.

She knew of another hooker who'd tried to make trouble for the pusher, and he'd cut her face. She didn't want to be scarred like that. Cold turkey would be terrible, but Cooper's switchblade was worse.

"You got the wrong girl. I never heard of this guy."

The three men exchanged glances, and the one with the mustache picked up a walkie-talkie from the floor beside his feet.

"Bob to Mary. Bob to Mary. Subject in custody. Refuses to cooperate . . . Right. On our way."

Where?

"Let's go, stupid."

The puncher put her works in a large plastic bag, and they led her out to the street. They walked her half a block to a gray Chevvy sedan, pushed her into the back seat. Two of the narcs climbed in on either side of her while the third joined a woman who sat at the wheel and without a word turned on the headlights, started the car, and drove west for two minutes. The silence was eerie.

"You feds?"

No answer.

"You don' look like San Paloma cops to me."

Nothing.

"Where we goin'?"

"San Diego," the woman at the wheel replied.

Dolores Camargo could see part of her face in the mirror. She looked beautiful, like a model or something. "San Diego? You're feds—D.E.A.," Dolores reasoned. "You didn't find no junk on me— not a gram. You can't hold me."

"We don't intend to, Dolores. We're going to let you suffer for three days, and then we're going to throw you right out of the country. You're an illegal immigrant."

"Puta."

"You're a little mixed up, Dolores. You're the whore," A. B. Gordon reminded her.

"You'll be back picking chili peppers in Sayula next week," the puncher predicted.

Madre de Dios. How did these people know about her hometown?

"And we're going to deport your ratty brother too. Little Pablo? The punk who works in that garage in Escondido? Out."

"He ain't done nothin', he's got a wife and two kids—"

"We'll boot 'em all out . . ."

They could do it. She'd heard of entire families being deported back to the grinding unemployment and hunger of Mexico. They'd starve. It was a nightmare. She began to shake.

"Unless you cooperate, Dolores," the woman at the wheel said in a surprisingly pleasant voice. "We've got nothing against you, Dolores. We want Cooper—"

The puncher caught her as she lunged for the door, pushed her back into the seat.

"That was crazy, Dolores," Alison Gordon said. "You could have killed yourself. We're doing forty. You want to die for some lousy pusher?"

Dolores began to cry, which signaled to Alison Gordon that it was over, Dolores would cooperate. She drove back to headquarters, patted the still-weeping girl as two of her men led Dolores Camargo into the trailer.

"We'll get him now, boss," the man with the raspy voice whispered.

"Set it up carefully, and let the local cops get all the credit for the

18

bust." She shook his hand, opened the door of the Porsche.

"What do we do with her when it's over?"

"Take her down to the de-tox center in San Diego. Maybe they can help her."

A. B. Gordon sighed as she put her key in the ignition. It was a goddam lie. The only thing she was sure of was that in three or four months Dolores Camargo would be back on the streets, peddling her body and shooting heroin bought from another pusher. The odds were that in a year or two she'd be as dead as Timothy Hessey, whoever he was. She thought about him as she drove north, wondered what was so special about him.

Perhaps Kaplan knew.

5

"I WAS JUST in the neighborhood."

"Don't be silly, Paul," the woman in the black bikini advised and added another handful of clay to the half-finished sculpture.

Even incomplete, the head was powerful and eye-catching—almost as arresting as A. B. Gordon herself. She noted the attorney's scrutiny for what it was, went on kneading.

"No idea you worked in your underwear, Babes, or I wouldn't have walked in on you like this. You ought to be more careful. Lots of burglaries in this part of Beverly Hills."

"Mr. Kaplan, meet Mr. Agajanian."

The lawyer turned to face a dark-skinned man in horn-rimmed glasses, a tan jumpsuit and sneakers—who was pointing some sort of automatic weapon at his navel.

"That's a Colt CAR-15. Throws a 5.56-millimeter slug," Alison explained.

"Wait a minute—"

"You set off two alarms on the way from the gate. Thanks, Andy."

The muzzle lowered some four inches, but Kaplan was still visibly troubled by the CAR-15, which he didn't see too often on the greens at Hillcrest Country Club.

"Hope I didn't intrude," the lawyer apologized nervously.

"Mr. Agajanian was going over my books. He's my accountant."

"I'd hate to meet your dentist . . . Say, could I ask for a Perrier?"

The accountant left the small studio to return to the main house and the ledger, and A. B. Gordon located a Carlsberg beer for herself and a Perrier for the attorney in the old refrigerator against the wall. Thinking about the sculpture and the alarms and the Armenian with the chopper, Kaplan realized that there was a good

20

deal he didn't know about this woman. He'd also never realized that she had such an extraordinary body, and for a moment he allowed himself to think . . . and changed his mind. "Thanks . . . hot day . . . honest, I was passing by . . . screening over at Ray Stark's in half an hour."

Stark had several fine Giacomettis in his backyard, she knew, and Paul Kaplan clearly had something on his mind. He always did. She sat back on a stool, drank cold beer and waited for him to do his number.

After a long sip of Perrier he began. "Wonder if you'd got some time. Need your help, Babes."

"I'm listening."

He mentioned a top TV star, reported that she was about to be involved in a rather gritty divorce and needed the services of a first-class private investigator—preferably a female who'd understand, empathize. It was all garbage. Kaplan was well aware that A. B. Gordon never handled divorces, and Alison Gordon knew that the TV star was still represented by the same shrewd, worldly counsel who guided Sinatra and several other major entertainment figures—not Kaplan.

What was the game? "Sorry, Paul, but I don't touch divorces."

Now he'd make his move.

"Can't blame you. Messy. Never mind. Hey, what's flying down in San Paloma?"

"The pusher goes to trial on Monday."

So it was still the Hessey thing.

"Good strong case?"

"Airtight. The Mexican girl set him up, and a local narco cop named Galindez made a perfect bust. Caught Cooper with eight ounces, told him he was under arrest. Cooper pulled a switchblade from his fancy boot and Galindez broke his wrist. Also kneed him in the crotch and shoved the muzzle of his .38 into Cooper's mouth."

"What'd he do next—set him on fire?"

"Sergeant Galindez read him his rights, naturally. I told you it was a perfect bust. That creep's going up before a tough judge, Paul. I figure Cooper's bought eight to ten."

"What about the guy who supplied Cooper?"

That caught her by surprise. "The wholesaler?"

"The super creep who kept Cooper and twenty or thirty other pushers in business," Kaplan said, voice rising. "The higher-up who sells kilo loads so the Dolores Camargos can go on dying by inches . . ."

She guessed what was coming, and it was crazy.

"Paul, the wholesaler doesn't mean a thing to me. I did my job, your check cleared and I don't like people shouting at me."

"You don't *care* about the wholesaler?"

"I don't, and don't you give me any pious routine about this 'merchant of death.' You don't care about him either, so put it right out on the table, dammit. Say it straight, or get out—now."

Kaplan sipped at his Perrier, cleared his throat. "*Someone* cares —a lot."

"Who?"

"Someone cares enough to spend whatever it costs—*whatever*— to punish that man. Right now I have in my pocket . . . a certified check . . . for $25,000."

It was crazy all right.

"Paul, this wholesaler—and we don't even know his name—is no baby. He's a pro, big league. Has an organization. Moves a couple of million worth of junk a year—"

"The twenty-five is a retainer, a down payment. You need more troops, special hardware, whatever—you got it. I can deliver another fifty grand in three days. Take the case. Please."

She shook her head angrily.

"Not for the money," Kaplan improvised, "for Dolores. For all the Doloreses—"

"Oh, shut up . . . you know, you're shameless," she told him. "You've got the scruples of a goddam werewolf. This is the cement shoes crowd . . . You really think you can con me into going against them with your hearts-and-flowers routine?"

"This is important. Trust me—"

"It cuts two ways, mister. You won't even tell me who Tim Hessey was."

"Don't know."

"Then ask that guy in New York. You know who he is, don't you?"

Kaplan glanced at his watch, hesitated.

"I want to talk to him myself," she announced. "No talk, no deal. You got *that*, Babes?"

The attorney put down his glass, took the check from his pocket. She waved it away.

"Good-bye, Paul."

That was 4:50 P.M. on Saturday. When she returned to her office after lunch on Monday, her secretary reported Paul Kaplan had left the phone number of a Mr. Knowlton. The area code was 212—New York City. She dialed immediately.

"Knowlton."

Cool cultivated voice, Ivy League.

"Gordon. Paul Kaplan give you my message?"

"Yes."

Controlled, noncommittal, impersonal.

"I'm listening."

Knowlton chose his words carefully, enunciated each one clearly. "I know nothing about the boy. We are a very large law firm, and we represent several of the biggest corporations and financial institutions in the world. A major client asked us to retain private investigators to look into this matter, and Kaplan recommended you. I gather you're doing a good job."

He sounded as if he'd rehearsed it.

"What client?"

"A client of unquestionable integrity and financial stability."

"What's the connection with the boy?"

"The client didn't say. Wish I could tell you more."

"So do I," she replied, and slammed down the phone.

She called a man named Frohlich, exchanged greetings and asked him to check out the number Paul Kaplan had provided. No problem. Frohlich owed her a favor and he worked in security for New York Telephone. Knowlton, Parks, Winston and Jacobson—Wall Street law firm. She thanked Frohlich and sent regards to his wife, then walked across the hall to the office of Feist and Shulman—two courtly counselors who had great tailors and a wonderful way with malpractice suits. It was in their library that she consulted the Martindale-Hubbell volume listing major law firms and their most important clients:

Pan American Airways.

Consolidated Chemicals.

The Seagram liquor companies.

Chemical Bank.

The CBS Television Network.

The Iranian embassy and United Nations mission.

Atlas Industries Ltd., the de Beers diamond syndicate and Remington Arms.

All were clients of the 105-lawyer firm whose senior partner was

Winthrop Knowlton, a former assistant secretary of state and president of the class of 1940 at Yale.

Checking the 1977 *Who's Who in America* told her a good deal more about Mr. Knowlton, his honorary degrees, clubs, books, wives and homes. It gave no clue as to who was so grimly committed to avenging Timothy Hessey, or why.

She'd have to find that out for herself.

IT ALL HAPPENED so quickly.

One minute Martin Cooper was standing at a urinal in the toilet of San Paloma's best steak house, and the next he caught a faceful of Mace and a karate chop that hurled him into blackness. When he came to he was blindfolded and naked. Nylon fishing line that cut his neck, wrists and ankles bound him tightly to a heavy chair. His eyes burned, his head hurt and he felt his heart pounding wildly.

"Pay attention, Marty," somebody ordered in a raspy voice, emphasizing the point by throwing a pail of ice water. The freezing impact made Cooper scream.

"He's paying attention now," somebody else said.

"Who are you . . . ?"

"Western Union. We got a message for you. Old joke, Marty, but don't laugh yet."

Somebody explained that they knew he bought from Fat John because the lawyer who took care of all Fat John's pushers was representing him, and somebody else announced that they wanted to find out how Fat John operated because they intended to help the wholesaler modernize his methods. After he stopped denying any connection with the wholesaler, Marty told them that anyone stupid enough to sell out John to another mob would be hit—inside prison or out.

Somebody else assured Cooper that they were nicer than Fat John. *They* wouldn't kill him if he was uncooperative—just leave him deaf and blind. Assuring the pusher that he'd "look good with a white stick," somebody suggested that they might also douse his legs in gasoline and drop a match, but, if he "helped," their friends in San Francisco had "connections" that could *probably* get him

25

paroled in three or four years. The maiming they could guarantee. They also promised Fat John would never know who had done it to him. There was a scent like perfume in the room, and for a moment Marty wondered whether any of these people were homosexual, though he surely had no prejudice against the gay community, which included several of his customers. It was police and sociologists he couldn't stand.

When the conversation focused down on whether they should apply their propane torch first to his right eye or to his left . . . when he felt the heat from the gas burner, smelled the scorching of the hair at his temple, he finally saw how fair and reasonable their proposal was. Whatever their sexual preferences or views on punk rock or the CIA, at least they weren't cops and maybe they would take over John's narcotics traffic. The chill presence of a gun muzzle against his stomach reminded Marty Cooper that Fat John had treated him arrogantly and unfairly several times. Indignant, inspired by terror, he began to recite names, contacts, drops, signals and methods into the Uher tape recorder he couldn't see. . . .

Even with all that information, the California State Police took five months to build a solid case against Fat John and his top associates. The narcotics agents worked hard and used every shred of a clue Alison Gordon gave them, but John had been a cunning, cautious pro for some twenty-five years. Key to his being the second biggest wholesaler south of Los Angeles was his strict security rules. Only one or two very slight slips by subordinates and a couple of wiretaps led to the indictment.

The state police's "series of lightning raids in six Southern California cities" wasn't bad and it did make the TV news shows, but only the *local*. (When it comes to a "series of lightning raids," it's the feds, the often-maligned U.S. Drug Enforcement Administration, who regularly hit the *network* news. Practice and timing are important, and physical activity is a must. Only a fool or an amateur would simply arrest "a major offender" as he steps out of a restaurant after dinner. The feds burst in at dawn, giving them a clean shot at the morning news as well as the six and eleven P.M. productions— consult your local paper for exact times.

Five hours after he was arrested, the wholesaler was free on $400,000 bail.

Three days later, the headless torso of a man—Caucasian, medium build and castrated—was found in a plastic trash bag on a road in Palomar Mountain State Park, ninety miles from San Paloma.

Local authorities first thought that this was another in the series of grisly murders being committed by "the Garbage Man," a catchy nickname fastened on the psychotic assassin by an imaginative journalist. The Garbage Man had trashed eleven victims during the previous twenty months, and since they were all male the theory was that the motive was sexual. This theory collapsed when the FBI identified the decedent's fingerprints as those of Russ (The Hammer) Charap, an antisocial individual with a yard long record of assaults and a known associate of Fat John Reno. It was on the morning this news arrived that a tall and very sincere Buddhist monk—who'd abandoned a thriving eyeglass store and the name Koenigsberg to find true peace—discovered most of the parts of another male—black, muscular and also lacking genitalia—while hiking to a sunrise service near Del Mar. When the head was found in a Kentucky Fried Chicken bucket, the Bureau of Criminal Investigation in Sacramento used dental X rays to ascertain that these pieces had been Junior Wood, a Nashville car thief who'd recently been the driver for Reno.

Only a few people outside the dope world understood.

A. B. Gordon was one of them, and she called Paul Kaplan to share it with him.

"What's this got to do with me, Babes?" he asked cheerily.

"You and your friend Knowlton paid for it. Fat John's cleaning house—just like Lepke did more than thirty years ago. He's wiping out people who may have betrayed him, or who might be muscled into testifying. He may kill more. The joke is none of these men had anything to do with the bust. He's murdering his stand-up guys. Funny, huh?"

"Hey, you can't blame me for this. The Hessey case is closed so let's forget the whole thing."

"Tell that to Fat John. He's facing fifteen in the slammer and he'll kill a hundred more to stay outside. You'd better let Mr. Knowlton know we may be up to our hips in hacked-up bodies. Is Knowlton a jigsaw expert? We may need him."

"Knowlton happens to be a very decent man, dammit. As a matter of fact, he's a vice-president of the American Civil Liberties Union."

"Perfect," she replied bitterly. "Maybe he can now defend Fat John. Personally, I hope the bastard gets five hundred years in solitary and nine kinds of cancer—"

"Lou Grade's on the horn from London," Kaplan lied. "You sound beat. Take a few days in the sun. 'Bye."

It wasn't such a bad idea. Might get the taste of good-guy liberals like Knowlton out of her craw.

She flew down to Puerto Vallarta to rethink and recharge, to relax as a private person at the civilized Posada Vallarta, where the pool was good and the drinks perfect. After evading the advances of two American advertising men and a German woman, she spent three fine days and nights with an amiable and much-traveled British Airways executive who, she thought, was probably a spy. She didn't care. They went on to Mexico City to enjoy the extraordinary anthropological museum, and it was there—staring at a magnificent Mayan carving—that she realized who Tim Hessey looked like. It was Mark, especially in the lower face and chin.

They had one other thing in common.

Both had died violently, long before their time.

7

WHEN SHE RETURNED to Beverly Hills she got involved with Tom, Dick and Barry.

Tom Wilson—the house goy at the William Morris Agency—wanted her to find the wife of the lead guitarist of PND. PND—nobody called the hot rock group by its full name of Post Nasal Drip—was booked to start a nine-city tour, and the lead guitar player wouldn't budge without his spouse. Gillian—a winsome lass with a family in Kent and a really terrific mantra that the whole Malibu crowd envied—had split.

Again.

Help? Please? Big bonus? Fast? There was also a TV special to be taped on the 17th, and on the 23rd PND had a good shot to win a Grammy Award. Oh yes, Gillian was blond, wore seventeenth-century prayer beads from Bengal and drove badly even when she wasn't high. She liked pizzas, Charlie Chaplin movies and men twenty-five or thirty years older than she was. A. B. Gordon found her up near Monterey, working her way through the Kama Sutra with a fifty-nine-year-old garage mechanic whose apartment was next door to a Pizza King franchise. The concert tour was a fabulous success, with at least a score of hospital cases after every performance. PND didn't get the Grammy, but the *Rolling Stone* cover moved more than a hundred and ten thousand LPs. . . .

Dick Horner was the assistant to the head honcho at Warner Brothers, a position which guaranteed him $85,000 a year and most of the mess. Dick had done business with A. B. Gordon before, and he had never groped her body or argued about the fee. Two reels of negative—reflecting about a million-three—had been stolen from a vault at the studio. The picture was scheduled for June release, and everyone knew "what bastards those exhibitors are." Not only couldn't the two reels be reshot because darling Barbra had other commitments, but some anonymous ghoul was offering to return them for one hundred big ones.

Could she?

Would she?

Very quietly, as usual?

It wasn't the butler. (California butlers don't have to steal, not with wages what they are in Bel Air.) Outraged by what she declared the "trashy sexist" covers on some albums put out by a Warner Communications record label, a film editor had filched the negative to raise money for the crusade against "chauvinist oppression." Considered talented, if disturbed and rather confused about the feminist movement, she was forgiven by the folks at Warners, who even contributed a tax-deductible $2,500 for her therapy.

. . .

Barry Fagan of Modern Systems wanted to find out whether somebody was bugging his offices and—if so—why. The best private investigator on the West Coast sent in a former U.S. government employee who knew about such technical routines, and he discovered that Modern Systems had been wired "to the sky." The listeners were being paid by the head of a rival firm, Contemporary Electronics. Contemporary was doing this to find out whether Modern was bugging *it.* Learning this, Mr. Fagan tried to hire Gordon Investigations for just such an assignment. He failed. . . .

During the seven weeks following her trip to Mexico, A. B. Gordon went to four concerts and a dance recital, made $3,855 on a stock market tip, sold a small sculpture to a producer at Universal and turned down an interview request from *People* magazine. She also read the report her assistant had prepared on Timothy Hessey. His father had been a brilliant architect named David MacArthur Hessey, and his mother was a Jean Sorensen. A neighbor in San Paloma thought the mother might have spent some time earlier in Virginia. The boy had been an outstanding student until his father's death. According to the obituary in the *Herald,* the father was a Dartmouth graduate and son of a Chicago advertising executive.

No answers here.

Not even any good questions—thank God.

"Want me to dig further?" the man with the raspy voice asked.

She hesitated—just a moment—shook her head.

"We've got other things to do. How're you coming on the Mengers case?"

"Looks like it's her shrink. The typewriters match exactly."

"Her *analyst* is sending those death threats? Why?"

"I think she's driving him crazy. Show you the file tomorrow."

On the day after next something freaky happened. Even though it was clearly in the "man bites dog" department, the story wasn't carried in either of Los Angeles' dailies or on any news broadcast. A prominent local psychotherapist cracked up and assaulted an even more prominent patient with a bottle of '71 Pomerol and homicidal intentions. Aside from a blind item in a *Hollywood Reporter* column, it was hushed up entirely. Several hostile jests coursed around the chic parties, at one of which Alison Gordon found herself facing Paul Kaplan.

"What a peachy surprise," he said.

"New blazer, Paul? *Nice.*"

"Man does not live by contracts alone. Friend of the groom?"

"The bride. We were in a college drama group—long ago."

"One of the best screenwriters in town, and my *newest* client. I was going to call you, Babes."

She finished her champagne, took another glass from a passing waiter who was working his way through ballet school.

"My phone's out of order. Call next month."

"It won't take a month to get your phone fixed."

She patted his shoulder. "Nice—the silver buttons are just right. Gold would have been pushy."

"What?"

She sipped half the champagne.

"Six weeks'll be better."

He telephoned the next day; she didn't call back.

And the next day and the next and the next.

He called her at home on the weekend, and she told him— truthfully—that she was busy with a new sculpture. Then Mr. Knowlton phoned from New York on each of the first three days of the workweek, and she didn't speak to him either. She was getting angry. *That* dream—the one she'd been free of for more than a year and a half—was back haunting her sleep. On Friday, just before lunch, the Buddha arrived.

A sixteenth-century Thai wonder, two feet high. The real thing —$3,000 or $4,000 at least.

How did he know? How the *hell* did he know?

It was Kaplan. She realized that before she found the note with two words: "Please? Paul."

She dialed his office number. "I'm sending it back," she said as soon as she heard his voice.

"Don't do that. It's yours . . . no matter what. You appreciate it, and you've earned it. If you never see me again, keep it."

The man was impossible, and the Buddha was so beautiful.

"You're terrible, truly terrible . . . What do you want from me, Paul?"

"Fifteen minutes—11:30 to 11:45 tomorrow morning. I give you my word. That'll be the end of it."

He arrived precisely at 11:30 the next day, waggled a finger at her. "I looked up that CAR-15 your man had. That's an Army *submachine gun* . . . they used them in Viet Nam."

"Thanks for the Buddha, Paul. Who told you?"

"Our friend—the screenwriter. She said you collect Oriental art. I see she's right," he said, gesturing to the wooden Ramayana and Cambodian ceramics across the dining room.

She drained her coffee cup, waited.

"Okay, Babes. Knowlton said to raise the ante. Hundred grand bonus. I told him money wouldn't do it."

"Do *what?*"

"This is big, very big. I said you weren't for sale."

She relit the dark cigarette. "That was sweet of you, Paul."

"Not sweet, realistic. I'm not going to horse you around anymore, Babes. Ain't got the time. I told him you might do it because you like to finish what you start. You're that kind of woman—"

"What kind?"

"Stubborn, proud—what the hell, *arrogant,* and full of a morality you don't talk about. That's you, Babes, like it or not."

It was all obvious manipulation, but she still couldn't totally resist it. "Forget the psychology, Paul. What is it?"

"The *importer*—the guy who brings this brand of junk in from the Far East. As I said, very big."

"You're insane."

"You did pretty well with the pusher and the wholesaler."

"Different ball game. Turning Cooper wasn't too difficult, but nobody's going to turn Fat John. He's got *his* morality. *Omertá*—code of silence. He'll spit in your eye and do fifteen years standing on his head, and he *won't* talk."

"Try something. Try anything."

"Why don't I just kill him?"

"Don't get crazy, Babes. I never said that. Look, you'd be doing a great public service—for the whole community. Go do your number with Fat John. He's out on bail. Work on him."

"Paul, I'll spell it out. This importer isn't just big. He's also bad. King Kong, Hitler, Idi Amin, Stalin and the Boston Strangler all wrapped up in one. This guy makes your crooked studio tycoons and corkscrew agents look like choirboys. I'm no expert on the dope business, but this character has to be somebody even the feds—with all their manpower—haven't been able to nail—"

"Try womanpower. Try yoga. Try prayer. Gospel songs, Canadian Air Forces exercises—whatever it takes. You can work with the feds if you like."

"What if they don't like?"

"They'll like. We can handle that . . . can I bum a cigarette?"

She walked across the room to the teak table, opened the top drawer and saw the photo—right next to the black box of Sobranies. She'd put the picture away three years earlier when she'd decided that she couldn't mourn anymore, and now she wondered what it was doing in this drawer. She didn't remember putting it here. She stared at the face, and wondered whether the apparent resemblance to that of the dead addict was real. Perhaps she was imagining it . . .

She took out the cigarettes, closed the drawer and returned to her chair by the picture window to study the swimming pool outside. After a few moments she put the box on the table near Kaplan.

"Something wrong?" he asked.

"Who knows? Listen, I can't imagine why you people think I can set up a man so big and so careful even the feds couldn't get him."

"You're more creative. I'm not buttering you up, Babes. You're trickier, slicker and—maybe—just a bit less scrupulous."

"From you, that's a compliment."

"It was meant to be. Come on, give it a try. It'll be the biggest operation you ever pulled off—"

She shook her head.

"For Chrissakes what the hell have you got to lose?"

"Lives. My people trust me, and I'm responsible to their wives and husbands and kids. This isn't a make-believe in some studio, Paul. If somebody gets a bullet or an ice pick, it's real blood and they're real dead."

"Right, you're playing hard ball. I sure don't want to know what you're doing. If the bar association asks, I can truthfully say I had no idea. You do whatever you have to do. *What-ever.* Don't tell me. Do it."

She got up, walked toward the teak table—stopped.

"It could take a year, Paul."

"Okay."

"Maybe two or three hundred thousand in fees—not counting any bonus."

"You got it. We'll throw in ten thousand more to buy extra insurance for your people."

"Will you come to the funerals?"

"Will you take the goddam case?"

She looked at the beautifully carved wooden archer that Mark had bought her in that steamy shop in in Chiang Mai. They'd found it in a back room, forgotten and covered with cobwebs. Weathered gray wood—the clerk hadn't understood why they didn't want the "new" model instead. Eight years ago.

God, she was tired of being alone.

"Well, Babes?"

"I've got nothing better to do," she said in a soft voice that didn't quite mask the bitterness.

Four days later she talked with a man named Bonomi, who commanded all the West Coast offices of the Drug Enforcement Administration. He was broad-chested, bright and working hard at hiding his lack of enthusiasm for cooperating with a female private detective. She guessed that the order had come from the head of D.E.A. in Washington. Knowlton would have that kind of top-level connection. He probably played bridge with cabinet members and sailed with the chairman of the National Committee. She did her best to reassure Bonomi that her people would merely try to help with "preliminary investigation," and that the important work and conclusion of the case would—of course—rest with the federal experts. Bonomi pretended to believe her. They both agreed that the entire operation was a *very* long shot, promised to keep "in touch."

The next day—while he was waiting in a line for dinner—Martin Cooper was stabbed to death in San Quentin Prison. Neither the weapon nor the assassin was ever found.

Fat John wouldn't talk.

The prosecuting attorney offered him a deal, which the obese wholesaler politely declined. Some men in his position might have laughed vulgarly or been defiantly abusive, but Fat John merely smiled and modestly pointed out that he couldn't help because he knew nothing about dope. He didn't even smoke grass. The indictment was an unfortunate mistake, as three of the most expensive criminal lawyers in the state would soon make clear.

No hard feelings.

Justice would surely prevail, for this was America.

Fat John wouldn't talk.

Maybe someone else would. Alison Gordon studied profiles on nine co-conspirators indicted with him, deployed nineteen operatives to focus on four who seemed possible. Phones were tapped, bugs were installed and people were followed. Pretty women were sent to cultivate those of John's henchmen who liked female company, and males to those who preferred men. A number of laws of God and the state of California were broken.

Results after five weeks—zero.

Results after a dozen weeks—zero.

Then it happened—sixteen days before the trial was to start. An operative following "Cue Ball" Carlson reported that the bald heroin packager had used a handful of change to call from a pay phone at Third and Cleary. The number dialed proved to be that of a charter pilot ninety miles north, and that man and his aircraft were under surveillance two and a half hours later. Watchers were stationed at San Paloma's airfields, the one used by the flying school and private pilots and the other strip south of town which had served a now defunct cargo service.

When Carlson arrived at that strip Friday night he saw the wing lights of the descending charter plane and he smiled. He stopped smiling when Alison Gordon pushed the gun muzzle into his back.

"Don't move. Just listen."

"I'm listening, lady."

"I've got three choices. Help me decide, Cue Ball."

The plane was down to five hundred feet, and the lady sounded mean. "Whatever you say."

Who the hell was she?

"You're jumping bail. Mexico, I presume. Don't argue. I can shoot you at point-blank range and get a medal for being a good citizen."

"Lady—"

"Shut up. If I don't kill you I can bring you in and you'll buy a couple of extra years for trying to jump."

She paused to let him consider, and sweat.

"What's the third?" he asked cautiously.

"You answer two little questions and fly like a bird. You'll be in Baja across the border in less than an hour, and no one will ever know you talked to some woman with no name and no face in the middle of the night."

"What questions?"

"Who supplies Fat John, and where does he live?"

The man groaned, the woman threatened, the man cursed, the woman reasoned, then let him hear the click of the safety catch on her gun being released. The logic in that sound was compelling, the plane was on the ground taxiing toward them.

"Carlson, this has nothing to do with John or his case. You won't be selling him. You'll be buying *your* way out, and John won't be hurt at all. Here's your only chance . . . your last chance."

"Kill him." A man's raspy voice.

The aircraft was only a hundred and fifty yards away, and the bag with $193,000 in twenties was still in Carlson's sweaty hand. Jumping bail was ethical—almost routine—in the junk traffic, and John would surely accept it coolly. When the plane was thirty yards away, Cue Ball Carlson told the lady the name and Los Angeles address, and was airborne four minutes later . . . (Nine years later he was duly smitten by an avenging angel and perished in Acapulco's second best brothel. Some people said it was tainted shrimp, others knew it was worldly retribution.)

The name that A. B. Gordon took to the D.E.A. was one Bonomi recognized, but while he appreciated the address, he wasn't that optimistic. The importer was high on Washington's list of "major traffickers," and among the three most powerful figures in the California underworld. It was rumored that he was wired in to Syndicate families in Arizona, Nevada, Ohio and New York. He never wore black silk suits or paid any attention to Mario Puzo's birthday —and the word "Mafia" never touched his lips. He was known simply as Mr. C., a title inspired by the first letter of his family name. Federal investigators had made three big and costly efforts to collect significant, solid evidence of Mr. C.'s despicable criminal behavior—three tries in eleven years.

Zip.

Lions 56, Christians minus 7.

They hadn't even come close to getting this man, and there was no reason to believe that A. B. Gordon would do any better. Bonomi, somewhat reluctantly, showed her the federal files on Mr. C. and his associates. There were sixty-six folders, seven full drawers of papers, blurred photos, transcripts of wiretaps and autopsy reports. Twenty-nine deaths in eleven United States cities, Manila, Tokyo and Hong Kong were attributed to Mr. C's organization, not including the junkies, of course. Nobody bothered to count them.

"So he kills people—"

"Some he kills, some he buys. Customs inspectors, lawyers, judges, politicians, even two of our agents four years ago. We estimate he's worth ten million dollars, maybe more, hidden in a hundred accounts and fifty different companies here, in the Caribbean, Switzerland and the Far East."

"And the only way is to get someone inside his setup."

"Right. The last time we tried it our undercover man was beaten to death with a baseball bat. It was supposed to look like a car accident, but it was a baseball bat. Every bone in his body was well broken . . . this man assumes that all his phones are tapped and that he's under constant surveillance. He's an expert on our methods, our equipment. He may have people listening to *our* phones. Don't let me discourage you, though. Maybe your agent'll get lucky, or maybe Mr. C. will have a car accident of his own. Some kid flying on uppers could wipe him out on the throughway and save us all the trouble."

"I don't believe in lucky accidents," she replied, and returned to her office. . . .

She called the number in New York the next morning.

"Knowlton."

"A. B. Gordon."

"Yes?"

"It's going to be very difficult, maybe impossible."

"We have great confidence in you. Do your best."

"I'll have to hire someone for a very dangerous job, which won't be cheap."

"How much?"

He might have been talking about the price of tomatoes.

"Fifty—up front. Not for me, for him."

"Kaplan will have the funds tomorrow afternoon. Anything else?"

"Why don't you send me the money directly?"

"Good luck."

Click.

If anything went wrong, the respected Wall Street firm of Knowlton, Parks, Winston and Jacobson would have no written or documentary connection with it. If something went wrong, her undercover agent would be battered into a pulp or perhaps drowned in a toilet bowl like one of Mr. C.'s other victims. Alison Gordon hadn't liked the icy Mr. Knowlton from the start, and each contact with him reinforced the first impression.

It wasn't going to work.

She was almost certain of that as she explained it to a highly intelligent black man named Elroy Evans. Evans had an IQ of 140, fantastic street smarts, solid experience in dealing with large and violent organizations, and a need for $50,000. He would play it cool, take no chances, move slowly and carefully. At the first sign of danger, he must run. She set those ground rules very firmly. Evans gave her his word that he'd comply, and she gave him a first payment of $15,000. . . .

He started in St. Louis, flashing some money in a nightclub frequented by the most affluent pimps and dropping hints that he'd had some trouble with "bad cats" in Chicago. He bought some cocaine, picked up a few tabs for champagne and drove west in a maroon '78 Imperial three weeks later. He spent a month in Denver, purchasing first one ounce of medium quality heroin and then three of the better smack. He gambled for high stakes, won and lost and left the city some $9,000 lighter. He was, of course, building an identity.

When he reached Los Angeles, he spent his nights at a variety of nightclubs before he showed up at Othello's—a bar where one of Mr. C.'s distributors often browsed among the hookers and bookmakers. Elroy Evans was now Dude Willis, and he had the flash clothes to go with the name. Dude Willis picked up a redheaded twenty-year-old who thought coke and black criminals were "a real kick," moved her into his $800-a-month furnished apartment and fed her twelve-year-old Scotch whiskey, drugs and lies. He could count on Karen to spread the word that he'd dealt dope and lived off a stable of women back East.

After a few weeks, he was sufficiently accepted so that he could buy an ounce of cocaine and two of heroin. It was Double Uoglobe brand—the kind that had killed Tim Hessey. Dude Willis complained that the price was a bit high, allowed he'd expect a better deal on the "key" he needed. A man who deals in "keys"—drug world term for kilograms—is taken seriously. Heavy money and connections are implicit. If the importers are the princes in the international narcotics traffic, then the key men are surely among the nobility in this ignoble brotherhood.

Of course, Dude Willis wouldn't-couldn't be a key man until someone decided that Willis had the money, the savvy and the connections to pay for and distribute a kilo or more of pure heroin. Artfully diluted many times, one key would provide thousands of individual "shots" for the street addicts. Mr. C. wouldn't come anywhere near the dope or the delivery, but Dude Willis couldn't be accepted as a key customer until Mr. C. had sized him up, checked him out and approved him.

A meet was finally scheduled. A car would pick up the under-cover agent outside his apartment house at ten P.M. the next evening, and would carry him to some place where Mr. C. would speak to him. The test wouldn't be one of those multiple-choice affairs—strictly pass/fail. Failure could be terminal. . . .

Two hours before the pickup, Alison Gordon and Bill Bonomi sat in the darkness of a third floor apartment across the street from the building where her operative lived. She'd established this command post and communications center several days before Dude Willis-Elroy Evans moved in, and one of her agents always manned the short-range radio in case Evans had something to report via his tiny transmitter. Three cars and a panel truck filled with alert D.E.A. men were parked within a few blocks, prepared to leapfrog each other as they trailed the pickup car to the rendezvous. It was standard surveillance procedure, and Bonomi had his own radio to keep in touch with them.

It was a warm evening, and even in his shirtsleeves Bonomi perspired. He was not armed; executives at his level didn't carry weapons. He looked at the beautiful woman—so cool and elegant in the linen suit—and wondered whether the report that she always carried a .357 Magnum was accurate. He'd never heard of a woman carrying such a heavy handgun, but this one was obviously *different.* If only a quarter of the stories about her were true, she was . . . hell, probably it was all exaggerated. . . .

They smoked and talked, and she said very little. She listened as Bonomi spoke about the years of bureaucratic battling between the Treasury and Justice departments for control of narcotics cases, the guerrilla warfare that finally led to the establishment of the D.E.A.

and the terrible press the new agency had received because of some early mistakes. She knew that the D.E.A. had many competent agents at home and overseas and she made sympathetic noises at his indignation about hostile journalists, at the same time that she recognized he was telling her all this mostly to ease his tension. It wasn't exactly news that indifferent congressmen and noncooperative U.S. diplomats had made American government policy on drug control a political football for most of the past half century. Of course, other countries—including many pious allies—hadn't done much better.

"Sorry about the speech," he apologized when he was talked out at last.

"It's okay. I'm edgy too. Have some more orange juice."

She poured them each a glass of the chilled sugar-energy, considered whether to tell him what two of her operatives had done the previous night. Although she'd forewarned him, criminal acts might bother this D.E.A. supervisor. She encouraged Bonomi to talk about how they might proceed if Mr. C. accepted Evans, which they discussed until five minutes to ten.

"They're here."

She looked down as Bonomi spoke, saw the brown Grand Prix pull to a halt across the street. She shifted uneasily and her gaze swept back and forth like a radar scanner, and Bonomi noticed.

"Right on schedule. They're always a couple of minutes early—just to check out the situation," he reassured her.

She shrugged.

"Everything's okay," he insisted.

She shook her head. *Something* wasn't right.

The man with the raspy voice confirmed her intestinal instinct a moment later. "Shirley's coming this way," he sang out from the doorway behind them. Bonomi turned, stared at the man and the CAR-15 in his hands.

"Got a license for that?"

"Learner's permit."

"Get back to the radio," she ordered. Then she opened her big pouch-purse and took out a small FM receiver set at 101.3 megacycles.

"Shirley is Mr. C.," she explained as she turned on the set.

"What's going on?"

"We bugged his car last night."

"Without a court order?"

"I *knew* we forgot something. You'd better alert your troops. It's the black Caddy. You know the plates."

Bonomi warned his units, and suddenly the voice of the importer sounded from her receiver. He was talking to another man about some phone call from Chicago and urging the driver to hurry. A D.E.A. car announced that the Cadillac was two blocks away.

Three minutes to rendezvous.

The big limousine pulled up behind the Grand Prix forty-five seconds later, and at that instant the lights went out in the undercover agent's apartment on the fifth floor. She could see four men in the Caddy. The one beside the driver got out, walked to the other car and said something to the man behind the wheel. Then he returned to the limo and Mr. C. spoke again.

"Soon as the spade son of a bitch comes out the door, give him both barrels. Both barrels—in the face. Teach those cops a lesson.

They *knew,* and there was no way to stop or warn Elroy Evans about the sawed-off shotgun that was waiting. That was when Bonomi found out the stories were true. At 9:59 she produced a .357 from her belly holster under her chic jacket.

"What the hell are you doing?"

"Cleaning my piece."

Before he could say anything else, she raised the window half a foot and swung the gun.

"Wait a minute—"

She didn't. She squeezed off three rounds, the last of which hit the Cadillac's gas tank. There was a blast, a geyser of flame, then another explosion. Chunks of metal, a cascade of razor-edge glass fragments, pieces of burning tire and human debris scythed through the air in a forty-five-yard arc. Windows shattered, and a Dr. Charles Moses—proctologist to the stars—was distressed when a shoe-clad foot broke his Tiffany lamp. The blast hurled the driver in the Grand Prix headfirst into his windshield, leaving him without either his senses or six teeth and bleeding from a face that only plastic surgery could restore.

People were screaming.

The D.E.A. radio crackled with a babble of voices.

Bonomi was shouting.

"Sorry," she said as she holstered her weapon, "gun went off by accident."

"*Three* times?"

"Hey, it's a car accident—just the way you predicted."

Now her man with the submachine gun was standing beside them, scanning with approval the carnage in the street.

"Go see about Elroy," she told him, and he did.

People were peering out of windows, and some brave or stupid souls—categories not mutually exclusive—wandered tentatively into the street. Bonomi was red-faced as he pointed down at the blazing wreckage.

"You . . . you just killed four people—"

She poured herself another glass of juice, heard the sound of sirens in the distance.

"Ambulances, fire engines, L.A.P.D. black-and-whites, goddam TV crews—they'll all be here in minutes," Bonomi shouted in an unusual display of temper.

She sipped.

"What're we gonna say, dammit?"

"You don't tell them anything, and I won't tell them anything. Okay?"

He ran out of the apartment to salvage what he could in the battlefield below. She drank her juice, considered her situation . . . she'd been hired to help put Mr. C. in a cell, not an urn. Did this mean she wouldn't get paid? After all, they didn't need her anymore.

Who did?

She mailed her final bill—$147,660 including the bonus—the next morning, heard nothing. Five days later she called Kaplan at noon, learned he was on a Pan Am jet to Tokyo. She dialed Knowlton, who was sailing somewhere in the Caribbean. Well, she should have expected it. Men were a lot different when they didn't want something, she remembered—but women were too. Yes, it was important not to turn bitter. Then the manager of her branch of the Crocker National phoned to let her know that a man had just given him—for deposit in her account—an attaché case containing $147,700 in fifty-dollar bills. The well-dressed messenger—about twenty-eight or thirty—had left before anyone got his name, but Miss Gordon was expecting this deposit, *of course.*

Absolutely.

Thanks for calling.

All cash, including a tip—or was Kaplan just rounding it off to the nearest hundred? Whatever you could say about Paul Kaplan, he wasn't cheap. The attaché case was probably Louis Vuitton. It didn't matter. The case was closed. Nearly half a million dollars had been spent, eight people were dead—and she still didn't really know why.

8

THE CARIBBEAN SUN was shining and the pool temperature was perfect, and The Old Man wasn't even breathing hard as he completed the fortieth lap. He was in excellent spirits as he climbed out and put on the terrycloth robe, but then he'd always felt good when he was preparing to do something terrible to his enemies. Looking at the long-legged full-bodied Miss Samantha White also pleased him, and he smiled appreciatively.

"You know," he said, "you've got a splendid head for business and an absolutely outstanding—"

"Yes, I know," she interrupted sharply.

"What's that British word?"

"Bum," she supplied, and tapped the clipboard, "and you've got a full schedule, general."

"Bum—sounds nicer than ass. Guess I'm lucky to have you working for me."

"You're paying $52,000 a year for the thrill. General, there are several calls to be returned. Baron de Rothschild in Paris, Oshiba in Tokyo, George Albion in Dallas, Ullmann in Zurich, McIvor at Citibank in New York and Prince Achmed—he's at the Savoy in London."

"After the briefing."

He slipped into his sandals, started walking toward the five-story building that had been a luxury hotel before he bought it as his home and corporate headquarters three years earlier. With the 9,000-foot runway only four miles away and the nearby ground station in constant touch with his own communications satellite, running the twenty-six companies in the conglomerate from this island was no problem at all.

"Anything else?" he asked as they approached the building.

She shoved her plastic ID card into the electronic lock to open the door, glanced at the clipboard again.

"Khalid—he called twice and sent another telex. He'll pay in gold."

The Old Man didn't answer, kept on walking.

"President Khalid is the head of a wealthy oil-producing nation," she pointed out, "and he's entitled to a reply to his request to buy Texons. After all, you've sold the missile to three other countries."

"Israel, Norway and Canada—not murderous bandits like that butcher Khalid."

He waved casually at receptionists, security men, executives and secretaries alike as they moved past the telecommunications center and the data-processing division humming with $7 million worth of IBM's finest computers.

"You know what I think of Khalid?" he asked her.

"Last week you described him as a . . . sphincter, I believe."

"Asshole," he corrected. "A copper-plated asshole—on wheels. Screw him."

"That doesn't come within my job description, general," she replied as they reached the doors to the briefing room, "so I'll just cable that we're in short supply at the moment."

He reached into the pocket of his robe, grunted irritably. The woman opened her purse, pulled out the cigar case and gave him a Larranaga. As he bit off the tip, she lit the Cuban corona and opened this security lock with the card. He puffed twice, grunted pleasure and bulled through the portal ahead of her.

The chamber was three stories high, with one whole wall covered by a huge map of the world. There were clocks showing the time in London, Frankfurt, Teheran, Calcutta, Tokyo, Los Angeles and New York. If it resembled the underground command post of the Strategic Air Command buried near Omaha, it was no accident. The Old Man had spent the final two years of his Air Force career on the SAC battle staff there. Associated Press and Reuters teleprinters stuttered in one corner, with a New York Stock Exchange ticker unreeling steadily nearby. Much bigger than the screening room, this place had seats for thirty. There was one extra-large leather swivel chair in the center, and this sixty-seven-year-old tycoon who'd been called The Old Man since he was thirty-two moved directly toward that throne. As he sat down, he glanced at his wrist. He still wore the stainless steel watch of a combat pilot.

"0800. Let's go, Milt."

Dressed in the white lab coat and horn-rimmed glasses that were part of his identity, Dr. Milton Steiner stepped forward on the platform beneath the map. Slim, earnest-faced, looking even younger than his thirty-one years, he'd been employed by The Old Man ever since he received his Ph.D. from Cal Tech at the preposterous age of twenty-one. Steiner was more than a boy wonder. He was—beyond question—one of the finest analytical minds of his generation.

"General," he said carefully, "I think we'd better clear the room. I'll run the projectors myself."

The Old Man nodded.

"This is a classified briefing," Miss White announced. "Clear the room, and secure the doors. No one will be admitted until the red light goes off."

The projectionist and two of Steiner's assistants left while she relayed the orders to Security over a bright yellow phone beside her, then pressed the switch which double-locked the steel doors. She picked up the clipboard, clicked her ballpoint pen.

"No notes and no tapes," Steiner said.

There had been "classified briefings" in this room before, but the security had never been this rigid.

"Disengage the recording equipment," the general ordered.

She obeyed, and for the first time since she'd come to this island she felt something close to fear. Steiner was the calmest and most conservative employee Atlas Industries had, which meant these extreme precautions signaled comparable danger.

"What have you got, Milt?"

"A high risk operation. A possible solution—if you really want to go all the way."

"All the way," the general said without hesitation.

"Estimated cost—three to five million.

"Forget the money. Let's hear it."

Steiner cleared his throat—twice.

"This would be illegal—*highly* illegal. I should warn you, general—"

"Don't warn me, dammit. *Tell* me. I'll decide.

Steiner moved to the podium, pressed the button that lowered a six- by ten-foot screen from the ceiling above the right wall.

"The pusher, the wholesaler and the importer have been eliminated. If you want to go all the way—"

"There's no choice."

There was something stark, even savage in The Old Man's voice, something far more ruthless than he'd ever sounded during his most rancorous business battles.

"Okay, we know the brand name—Double Uoglobe. Research tells us the opium for this is grown up in northern Burma—in the Golden Triangle." As Steiner spoke, he turned off the lights and turned on the slide projector. A map of upper Burma, northern Thailand and southwestern China jumped onto the screen.

"The Golden Triangle," he repeated, "major source for Asian opium for decades. Isolated country, remote—hard to police. Hill tribes up here growing poppies for half a century or more, selling the raw opium to traders—mostly ethnic Chinese. They buy two kilos from one village, four or five from another—pay the farmers $35 or $40 a kilo. We're getting film on this in a couple of days. A French crew made a documentary up there five years ago."

"Get to the plan, Milton."

"Right. The stuff—all the small shipments—is bought up by big people with money, men, weapons. Modern weapons, even heavy machine guns and mortars. The men who bring this opium to the refineries—secret jungle labs along the Thai frontier—are mostly survivors of a couple of Chiang Kai-Shek's Nationalist armies, driven across the border by Mao's troops well over twenty-five years ago. Here, we've got some stills." Nine photos of Asian soldiers followed in swift succession, and then he clicked the map back onto the screen. "There are a couple of assembly points up here—deep in the Shan hills—where the convoy is organized. The Double Uoglobe people seem to prefer one or two big convoys each year, very big."

"How big?"

"Maybe eight hundred mules escorted by a thousand armed men —all C.I.F., Research says."

"C.I.F.?"

"Chinese Irregular Forces—that's what the CIA calls them. The CIA knows them pretty well, used them for a gang of intelligence missions along the Red Chinese border. Chiang used to reequip them by cargo plane from Formosa. Official story is those flights stopped maybe ten years ago. Could be true, but they're still getting weapons, ammo, all kinds of supplies from *somebody.*"

"Uncle Sam?"

"General, I deal in facts—not conjecture. Yes, it could be the CIA and you could be going head-to-head with some very powerful people in Washington. We hope to have more *facts* soon. Research is working on it. Well, they put together the convoy and come down through this area. They know the terrain, and they're tight with people in every village. Growing opium up there is like raising chickens—no big deal. Nobody considers it either immoral or criminal. It's a cash crop, like rice. They're poor and they need the money, and they don't have any notion about people ten thousand miles away killing themselves with white powder."

"Milton, I don't pay you $80,000 a year to read me the goddam *National Geographic*. Can we please cut the anthropological crap and get back to the facts of the convoy?"

She heard the scientist suck in his breath.

"Well armed, excellent intelligence and safe because they've paid off or scared the cops or soldiers on both sides of the border. No ground force can get within forty or fifty miles of them undetected. Probabilities of success for ground assault mounted by either local military or any mercenary troops you could infiltrate— almost zero. That's a *fact,* general."

"You see what he's driving at?" The Old Man asked excitedly.

"Only that the convoy can't be attacked."

"On *the ground* . . . spell it out, Milt."

The scientist cleared his throat again, filled the screen with a detailed map of a much smaller region of The Golden Triangle. "Most of the time the big convoy slogs down this route—through this valley. The Meo tribes up there call it Dead Moon Valley."

Suddenly she realized what Steiner was saying. "It's crazy—"

"Brilliant, I'd say . . . Large target, moving at a mule's pace, bottled up in the goddam valley. *Perfect,*" the general countered.

"It appears . . . on the basis of all data available, computer analysis and logical review . . . that the only solution—"

"Don't listen to him," she pleaded.

"The only solution," Steiner continued slowly, "is an air strike."

"You'll go to jail," she warned hopelessly.

"Air strike." The Old Man's voice filled the room like a celebration.

"A base would have to be established somewhere in northern Thailand, and appropriate attack aircraft assembled. Planes with a range of at least twenty-five hundred miles, good bomb load and significant strafing capacity. Aircraft with multiple machine guns and able to operate at low level at speeds of less than two

48

hundred miles per hour on strafing runs."

"There's no such plane," she argued.

"There used to be. Tell her, Steiner."

"The Boeing B-17."

"*My* bird."

Now the lights were on, and she could see the passion in The Old Man's eyes. He was somewhere back in World War Two, leading his Fortress squadrons against the enemy—the best enemy he'd ever had.

"It doesn't exist," she said. "Nobody's made them in thirty years."

"The last B-17G . . . Air Force serial number 85841 . . . was built in 1944," Steiner read from his notes.

"Sure, the G model carried 13 heavy .50s. That enough machine guns, Milt?"

"I think so. The basic M-2 heavy machine gun that was standard equipment laid down 850 rounds a minute. If we upgrade to the postwar M-3s, they'll deliver more. 1,350 to be precise."

"You're going to start a goddam war—"

"They started it—the day the boy died. How many birds will we need?"

"Four, plus two in reserve," Steiner estimated.

"Can we get 'em?"

Steiner looked at his pad again, nodded.

"I believe so. It'll take some doing—"

"Do it."

"There's the matter of personnel. Flying crews and maintenance teams. We'll need professionals."

"We'll buy them. It's going to be tremendous!"

Steiner coughed. "Not for you, general. This high risk operation will demand a younger field commander, a leader—not a strategist."

The Old Man was on his feet. "What the hell are you talking about?"

"You're not the right man for the job. That's a *fact.* You can't go. You can plan it, but you can't lead the strike."

"And I say you're full of crap, I'm not that old, dammit."

Steiner took off his glasses, rubbed his eyes. "General, you know damn well I'd do anything for you . . . after what you did for my father—"

"Forget your father, you don't owe me anything."

Steiner put on his spectacles, faced the general. "I owe you, and

49

I like you—and I like working for you. One of the things I owe you is my best shot. Okay, here it is. You're too old, and there's no *logical* reason for you to run this high risk—"

"And you can shove your computers and your actuarial tables . . ."

He paced up and down, glaring furiously at all of them, looking like a defiant eagle, a defiant *old* eagle.

"Milt's right," she said quietly.

"Bull!"

"It's a question of responsibility," Steiner pointed out. "Dozens of lives will be risked. General, we need the finest . . . the most experienced . . . the best B-17 pilot in the world."

The Old Man puffed on the cigar for several seconds.

"Okay, Milt, I'll get him."

9

THERE WAS no such man.

There probably never had been, and if the Harry O. Logan described in the report had ever existed he was very different today. In today's world of slick and evasive males who danced and lied well, worried about their figures and dodged commitment as if it were a terminal affliction, it was hard to believe that the person described in Elroy Evans' report had ever existed. If there had been such a flier long ago, by now he was sure to be a balding, foolish stereotype who told war stories when he was drunk and fooled around with other middle-aged men's wives when he wasn't.

There were no more knights in shining armor.

There were no more cowboy heroes on white horses.

The file on the car seat beside her—and the perfect man those pages treated—had to be fiction. This was the time of the anti-hero, and Alison Gordon knew it. It didn't matter. She was on her way to La Jolla to spend the weekend with her sister, and it was always easy with Jan, her amiable husband and the twins who were very pretty and very twelve. San Paloma was only twenty miles from La Jolla, so with a little luck she'd be finished with Logan by a quarter to one this balmy Friday and eating lunch with Jan thirty or forty minutes later.

SAN PALOMA—3.

She tensed when she saw the sign. This was where it had all begun. It wasn't entirely over . . . Fat John's expert counsel were appealing his conviction on a dozen technicalities and only God knew what had happened to Dolores. Probably only God cared. Neither Kaplan, nor Ivy Leaguer Knowlton in New York nor the mysterious client who'd paid them all gave a damn about an addict-whore. She found the turnoff for the flying field, directed the Porsche to the San Paloma Flying School. It even looked like World War Two—with the sign OFFICE in front of a small Quonset prefab and a larger Quonset hangar thirty yards away.

When she found the office empty, she walked past the two parked cars—the '78 Fiat Spider so jazzy in bright red and the blue '74 BMW—to the hangar. A man who might be fifty-five and could be Logan was working on an engine. He was wearing mechanic's overalls, a wrench and almost no hair at all.

"Logan?"

He pointed up at an Apache swooping down to land.

"You a student?"

"Of life," she answered, feeling as brittle as she sounded.

"Logan used to be a student of *Life*, but he let his subscription expire."

The small plane taxied noisily toward them and stopped. Two people emerged. One was a trim looking woman in expensive, tight-fitting clothes, a blond.

"Bottle job," the mechanic said of the peroxide lady. Another forty-five-year-old trying to pass for thirty-five.

The man who jumped to the ground was wearing a pilot's coveralls. He was tanned, at least six feet tall and no more than one hundred eighty pounds. Everything about him was lean, even the way he moved. Logan would be fifty-four, and this man looked a decade younger. He said something to the woman as she climbed into the Fiat, then walked into the office. The detective followed moments later.

"Logan?"

He nodded.

"Harry O.?"

He nodded again.

She recited the first three digits of his Air Corps serial number, and he finished it correctly.

"349th? 100th Bombardment Group?"

"Yeah, the Bloody 100th," he said as he sat in the wooden swivel chair behind the desk.

Three Distinguished Flying Crosses, four Air Medals, Silver Stars and two Purple Hearts—136 missions over Nazi Germany and this incredible character looked like a movie star playing a high school football coach. The touches of gray at the temples only helped. "Major Logan, my name is Gordon."

He gestured toward the electric percolator on the metal table against the wall.

"Black—with one sugar," she replied.

He poured two cups, added a white lump to one and handed it to her. "How can I help you?" he asked.

"I'm a private investigator."

He shrugged, smiled. "If Dr. Knittel thinks his wife has been—"

"No, major. Nothing like that. I don't handle divorce cases . . . You make a good cup of coffee."

"All Colombian and lots of it. No secret. You really a private investigator?"

She showed him her license.

"You didn't have to do that. Miss Gordon, what can I do for you?"

His voice was warm, his eyes direct. No California macho charm. No wedding ring either.

"Make a phone call. Collect. Don't ask me what it's all about, and don't laugh. Somebody hired my agency to find you, and to ask you to please phone."

"I wouldn't laugh at a lady who looks like you and says please. Where am I supposed to call?"

She handed him a slip of paper.

"I checked the area code. It's Miami," she said.

"And who do I ask for?"

"Vandal."

He stiffened. *"Vandal?"* His face didn't show the impact but his eyes did.

"You know him?" she asked.

"I used to."

A Nazi propaganda broadcaster had denounced the 100th as vandals after two devastating raids in 1943, and the general had defiantly taken that epithet as his code name. It all came back in a split second . . . Logan in one plane and The Old Man in another, flying almost wing-to-wing through the antiaircraft fire. That was before the Eighth Air Force brass had grounded The Old Man as too valuable to risk on combat missions over enemy territory. Furious at being pulled from combat at thirty-two, The Old Man had offered to give up his star to fight and the commander of the Eighth had told him to grow up. The Old Man hadn't liked that. They'd argued bitterly until Doolittle, who had one more star and limited patience, had pulled rank and given a direct order. The Old Man admired Doolittle, but he'd never forgiven him.

Vandal.

The name suited him.

Battle was his natural habitat.

Logan looked at the number of the slip of paper she'd given him, made the call.

"Atlas," the switchboard operator in Miami announced.

"Extension 100."

Unaware that his call was being routed to the island by private communications satellite, the flier listened to the clicks and beeps and wondered. Miss White was on the line forty seconds later. He told her who he was, who he wanted. He waited.

"Hello," a man's voice echoed.

"Vandal?"

"Yes. Is that you, Blue Leader?"

Nobody had called him that for more than thirty years. It all came back, and he winced under the shock. She saw it clearly. Something was clearly happening to Logan, Harry O.

"Yes," Logan replied. "How are you, sir?"

"Okay. You?"

"All right."

"Blue Leader, I need you. I've got a special mission. Very tricky, very dangerous. I won't crap you. It's a high risk operation."

They'd always given him those. "I see," Logan answered.

"Four to six months' work. $250,000. This isn't business, Blue Leader. It's personal."

The whole war had been personal to The Old Man. "Flying?"

"Of course. Why else would I need you? I can have a Learjet pick you up at San Diego tomorrow at 0900. Okay?"

Logan looked at his open appointment book, saw that he had a nine A.M. lesson scheduled for Gary English, the big-mouthed owner of the largest shopping center in the county. English had a lot of money, prejudices and exaggerated notions of his own importance. Avoiding him would be a pleasure.

"Sure."

"It'll be a company bird—Atlas Industries. That's me. See you for dinner tomorrow night. Thanks."

The Old Man was mellowing, Logan thought as he put down the telephone. He never used to observe such amenities as "please" or "thanks."

$250,000.

What in the world could it be?

Logan returned to the plainly furnished office of the San Paloma Flying School, and to the very attractive woman sipping his coffee. Her large brown eyes were radiating curiosity, but she was too much of a lady to ask.

"Old friend," he told her, and reached for his cup.

"You don't lie too well, Logan. Stick to flying."

There was something unreasonably boyish about his smile, something so likable that it made her uneasy. She wasn't ready for this kind of appealing directness, and besides, it was ridiculous in a man of his age.

"Logan, may I give you some free advice?"

"Sure."

"You won't take it," she predicted. "You never did. I know about you. You'd have been a general if you weren't so damn stubborn—"

"I do my best."

"Logan, that was Atlas in Miami."

"What's the advice?"

"I checked out the phone number. Listen, Atlas is one of the clients of a powerhouse combine of Wall Street lawyers. Senior partner named Winthrop Knowlton."

"Never heard of him. More coffee?"

"If this thing is what I think it is, it's very bloody business. Eight dead already."

It had been some time since he'd met a female who seemed to care *about* him—not just *for* him—and it was puzzling that this woman was even the least bit concerned. "What do you think it is?"

"I can't imagine. I get $400 a day to be clever, and I don't have any idea what the next step is—but I'm sure it's dangerous."

Logan nodded. "He said something like that."

"And you don't mind, you probably like it."

"Would you care for some lunch?"

Neither the man nor his future were any of her business, Alison Gordon reminded herself. She was also much too realistic to waste another minute with this leftover hero. She stood up to leave.

"No thanks . . . Logan, it isn't the good guys against the bad anymore. Don't you read the papers? It's a different world."

He nodded, and she walked to the door.

"Miss Gordon, I hate to eat alone."

Why did she hesitate?

"I'm having lunch with my sister in La Jolla. Take care, Logan."

It had been stupid of her to say anything, she thought as she opened the door. She wasn't his mother. He was old enough to look out for himself. He wouldn't, of course. It was all spelled out in the file. He'd never had the sense to put himself first or even near it. She would be reading his one-paragraph obituary in the L.A. *Times* in a month or so.

"You like chili?"

That made it easy. She hated chili. It bothered her gut almost as much as naive heroes. "No, thanks."

"I wish you would. You could phone your sister, and we could talk over lunch?"

What was there to talk about?

"Do *you* like to eat alone?"

Alone. What the hell did he know about being alone? The word echoed and reechoed inside her. She swallowed to force down the pain, reminded herself he hadn't intended to hurt her. Well, maybe she could reason with him. . . .

She telephoned Jan, and he drove her to Anita's Chili Parlor in his dusty BMW. The restaurant had a dozen tables and a large cheery woman who was the owner-cook. She welcomed Logan warmly, took their order and left them alone with two icy bottles of Mexican beer. The food came quickly and they talked over lunch —the best chili Alison Gordon had ever tasted. None of it made any sense at all. He wasn't the simple warrior that he was supposed to be. He knew about sculpture, jazz, the laws and the creatures of the skies and seas.

"My son teaches marine biology—and his father," Logan explained.

Child of the first wife. The report said he'd been divorced twice. She thought about the fat file. Maybe she shouldn't have called him "major." After all, he'd been a full colonel—a "bird" colonel in Air Force jargon—before he retired in 1962. The dessert was cream cheese and guava. It was good, and so was the coffee.

"Logan, let's talk about Atlas now."

"I'd rather talk about your work. Sounds very interesting."

"I don't want to pry."

"Bet you meet some unusual people—all kinds, huh?"

He was a handsome man, but not like those suave peacocks who knew that they were good looking and all the latest jokes.

"I never met anyone like you—not recently," she replied frankly.

Some men would have preened or mouthed some clever remark. He only looked at her—directly. "Is that good or bad, Miss Gordon?"

"Don't call me 'Miss Gordon,' dammit. I'm over thirty and I'm a . . . a widow." She stumbled on the word, she hadn't used it in years.

"I didn't mean to offend you. Sorry."

"Don't apologize, Logan. You haven't done anything. I'm trying to help you." She felt angry, but why?

"Would you like a brandy?"

"No . . . sure."

He held up two fingers, and Anita started pouring.

"Logan—"

"It must be rough being a widow—I mean, so young . . ."

Here comes the pass.

She was wrong again.

"Logan, you're an intelligent man. You know a lot of things besides flying. You've got a business—your own. Why do you have to get involved in other people's? All through the war you took on messes that weren't yours—always Mr. Nice Guy. Why do you have to be such a goddam hero?"

"I'm no hero."

"It's all in your file. Dammit, you're the second-most-decorated man in the history of the Air Force—"

"Don't hold it against me."

Anita put down the brandies, rippled away.

"Look, I don't know what you're sore about," he said. "I don't see that I've done anything wrong—"

"Not ever? Why are you running this half-ass flying school in Nowhere, California?"

"Like to fly."

"You could have gotten a job with any airline—years ago."

"Had some offers," he admitted, and sipped his cognac.

"Well?"

"Don't like big companies. Not knocking it for other people."

"But not for Logan. How about non-flying jobs? You were a famous hero. Any offers?"

He nodded.

"Good money?" she demanded.

He shrugged. "I earn enough to get along."

"And pay income tax on every cent of it. You probably never

jumped a traffic light or someone else's wife in your whole damn life. Don't you understand?"

"Hey, I'm no angel. I drink, play cards, swear. And enjoy women."

She tasted the brandy.

"Logan, I'm not calling you a sissy or a fool. I'm saying that you put other people first. You gave away most of what you had in those two divorces."

"They needed it, or at least wanted it, more than I did—"

"And now you're getting involved with this Vandal because *he* needs and wants you?"

"We'll see. You know, I'd like to look at your sculpture some time."

The tone in his voice said it wasn't just an opening ploy in a seduction attempt. He meant it. "You never will—not if you get involved with Vandal. Don't be a hero, Logan. Heroes die."

"Leslie Fiedler," he said. "I read the interview in the *Times.*"

Literate too. Too much.

"Would you excuse me for a minute?" he asked suddenly.

She shrugged, and he went to telephone young Joe Carty to ask him to take over the flying lessons while he'd be gone.

Moments after he walked away, Anita came to the table with the brandy bottle.

"No, thanks," Alison Gordon said.

"On the house."

"For Logan?"

"Sure, he's my friend. He'd never get a check here—but he insists."

"You owe him?"

"Miss, I owe Harry Logan my son's life. It was Harry pulled him out of a burning car three years ago. No one else had the nerve. It was going to blow any second. I owe him. I like him too . . . You like him?"

Who wouldn't? But dammit, heroes never learned. She realized she'd never reach him. He couldn't be changed. Handsome, intelligent, compassionate, honest—and doomed. Too damn much.

This was the man she'd dreamt about when she was fourteen. He was probably good in bed too. Something deep inside her moved when she thought about him as a lover, and she frowned at that. It was simple hormones, she told herself. Animal chemistry and living alone so long could do that to a woman—even one as world-wise as

A. B. Gordon who got $400 a day and damn little else. Yes, he'd be kind and gentle in that too, she suspected—

No, it was all schoolgirl fantasy. She was embarrassed to find that she was still vulnerable after all these years. Under the calluses, she still hoped and even yearned. It was nonsense, of course. Logan had plenty of flaws. He was no better than all the other men who'd passed through her body and life. Even poor dead Mark hadn't been perfect. It was plain foolish to care about Logan as a man. After all, she knew so little about him—

Harry O. Logan, the perfect stranger.

Impossible. That closing line Billy Wilder and I.A.L. Diamond had written for *Some Like It Hot* was true. "Nobody's perfect." She'd wasted two more hours of her life—again.

"Like to go swimming?" he asked when he returned.

"I've got to get up to La Jolla."

He drove her back to the airfield, watched her slide into her car.

"See you," he said.

"Take care of yourself, Logan—Harry O."

She started the engine, and saw him signal he had something more to say.

"Yes?"

"What's your name? What does the *A.* stand for?"

Why should he care? "Alison."

"Alison." He repeated it and nodded.

She couldn't—wouldn't—wait any longer. She didn't look back as she put the car into gear. She didn't want to face Harry O. Logan anymore. The noise of the powerful engine and the movement helped, and a few minutes later she pointed the Porsche up the coastal road, wondering if she'd ever see this obsolete, disturbing man again.

10

JAN, HER OLDER SISTER by three years, lived in a small but comfortable house on a charming hill in the town of La Jolla—one of the most scenic and gracious communities in Southern California. Her twin daughters were blond, unspoiled, cheery students always in the upper quarter of their class. They were blessedly free of physical blemish or social prejudice, they sang folk songs and swam well and raised money every year for UNICEF and the Red Cross. They clearly loved their sensible, freckled mother, whose gifts as a potter brought in $6,000 annually to complement their father's salary as head of the high school's science department. Dad was great too, and so was the mutt dog named R2D2.

A loving family—all pleased to see A. B. Gordon.

For her it was always relaxing and comfortable to visit these affectionate and rational relatives—the only ones she had this side of the Rockies. She felt safe here. Here she could forget—briefly—about the so shrewd and powerful people and her gritty work. There was no pressure in this loving house, no ugliness. The first thing she did after she dropped her weekend bag on the bed in the spare room was to put away the .357 and holster, and after two glasses of crisp Mondavi chablis and an hour of family talk she felt better than she had in months.

Jan's lanky husband came home while the women were picking the vegetables for dinner in the garden, and while he cut up the salad the sisters prepared the stew together and enjoyed his stories of adolescent pranks and assorted nonsense. The women laughed and the twins set the table, and life seemed livable. More wine flowed . . . Now there wasn't any Beverly Hills or New York or Atlas Industries, or that other place of long ago far away.

No dead addicts, burning cars or heroes of any kind.

There were fresh peaches for dessert, fine espresso and no problem, until Jan casually asked why she'd missed lunch.

"I had an accident." Alison said grimly.

Jan Kelleran recognized the look on her younger sister's face. From the time Alison had been eight, that expression had signaled deep upset and conflict.

"The car?" Arch Kelleran put in.

"Archie, don't let me stand between you and General Electric," his wife said, and pointed toward the kitchen. He understood both messages—the need for private sister-to-sister talk, and the time for loading the dishwasher. He left without a question.

"It wasn't the car, was it?"

"Sis," Alison said, "I ran head-on into something much worse."

"Must have been some collision. You look as if you hit a stone wall."

"Worse—an extraordinary man. Smart, decent, strong and handsome—"

"Did he ignore you or rape you?"

"Neither. This isn't too funny, Jan. Don't laugh."

"How can I laugh," Jan said, "when you seem ready to cry? He sounds great to me. What's wrong with him?"

"Nothing—except his line of work. He's in the hero business, and I don't have much experience with heroes. I think I blew it."

"What happened?"

"I tried to change him—over lunch. What kind of an idiot would try to change a man in his fifties at lunch? Well, it wouldn't have worked anyway."

"In his fifties?"

She nodded. "He isn't like any of the men I know. He took me to a chili restaurant. I hate chili. It was wonderful. Does any of this make sense? Do I sound drunk or something?"

Her sister nodded, refilled the wineglasses. "Something. I think they call it love. You remember love?"

"Not really. Anyway, I don't believe in the tooth fairy or love at first sight anymore. I'm too old and as you know, too sophisticated. I'm the most goddam sophisticated rational person you know. I don't even believe in love at fourth sight. What do you think of that, big sister?"

"I think you're in trouble."

Alison nodded twice.

"Why couldn't he be like the other men I know? Who the hell needs a fucking hero—a perfect fucking hero?"

She sipped her wine.

"Sorry about the language, Jan."

"Come off it. I'm your *big* sister, remember. You want to let loose a little, let loose."

"I don't want to let loose. I want to forget him, and what a damn fool I was. I know all about men. I've used them, fooled them, exposed them, analyzed them, laid them . . . and killed them. This idiot flier I tried to reason with—for his sake. That was my big mistake. I felt sorry for him. I wanted to save his life."

"And what did he want?"

"Don't worry," she said as she brushed her napkin across her eyes, "I'm not going to cry. It would be too preposterous for a sensible woman in her thirties—a shrewd woman widely respected and well paid for her keen thinking—to cry for a damned total *stranger*. It's probably the lunar cycle. I always get a bit funny when my period's coming on."

"No, you don't. You never did."

"Listen, Jan, I've learned my lessons. It's okay to have a man in your bed, but not your guts. Men hurt you."

"So do car doors. Why don't you call him?"

"Because I'm too smart—and he's dumb. He wanted me to go swimming. That was a dumb idea, wasn't it? Harry O. Logan, beautiful but dumb. A dumb dream, and I'm too old to have such dreams . . . Maybe this is just all overwork. I'm exhausted, Jan."

"Scared too. Nothing to be ashamed of. Logan? The pilot who found that lost kid up in the mountains last year?"

"Sounds like my Harry. I'm not scared of him. I'm much smarter than he is." She yawned. "No, I'm tired. Think I'll go to bed. Stay in your own damn bed, Logan—you dummy."

The doorbell rang. He was wearing an open-neck sport shirt, "summer uniform" pants and that damn smile. Dazed, she made the introductions automatically. He'd probably tracked her via the phone call from his office, but why was he here?

"I was just driving by," he said, "and I still wondered whether you might like to go swimming."

He never gave up. A true-blue romantic. Did he really think she was some dewy schoolgirl?

"If it's too late I could come back tomorrow."

He would, too.

While her sister and brother-in-law exchanged poorly camou-flaged glances, Alison Gordon got to her feet and said something in an almost inaudible voice. She was just as baffled as they were—a condition that continued even after she collected her swimsuit and joined Logan in the BMW.

"Why did you do that?" she asked as they turned onto the main highway.

"I was worried about you. You seemed . . . sore about something, sore and tense."

He was telling the truth.

"You're worried about *me*, Logan?"

"Somebody's got to, and I think I'd be good at it."

She laughed and he drove and they listened to three of the best Gerry Mulligan singles back-to-back in some special "salute" on a nearby station. The beach was deserted when they got there. She changed behind the car, plunged into the cool surf at the same moment he did. They swam for some twenty minutes and he took her hand as they walked back onto the sand. It seemed so natural that she didn't react at first, then stiffened and broke the clasp.

The only thing for her to do was to say it directly.

"Logan, this isn't going to work. We're too different."

He shook some of the water off—almost like a dog, and his eyes were bright in the moonlight. She felt her breathing quicken.

"Aside from the little age gap, I don't think we're so different."

"That's it," she said quickly.

It was a lie. His extra eighteen years didn't matter a bit.

"How old are you?"

He shouldn't have said that. It was unfair, and she nearly stum-bled.

"I'm too damned old for you, Logan—"

"The hell you are."

He took her in his arms, and he kissed her until she stopped crying. He comforted her, stroked her until there was nothing be-tween them. They made love twice, then swam again—naked in the rising sea. . . .

"This is a big mistake," she told him as they entered his house shortly before midnight.

"I don't think so."

He kissed her again for a long time, and they slept in each other's arms until the alarm rang at six. Neither of them had slept that well for years.

11

SHE DOZED with her head on his shoulder most of the way. The flight was tranquil, Miss White's greetings at the airport were pleasant and the eighty degree temperature relaxing as they drove through the humid Caribbean night to the Atlas compound. Even the men at the guardhouse, where the driveway from the two-lane road began, seemed friendly as they opened the metal portals and waved the sedan through.

Eight-foot stone walls.

Sentry posts and steel gates.

The Old Man was still maintaining perimeter security.

When they climbed out of the car at the main building Miss White told the driver to unload the baggage from "the boot" and opened the door to the residence/headquarters with her plastic card. They followed her into the air-conditioned comfort, saw what had once been a hotel lobby. A chime began to sound—loudly.

"Metal detector. Are you armed, Mr. Logan?"

"*She* is."

Miss White couldn't fathom why he was grinning, but then the strangest things seemed to amuse Americans. She pointed at two uniformed men—pistols in their hands—at the head of the stairs.

"Would you be kind enough to leave the weapon with these security people?"

"No."

"Miss Gordon needs her weapon," Logan explained," because she's *my* security. She's terrific."

The general was going to *adore* this. The woman with the M.B.A. from Columbia assured the guards that Miss Gordon was authorized to enter all areas with her "small personal revolver."

"It's a .357 Magnum," the detective said, and flipped back her jacket to expose the powerful handgun.

"Don't flash, honey. I told you that a thousand times." Logan patted her head, turned to Miss White. "I'm crazy about her. She's a miracle," he confided.

And A. B. Gordon loved it, and didn't care who knew it. They were never more than a foot or two from each other, never out of physical reach—joined as if by an invisible cord. If Samantha White's memory served her, this was love—acute, marvelous. She found herself smiling benignly—and a bit enviously—as she led them to the suite where The Old Man was waiting impatiently.

"Hello, general."

"Hello, Harry. What's *she* doing here?"

Samantha White winced at the rudeness. "Miss Gordon's with Major Logan."

The Old Man shook his head angrily, and Logan made the introductions.

"A. B. Gordon, this is M. E. Steele, Major General, U.S. Army Air Corps, Retired."

"Abie Gordon? We hired a detective named Abie Gordon ten or twelve months ago. Some smart Hebrew in Los Angeles . . ."

"That's me, Maxie, though I'm not Hebrew and I work out of Beverly Hills, to keep the record straight."

"She's smart, though," Logan said.

M(axwell) E(merson) Steele was flabbergasted. Only his Aunt Harriet had called him Maxie—a name he detested—and she'd been dead thirty years.

"It's ten after nine. Don't you think we ought to start dinner?" suggested Miss White.

"I want to get this straight. Harry, this is a very confidential deal. I'm sure the lady's charming and capable but—"

"Who's Tim Hessey?" Alison demanded abruptly.

Steele controlled his rage, moved to a sideboard and poured three fingers of Jack Daniels, which he half-destroyed in a single gulp. Miss White found it all fascinating . . . nobody ever spoke to The Old Man like this.

"What would you like, major?" she asked.

"He retired as a colonel," Alison announced. "He drinks Glenfiddich on the rocks. I'll take a dark Carlsberg, if you've got one."

Better and better, Miss White thought as she phoned the bar.

"Who *is* Tim Hessey, general?" Logan added.

"My grandson."

"Oh my God." Alison Gordon sighed and walked across to pour herself a bourbon. She took in a big sip, swallowed and shuddered. "I thought his mother's maiden name was Sorensen," she said.

"She's had a lot of names . . . I suppose I ought to thank you for what you did," Steele said slowly

She drank more bourbon, shook again. "That's terrible stuff. How can you drink it?" and finished what was in her glass. "General," she said as she surrendered to a couch, "you probably don't know what the hell you started."

"I'm not finished. That's why I need Harry—"

"You need *us,*" she corrected.

"It's a flying job. Tricky mission. Four-engine birds. You'll be the flight leader, Harry."

The woman refused to be ignored.

"We're together, Mister General, and you're damn lucky. You need me almost as much as Logan does."

"Is she always like this?" Steele said pointedly.

"I haven't known her that long. You ought to listen to her, general. She's extremely intelligent. It was her mind that first drew me to her."

"When was that?"

"Around lunchtime yesterday. Destiny, I guess."

Steele finished his bourbon, poured more sour mash, shook his head.

"You take your gout pill, general?" his assistant reminded him.

"Christ Almighty, no. I didn't. Don't nag . . . Are you on her side?"

"What side is that?" Miss White inquired politely.

"The smart side," Alison Gordon broke in. "I don't know what you're planning, general, but it's got to be big, dangerous, and probably illegal. Nobody offers $250,000 to walk an old lady across Santa Monica Boulevard. A large covert criminal operation? Right? Okay, that's what I'm best at. I've got a lot of experience."

"Such as?"

"Seven years with The Company. The Agency. The CIA—the professionals. Not pushing memos in Virginia, general, but in the field. Two years in Africa, three in Viet Nam and two in Thailand. Where have you been lately?"

"Get her out of here—"

"I think we'll need her," Miss White put in seriously. Then she gave him his gout pill.

66

The argument raged, the drinks arrived and the dispute continued over an excellent dinner of Bahama rock lobster, sirloins flown in from New York, the green vegetables on which Atlas' nutritionist insisted and the pecan pie from the recipe of that fine restaurant in New Orleans. It was over the Irish coffee that the general touched on the specifics of the mission.

"We'll be using 17s, Harry. Gs—we're out buying them now."

Logan was clearly interested, and pleased.

"What's he talking about?" Alison asked.

"The G model, the most advanced of the B-17 bombers. That was my plane. 1942 to 1945, 136 missions."

"Best years of your life . . . of all our lives," Steele said. "What have you been doing for the last fifteen years, Harry? Nothing worthy of you, I'd wager. You were the best, Harry. Here's your chance to do something great . . . to be someone great . . . again." He was also, of course, talking for himself.

"Is he talking about a *bombing attack?*" Alison demanded.

Miss White nodded.

"Get the nets. This old guy's crazy."

The general seemed not to hear her, was completely immersed in the project. "You're the ideal commander for this, Blue Leader. It's bombing first, then low-level strafing. Remember that strike on the *stalag?*"

Logan put his hand on Alison's. "I was shot down in January of '44—over the Saar. Spent three and a half months in a prison camp for air crews, a *Stalagluft.*"

"They couldn't hold Blue Leader," Steele said, once again talking about one of his boys . . . his best one . . . "Broke out, fought his way out to some Yugoslav partisans on the Adriatic. He was back flying a week before D day."

"That camp was pretty bad." Logan was back in it too. "The S.S. guards . . . real sadists. Had to try to stop that—"

"With 17s. It was beautiful," The Old Man remembered. "On the way back after a raid on some rail yards, took his flight a hundred and thirty miles out of the way and blew the crap out of those guard towers. Barreling in at one hundred feet, machine guns blasting. Shot the shit out of those S.S. bastards. Two low-level passes and the guard towers were kindling."

"The brass didn't much like it," Logan said quietly, and reached for a cigar.

Steele nodded. "They killed your promotion. You were set to go up for light colonel and they stepped on it."

Logan lit the Don Diego.

"You should have got a medal, Harry. You damn well should have had a star . . ."

"What happened at the camp?" Miss White asked.

"Treated our boys a lot better after that. Every guard in Germany knew better than to screw around with the 100th after that. You did it, Harry. Now you can again—"

"I'm not mad anymore, general."

"*I am.* There's only a couple of things I do better than you. Holding grudges is one of them. I told you this was personal."

Steele looked at his assistant, who walked quickly to the door and locked it.

"Okay, what's the target?" Logan asked.

"Dead Moon Valley—in eastern Burma near the Thai border."

Alison Gordon finally understood.

"What's in the valley?" Logan asked.

"Tell him, general. Tell him how far your vengeance has to go," Alison said.

"My grandson died of an overdose—Double Uoglobe brand heroin. Your friend here helped punish the pusher, the wholesaler and the importer. Did a pretty good job, I have to admit. Now I want the source."

"He's nuts, Harry."

Steele ignored it. "That poison comes out in big convoys once or twice a year. Maybe eight hundred mules carrying opium, armed escort of up to one thousand armed mercenaries. I want to hit them in the valley."

"He wants to kill one thousand *men* to get even—not Nazis. Some of them Shan or Meo tribesmen, some Chinese Nationalist leftovers just trying to survive. You want to butcher them, Harry?"

"It's a damned murder caravan—it brings death to thousands of kids here, in Britain, a dozen countries in Europe and Asia. I say kill the killers—"

"So that's the mission."

The general nodded, relit his own corona.

Logan turned to Alison. "In a way he's right . . . it is my last chance."

"*I'm* your last chance, Harry—and you're mine. But you want to be a hero again? All right, we'll do it."

The Old Man actually beamed.

Logan too. "That $250,000 ought to come in handy, now that I'm taking on an expensive lady."

She loved him too much to tell him he was lying.

"$300,000," she corrected him. "You'll need a cover operation to camouflage the whole deal, and tight professional security. The extra fifty's for me—"

"Who said *you're* going?" Steele broke in.

"I did. Maybe I can help Harry get out of this alive. You wouldn't get a plane off the ground without me, dummy."

"Why should I pay you? You'd go anyway—for him."

"You're right . . . but you're not cheap. You're not *that* much of a businessman, are you, general?"

"You better be as good as you talk, young lady."

"I'm like Logan, general. I'm the best."

Steele sighed, looked over at Logan. "Well, Blue Leader, are *you* with me?"

Logan deliberately avoided her eyes, focused on Steele. "I'm with you, general. We'd better get to work right away. Buying planes won't half do it. We'd need spare parts, ammo, bombs. Crews—ground crews and flying personnel. We'll need radios, trucks and jeeps, uniforms, probably a couple of cargo planes."

"Whatever you say."

"We'll need a lot more intelligence, and we'll need a place to train—some jungle area. I think I know the spot."

The Old Man was delighted.

Blue Leader was back at war. They both were.

With Blue Leader leading the attack, they couldn't lose. Those death-dealing bastards were good as dead.

12

THE GENERAL LIFTED his goblet, looked to Logan.

"You call it, Blue Leader."

Logan didn't hesitate.

"Maximum effort."

"Maximum effort!" Steele echoed, drained the cognac, then laughed and explained. "That's what I used to tell them before important strikes—maximum effort. They took my initials—M. E.— and called me that. Maximum Effort Steele—I wasn't supposed to know. Hell, I was proud of it."

Logan relit his cigar, nodded.

"It'll be just like the old days," Steele said expansively.

"No, it won't," Logan told him. "It won't be World War Two and the Eighth Air Force," Logan said, "and we'd better face it right now. We'll be a small unit with no backup, no fighter escort, no great military machine or industrial power behind us. In fact, the United States will be against us."

"So will Thailand, Burma and every other government," Alison Gordon added.

"We'll have no friends, no allies," Logan went on. "Every man, woman and child . . . every cop and every crook . . . every beggar and banker . . . every intelligence outfit in Asia will be our enemies—"

"*Wait* a minute—"

"There's more, general. In '45 we smashed them with thousand-plane raids, and if we didn't wipe out the targets, we'd come back in a couple of days with another thousand or the RAF would. This time we'll have one shot. Whether it works or not, we'll have to bug out like bandits the minute it's over."

"It'll *work*," The Old Man insisted.

"If you haven't already blown it," she said. "Who else knows about this?"

"Steiner—our senior analyst. It was his idea," Miss White told her, "and we didn't tell anyone else."

"How do you know? When was this room last swept for bugs?"

The general pointed at his assistant. "Tell Security to sweep again in the morning."

"We're leaving in the morning. Please call Steiner now," Logan said, "and tell him to bring whatever target data he's assembled. We're moving the operation out of here at 0900. Lay on a flight, will you?"

"Where the hell are you going?"

"Costa Verde."

Logan had served as U. S. air attaché in that Central American dictatorship just before he retired, and then had helped start that banana republic's regional airline. That too was in his file.

"We'll set up a Bahamian or Panamanian holding company to handle the money and the planes," the ex-intelligence agent, thought aloud, "and we'll call it—"

"Aero Central," Logan suggested. "The corporate shell already exists. A charter outfit by that name collapsed two or three years ago. We could buy control for forty or fifty thousand."

"Cash," A. B. Gordon specified. "No checks to be traced. About those bombers—you haven't bought any yet, have you?"

"We're looking," Steele told her.

"Stop—right now. Telex your people to call it off immediately. There mustn't be any connection between Atlas and those planes. *We'll* buy the planes."

"How're you going to find them?" the general demanded.

"You wouldn't want to know," she assured him. "We'll be opening a Swiss account in three days. I'll get you the name of the bank and the number. We'll need a million. Make it a million-two in Swiss francs or Deutschmarks. I don't even want U.S. dollars in the account. Can you meet me with the cash in Zurich—Thursday at noon?"

A startled Samantha White looked to the general.

"She'll be there," he said, nodding toward Miss White.

"Main railroad station," Gordon instructed.

"Do I get a receipt?" the general said with a straight face.

"What you get is your revenge," Logan told him. "Don't you

understand? Alison's trying to protect your ass. No pieces of paper to tie you to this operation. Al . . . your friend who sells B-17s? Can he get us bombs and ammo too?"

She laughed. "Anything your little heart desires," she promised. "Red Army jockstraps, West German tank parts, Egyptian naval mines or Chinese warheads—he can deliver if the price is right. He's got nine names, twelve passports and a delightful sense of humor. He buys weapons and corrupts officials the way you change your socks—every day."

"Just the man we need," Logan said.

"One of my favorite rogues."

"Maybe you'd better take a million-five," Steele thought aloud. "This guy sounds like a one-stop. Can he be trusted?"

She laughed again. "He can be trusted to screw anyone if he thinks he can get away with it. If he thinks you're not going to kill him, he'll overcharge you or short count you or maybe sell a load of the same hardware to the other side. I've known him for years. It's never dull—he'll get the stuff."

Those years of CIA training had stopped her from mentioning the name. Which was good, Logan thought, because they'd need only professional, total security.

"You don't think he'll cheat you?" Steele asked.

"General, he knows I *will* kill him."

He believed her. Startlingly beautiful, and just as tough . . . Steele had never met this combination, and for a moment he envied Logan, who wasn't one-thousandth as rich or powerful.

While Miss White summoned Steiner, Logan and the general talked about the top B-17 crewmen and how they might be located. Steele was still "wired in," he said, to several senior Air Force officers at the Pentagon, but it would be too dangerous to use them . . . one of them might make the connection later, after the raid. There must be no link between the strike force and Vandal.

The reunion book . . . that was it. The alumni of the 100th had assembled every ten years since 1945 to relive the "glory days," and after the '75 meeting in Dayton Bob Young had sent out a mimeographed directory with the home addresses of more than two hundred surviving veterans who either attended or sent their regrets. Miss White, her fine legs noted by Logan as she walked, left to Xerox the list as Steiner arrived with two bulging canvas weekend bags.

"Milton, this is Blue Leader," Steele said. "He's our man—the one I promised."

"The best B-17 commander in the world?"

"The same. He's leading the strike. Give him the stuff you've collected."

The scientist eyed Logan for several moments, put down the suitcases and stepped forward to shake hands.

"I think it'll work. It ought to," Steiner said.

"Don't sweat it. We'll gut 'em."

They shook hands.

"This is just preliminary research," Steiner told him. "You'll need a lot more. More recent maps, more detailed photos."

"We'll get it. One more thing, Milton."

"Yes?"

"It's a brilliant idea. Thanks."

Dr. Milton Steiner allowed himself to smile. "What are you going to call it?"

Steele opened his mouth, but Logan spoke first.

"Hacksaw Two."

The Old Man blinked. Hacksaw had been the code name for the attack on the Düsseldorf munitions plants—the raid in which his younger brother had died. Logan was doing this to honor Jeff, to make his commitment clear.

"Okay, general?"

"Hacksaw Two. Sure." He was obviously pleased.

Steiner departed, Miss White returned with the Xerox copies, and Alison Gordon thought about what had just happened. The command of the operation had changed hands. Harry Logan was in charge again—after all those years. Ten minutes later he led her upstairs to bed, and he was in command there too. She didn't mind at all—so long as he anticipated and fulfilled her every wish as he did, made love with intense attention to each nerve and whim. It was as if they were Siamese twins joined together in total communion. He loved giving her everything she wanted . . . it was what he wanted too. She didn't feel he was just inside her. He was part of her.

How could it happen this fast? In less than forty-eight hours they were bound together beyond all reason or expectation, and she *knew* that this was *the* man. Nothing would separate them as long as they lived—she'd do *whatever* was necessary to keep Harry O. Logan beside her. Dead Moon Valley lay ahead; no one could predict how much time they'd have. She coiled her legs around him once again, and she shivered as he whispered her name in the darkness. He felt grateful beyond words to have found her after all these years, and then he lost himself in her magic.

13

I<small>T WASN'T</small> until after the Learjet jumped into the sky precisely at nine the next morning that Logan explained why they were flying to Costa Verde. Not many people wanted to go to Costa Verde, a small and steamy nation with more army camps than tourist hotels and one of the lowest literacy rates in the hemisphere. It took Haiti and Uganda to make Costa Verde look good in those United Nations studies. There was enough fruit and fish there so that few people starved, but education was minimal, medical care poor and civil liberties just words in that parody of the American Constitution some early president of Costa Verde had signed during a bout of malarial confusion. Bribery and tropical fevers were still team sports in this country, despite the progressive leadership of the current president—José Fabrega Enrique O'Brien Garcia.

As Richard M. Nixon proved, there are all kinds of presidents. There are smart ones and fools, bastards, populists, crooks, statesmen, womanizers, drunkards, philosophers, ex-terrorists, saints, mediocrities, heroes, cowards, orators, mumblers, stumblers, pompous asses and individuals of true religious dedication. Presidents come in all colors, sizes, ages, sexes and ideologies. They speak in many tongues—usually forked. Apaches and Sioux have—wisely—never trusted presidents or used car salesmen, referring to them as Great White Mothers.

Like most other presidents, the chief of state of Costa Verde was a true patriot who loved children and spoke of the glories of democracy. He'd been elected by his peers—both of them. His father, General Hernan Garcia, had been the president and his uncle Ricardo had been head of the army, and they'd agreed with the first lady—who had a big mouth—that José would run the business better than his older brother Miguel, who collected teenaged Indian girls, antique pistols and social diseases. His mother—a deeply pious woman who always kept fifty or sixty machine guns and a couple of antitank weapons in the cellar—had blessed the selection of José. To prepare him for his complex responsibilities she'd taught him about Swiss accounts, the importance of good relations with the Associated Fruit Company and how to make laundered contributions to the campaigns of American senators.

"He's quite a guy," Logan said as they unpacked their bags in the Simón Bolívar Suite of the Hotel Nacional-Sheraton.

"A prize prick, I hear," she replied matter-of-factly.

"A dictator—sure. A rough cob—absolutely. A tyrant—first class. But why don't you meet him before you call him a *prick?*"

She hung up her spare skirt, turned. "I didn't call him a prick, Harry. I just said that's what I heard. I'm used to dealing with that sort of person. After many years in the C.I.A. and my tour on the Beverly Hills circuit—well, pricks are strictly routine."

Logan winced.

"My language bother you, Harry?" she asked pleasantly.

"I'm getting used to it. You're the new woman, right?"

"I'm *your* new woman, Harry," she answered, and kissed him on the side of the neck. He took her in his arms, and their bodies joined from lips to thighs. His hands moved down her spine to that place in the small of her back, and she made her happy animal sound. In a moment, the growl turned to a sigh.

"I've got a great idea, Harry."

"All your ideas are great," he said as he stroked her.

"This is one of my greatest," she answered, and squirmed.

He kissed her again.

"What time are we due there?" she whispered.

"Soon. Save the great idea."

"I don't want to. Harry, why don't we—"

"We will. Later."

She disengaged herself, patted his face. "Couldn't El Presidente wait half an hour?"

The president of Costa Verde did, and he didn't seem to mind. He was plainly delighted to welcome them to the palace, a white-walled confection of a Moorish monstrosity with tough little soldiers manning sandbagged posts every thirty yards along the exterior fortifications. The office of El Presidente on the second floor was huge, and the man himself was appropriate for it—he was at least six feet two, two hundred forty pounds with a large head adorned by an outsized macho mustache.

"Mr. President," Logan said as he prepared to make the introductions.

"You got a lot of balls, Harry," the president roared amiably.

"I'd like you to meet Alison—"

"Keeping the president waiting while you screw your brains out . . . goddam, Harry, you haven't changed a bit!"

It took Logan a moment to understand, then, "You had the room bugged—"

"Not too well, either," she judged. "That mike in the molding over the bed was pretty crude. I spotted it the moment we dropped our bags. The primitive device built into the phone was—I don't want to hurt your feelings—embarrassing."

Garcia threw his arms around the flier in a classic Latin *abrazo*, stepped back and studied A. B. Gordon.

"That's some helluva broad, Harry."

"Some helluva broad," Logan agreed. "Alison Gordon, may I present President José Fabrega Enrique O'Brien Garcia—general of the armies, supreme commander of the air force and chief of naval operations of the Republic of Costa Verde."

"The fellow you called a prize prick," Garcia added.

"An honor to meet you, Mr. President. Have you got any cold beer?"

"She's beautiful, Harry. I mean it. Harry . . . Harry, it's great to have you back." He ordered the beer and the malt Scotch for himself and Logan, then he gestured for them to sit down. "It's been terrible since you left, Harry."

"I read about the guerrillas."

"Nah, nah—we can handle those idiots. I learned that back at Fort Benning in '48. My old man sent me there—basic training for Central American presidents. My boy, Diego, went to the Stanford Business School instead, and all he brought back was a lot of crap about accounting and cash flow and profit centers. How the hell is he going to run the family business?"

"The Republic of Costa Verde is the family business," Logan told her.

"And he'll run it right into the ground," Garcia said gloomily. "He wants to *talk* to the students. Some bullshit about participatory communication and—hell, it's rubbish. He even wants to give land to the Indians. I don't sleep nights, Harry. My wife's in Paris buying

Diors, the college kids are raising hell and those moronic Cubans may try to ship in another load of guns any day. I don't get much help from the U.S. either."

"Sounds grim," Logan agreed as the drinks arrived.

"That's not all. Harry, I haven't had a decent game of poker since you left. That new American ambassador? I think he's weird or something. Wants to play backgammon. What kind of game is that?"

"Quite popular in fashionable circles now, Mr. President," Alison said.

"Tell her to call me Joe, will you?" Garcia said, and shoved an open humidor of Upmanns toward the flier.

"Sure. Joe—Alison. Alison—Joe."

Logan extracted a corona, bit off the tip.

"Take a handful, Harry. Damn, it's good to see you. What are you doing these days? How long can you stay? You can move in here, you know."

"Joe, we're here on business. We need your help."

The president lit his own cigar, gestured broadly. "You got it Harry. What's the deal?"

"That airstrip at Puerto Linda down the coast—the one the fruit company used?"

"Yeah?"

"I want to borrow it for eight or ten weeks. Training some fliers for a movie. Alison's from Hollywood, you know."

It figured, Garcia thought. He was a tit man himself, and she was well endowed like those movie actresses. "No sweat, Harry. When is the plane coming in?"

"Soon. But not one. Six B-17s."

The president remembered. "Four-engine jobs. The Brazilians had some fifteen years ago—search-and-rescue patrols at sea. This a search-and-rescue picture, Harry?"

Logan blew a smoke ring. "World War Two—how we beat the Japs. They'll be rigged as combat aircraft, machine guns and all. Very realistic."

"Nostalgia's big right now," she added.

"Sure. I always liked war pictures myself—those and the cowboys and Indians. Sounds great. Who's making it? MGM? Warners? Columbia?"

"It's a new company. You never heard of them."

Logan's tone was now saying more than his words.

78

"How realistic?"

"Real bombs and live ammo. We'll only do *rehearsals* here, Joe. We'll do the actual shooting in Asia later."

"Sounds like a big deal, Harry."

"The budget's over four mil," Alison said.

Garcia thought, then shrugged. "Six bombers—people are gonna notice them."

"Nothing secret about this," she assured him. "Publicity's good for a film. You'll read about it in all the papers when we start shooting. You'd better. We're hiring one of the best press agents in Hollywood."

She was playing it very well. All so cool and casual now, very different from the woman whose animal cries had sounded less than an hour ago.

"Well, I hope you make a million," Garcia said as he stood and splashed more Scotch into Logan's glass and his own. He didn't notice her eyeing the flowers by the window.

"Here's to the movie," he toasted, and stepped forward.

He sipped, and she dived across the room to knock him sprawling. The window shattered as he fell, and now they heard the staccato hammering of automatic weapons. Eight bullet holes desecrated the oil painting of his grandfather on the wall—slugs that would have killed him if she hadn't intervened.

"Mierda!"

The president of Costa Verde started to rise—but she pushed him to the floor again.

"Stay down."

Somehow he wasn't surprised to see the .357 in her right hand. There was more firing—from several weapons, at least a dozen bursts as the guards joined the action. The shooting continued for almost half a minute, then ended as suddenly as it had begun. A moment later the door was swung open to admit a young captain and two sergeants carrying U.S. M-16s. She maneuvered her heavy handgun to cover them, but Garcia held up his hand.

"It's okay, Alison. Okay, you understand? What the hell's going on out there, captain?"

The young officer hesitated. "A sentry on the wall, Mr. President. He went crazy, or something. He only joined the guard detail this week."

Garcia knew that it hadn't been insanity. The craziness was in those college kids and their revolution talk . . . it was getting to people, even some of the soldiers. He waved the uniformed trio to leave, turned to Alison. "Thanks for the shove. You've got some eyes, Alison."

"You're welcome, Joe." She holstered the Magnum and adjusted her skirt.

"I'd be dog meat if you hadn't—Harry, come do your movie. Anything you want . . . make it as realistic as you like. Stay as long as you want. I like this lady, Harry. A real lifesaver."

"For me too," Logan said, and reached for her hand.

They left Costa Verde in the Learjet at seven that evening, half an hour after the report on their visit to the presidential palace reached Dr. Lawrence Zimmerman. Cousin of a famed rock star and himself a Phi Beta Kappa from Cornell, Dr. Zimmerman was the assistant agricultural attaché at the U.S. Embassy and a serious collector of pre-Columbian artifacts. He was also the station chief for the Central Intelligence Agency in Costa Verde.

14

In Madrid, a man may be identified by the *tapas* bar he frequents. In due course as social progress advances, this will no doubt apply to women too. In Hong Kong, the name of one's tailor and the firm that makes one's shirts are considered significant, and in both greater and greatest Los Angeles one is judged by his/her car and swimming pool. Frankfurt is traditional, relying on cash and mistresses as units of measure. London still goes by the club to a large degree, despite the depredations of socialist playwrights and Cockney rock stars. Everyone knows that almost anyone can join the Royal Automobile Club, but membership in the Atheneum is largely limited to writers, bishops and senior civil servants.

In Paris, it's the café that counts. Whether you sip coffee, Beaujolais, fiery Marc from Normandy or *le Scotch,* it is where you imbibe that establishes your identity. *Les vedettes du cinéma* drink at the bar of the Hotel Georges Cinq, editors at the sidewalk tables of the Deux Magots, lesbians at that charming place on Rue des Martyrs and chess freaks at Chez Gustave. There is nothing distinctive about the exterior of the Left Bank café named in honor of the late Monsieur Flaubert, a novelist much admired by a Breton named Rapicault who founded this establishment in 1928. The interior wood-and-mirror decor is typical of at least sixty other cafés here in the sixth arrondissement. It is the steady customers—*les habitués* who come in regularly—who make this place on the Rue du Dragon special. They are all serious chess players. Earnest men and women ring the boards that adorn almost every table, and there is little conversation—even when gray-haired Madame Cécile brings a *filtre* or a *fine* to one of the combatants. The warriors range from nineteen to eighty-nine—fierce young students, aging directors and

81

ageless actresses, smugglers, poets, photographers, pornographers, musicians, free-lance spies and businessmen. No one asks what business one is in or what passport one carries. Race or creed, accent or affluence mean nothing at Chez Gustave. Fame, beauty, sexual talents also count for little. Chess skills, cunning and concentration, are all that matter here.

There were sixteen people ringing or studying the boards as Harry Logan and Alison Gordon entered, and the only person who noted the arrival of the Americans was a bony, gray-haired woman who stood behind the bar slicing ham.

"Madame Cécile," Alison told him softly.

"Nice lady?"

"She cut the throats of two Gestapo agents in 1944—probably with that knife. Care for a sandwich?"

"Later."

The woman behind the bar nodded in recognition.

"*Bonjour*, Alison," she said, and reached for a plate.

"*Bonjour, madame.* How's *le minou?*"

Not all Americans were uncivilized. Madame Cécile was pleased that her old customer had remembered the cat. The owner of Chez Gustave hadn't seen the American girl for nine years, but she hadn't forgotten what she drank. She filled a wineglass with Byrrh, set it down on the bar, then gave a Gallic shrug. "Who knows about a cat?" She appraised the couple. "They sleep a lot. They're worse than men, *n'est-ce pas?*"

"Much worse," Alison said, and smiled at Logan.

"Is this your man?"

"This is my man. His name is Harry. Harry, this is Madame Cécile."

The French woman wiped her hand on her apron, thrust it forward. Logan was surprised by her powerful grip, and she was impressed by his as well.

"*Soldat?* An officer?"

"Not lately," Logan told her.

"Not so long ago either. A man's grasp tells a good deal, Monsieur Harry. *Eh bien,* will you drink?"

"Whiskey, please."

"Malt whiskey," Alison further specified.

Madame Cécile smiled, pleased that Alison took such care of her man. The way that he stayed close to her was good, and the look in his eyes said that he cared too. She poured the Scotch and began to talk about the cat. He was twelve years old now, still prowling the night and fathering kittens as far as the butcher shop on the Rue des Sts. Pères . . .

As she talked, Logan noted Alison scanning the chess players in the mirrors, drank his Glenfiddich and wondered who were these people at the boards?

The portly man with the gold watch chain across his belly? The young Arab in metal-rimmed glasses? Was the busty brunette who did wonders for her Notre Dame T-shirt an artist's model or an Israeli courier? That mustachioed man whose Italian tailor had done wonders for him—was he a rare-book dealer or a gold smuggler? They were probably all law-abiding citizens whose only vice was chess, and it was silly to romanticize. He lit a Don Diego, returned his focus to the conversation beside him.

"A good man and a good cigar. There's nothing like the aroma of a good cigar," Madame Cécile reminisced.

She hadn't asked one question. One did not make inquiries in Chez Gustave.

"By the way, madame," Alison said casually as she finished her aperitif, "if you should see Emil . . . by chance . . . please say hello."

"Of course, but he doesn't come in that often."

Alison Gordon stood up, patted Logan on the arm. "Let's wander over to Lipp's, I'm in the mood for Alsatian food."

Logan paid the bill, and they both shook hands with Madame Cécile again before they left. As they walked up the narrow street lined with small shops, restaurants and bookstores, Alison told him about the history of the café—how it had been a World War Two hangout for Resistance types and black marketeers and later a popular haunt for British, American and Scandinavian writers and painters in the fifties. The lovers turned right at the corner into the bustle of the Boulevard St. Germain, and four minutes later were studying menus in the restaurant Lipp. The big *serieux* of dark beer went well with the spicy sauerkraut, ham and sausage combination, but Logan wasn't really satisfied.

"Now where do we look for your hardware dealer?" he asked.

"Nowhere. He'll be along as soon as the game's over," she assured him as she finished the last of the *choucroute*.

"He was there?"

She nodded, brushed her lips with the cloth napkin.

"Why didn't we—"

"He's shy. Ah, Emil—come join us for a bite."

It was the plump man with the gold watch chain.

"I couldn't impose," he said in some accent tinged with the sounds of Eastern Europe—perhaps Poland or one of the Balkan nations.

He bent ponderously to kiss her hand, grinned like some naughty philandering husband.

"You grow lovelier by the minute."

"By the year, Emil. You still flatter beautifully. Emil, this is my friend, Harry . . . my very good friend."

"There's nothing more precious than good friends. What a pleasure to see you, my dear."

He sighed massively, and—with great care—lowered himself onto a chair.

"You won, of course?" she asked.

"Naturellement, but the competition isn't what it used to be."

"Maybe it never was," Logan said.

"A philosopher? How splendid!"

"A flier," she corrected.

Logan signaled to the waiter, and the man with the gold chain consented to order a double portion of *cervelas* sausage, a cassoulet of white beans and duck and a large stein of beer. Followed by another *serieux,* two pastries and a pot of tea. It wasn't until he squeezed the lemon that A. B. Gordon raised the question of business.

"We're here to do some shopping, Emil, and perhaps you might advise us."

"Shoes? Ties?"

"Aircraft," Logan said.

"Try the *mille-feuille,* just a forkful," the fat man urged.

"B-17s . . . the G model . . . six."

"Is he joking, Alison?"

She shook her head.

"We're making a movie," she said.

The chess master shoveled more pastry into his surprisingly small mouth, grunted.

"Who isn't?" he replied as he chewed. "Very popular. They say it's an art form now. You believe that?"

"17Gs rigged with thirteen .50-caliber machine guns each, bombs, spare parts, napalm canisters—I've got a whole shopping list," Logan told him.

"Try the Galeries Lafayette. Sale on Franck-Olivier blouses this week," Emil told Alison. "Numbers you'd pay $65 for on Madison Avenue are going for $22."

Logan ignored the evasion. "At least a hundred thousand rounds of machine gun ammo for those .50s. Couple of four-engine cargo planes . . . old C-54s or 130s if you can get them, half a dozen medium trucks and ten jeeps—World War Two models or look-alikes."

"Ought to be a wonderful movie, colonel."

"I never said he was a colonel," Alison told him.

"I've done business with a thousand of them, haven't I? Easy to spot. Very erect and determined, know exactly what they want and not as dumb as generals. I've met generals—*unbelievable.*"

Alison refused to be deflected.

"We'll need some other things, Emil. We pay cash. Swiss francs —up front."

His pudgy hand moved quickly to his face, just masking a belch.

"I simply don't deal in such items anymore," he replied. His eyes darted to the dessert tray, and she saw that he was considering another pastry.

"Don't," she advised. "You wouldn't want to get fat, would you?"

"How thoughtful you are, my dear . . . and I'm sorry I can't help. I've dropped those lines, you see. Machine tools or industrial diamonds, certainly. Maria Theresa silver thalers or gold bullion, all you wish. How about three nice tankers in wonderful condition— cheap?"

"Captains were old Liberian ladies who only sailed them to church on Sundays?"

"Not bad . . . for a colonel. Alison, you *must* have heard I don't handle such merchandise anymore. Your *company* is well informed."

"I haven't worked for that company in years, Emil. I'm in business for myself, in Beverly Hills."

Emil dabbed at the pastry crumbs on his lips.

"Two freight cars of Courvoisier—lost, so to speak, on a siding near Lyons?" he offered.

She shook her head, smiled and lit a cigarette.

"Nine hundred Sony color sets—seventeen-inch beauties—with a bill of lading that's a genuine work of art?"

She shook her head again. He reached inside his velvet jacket, pulled out an elegant wallet of lizard.

"Put your money away. You're our guest."

Emil looked baffled.

"Don't argue with Harry. He's very old-fashioned."

It wasn't fair of the Americans to be so terribly nice. "I'll ask around," Emil offered.

"We need it soon. Going to be one *helluva* movie."

Was this colonel determined or crazy? Emil thought of his own experiences with Arabs, Africans, Israelis, Slavs, Latins, and half a dozen kinds of Asian. It was difficult to tell with them this committed. This one was quiet and had good manners, but he was—most surely . . . fierce. He was someone to be taken seriously.

She said they'd check back at Chez Gustave in two days, and Emil thanked them twice before he waddled toward the exit to the Boulevard St. Germain. She turned to Logan, saw him smiling. He wasn't at all discouraged.

"We'll get the hardware from somebody else, hon," he predicted, and gestured for *l'addition*. "There are dealers in Zurich too, aren't there?"

She leaned forward, kissed him.

He had enough sense not to ask why.

He paid the check, and when they reached the street he pointed at a trio of taxis lined up fifty yards away. They were due to meet Samantha White, the general's assistant, at that Swiss rail station the next day, he recalled as he opened the cab door. He'd phone from the hotel about the airline schedules.

"Tomorrow morning," she said as if reading his mind.

"Why not this afternoon?"

"Are you crazy? You think I'm going to pass up those blouses?"

Logan held her hand all the way across the bridge and through the honking traffic to the big department store on the Boulevard Haussmann. She bought three blouses, and he reserved the seats on the nine A.M. Air France flight, and they took a shower together in the hotel before they made love.

At CIA headquarters in Virginia, a clerk routinely opened the pouch that had come in from Costa Verde. He removed the contents to send them up to that bright young analyst just assigned to keep an eye on Central American ferment, the Puerto Rican guy with the M.A. from Tulane. Costa Verde, Nicaragua, Guatemala—they were all heating up fast. They weren't sleepy "banana republics" anymore. Students, Cubans, labor leaders, Sov-sympathizers, reforming or radical priests, guerrilla instructors, ambitious junior officers—they were all pushing, planning, menacing the status quo.

Some kind of change was in the air, and simplistic and powerful men who never listened to the agency anyway were demanding that the CIA predict precisely what and when it would be. Central America wasn't on the back burner now.

Every report that came up—even those from bombastic types such as Zimmerman—was being scrutinized carefully. There was no telling what you might find—even in a nothing place as damp, dull and dreary as Costa Verde. If there was anything at all in these dispatches, Arthur Castillo would find it in due course. The kid was an ambitious type, an eager beaver who doubled-checked everything.

Including names.

15

IT WAS COLD as the horse climbed steadily up the twisting road, and the Haw merchant buttoned his quilted Chinese cotton jacket as he fought down a shiver. The Meo tribes who chose to live in these chilly green hills couldn't take the humid heat of the valleys, the rider thought, and he thanked lord Buddha for that. It was only the Haw traders like himself—determined small businessmen whose families had bought the Meo's only cash crop for nearly a century —who had access to the gum of the poppies the illiterate tribesmen cultivated.

The merchant now saw the spirals of smoke rising near the crest, and he understood. There were many tribes dispersed across these remote hills in northeastern Burma, Lahus, Yaos—those filthy Akhas, rebellious Shans, Karens and Kachins who still revered the bold men of the Office of Strategic Services who'd armed them to fight the Toyko people in World War Two, and the Meo, who were spread across north Thailand, Laos and Viet Nam, and were the best of the opium growers, as well as the worst farmers. This was the usual November smoke, signaling that the Meo had chopped down their trees and were burning the stumps to clear the land. They'd put in a crop of rice first, and then the poppies.

Slash-and-burn each November for three years.

Then the earth would be exhausted, and they'd move the whole village a few miles to repeat the primitive process.

The Meo were hard workers, brave soldiers and good citizens of the eighteenth century. The Haw, whose ancestors had migrated from southern China two centuries earlier, liked to do business with these simple folk. They were like cows, the trader reflected, easy to milk in a dozen ways. The Haw lent them money at exorbitant rates of interest, and they never complained. The Chinese traders sold them salt, sugar, matches, oil lamps and other essentials that couldn't be grown—at prices thirty percent higher than those charged down in the valley towns. The Haw lived halfway up, and the Meo preferred to be exploited by them rather than face the lowlanders' jokes about the colorful and "old-fashioned" Meo "costumes," massive silver necklaces and odd fezlike hats.

There was nothing quaint about their guns. Even the poorest village had a dozen or more American M-1 rifles, sturdy World War Two weapons in good condition. The Meo could be exploited economically, but they were not to be pushed around physically by anyone—not even an army. The Haw trader and the whole Golden Triangle knew of the savage Meo battles against Thai engineers and soldiers who foolishly tried to build a highway right through the tribal poppy fields in Chiang Mai province. The fighting had been bitter, and probably unnecessary. It was merely a question of knowing how to deal with the hill tribes, a matter of respect. Most government officials and military officers in all the nations here treated them like barbarians, which made it easier for the Haw merchants to profit from their fear and anger.

The trader reined the horse to a halt, listened.

It paid to be careful in these green hills. This whole region was a no-man's-land of armed tribesmen, money-hungry rebel bands seeking funds for better weapons, so-called gendarmes who were little better than bandits, and a variety of bandits who were no good at all. Only last week, a bus had pulled into a town less than sixty miles from this ridge with every passenger and the driver stark naked. The bandits had taken everything, leaving only their fillings and religious amulets. That group of travelers had been lucky— sometimes the marauders left corpses.

The Haw loosened his 9-millimeter automatic in its holster, nudged his mount forward. He'd be safe when he entered the village so long as he observed the Meo rules and customs. They were animists with witch doctors and a complex religion, and there was a whole code about sex and women. The trader's father had taught him these things, passing on what his own father had learned from an earlier ancestor.

Now the terrain was level, and the Chinese merchant sensed that the settlement was near. The horse moved a bit more rapidly, pleased that the long ascent was over at last. And there it was . . . thirteen or fourteen large thatched shacks with a cornfield behind them. It was still damp up here despite the altitude—a sweaty tribute to the acute humidity that blanketed the whole region. The Meo—perhaps twenty or twenty-five were in sight feeding pigs, weaving, cooking, nursing children—did not appear to notice the clamminess at all—their attention was focused on the stranger.

The headman came forward from his big house, and the ritual began. Formal greetings were exchanged, as they had been in such meetings for hundreds of years. The man who led this group of Meo wore the black cotton trousers and flower-pattern sash that his tribe had favored for so many generations, and the words that the merchant spoke were no different than those uttered by his father and grandfather on arriving at just such a village. The headman spoke to a middle-aged woman, who returned with earthen bowls of boiled rice and roast pork. There was tea, and then there was talk of trading. The Haw waited politely until the headman mentioned that the supply of matches and candles was dwindling, and he nodded when his host mentioned that more cloth was needed for the New Year.

Three kilos.

6.6 pounds of gum opium—that was all one might reasonably expect this isolated group of tribesmen to grow—tribesmen and tribeswomen . . . the women here played a major role in tending the animals and the fields. They were big, strong women, stronger than the Burmese or Thai down below. The trader's brother was married to such a Meo woman, one of four daughters of another headman.

The bargaining began, and when it was over the trader handed over half of the goods that would pay for the opium. The other half would come when he returned to pick up the dark balls in February when the poppies had been harvested. There was nothing to worry about here. The Meo were honest, and they would deliver.

Now more formalities—ritual but essential. The Haw thanked the headman for his hospitality, remounted and started down the mountain. It was as he left the village that he saw a pretty girl of sixteen, and he thought of his stupid cousin who had tried to win such a juicy creature and then attempted to take her by force. She had beaten him off unassisted, and then the men had tried him for his crime. They could have killed him under Meo custom and law. They could have tied his legs to a pair of oxen, fired off their rifles to scare the animals into tearing him in two. But they had shown mercy because his cousin Feng was the son of an old and familiar merchant, so they thrashed him with clubs and took his money and weapon before chasing him away. He could never return, of course. He could never deal with any Meo clan in these hills again; word of his barbarism had spread. Now he kept a shop down in the valley, barely eking out a living and shunned by all the Haws he'd embarrassed . . . The trader nodded politely to the girl, masking the desire that could threaten his business. She blinked noncommittally at the outsider, exactly as a good and proper Meo girl should. The merchant rode on, thinking of the next cluster of houses nineteen miles away. That village's land was already losing its fertility, and this was that tribe's last year there. It would probably produce only two kilos this harvest.

Three kilos here, two kilos there.

Bought from the Meo at $40 a kilo, and sold to his Uncle Wu— the wholesaler down in the town—for $67 perhaps $68 each. It was a decent profit, and the price his uncle got did not bother the man on horseback at all. Everyone was entitled to make some money. The trader knew that somebody was reselling the balls bought from his uncle, and he had heard that there were men near the border who did something to cook the gum into powder. It was white, people said, and much more valuable than the gummy drippings scraped from the poppy pods by the Meo. Strangers in distant cities were rumored to pay as much as $2,000 for a kilo of that white powder, but the Haw merchant had not been fooled by those fairy tales. He was no child. Why would a man pay so much for crystals made from the milky sap of poppies when anyone could grow them in a thousand places?

Still, men killed for those balls of gum. One had to be wary, and the trader took no chances as he guided his mount toward the next ridge across the green-clad valley. He kept his hand on his gun, aware that there were four other villages on his route and it would be more than two weeks before he slept with his wife in his own bed in the town on the river. She was not as young or rosy as that Meo beauty, but she was warm and loving and patient. Patience was important. His people had known that for more than three hundred years. Whatever side of those man-made borders they lived on, they were—after all—Chinese. It was a great culture of scholars and scientists, bankers and merchant princes around the world. Now it was again a great power, as it had been centuries before. Whatever his politics, a Chinese could be proud of that.

As darkness drew near, the merchant resolved that he would tell this to his children once more when he got home—and rode on through the tropical forest he knew so well. His father had traveled this circuit, and his son would follow. If he were honest and kept faith with the tribes, if he delivered proper count and good quality, there was no reason that the trade should not continue. The Meo needed the salt and candles and lamps, and the prices on the opium kept rising. No one had ever been able to stop this traffic, or even seriously to dent it. It had never been difficult to pay off police or public officials in this part of Asia, so the future of the trade was safe.

Who could stop it?

Who in his right mind would even try?

16

THE SWISSAIR FLIGHT from Paris the next morning was on time. So was Miss White.

Precisely at noon, she gave Logan a heavy Pan Am flight bag in the Zurich rail terminal and walked away nibbling on a delicious bar of Lindt bittersweet chocolate. Some sixteen minutes later, the money was counted in the office of a Herr Schrager in the downtown Haemmerli Bank. As neutral and nonaligned as his country, the gray-suited Swiss showed no emotion as he computed the total.

"In U.S. currency, that is $1,502,004.37," he said with the nonchalance of a man who had opened dozens of numbered accounts with huge cash deposits. When the code name and other security arrangements were completed, he gave the flier a receipt and bowed courteously to the attractive and well-dressed woman who spoke such good German. Herr Schrager was polite to everyone with money, even those Japanese who were doing cheap knockoffs of fine Swiss watches. When Logan inquired about a good nearby restaurant, the banker helpfully suggested one that specialized in game—and saw them to the street to point the way to his cousin's establishment.

After some first-rate venison and dumplings, pastry and coffee, the Americans found their way through the snow-covered streets to a post office and Alison Gordon began telephoning. She spoke carefully, conscious that bitter and dangerous men might be tapping the lines of these arms dealers:

Salabert in Lausanne was *"en vacance,"* which could mean that he was out of the country buying more hardware or perhaps in jail.

Signor Arbolino in Trieste was in the hospital—"a tragic good accident." Some dissatisfied customer had perhaps put a bomb in

93

his car. Weapons merchants' accidents were rarely accidents.

Klaus Haberman in Hamburg—one of the biggest, she remembered. "Emil split an African deal with him in the sixties—"

"Let's go see Emil."

The security at Zurich Airport is the tightest in Europe. Each outbound bag is examined, and each passenger taken into a screened booth for a thorough body search. There are police with submachine guns at the exit to the field, and more near the plane. Property values and the tourist trade are terribly important to the Swiss, who may have missed World War Two but stand ready to fight heroically for what really matters. Promptness is also cherished by the virtuous Swiss, so the plane left exactly on schedule, and at 5:50 Logan and Gordon were ambling down the Rue du Dragon toward the chess players' cafe.

Emil was not there.

Nor was there a message for them.

Logan was silent as they wandered out, and said nothing until they were nearly at the corner. "There are two 17s down in Texas —Harlingen, Texas. Funny outfit called the Confederate Air Force. Flying buffs. I heard there's another in England. Company named Euroworld at Duxford in East Anglia."

"Will they sell them?"

"We'll find out. If they won't, we'll locate some others. We don't need that goddam Emil."

There he was.

Fat, smiling, munching on a pastry.

"Good-evening, *mes amis*," he said grandly. "You're looking *merveilleuse*, Alison—so why is the colonel scowling? If I were fortunate enough to be . . . associated . . . with such a beautiful woman, I would never scowl—"

"Klaus Haberman," Logan said impatiently.

"What is he talking about?"

"We'd like to get in touch with him, Emil," she explained.

"He has terrible manners."

"Does he have B-17s?" Logan demanded.

Something mischievous flickered in the fat man's eyes.

"I think I owe you an apology," he said.

She understood immediately. "I don't lie to friends."

"I had to check. It is that kind of world."

She put one of the black cigarettes in her holder, and the fat man with so many names hurried to light it with his gold Dunhill.

She smiled. "Emil's going to help us, Harry."

"With Haberman?"

"With the planes."

"I've found two already."

Logan pointed accusingly at the fat man. "You said you didn't—"

"He's making an exception—for an old friend," she soothed.

"I'm sentimental," the arms dealer confessed.

"An old friend who doesn't work for The Company," she pointed out wryly.

Now it made sense.

"I wouldn't sell *them* a used condom—excuse the language, my dear."

"Of course."

"You hear what they did to the Greek? Georgiades was one of the worst men in Europe, but they shouldn't have done *that.*"

"Damn right," Logan declared, and she patted his arm.

"Frankly, he was loathsome," Emil admitted, "and his table manners were disgusting . . . I didn't realize you knew him, colonel."

"I didn't—but I know 17s. Let's talk about them, Emil."

Emil forgot about Georgiades. "Hard to find. Rare birds, you might say."

He was setting the stage for inflated prices, the bargaining would come later. He reported that the planes had been stripped of their battle gear years earlier, but were still in "reasonable" condition. Until five weeks ago they'd been moving meat and salted fish between the Persian Gulf and Mombasa. Unable to compete with newer cargo aircraft, they'd been flown to England for overhaul and resale.

"They are at an airfield in Norfolk—a place called Thorpe Abbotts."

The shock showed clearly on Logan's face.

"139," he said.

"What is it, Harry?"

"Station 139 was the Air Corps designation for that field at Thorpe Abbotts near a town called Diss. That was *our* base. I remember the first strike that took off from it . . . 25 June 1943 . . . targets near Bremen . . . God, we were green, we lost thirty men that day . . ."

Neither Alison Gordon nor Emil spoke.

"In July we hit those U-boat pens in Norway. We only lost one crew that trip. We were learning . . ." He shook his head, braced and came back to them. "When can I see these planes?"

"I'll make some calls in the morning."

"What about tonight?"

The arms dealer began walking toward the Boulevard St. Germain.

"What about tonight?" Logan insisted.

"Tonight is impossible—tonight you are my guests for dinner at Laserre."

The foie gras *frais*, the crayfish, the duck—all were excellent. Emil pretended not to notice that the Americans were holding hands and touching, and after two glasses of wine he found himself wondering what they could possibly do with six antique bombers. It had to be something bizarre. They weren't adolescents. These were adults, deeply committed to each other, and to some plan that unquestionably had to be *fantastic* . . . It was intriguing. The additional bottle of Calon Segur '71 helped the arms merchant maintain a civilized conversation and avoid prying. He spoke of the odd sweaters worn by the American president, the effect of last year's drought on the Bordeaux pressings, the latest British sex scandal and that week's Italian kidnapping—anything to steer clear of improprieties. He was a perfect gentleman.

At 10:20 the next morning Emil kept his word and telephoned, and just before 3:00 that afternoon, the "airbus" carrying Logan touched down at Heathrow near London, where the hired car was waiting. It was almost dark when he reached the outskirts of Cambridge, and a light drizzle fell steadily, reminding him of so many English rains so long ago. It was all very immediate, as if it literally were only yesterday. He still remembered where every bomber base, fighter field and emergency strip had been. And suddenly a name jumped into his mind.

Austin.

Scott Austin—his plane had gone down on that first raid. Harry Logan tried to remember the names of the other young men who hadn't come home that day he'd never forget. It had been gray and cloudy like this one.

25 June 1943.

He was lone in the Jaguar and there was no one to judge him, but he still strained to fight back the tears. He looked up, and for a terrible split second the whole sky was filled with Flying Fortresses. The roar of their massed engines was deafening.

Ghosts.

They vanished, and—without warning—he missed A. B. Gordon very, very badly. She'd be stepping from a Concorde at Kennedy in a few minutes. It hurt to be away from her—even briefly . . . and he thought about other women who were separated forever from their men, the aircrews who'd died in that ancient and almost forgotten crusade. The young students and snotty journalists were wrong. It wasn't just musty history. It was *still* important. *They* had not burned up for nothing.

He was still brooding when he checked into the hotel near the university. Some things hadn't changed. There still wasn't enough heat in the room and the food was barely mediocre. The bed was hard . . . which wasn't the reason he slept badly. How could it be otherwise if she were not beside him in the chill night?

17

THE PAINT was peeling in a dozen places.

The left wing drooped visibly, and the right tire was so worn that he could almost see the inner cord.

Old, battered and beautiful.

Logan looked at the aged flying machine, thought how small it seemed in comparison with modern aircraft. 74 feet 8.9 inches long, wings 103 feet 9.4 inches across, it had been a giant then—the monarch of the skies. Curtis LeMay, the cigar-chewing chief of staff who bombed Japan to its knees, had called it "as tough an airplane as was ever built." Ira Eaker, who had three stars and a mind like a computer, had rated the 17 as the number one weapon in anyone's aerial arsenal.

"The best combat airplane ever built," Logan quoted.

"Our Lancs weren't *too* bad," Ashley observed quietly.

It was all right for Keith Ashley to laud the Royal Air Force's Lancasters and Halifaxes, both good machines flown by able crews. Ashley was British, and Harry Logan was old enough to respect patriotism. He wouldn't argue the merits of the 17 with him any more than he'd debate with Americans who'd flown 24s. The B-24 was a sturdy bomber, but the 17 was the *best*.

"Not bad at all," Logan agreed. "You fly Lancs?"

The ruddy-faced managing director of Norfolk Aircraft Ltd. nodded, smiled. "Don't have to ask which brute was yours," he said. "I think there used to be a chin turret up front—there."

"Power operated with twin .50s—the G model. Mine was called Dirty Dora," Logan remembered as his eyes swept the familiar field. He could almost see the rows of 17s taxiing for takeoff, and now there was one silent relic squatting in the gray morning . . . "There's another, isn't there?"

Ashley pulled a briar pipe from the pocket of his duffel coat, pointed at the corrugated metal hangar sixty yards away. As the two men walked toward the building, Logan talked about his days at this base and the Briton packed tobacco into the pipe's bowl, listening. Ashley's white hair testified to his approaching fifty-ninth birthday, but he wasn't so old, or bad-mannered, that he'd interrupt someone else's war stories.

"I'll torch up and catch a few puffs out here," he said as he drew his lighter and gestured toward the door. "Be along in a sec."

Logan entered, closed the door. This machine was in even worse condition. One engine was gone and another had no propeller. That could be fixed, if the electrical and hydraulic systems were basically sound. He had to see for himself—from inside. He felt strange— oddly self-conscious—as he circled the old bomber to where he could swing up and in. He hadn't been inside a 17 for more than twenty years. He stepped forward.

"What the hell do you think you're doing?" somebody shouted.

Somebody had a southern accent, and Logan turned to face a short wiry man in mechanic's work clothes. He had a mustache, a dark tan and a look of concentrated belligerence.

"My name's Logan."

"I don't give a crap if you're Clint Eastwood, mistuh. Stay away from *my* airplane—"

"I thought Ashley owned this ship."

"I fly it. It's *my* bird. If you're one of those cotton-pickin' vultures out to cannibalize her for the parts, forget it. She ain't ready for the scrapyard yet. You *read* me?"

"No, but I hear you. So does everybody else for three miles. What did you say your name was?"

"I didn't. What are you doin' screwing around my bird?"

Logan heard the laugh, swiveled his head.

"I see you've met Mr. Mayberry," Ashley said. "He knows a lot about that machine, I believe."

"Five and a half years, Yankee!"

It had to be done, and better now than . . . "Stick it," Logan told Mayberry.

"We say stuff it in Britain," volunteered Ashley, hoping to break the tension.

"Thanks. Stuff it, Mayberry—sideways. Now kindly shut your face and listen—"

"To what? Who the hell are you?"

"I told you. My name is Logan. I want to buy this bird to *fly* her, not to dismantle her. I wouldn't do that to a 17, dummy. I used to fly 17s myself . . . lot of missions, out of this field."

Mayberry looked at him suspiciously. "The 100th flew out of here, I heard. Were you with—"

He stopped in mid-sentence, stared, and Logan nodded.

"*Harry* Logan of the Bloody 100th? Ot-to, this is Harry Logan."

A blue-eyed man who'd come in with Ashley shrugged, and Mayberry thrust out his open palm to shake hands.

"Pleasure to meet you, Logan. I was out in the Pacific with the 19th, but we heard 'bout you. Our skipper said you were the best B-17 pilot in the world."

"Thanks, and how about you? You fly as well as you talk?"

"Better. Don't mean to sound boastful, but if it's got wings, I can fly it. 17s, 24s, C-47s, 54s, DC-6s, Martins, Lockheeds, British, French, even German birds. Ot-to here taught me Junkers. We were . . . hauling hardware in Africa."

Gunrunners were fine, they'd have no qualms about breaking laws for money.

"Hey, Ot-to, meet Harry Logan, This here's Ot-to Kopf. Means *head* in German. He's a Kraut."

About thirty-eight, probably six feet, alert and calculating—it showed in those azure eyes.

"I don't care if he's a Martian, so long as he knows 17s. I'm hiring pilots for a war movie. Four, five months' work. Good money."

"We got two thousand a month last job," Mayberry tested.

"I'm paying double. You in?"

"You know it."

Logan looked at the German.

"I'm from Cologne," Kopf said too slowly.

"He doesn't care where you're from," the southerner said, not understanding. Logan did, though. He'd been through this kind of thing before. One faced it head-on . . . "Herr Kopf cares where I've been."

"American air raids killed my father and two of my sisters. Did you bomb Cologne—January, 1945?"

"My squadron hit Cologne two or three times. I don't know about that particular strike, but we dropped a lot of tonnage."

"Tonnage? You talk about tonnage? What about *people?*"

"We probably killed a lot of people. Difficult to tell at 22,000 feet.

You flew bombers, Ashley. Explain it to him if you can."

Ashley sucked on his pipe.

"Tell him."

"I'll tell him my family was wiped out in a place called Coventry. German bombers did that. November 14th, 1940."

"Your father a bomber pilot, Otto?" Logan asked.

Kopf shook his head. "Antiaircraft gunner. He was forty years old. They put the older men in flak batteries."

"Yes . . . to shoot down our bombers. Listen, Otto, I'm sorry your father's dead. I'm not the least damn bit sorry that some American plane destroyed a hostile flak battery, and I don't regret bombing Cologne. If the Nazis came back, I'd blow Cologne to hell tomorrow."

"I remember the fires—" Kopf persisted.

"Forget the fires."

"I can't."

"Then remember all of them," Logan said angrily. "Warsaw and London, Rotterdam, Kiev, Chungking, and Tokyo too. Have a good sick time. You want to hate? Okay, I helped smash up a *dozen* German cities—three dozen. Frankfurt, Hamburg, Düsseldorf—I remember that one. Stuttgart, Munich, Bremen. You have any relatives in Bremen? I may have burned them up too—"

"You bastard—" He raised his fists, and Mayberry grabbed him. "Take it easy, Ot-to. Easy. Use your head, man. Odds a million to one he didn't have nothing to do with your folks, boy. Crissakes, get ahold of yourself. 1944 was a zillion years ago."

Kopf stopped struggling and Mayberry released him.

"What about this war movie?" Mayberry picked up quickly.

Kopf was still breathing hard. The anger, pain, still in his eyes.

"Thousand a week. Seventeen or maybe twenty weeks' work. Central America. Jungle story. U.S. against the Japs," Logan told him.

"Good money." Mayberry nodded. "No problem. That wasn't your war, Ot-to. Probably got some great-looking actresses. Blonds with fine jugs, right, Logan?"

"Could be."

"Just like the chicks back home, Ot-to. We'll pick up a sweet twenty grand and maybe go see some of those juicy German ladies. Waddya say, man?"

The fires were dimming some. *"Jah,* the pay would be good . . . if you still want me, Logan, I can assure you I am not always so

. . . emotional . . . and I have more than eight hundred hours in B-17s . . ."

"Knows the bird from top to bottom," Mayberry added.

It was a risk, but there was no time. Logan made the decision. "Okay, how long will it take to get these birds airborne?

"Nine or ten days, and maybe $28,000 or $30,000 worth of parts and labor," Mayberry said with enthusiasm.

Logan was watching the German closely. "That right, Otto?"

"Jah, Beau's correct."

"That's me, suh. Beauregard Mayberry the Fowth. You can call me Beau, suh."

The bargaining began. There was—for practical purposes—no market for B-17s, no demand for the aged machines except from nostalgia buffs such as the Confederate Air Force or some film producer out to recapture World War Two. On the other hand, if some person or firm seriously wanted or needed one or more of the historic bombers, there were damned few left. The negotiating started with Ashley asking $175,000 apiece and Logan offering $85,000. They shook hands four minutes later on $220,000 for the pair—"as is,"—and the Briton agreed to help find the spare parts required to put both planes into the sky safely.

Mayberry cleared his throat, coughed. "Well, suh, now that's settled, Ot-to and I ain't been paid by anybody for more'n a month now an' we got a touch of the shorts."

It sounded almost venereal the way he said it.

"It's just a small thing. Don't want to impose on your generosity but it would sure be mighty fine, mighty damn fine, if you could sort of advance us maybe £300 for walkin' around money. Just a kind of loan, you might say, general . . ."

"General?"

"Well, suh, it's your air force, ain't it?"

Well, he guessed it was, and it felt good. And this time they'd do it his way, with no interference by politicians, bureaucrats or promotion-hungry brass busy protecting their own asses. After all these years, he was finally in command—leader of a very strange strike force of adventurers, without a flag or a country. Yes, in the way it counted, he was a "general" at last, even if it had to be kept a secret.

While Harry Logan was feeling as alive as he had in years, Capitaine Guillaume Rimbaud was feeling only slightly relieved from his usual boredom. Rimbaud was a distant relative of the famed poet, but his world was not that of literature, art or madness. This Rimbaud had a regular job—one that would surely offend his great third-cousin. He was a soldier-civil servant in a branch of the French government known as the SDECE, and spent eight hours a day drinking inferior coffee and reading endless transcripts in an office on the third floor of a dreary building on the Right Bank in Paris.

The sign on the old stone pile said Département de Transport but Rimbaud knew little about trains or highways. The SDECE preferred a discreet anonymity, since the location of the electronic eavesdropping and wiretap headquarters of the Service de Documentation Extérieure et de Contre-Espionnage was supposed to be secret. Most of the transcripts of the wiretaps were routine stuff about stomach problems, checks in the mail, group sex and the childishness of the British and Americans. The occasional bit involving cocaine, stolen cars or real estate deals brightened things just a trifle. Rimbaud had found his current flat on the Ile St. Louis via a wiretap, so he could not condemn the operation entirely. Still, surprises or mysteries were all too rare.

Now what the hell did *this* mean? A subject code-named Chopin was trying to find and purchase obsolete B-17 aircraft. He told people that these historic machines were needed for a film, which *might* be true. If so, that would be most unusual, for Chopin was one of the most accomplished and systematic liars and conspirators in the international weapons trade.

"Merde."

This scrap of information was just another fragment probably worthless to the SDECE. Still, the SDECE might trade or sell it to someone else. That was the interesting part of this game—the maneuvering and dealing. The Soviet KGB liked to collect all sorts of information, and—even with their budget cuts—the Americans were still paying ridiculous prices for everything, including old telephone directories and photos of the Polish military attaché entering that brothel on the Avenue Foch.

It wasn't much—this old-airplane thing—but someone would buy it. Capitaine Rimbaud looked at his watch, reached for the phone to call his lover about the five P.M. rendezvous—and stopped. It was too dangerous. Some bastards—in one secret service or another—might be tapping the line. *Cher* Jean would have to wait.

13

MOST GOD-FEARING PEOPLE respect the Old Testament, the New Testament or both. The two publications that awe the Hollywood folk are *Daily Variety* and the *Hollywood Reporter*, trade papers hustling the latest entertainment news and gossip to the faithful five times a week. The story broke first in the *Reporter* column of a very well-informed journalist named Hank Grant.

"Sheik Omar Baroodi, who collects Rolls Corniches like some folks stash matchbooks, in from London with a cool ten million for a film fling. Don't call me, chums. Call him."

Three days later, *Daily Variety* scooped the entire free world with news that "Young Sheik Baroodi's mulling a five-flick deal, and Numero Uno'll be a World War Two blockbuster." Several unemployed producers, five screenwriters with heavy alimony and four directors who admired the symbolism of World War Two nearly drowned in their Jacuzzis on hearing this, and the switchboards at all the best hotels lit up madly as they tried to find the affluent Arab.

Then savvy syndicated columnist James Bacon told readers in forty-four states that "Sheik Baroodi wants his oil-bucks pappy to buy him a movie company, but Dad insists his scion warm up with a couple of pictures first. Tough luck, sonny." The next morning Rona Barrett thrilled millions of TV viewers with the "flash" that "Sheik Baroodi is dickering with superstar Bobby Redford and super-scripter Bill Goldman for his air-war epic. Biggies at other studios are seething." More than three hundred papers carried the Earl Wilson item that Liza Minnelli had no intention of wedding "either the amorous Arab or that millionaire Brazilian urologist."

The engine behind all this inside information was an energetic publicist named Bernard Peshkin, who'd lost most of his hair and all his illusions since leaving Brooklyn twenty-six years before. He was inventive, amusing, unscrupulous. Having learned his trade in the public relations ranks of MGM, Rogers & Cowan and the Warners conglomerate, he now ran his own firm to support the owners of the Santa Anita racetrack and Nate & Al's deli—the only place in the state where one could buy a decent pastrami sandwich. Alison Gordon had known him for years.

"We met on the Concorde," she explained to Peshkin after making the introductions. "He wants to make a couple of pictures, Bernie, and I told him he needs a top-notch publicist to be taken seriously."

The Beverly Hills Hadassah might not like this, Peshkin thought, but the sheik's gold Rolex looked real, and that suggested sincerity.

"Would $800 a week be all right?" Baroodi asked.

He had a nice smile, and the roll of hundred-dollar bills he pulled from his pocket made an excellent first impression. Before the press agent could compliment him on his good manners, Baroodi peeled off $8,000 and put it on the slab teak desk.

"My father wanted me to go to the U.S.C. film school," he confided, "but I'd rather skip that theoretical stuff."

"Plunge right in—best way to learn," Peshkin enthused. "Nothing beats on-the-job training. You're gonna make one helluva producer. I got a feel for these things, sheik."

"Call me Omar."

Good-looking kid, the press agent calculated, and with all that loot and a couple of pictures cooking there'd be no problem in lining up the most voluptuous starlets as dates for the poshest parties and charity balls—maybe even that $1,000-a-plate World Hunger banquet next week. Peshkin got along with people of every sexual, dietary and metaphysical persuasion—but it would be a trifle easier if Baroodi enjoyed women.

"Omar, you dig chicks?"

"I've got to go," A. B. Gordon interrupted, and went swiftly away.

Peshkin helped his new client rent a suite of offices on Wilshire Boulevard, lease a furnished house in Bel Air for $3,500 a month and hire the standard crew of chef, butler, maid, gardener and bodyguard-chauffeur. The executive secretary had great legs and the story editor the wisdom that came after four years and a minor ulcer at Paramount. Fully staffed, the dashing young Arab escorted dramatically endowed blonds, brunettes and redheads, a six-foot black model who shaved her head and a white opposite number whose hair, when down, tickled her rear, to a different fund-raiser, premiere or other media event every night of the week. Peshkin spread the word that *this* Arab tycoon despised the hateful bastards who wanted to murder Israel, and—when the L.A. *Times* ran the photo of the sheik with Shirley—at the anti-nuclear gala—influential women with excellent face-lifts began inviting him to private screenings at their million-dollar homes. Top talent agents, interior decorators and real estate brokers shared investment tips and obscene jokes with Baroodi, and he was offered more properties— beach and literary, drugs, assignations and tax shelters—than any nine producers could handle.

Alison Gordon watched and waited restlessly. She tried to keep her mind occupied with two routine cases and locating key alumni of the Bloody 100th, but her viscera wouldn't cooperate. In the office or in the shower, at the wheel or trying to sculpt—day or night, it was always the same urgent question. Where the hell was Harry Logan? Why wasn't he here—touching—now?

The curt cable from Hamburg announcing that he'd phone from New York on Thursday made her cry out in joy, but seconds later she was wondering what he'd been doing in the German port. This reverie was broken by the telephone call from Bonomi. She hadn't expected to hear from the D.E.A. executive again.

"Gordon . . . Fine. What's up? . . . Who's the contractor? . . . How much? . . . I see . . . Those your people in the '76 Ford? . . . And the blue Dodge? . . . I appreciate your concern . . . I'm always careful, but thanks anyway . . . Right. Bye."

She hung up the phone, put out her hand.

"Five bucks," she demanded.

"Those meatballs are *federal?*" the man on the couch said in the raspy voice he'd brought back from Saigon.

"You made the bet, Don."

He fumbled in his pocket, grunted. "We spotted them three days ago. Worst surveillance I ever saw. Boy Scout shit."

"You sound like an outraged taxpayer. Where's my five?"

He threw a twenty-dollar bill on her desk. "You got change?"

She shook her head, blew at the paper currency and saw it flutter toward him. "Buy me a bottle of wine," she said, and flipped on the intercom to tell her secretary to dial her man Elroy Evans in North Carolina. She waited for Don Hovde to ask why federal agents were following her, but he didn't. Suddenly it was all clear.

She picked up the phone, and the undercover agent's voice sounded in her ear.

"What's happening in L.A.?" he asked.

"It's hot, could get steamy where you are, Elroy."

"I'm listening."

"Remember that auto accident? Those people had some friends, and they're angry. They're offering twenty thousand for whoever was responsible. Open contract."

"That's downright un-Christian."

"Elroy, this is no moment for theology. Pack a bag. I want you at National Airport in Washington tomorrow. There'll be a ticket in your name at the Eastern counter. When you get to San Juan, check into the Racquet Club near the airport. I'll wire some money. Stick close to the hotel and stay away from the casino. These creeps have friends in Puerto Rico too."

"I'll miss church this Sunday for sure."

"About twenty Sundays . . . You're on the payroll—overseas duty. Thousand a week. Any questions?"

"Not at a thousand a week. *Ciao,* foxy lady."

"Ciao," she said, and turned to confront Hovde. "You knew?"

"It's been on the street a couple of days. Yeah, I heard . . ."

"But didn't say a word. Just what did you hear, Don?"

He cleared his throat. "Rumors, cheap talk. They say there's a twenty-grand contract out. Maybe some Syndicate guy named Pete Anthony took over the junk setup. Could be his twenty. Who knows?"

She stood up, pulled the .357 from the desk drawer and checked the clip.

"You never were a good liar, Don. Let's have it all." She put the weapon into the belly holster.

"Move away from the window, will you?"

"He's that bad? You should have told me," she said, and slid her swivel chair out of the line of fire.

"I was trying to handle it myself. Ran a little recon, found where he lives, where he works, where he hides his mistress, even where he takes steam baths. Just in case—"

"In case of *what?*"

"In case we have to blow him up."

"What're you going to blow him up with? A bazooka? A 105 howitzer?"

"Claymore."

It figured. The three and one-half pound antipersonnel mine had been widely used in Viet Nam, and was still a standard weapon in the arsenal of many U.S. military units.

"You'd really do it, wouldn't you?"

"Listen, you've got to see it in perspective. Preemptive strike. Perfectly legit. All the governments talk about it. Hit them before they hit you."

"Don, we left all that crap behind on the other side of the Pacific. I know everyone in this office used to work for the Agency, but we don't anymore and we're not in the middle of a bloody war either."

He nodded, but she could see he wasn't budging.

She tried again. "Describe a Claymore."

"Seven hundred small steel balls embedded in a plastic matrix at the front of a curved polystyrene case. One and a half pounds of C-4 explosive behind the matrix. Range of steel balls on detonation, fifty-five yards in a sixty-degree fan-shaped arc."

Letter perfect after all these years.

"Now describe me."

"Maybe five five, light brown hair, brown eyes, great cheek bones. Sort of high class. Patrician—that's the word. Fine legs, super body. Could be three or four pounds overweight but in the right places. Real good set of—"

"Don, that's not what I'm talking about and you know it. Talk about me, not my tits."

"I didn't use the word, you did. Okay . . . You're very smart, considerate and practical. You're a very good shot, and real strong for a lady."

"That's right—*lady,* Don. I don't believe in casual violence. Never did, did I? Only when absolutely unavoidable, remember?"

He nodded. "Sure, you were always a . . . a lady. Swell clothes too —"

She lost her temper. "So what made you think a *lady* would buy blowing up some son of a bitch with a Claymore in downtown L.A.?"

He considered that, then: "I wanted to protect you, Al. It's part of what I do."

She walked around the desk, patted his cheek. "I know, I appreciate it, but no thanks, Don. Look, I've got to go out of town in a couple of days. Be gone—out of the country—for a few months. It'll all blow over by then. Want to come with me?"

"When I wrap up that Stigwood thing. End of the month, I figure."

"Fine." She started for the door, but something stopped her. It had no name, but it was located just below her navel. "Would you do me a favor, Don?"

"Anything you say."

"I want to protect you too," she said. "There could be trouble if that damn thing got into the wrong hands. Somebody could steal it, or it might go off in the back of *your* car. Humor me. Take out the detonator, and bring in the Claymore tomorrow—*please.* . . ."

He delivered the weapon in a wooden box the next morning and handed her a plastic soap dish containing the detonator wrapped in puffy cotton batting. She thanked him, and her smile of relief was a delight to see. She was a wonderful person, a loyal and lovely woman who'd do anything for her friends. Hovde was embarrassed about having disturbed her by mentioning his plan for this Claymore. She was so sensible, so intelligent. He had learned his lesson.

He would say nothing—not a word—about the other six Claymores in the footlocker in his garage.

19

THE EXPLOSION hurled the car over onto its side.

The driver died instantly, and when the man beside him tried to climb out "El Stalin" shot most of his head away with a burst from the M-16. Jesus X. Gallardo was fond of the stirring nickname which his revolutionary activities had earned him, and of the American infantry weapon stolen during an earlier foray against the despot's soldiers. One of the main objectives of this jungle ambush was to "liberate" more guns for "the people's struggle against imperialism."

Despite this preoccupation with revolutionary rhetoric, the talents of El Stalin were not limited to simplistic Marxist slogans. His gifts for guerrilla warfare were substantial, far greater than his abilities as a philosophy student during his three years at the University of Costa Verde. El Stalin had earned the command of the MPO-13, the Popular Movement of October 13th, by staying alive. Many of the other leftist students—including a dozen who had studied Mao's little red book and the Cuban manuals on mobilizing the masses more carefully, had been eliminated by President-General Garcia's regulars in the previous two years. The Workers Liberation Front of Carlos Ordaz—all seventeen of them—had been slaughtered during an ill-timed assault on a rural police station, and Felipe "Toro" Saldana was half dead in a cell—sole remnant of the Peking Brigade.

El Stalin's unit had discipline and training, especially in marksmanship. A moment after the blast smashed the army staff car, the troopers in the truck behind it jumped out and began firing. Skinny Luis Lantero dropped one of them, confirming the wisdom of naming him deputy commander of MPO-13. Clara Velez shot a corporal in the stomach, and the Bonilla brothers threw grenades that drove the soldiers back in panicky flight. One chunky sergeant squeezed off a round that spun Chico Duarte against a tree, his shoulder smashed. His mouth was unaffected, however. Nothing had ever shut up bespectacled Chico; not even his law school teachers. This time he cursed—loudly.

None of the combatants on either side said anything quotable, but there was a good deal of shouting, some screams of pain and/or fear and an exchange of small-arms fire that lasted another forty or fifty seconds. The three surviving soldiers retreated around a bend in the winding two-lane road, ending one of the less memorable military actions in Central American history. Reminding himself that Fidel had begun with such small raids, El Stalin led his twenty-one "freedom fighters" out of the underbrush to collect the booty.

"Hurry up! Move it! Move it!" he ordered.

The staff car was on fire, and the fuel tank could blow at any moment. Equally menacing was the danger that a mobile patrol— perhaps one with an armored car—might arrive without warning.

"Two minutes! Two minutes!"

His rule of thumb for survival was simple, and it worked. No ambush should take longer than five minutes from the first shot to the last guerrilla fading into the jungle. This wary approach to fighting the imperialist lackeys and running dogs was a major reason that MPO-13 was still in business. While nubile Clara Velez tied a bandage around the wounded rebel's shoulder, the others rushed to unload the cases of M-16s from the truck.

"One minute, comrades!"

They picked up the boxes, and were back in the dense tropical forest a full thirty-five seconds before the deadline. El Stalin was delighted. His loyal fighters were getting better every week, and with these new rapid-fire guns they would be much stronger than those stupid liberals of the National Freedom Army who opposed communism as much as the fascism of the Garcia regime. After dog-trotting more than a mile through the steamy afternoon, El Stalin saw that his brave band was exhausted and signaled a halt.

They sighed in relief as they put down the booty. Six boxes of modern automatic weapons. Real firepower.

"Open them, comrades," commanded El Stalin.

The Bonilla brothers used their steel machetes to pry up the tops, and everyone stared. Uniforms—not guns. There was not a weapon in any of the boxes—not even a bayonet or a can opener. Luis

Lantero opened his mouth to speak, and they all heard the blast.

"That will be the gas tank," Lantero guessed accurately.

"*Sí*, but what the hell is *this?*" the younger of the Bonilla brothers said.

"Something we can use," El Stalin assured them . . . He had to hide his own disappointment, to conceal his rage that his spies' information had been wrong—again.

"We were going to use those M-16s to destroy the Yankee warplanes," the wounded man reminded him bitterly. "You think the report on those bombers was wrong too?"

The commander of MPO-13 smiled benignly, adjusted the cap that he thought made him look so much like Fidel.

"Faith—we must have faith in our brothers, comrades. Our intelligence people are doing their best. No one is perfect. If they send word from the palace that the imperialists are bringing in B-17s with mercenaries to support the butcher Garcia, we must respect them. They are risking their lives for *la revolucion.* Don't worry. We'll destroy those planes . . ."

"With uniforms?" Chico Duarte challenged.

It was the pain, of course. Still, only a clear sense of Marxist objectivity stopped the leader from closing the ex-law student's large mouth with a gun butt. He forced a tolerant smile to show his mastery of the situation. "I have a plan," he announced confidently, and gestured to his fellow guerrillas to pick up the crates and resume their trek. It was still seven miles to their hideout, and by the time they reached the camp El Stalin would really have to present some plan to them. It would come to him. It better. Whatever the cost, the American bombers had to be destroyed.

20

"HE'S DYING," she blurted.

Logan blinked under the impact. The transatlantic flight on Pan American had been pleasant, the customs and immigration processing smooth and the drive up into Connecticut a scenic reminder of the glories of New England in autumn. The traditional saltbox house on the wooded acre just outside town reflected a sensible and attractive life style. There was no pollution or industrial ugliness in these hills, and Logan had been feeling good in the crisp November air as he rang the bell. He was completely unprepared for *this,* and for a moment he could only stare.

"You knew he was sick? That's why you're here, isn't it?" the pretty woman in the red bandana asked.

The hair under that covering was also red, Logan remembered. The plaid work shirt and jeans fit well enough to show a figure other women in their forties had to envy, but the pain in her face was something no one would want.

"I had no idea," Logan told her.

Sid Carpenter had been one of the finest bombardiers in the whole Eighth Air Force, and one of the luckiest. He'd survived four burning airplanes, including two that ditched in the icy English Channel. He'd been equally lucky in finding and marrying this loving intelligent woman, a cheery and capable partner whom nothing rattled.

Now she stood in the doorway, shaking.

"Take it easy, Betty."

She nodded, but she kept shuddering in anguish. Logan couldn't find anything to say, so he reached out and she came into his arms and he held her for nearly a minute until the sobs quieted. Then she

113

took off the bandana to dry her eyes, unleashing her shoulder-length hair.

"I wanted to cut it, Harry, but he likes it long . . . no, that's only half true. I was always vain about my hair."

"Always," Logan agreed, and followed her into the house.

It was comfortably furnished in a style decorators might call Colonial, and there were shelves jammed with books everywhere. Sid Carpenter had always loved reading—British novels, American history, French plays and all kinds of poetry. Without thinking, Logan walked to the crackling logs in the fireplace like some heat-seeking animal.

It didn't help.

The chill of fear dominated the room.

"What is it?" Logan asked.

"Leukemia. Only a miracle can save him."

She opened a walnut hutch, pulled out a bottle of Scotch and poured stiff drinks into two glasses. She gave one to Logan, and before he could sip she downed half of hers.

"I drink now, Harry."

"I always did."

They both drained their glasses, looked at each other numbly.

"Harry, you brought him home a lot of times when it was impossible. He told me about those flights. He said you could do anything."

Logan looked around the room uneasily.

"Harry, make another miracle!"

"I'm only a flier, Betty."

She dropped into an overstuffed armchair, started shaking again. Logan clenched his fists, resisting the impulse to smash something. Sid Carpenter had been the Good Guy, the one who helped everyone else. He couldn't be more than fifty-eight.

"Where is he?"

She pointed at a door in the corridor.

"In his shop—downstairs . . . Harry, what am I going to do?"

Logan put down his glass, started toward the hall.

"Harry—*he doesn't know,*" she whispered.

Logan walked to the door, opened it and made his way to the basement workroom. It was filled with lumber, tools, two lathes and a large workbench. Sidney Carpenter—a little grayer and much thinner than when Logan had last seen him—was busy with an electric sander. He saw Logan, turned the tool off and held out his hand.

114

"Good to see you, Harry. What do you think?"

Logan studied the wide slab, guessed.

"Terrific. Tabletop?"

"Not a bad guess for a guy who never gave a damn about wood. Great surprise when you called yesterday, you don't get east too often, do you?"

"First time in four or five years. Okay to smoke?"

"Sure. Try that stool. I made it. Sid Carpenter enjoys working with wood. Some joke, huh?"

Logan lit a cigar, perched on the stool.

"How're the kids, Sid?"

"Great. Billy's a lawyer—got a job with the state government in Hartford. Donna's twins are five now, so she's going back to work next month. She's with the old firm, you know.

Logan tried to recall, couldn't.

"Boeing," the ex-bombardier explained, and smiled. "The folks who made our 17s. She'll be helping design the circuits for a big new jet. 767, I think. What the hell are you doing?"

"That's what I'm here about," Logan began as he looked around until he found an ashtray. "Been hired as tech adviser for a picture —big movie about World War Two in the Pacific. I'm supposed to round up the crews and the 17s."

"I'll be damned. 17s, huh? Didn't know there were any left. You're still hooked on flying, huh?"

Logan nodded, puffed on the Don Diego.

"That's what I seem to do best. Going to be a real authentic picture. Need top people. Maybe four months work at a thousand a week—and a fat bonus. What do you say?"

Carpenter picked up a piece of sandpaper, smoothed the wood carefully.

"Beautiful, isn't it? . . . No, I don't think so, Harry. I've got something else to do—something important. I'm dying, Harry."

Logan held his breath.

"She thinks I don't know, so I pretend I don't. No reason to make her suffer more, right?"

Logan tapped the ash from his cigar.

"I guess," he answered, and shook his head.

Carpenter stroked the wood. "Fine piece of oak. I should have gone into cabinetwork, Harry. Wood was my first love, but my dad talked me into joining him in the insurance business. Nice money . . . but I never really cared much for it. Wasted thirty-two years

. . . Say, you want a beer? Old times' sake?"

"Sure."

Carpenter took two cans from the old refrigerator and they drank from the metal containers.

"She called you, didn't she?"

"No. I gave it to you straight. It's a movie. Too bad you can't— hell, why don't you? You could teach some of the kids—"

"Thanks, but I'll finish up here. With her. I'm still crazy about that lady—after all these years. You going to see some of the other guys?"

Logan nodded.

"Give 'em my best. Tell 'em I had a—well, you know. Sorry I won't see your movie . . . Hey, *maximum effort?*"

"Maximum effort."

They drank, shook hands and Logan walked upstairs to say good-bye to Betty.

"What did he say?" she asked.

"Maximum effort."

She was crying again as the flier left.

Logan drove south swiftly, although he was in no hurry to see Geoffrey Van Bokkelen again. He'd never been in a rush to see Van Bokkelen, even when they'd flown together in the 100th. The rather haughty scion of one of Wall Street's wealthiest families had been great in battle, but—beyond any question—the most unpopular man in the outfit. The appointment was for four o'clock, and Van Bokkelen was the sort who'd be nasty if you were a minute late. Traffic was relatively light until Logan reached the edge of New York, and it was 3:53 when he parked the Hertzmobile a block from the Van Bokkelen townhouse on East Sixty-eighth Street. He rang the bell at 3:58 and at 4:00 the butler ushered him into the high-ceilinged living room where Van Bokkelen was waiting.

Tall and trim.

Same curly blond hair, same appraising look.

A glass in his hand—still ready for anything.

Nothing, in short, had changed much. He had hardly aged at all. It was incredible, but Geoffrey Van Bokkelen could pass for a man fifteen or even twenty years younger. He wasn't wearing that uniform anymore, but the elegant silk shirt and Italian slacks clearly stated his new identity. Rich, monied and radiating the vigor of the best beaches, health clubs and international resorts, he had the air of a well-fed tiger. Which was appropriate, because it went with the lion's head and other big game trophies on the walls of this large and expensively furnished room.

He registered Logan's survey, smiled. "Glad you like it, Harry. Champagne?"

"Sure, okay."

Van Bokkelen reached for a bottle of Dom Perignon.

"I remember," Logan said, examining the label, "you swore you'd never drink anything else when you got home—and *some* home."

Van Bokkelen handed him the glass, flashing perfect teeth. "Home is where the heart is . . . Drink up, Blue Leader."

Logan sipped the chilled wine, sat in a large rocker.

"Make yourself comfortable. That was my granddad's favorite chair. I keep it because I'm sentimental, as you'll remember."

Logan studied the display of rifles on the far wall. "Bullshit. You were the only guy in the outfit who *enjoyed* the war. You're a natural-born killer, Van."

Van Bokkelen finished his drink, refilled the crystal. "That's no way to talk to a man when you want something from him, Harry."

"A *very good* killer. Okay?"

"That's better. Compliments are always appreciated, especially from an expert. You were damn good yourself. In fact you were the best pilot we had, I admit it, but I don't—I *never* liked it."

"You were a fine pilot, Van."

"I would have been the best if it hadn't been for you. I was always jealous of you . . ."

Logan decided to change the subject. "Read about you last year," he said.

"The air race?"

"The guy you beat to death in the park—with your fists."

Van Bokkelen's smile stayed in place. "Hands, Harry. Karate. I'm a black belt, and he was a mugger with a knife. Self-defense."

"You didn't have to kill him, did you?"

"You trying to provoke me, Harry? This is some way to talk to your host—your old wartime buddy."

Logan drained his glass, rose and poured himself more champagne.

"Help yourself, buddy. There's a cellarful. I'm a very wealthy man, relatives keep popping off and leaving me millions. You know how rich I am?"

"Rich and bored. Five wives. Stunt flying. Mountain climbing. Big game hunting. Crap."

"Man is a hunting animal, Harry—"

"Crap. I'm here to do you a favor. I've got a *job* for you."

"Are you kidding?"

Logan shook his head. "Exciting, dangerous—a little crazy. Flying B-17s, not toy racers. I've got a war for you, Van. For real."

Excitement flushed the millionaire's face pink, and he sat straight up.

"You interested?"

"How do you know you can trust me?"

"I know how badly you want this—*need* this. Live ammo, real bombs. You'd sell your mother for this."

"My sister. My mother's dead. What the hell is it?"

"Killing people—bad guys. Like the old days. Nobody you ever heard of, though. I'm putting together crews for six 17s."

"Could you use a P-51? That's what I race."

With a speed of 442 miles an hour, range of 1,710 miles and operational ceiling over 42,000 feet, the old Mustang fighter might be ideal for photo-reconnaisance, Logan thought. It would fit neatly and inconspicuously into the World War Two-movie cover story. Perfect.

"Might come in handy . . . The cover is we're making a picture —*Vengeance Squadron.* Big budget. We'll train in one place, shoot the film in another, and then we'll fly on to our war. I can't tell you where—"

Van Bokkelen was on his feet. "I'm not asking. Sounds fantastic. When do we start?"

"Soon as I round up the birds and the crews. You haven't asked about the money. It's a thousand a week. I can't say whose."

"Don't care. Forget the money. I'm worth more than twenty—"

It was $22 million, to be exact. A. B. Gordon had checked.

"You're worth a thousand a week, just like everybody else. No charity, no favors, no special privileges for rich playboys. No bullshit either. I'm in command. Tight security. You breathe one word of this and—this is for real—you're dead."

Van Bokkelen smiled again. "You'll kill me, right?"

"No, my lady friend will. That's her department."

"Some lady."

"Some woman," Logan said, and realized again how fiercely he missed her. "Get your 51 gassed up, Van. I'm on my way to sign on

118

the others—pilots, navigators, the works. Got a date with Jimmy Frankenthal in forty minutes."

"You're eight months too late."

Van Bokkelen was right, and Logan sensed it as soon as he entered his ex-navigator's apartment in the high-rise on West Seventy-ninth Street. She was pretty, about thirty-eight or forty, and shining with love for James Morris Frankenthal. He was all aglow too. Her name was Winifred, Frankenthal explained, and they'd been married eight months and six days. She made gold jewelry, interesting Celtic pieces. She also made Jimmy Frankenthal wildly happy. The marvelous second-wife-new-life syndrome—Logan had seen it before. Nothing could touch it, and he didn't want to, anyway. Jimmy Frankenthal was living and enjoying his own dream after so many difficult years of marital struggle, and Logan was neither stupid nor selfish enough to attempt to pry him away. Logan's own dream—of flying the Forts one more time against identifiable enemies of decency wouldn't tempt his former navigator in the slightest.

"It's great to see you so happy," Logan said truthfully.

"Love conquers all, Harry. My ex-mate has the big co-op on Riverside Drive, the car, the summer place in Easthampton—and I've got Win. I'm the lucky one, right?"

"Luckiest I know. You've got it made, and I've got to get back to my hotel."

They wouldn't hear of it. They made him stay for dinner and much good California Pinot Chardonnay, and Logan was glowing too as he walked toward Broadway at ten o'clock to find a taxi. It was drizzling, and he barely heard the leggy tart who called out from the doorway of the bakery on the corner. Circling a pair of Hispanics arguing beside the newsstand, he *just* missed the traffic light. Passing cars splashed water, the wind slashed in from the Hudson only a few blocks away and the glow began to fade. He glanced downtown for a cab, saw the huddled mass of an aged "bag woman" and her worldly possessions in a doorway. A tall transvestite wobbled into sight on ridiculous high heels, and Logan wondered glumly whether the man realized how idiotic he looked in the bouffant blond wig.

It had not been a good day for Hacksaw Two, and the goddam rain and the local scene were beginning to depress him. Maybe he wouldn't be able to collect the crews and the bombers. What could he do with two aged and unarmed relics, a stripped-down Mustang and three pilots? Maybe it wouldn't work. Maybe the whole plan was impossible . . .

The light changed, and he crossed Broadway to find shelter in a doorway beside a bank. He finally flagged a taxi, which splattered his trousers as it jerked to a halt. By the time the cab was passing Lincoln Center, Logan had made up his mind. He'd get another plan—a fall-back scheme. If Hacksaw Two had to be abandoned, he'd construct another operation with her. She knew the area. "Covert operations" had been her specialty . . . Maybe they'd have to mount a lightning ground assault or an air commando drop, or perhaps he could pull it off with just a few aircraft dumping those murderous new cluster bombs. Whatever it might come to—plan B or plan C or even plan Z—he'd given his word, he wasn't about to abort the mission.

21

THERE ARE status places to work in every organization, and the federal government is no exception. For example, Washington is more prestigious than Oklahoma City. In the nation's capital itself, it is classier to serve civilly in the Department of State or even the Pentagon than the Department of Agriculture or Postal Service, which somehow lack charisma. There are further distinctions within the Pentagon—the intelligence hotshots in the high-security area of the D-ring of offices and the top level planners in the C-500 suites barely talking to the procurement staff located in those unfashionable B-ring jungles.

Near the bottom of the social ladder are the diligent folk in the Arms Export Control Division, whose quarters are simply and literally the pits. They toil in a windowless basement, where they get neither sunlight nor respect. Mr. Randall Burlinghame, who had bifocals and four years to a pension, was accustomed to these working conditions. He had the best attendance record in the division despite his back problems, and he took his responsibilities seriously. It wasn't merely the lure of those cheap and nourishing tuna and cottage cheese specials in the cafeteria that got him to his desk five minutes early every morning. Burlinghame cared, he was fascinated by every odd bit of information that came to him as deputy chief of the Far East section, AECD. A former Baltimore high school teacher, he was still convinced that reading broadened the mind.

He could never understand why some people considered his job boring. Here was a report that Barabas Surplus Supplies, Inc. of Tampa, Florida, had sold 312 bombs—obsolete 500-pounders the Air Force had peddled cheaply nine years ago—to the Golden Crescent film company for a World War Two movie to be made in Thailand. Burlinghame smiled as he recalled reading about the picture—*Vengeance Squadron*. He was proud of his memory, and often impressed people by rattling off the names of all seven dwarfs and every one of Elizabeth Taylor's husbands. Everything was in order. Export license, bill of lading, shipping documents. Randall Burlinghame cleared his throat, stamped the final permit and signed it with a flourish. He especially liked this part of the job, for his fine clear signature still won him many compliments.

Copy to Karnow at State.

Copy to Fanelli at Commerce.

Copy to Tyrone at CIA, Eliason at Air Force and Mrs. Munk in Central Files.

Randall Burlinghame looked at the wall clock, sighed in anticipation. It was eight minutes before noon, Thursday, and Thursday was when the cafeteria featured that delicious tomato surprise.

22

THE STRANGER was short, Caucasian, about thirty and bleeding from his left ear. He was also unconscious, a by-product of a savage blow to the head with the stock of a submachine gun. He could easily have been killed—trespass is a heinous crime in Beverly Hills where tempers run as high as mortgage rates. . . .

It happened quickly. Alison Gordon was curled up on a couch in her living room, speaking on the telephone to the best B-17 pilot in the world. It was midnight in that cold windy city on Lake Michigan, but ten P.M. her time. Logan's voice warmed and excited her—and then she heard the soft chime of the alarm system, and she thought about that $20,000 contract.

"Just a second, Harry," she said.

She put down the phone, picked up the .357 and flicked out the lights. Elapsed time—eight seconds. She dropped into a crouch, circled to the corridor and made it out the back door in under half a minute. She was just outside when she heard the noise. Reacting as she'd been trained, she dived into the bushes and rolled over with a good two-handed shooter's grip on the Magnum.

Too late.

She heard the low whistle that was Agajanian's "all clear," the same signal her CIA team had used in Viet Nam. Still wary, she kept low as she turned the corner of the house—ready to fire instantly.

"He's cold," her armed accountant assured her.

She pointed the Magnum at the prone stranger.

"Who is he, Andy?"

"Driver's license says Joel Strega, born October 12th, 1947. That makes him a Libra."

She thrust out her free hand, and Agajanian gave her the trespasser's wallet. Aside from $64 in cash, two joints and the business card of a massage parlor named Paula's, it was empty.

"Anything else?"

Agajanian handed her a switchblade knife and a .22-caliber pistol.

"That's it. No credit cards, no military discharge papers, no medical insurance ID—no real ID at all. I don't like it."

She studied the two weapons. "What do you think?" she asked.

"Throw him in the pool."

"He'll drown."

"Accidents happen. Armed intruder breaks in, tries to steal your art collection and falls into the pool. Tough titty."

"Maybe he's just a burglar."

"Maybe he's a hit man after that twenty grand. That .22's an assassin's piece. You don't *know* he's a burglar, do you? If this had happened in Saigon—"

"This is Beverly Hills."

"Not so different. The hit men here wear better clothes and use different weapons but you could still get killed, real easy. You said so yourself last month."

He took a handkerchief from his pocket, started to wipe his fingerprints from the knife and gun.

"That was a figure of speech. Listen, I suppose Don told you about that contract . . . well, it's just street talk—"

The bleeding man groaned, and Agajanian started for him.

"Don't get crazy," she ordered. "Leave him alone. What the hell were you doing here at night anyway?"

"My shift."

"You mean you guys are guarding me around the clock and I didn't notice it?"

"Not bad, huh?"

"How many of you are in this?"

"All of us. It's no sweat. Six people—four-hour shifts. If you don't like the pool idea, I could drop him down on the freeway and the cars would—"

"Andy, I've got to get back to the phone. Call the cops."

"They're right outside. They've had the house staked out for days."

Agajanian handed her the machine gun, picked up the limp body and carried it out to the gate. He dropped his burden like a broken toy, opened the barrier and lifted the trespasser again. He walked to the car parked in the shadows where the three D.E.A. agents watched.

"Miss Gordon said to give you this."

"What is it?" the driver asked.

"Armed intruder."

"Who're you?"

"The gardener. I found him on the lawn."

Agajanian threw him on the hood of the car.

"What is this crap?" the driver demanded.

"You're the garbage men, aren't you?"

One of the men in the back seat suggested Agajanian have sexual relations with himself.

"Well, I'll just have to dump him somewhere else," Agajanian announced. He carried the body to a large plastic trash bin, dropped it in and strode back to the car.

"These are his," Agajanian announced, handed the driver the knife and the .22, and walked back to the house to rejoin his boss in the living room.

There was only one small lamp on, and she was sitting against the wall, pointing the machine gun at him as he entered.

"Sorry," she apologized.

"It's okay. You know, that trip out of the country might be a good thing for you."

"You want to come?"

Agajanian nodded. He was ready to go wherever and whenever she wanted—without questions. He trusted her completely.

"Here's the deal," she said, and told him the whole story of Logan and General Steele and Hacksaw Two. She trusted him completely too.

"You said you'd never go back to the Far East," he reminded her. He didn't mention the nightmares, the terrors . . .

"I'm in love with Harry Logan."

Which explained everything.

"He's a terrific person, Andy . . . I've got to go with him. You believe in old-fashioned corny stuff like destiny, Andy?"

"I believe in everything."

"You believe in this mission?"

"The mission *sucks*. When do we go?"

"We can do it," she insisted. "He just phoned from Chicago. He's been signing up aircrew in the midwest for the past couple of days. Got a United captain with more than twenty-one thousand flying hours—"

"Why would he leave a good job for this *nut* deal?"

"He was sixty in July, they retired him. There's another man whose name you might know—Bart Kendall."

Agajanian thought, remembered. "The TV news clown who used to work on NBC?"

"ABC," she corrected. "He was in the 100th too. He was pushed out in that big network shake-up in '77, hasn't worked since."

"A worn-out jet jockey and a pretty boy who lost his job to some chick with big boobs. What a hard-case crew this is gonna be."

She stood, handed him the machine gun. "There's plenty of work here if you'd rather stay. I won't blame you."

"I'm going. Don's going, and Elroy's halfway there. Maybe you ought to invite his cousin to join the party."

"Mercer?"

"Master gunsmith. Real pro with all kinds of automatic weapons, even those big .50s. This could be just his sort of gig. Mercer Davis is a poet, you know."

"What?"

"Only poets, lovers and crazies are gonna like this one. You sure you're in love?"

"Crazy in love. So's Logan. Andy, he said this is his last chance—and I mean to see he gets it. When it's over, we just might settle down somewhere—"

Agajanian shook his head. "Didn't know it was this bad."

"*Good,*" she corrected. "It's going to work. We've been very careful. Not a single mistake so far."

Agajanian shook his head again. "I can think of one right off," he said as he reached for the pack of cigarettes on the small table.

"What?"

"Should have drowned that bastard in the pool."

He lit the cigarette, picked up the machine gun and walked out into the darkness to resume his watch. If he was right, another assassin would come, and there was no way of predicting when. The only thing certain was that she loved a flier called Harry Logan, and both of them obviously believed in miracles. Maybe it wasn't so bad. He hadn't seen her this happy in years. How long it would last was another matter. In her heart she had to know the truth.

Hacksaw Two didn't have a chance.

It was a suicide mission, and the real miracle would be if any of them got out alive.

TOBY HAYWARD wouldn't come: He had three children and tenure and he dared not risk a full professorship at the University of North Carolina by walking out in the middle of the academic year.

Walter Kelleher couldn't come: He'd been driving his taxi into Boston from the airport when the vehicle was nearly totaled by some imbecile at the wheel of a refrigerator truck filled with lobster tails. Kelleher was almost totaled himself, and would be in traction at Peter Bent Brigham Hospital for ten weeks more.

Curtis Keepnews was "intrigued by the notion." Not only was he a movie buff but his daughter was writing documentary films for the United Nations. But he was representing Kodak in an extremely complicated antitrust suit and the trial could easily run another four months. He was delighted to see Logan again, and the lunch at the Harvard Club wasn't too bad either.

The flier was on the telephone most of the afternoon, calling Tucson, New Orleans, Nashville and Paris. The news from the portly arms merchant on the Left Bank was mixed. The "office equipment" had already left Hamburg by ship, but the search for "another of those antique aircraft for the museum" was dragging. A rumor that such a vintage machine might be found in Argentina was being investigated by associates, and Logan was invited to telephone again in three days.

At seven that evening Logan walked along West Tenth Street in New York City's Greenwich Village. Much of this part of lower Manhattan had deteriorated from a warm and creative community of writers, painters, musicians, theater folk and small business people to a noisy gaudy circus for tourists and assorted freaks. West Tenth, however, still had some of the solid real-humans-live-and-work-here quality. It made sense for Charlie Clarkson to rent a floor in a sturdy four-story brownstone on this street. It was clean, well kept and stable. There were no all-night fast-food joints or garish "head shops," no sly dealers peddling drugs in the building corridors or drunks urinating in the doorways. Trendy adolescents from other places did not come to this part of the Village to seek companions, and thrill-seekers intent on outraging their bourgeois parents in the suburbs took their pitifully pretentious pleasure farther south or west in the area.

There were flower boxes on the window ledges of these houses on West Tenth, and when Logan was buzzed in, he found the ground floor hallway was immaculate and freshly painted. He walked up the flight of stairs to the door marked 2B, knocked. Clarkson had put on weight, as people do in their fifties. He was more than plump though. He was soft, like a very large infant, and he had little more hair than a six-month-old baby. Age often takes its toll of men's scalps too, Logan thought, but there was something more.

"Charlie, Charlie, it's good to see you," Logan said. The extra bulk hardly mattered, Logan had always respected—and liked—this Kansas farm boy for his quiet strength and integrity. Clarkson hadn't made as much noise as some of the others, but he was one of the calmest in battle and among the most capable.

"Come on in, Harry. How long has it been?"

"Too long. Say, this is nice."

Someone with excellent taste had furnished the flat. The abstract prints, the light wood frames, the lamps, drapes, chairs, the modern couch and the bookshelves that filled a whole wall all worked splendidly. Nothing in the room was that expensive—not even the brass-and-glass coffee table—but it was all discreetly attractive.

"It's our idea of quiet contemporary. You still drink malt Scotch, Harry?"

"Sure. You hangin' in with the sherry?"

"Hanging in," Clarkson said, and poured the drinks. He seemed a bit reserved but he had been back then too. Probably just tired at the end of the day. The life of a New York City math teacher—even in a private school such as the progressive one that had employed Charles Wilton Clarkson for the previous sixteen years—could be demanding.

Clarkson's hand shook, and drops of sherry spattered the coffee table. "Sorry. Getting old, I guess."

128

"You've got a tough job," Logan said. "Kids today are a lot harder to handle, I hear."

Clarkson put down the glasses, shook his head and sat down. "Only some, Harry. We've got a lot of good ones too. It was difficult eight or ten years ago, but most of that's gone."

"The revolution's over," Logan agreed, and lifted his Scotch.

"It wasn't all bad, Harry. Those kids had some good ideas in among the craziness."

"Some damn good ideas—real old ones. Funny, they thought they invented them . . . Hell, they did remind us, and that's worth something. Want to drink to honesty, clean water and no bullshit?"

Clarkson smiled. "And love?"

Logan thought of Alison in California, and nodded. "And love . . . You know, I've been making more goddam toasts in the past two weeks than I did in the last ten years, but this is the first to love. I must be getting old too."

They drank.

"Not you, Harry. You're the youngest man your age in the world. You could pass for forty."

"*That's* love. I found a fantastic lady, or rather she found me. She's in the finding business, and she is a real winner. Can we drink to love again?"

"Why not?"

They sipped, talked about flying. They were reminiscing about their first battles in the sky when a door behind Clarkson opened and a sandy-haired man entered the room. He was nearly six feet tall, lean and tanned—almost too handsome. He must have been in his thirties, but he had a boyish look and moved with the stride of a college boy. There was something self-consciously confident in his large grin.

Clarkson, seeing the expression on Logan's face change, turned immediately, and his look changed too. "Alex, this is an old friend of mine—Harry Logan. We flew together in the war."

The theatrical grin reminded Logan of those cocky male starlets —there was no other word—who dressed up the cop series on television, the ruggedly handsome androids manufactured in some secret lab beneath the MCA tower.

"Harry, this is Alex Howard."

Fine teeth, curly hair, open-necked sport shirt.

Actor, or maybe a model.

Strong handshake, tweedy after-shave lotion, radiant health, contact lenses.

"Pleasure," the younger man announced in a voice still tinged with Virginia. "I've only known Charlie five years myself."

"Six," Charlie corrected.

Howard flashed another of his thousand-watt grins. He wasn't a fraud, Logan realized. He really meant it. He wanted to be friendly with/to Charlie Clarkson's old comrade-in-arms.

"Was he a good soldier?" he asked amiably.

"First-class. Smart, gutsy, totally reliable.

Howard checked his own appearance in the mirror, patted his roommate on the cheek. "He's still a wonderful person, Harry."

Clarkson fought to suppress an embarrassed blush. "What time will you be back?" he blurted.

"Half an hour after the curtain falls. It's 'off to work we go,' " Howard chanted in cheery send-up of the seven dwarfs' song from the vintage Disney film. He winked, danced comically to the door and departed—stage left.

"Nice guy," Logan said as he returned to his drink.

Clarkson didn't reply for several seconds.

"Harry, he's my . . ."

More silence.

"We're lovers, Harry."

"I could see that . . . Actor?"

Charlie stared at him intently.

"Didn't you hear what I said? I'm gay."

Logan finished his Scotch. "I heard you, Charlie."

"I always was—even back in the war."

Logan nodded again. "I know. I guess I knew then, if you're keeping score. May I?" Without waiting for an answer, he poured two fingers of the Glenfiddich into his glass.

"You never said anything, Harry."

"Charlie, they used to bust homosexuals out of the service remember? Section 8 or a dishonorable discharge, that was standard operating procedure. What do you want from me—a speech?"

"I want to know the whole thing, and I'm asking you to tell me."

"Okay. You were a good pilot and a good friend, and I never gave a crap about your . . . what do they call it . . . sexual preferences. Hell, the language keeps changing and I'm no politician. I'll just give it to you straight—no pun intended—okay?"

"Okay."

"You say you're gay? Back then they'd call you queer, a fruit, a goddam faggot. People used to say things like that, Charlie."

"A lot of people still do. I'm gay, Harry, but I'm no faggot. A faggot—"

"Charlie, I don't care. You never had to explain or defend anything to me. I don't believe in calling people names because they're different from me—unless they're s.o.b.'s. You never were an s.o.b."

Logan reached for two ice cubes, dropped them into his drink. "Listen, Charlie, I don't turn in my friends—no matter what their goddam preferences are. You don't steal or sell dope or betray your country. I don't care if you're a vegetarian, a Republican or a Hare Krishna. There were a lot of idiot rules in the Air Corps, probably still are—in *all* the armed forces."

"Thanks, Harry."

"For what? This is no time to crap each other. I'm no saint, and you aren't either. Let's not kid each other. I accept you as you are, your right to be whatever you want. I admit it—I understand this gay number *here,"* he said, and tapped his head, "but not *here."* He touched his stomach. "It's like those Einstein equations. I learned them at college, but I still find it hard to believe them. Doesn't matter. Times have changed. You don't have to hide or justify your thing anymore, right?"

"Harry, I lost three good teaching jobs—in other states—"

"Cheer up. Now you can wear a button or march in a parade, if you want to. I'm sorry, that sounded flip."

Clarkson finished his sherry. "That's not my style. The younger guys do that. I'm just an old-fashioned gay."

"Sounds like a song title . . . Charlie, I'm sorry about the bad times you had. Now you're okay, with a decent job, nice place here, and Alex seems like a good guy."

"He's very nice. He's an actor, as you guessed. Mostly off-Broadway. Does an occasional TV commercial too. Not so many now, though. He's thirty-nine."

"Doesn't look it."

"He'd like to hear that. He's a bit vain, you know. He wouldn't want me to tell you he makes most of his income from selling shirts at Bloomingdale's. He still hopes he's going to be a star."

"Just like everyone else. What's your dream, Charlie? You tell me your dream, and I'll tell you mine. That *is* a song title, I think."

Clarkson walked to the table, poured himself more sherry.

"I want to get him out of here. There are some bad people in New

York—bad gay people. They want to get Alex into some terrible things. They're into leather, pain. They tell him they can help his career, find him parts. They want to hurt him. I told him, but I can see he's tempted. He's not as strong as he seems, Harry."

"How're you going to get him away?"

"I want to open a bookstore down in Key West. There's a good gay community there, and people aren't hostile. I think there's even a local theater group. He used to work Christmases at bookstores, you know, and I was an assistant librarian myself for three years."

"When will you go?" Logan asked.

"When I get another $40,000. There's a bookstore for sale for $55,000, and our savings account has fifteen in it now."

Perfect. Here was his chance to recruit an excellent B-17 copilot and help his friend at the same time.

"Now I'll tell you *my* dream, Charlie, and I think you're going to like it. There's $50,000 in it for you . . ."

Deal. Logan was on the 8:05 A.M. American Airlines flight to Nashville to see Billy Bob Kinkaid, and by dinnertime was flying south to Tucson. Nine minutes after he started trying to eat one of those reheated-frozen meals—6:05 P.M. Los Angeles time according to that night's news broadcasts—somebody fired a concussion grenade into the private office of the president of the Pacific-Apex Novelty Corporation. The head of the downtown Los Angeles firm had left only a few minutes earlier, which probably saved his life. The usual number of variously garbled accounts were reported by assorted print and broadcast journalists, but they all agreed on one point—Mr. Peter T. Anthony, forty-seven-year-old president of Pacific-Apex and a resident of Pasadena, had come very close to dying.

He had no idea as to "who might do such a terrible thing." That's what he told the press. Lieutenant Casper Ottinger of the L.A.P.D. disclosed that the grenade fragments indicated use of a military weapon, and—of course—the investigation was continuing.

24

AT HALF PAST TEN the next morning, Alison Gordon looked down from Mr. Spinoza's helicopter at Mr. Spinoza's splendidly landscaped estate on Mr. Spinoza's private mountain ninety-seven miles north of Los Angeles. Not too many Americans owned mountains, but relatively few individuals in the U.S.A. had as much money as Mr. Spinoza. Only forty-three, according to the latest studies of the Internal Revenue Service and the Federal Bureau of Investigation, both of which had been sincerely interested in Mr. Spinoza, his enterprises and associates for more than a quarter of a century. Neither the IRS nor the FBI was absolutely certain about how much money he had, for Mr. Spinoza went to great lengths to maintain his privacy. Why else would he live on this inaccessible peak in a house crowned with radar to detect approaching aircraft? Why else was the machine gun post on the roof manned around the clock?

These weren't, of course, the sort of questions a lady would ask her host, and when she faced him in the large marble-floored room with the Steinway grand and the wall of books she respected the amenities. It wasn't merely that Mr. Spinoza had $92 million—or was it $116 million—when he retired. Even now, two years later, he was one of the most revered and feared men in the international crime syndicate though he hardly looked dangerous in the open-necked work shirt, corduroy trousers and loafers.

"Thanks for sending the chopper," she said politely.

"You said it was urgent," the short, smiling "Professor" replied. Top underworld figures in a dozen countries still respected his shrewdness, still spoke of the cunning of the Professor. At sixty-six, his smile was benign but his eyes told a different story. The look of the falcon remained—alert, tough, predatory.

"A cup of espresso?" he invited and gestured toward the gleaming metal machine on the sideboard.

"Thank you."

The cups were Sevres porcelain, the coffee strong and delicious. She said so, complimented the gardens and the house.

"I'm glad you didn't tell me how well *I* look," he said. "That's what people usually say to men my age. How can I assist you?"

Most men would have said "help," but he was too polite.

"I have a problem. It's basically one of communication."

"So many are."

"Something happened last night. You may have heard about it on the radio. There was an incident—a *violent* incident—in Los Angeles. A grenade smashed up the office of a man named Peter Anthony."

His face showed no recognition.

"Yes?"

"Perhaps I should start from the beginning. You know my business, of course."

"Very well. I haven't forgotten what you did for my daughter four years ago. You're good at your business, *very* good, Miss Gordon."

"Thank you. Well, I was working on a case—doing my job—and several of my colleagues were involved. It started out with something small and routine, and it got a lot bigger. Without boring you with the details, a situation developed—suddenly—in which a man was about to kill one of my people with a shotgun. I couldn't permit that."

Spinoza nodded. One had to take care of one's people.

"I had to take action, and I did. The man with the shotgun and others in the car with him—it was unfortunate."

"These things happen. What about this Anthony person?"

"May I smoke?"

Courtesy—he liked that. He handed her the Florentine silver lighter.

"It wasn't anything personal, but Anthony doesn't see it that way. He's put out a contract—$20,000—on me."

"Stupid."

For a moment the old savagery showed on Spinoza's face.

"My people don't like it. A few days ago a trespasser was found on my grounds with a gun. My friends think he was after that $20,000. They could have killed him, but I stopped it."

He nodded, and wondered what she wanted.

"It's possible that it was one of my people who fired that grenade into Peter Anthony's office as a warning. It was a concussion device rather than a frag bomb, and it was delivered just after normal business hours when the office was empty. Logic says that it wasn't intended to kill Mr. Anthony but to give him a message."

She could have been discussing a mathematical formula or the electoral process of Sri Lanka.

"You mentioned communications," Spinoza said.

"I did. I'm considering what should be done next to settle this misunderstanding, and I'm evaluating a number of options. I realize you wouldn't know a person as crude and stupid as this Anthony, but perhaps you might be acquainted with some individual who might have some occasional contact with him. Maybe a communication could be passed along. After all, you deal with so many people in your business and in all your fine charitable activities."

Nice. The reference to his philanthropies was a graceful touch. Spinoza was impressed by her tact and class. Rarities in the world of thugs and loudmouths. Very admirable . . . "As you say, Miss Gordon, I've never heard of this man."

She sighed, wistfully. "Sorry to have troubled you. It was good of you to see me, I'm sure you're busy—"

"I'm learning to play the piano—at my age. Never had the time before. I'm not too good at it, but I'm having a wonderful time."

"I'd love to hear something," she said.

He wasn't fooled for a moment, but he was pleased. He walked to the bench, sat down and lifted the piano lid.

"I only know a few pop pieces. I'm not up to Mozart or Vivaldi yet."

"Anything you like."

He played cautiously for a few bars, then abandoned himself to the bouncy melody. He shook his head at each error but never lost the joy or the momentum, and he finished with a grand flourish and a shy grin.

" 'Sunny Side of the Street,' " he announced breathily.

"Fine and dandy."

"That's Gershwin. I'm coming to him next. Those Gershwin brothers—they were *something.* I'm not knocking Jimmy McHugh, you understand. He wrote so many great melodies—a genius. You read that book by Fats Waller's son?"

"Missed it."

"The boy says his pop wrote 'Sunny Side of the Street' and sold the tune to McHugh," Spinoza reported as he mopped his brow with a handkerchief, "but I don't know."

"It's a swell song no matter who wrote it. I wish I had your time to read, Mr. Spinoza. You must be enjoying it."

"I'm reading everything," he said proudly. "History, poetry, biographies. Some Greek plays, too. Aeschylus—he was terrific."

They talked about the poverty of today's novels as they strolled toward the door.

"If I should run into somebody who knew this Anthony, what would the message be?"

"Just mention the options, and my desire for peace and quiet."

They were in the foyer, passing two suits of fifteenth-century armor any museum might envy.

"The simplest would be to put out my own contract on *him*, $40,000. Or I could let my associates burn him. They've all kinds of hardware, Army stuff. One of them wanted to blow his house up with a land mine, or was it that blue Mercedes he drives to work? Or I could burn out his office, house and car—*and* the flat near the Hilton where he keeps the Dutch blond. All in one night—clean sweep. Just a thought. Of course, it would attract a lot of attention. Might even start a big investigation of Mr. Anthony and all his friends. Those federal cops are always looking for publicity."

An extraordinary woman. She could have gone far in his organization.

Indeed, any organization—or man—would be fortunate to have her. Anthony was an imbecile to wage a vendetta against Miss A. B. Gordon and company. Her reputation was obviously deserved. No telling what she would do, how far she would go. The risks were too great. Anthony would have to be stopped, immediately. Putting out a contract on *him* for twice as much was a marvelously ironic idea, Spinoza thought—and he nearly smiled.

She thanked him for the espresso again as they neared the helicopter, and they shook hands.

"This concussion grenade? I'm curious. How would such a device be shot into an office?"

"M-79 grenade launcher. 29 inches long, just under six and a half pounds loaded. Muzzle velocity—250 feet per second. A lot more accurate than the old M-7. Better sights too."

"You've fired this weapon?"

"Several times. Give my best to your daughter, Mr. Spinoza."

Class—to the last moment.

He watched the rotorcraft rise, waved as it moved noisily into the late morning sky. If only his own daughter had the sense, the poise, the strength of *this* woman. Something about her reminded him of his late dear wife, his faithful helpmeet of three decades. It wasn't merely the intelligence and ability to cope with problems. Ah yes, she had the same calm thoughtfulness, toughness, and the same splendid ass. Comforted by this recognition, Spinoza walked back to the house and played two other McHugh melodies—"I'm in the Mood for Love" and "Don't Blame Me"—all the way through, with just one mistake.

Next week he'd start on the Gershwin.

25

IT WAS searing hot. The afternoon sun beat down like a blowtorch. Perhaps the patient people who lived in this part of northern Mexico were accustomed to these temperatures, but Logan felt almost nauseated as he pointed the car toward the foothills of the Sierra Madre Occidental. This was Sonora—sandy and scorching. He vaguely remembered that there were lilting songs about Sonora, lovely laments written by lonely romantics about their native state. Perhaps the beauty was in the eyes of the beholder, or perhaps those tender lyrics were penned in a comfortably cool recording studio in Mexico City. Someone had told him how "I Left My Heart in San Francisco" was created in Brooklyn, Logan recalled as the sweat poured down his face and chest.

He had rented the car in Tucson and an hour after he'd crossed the border the faulty air conditioning had collapsed. Now he was driving through this furnace with his shirt stuck to the seat, sucking at a tepid bottle of Carta Blanca to replenish his body fluids. He had bought four cold beers in Guaycora a few hours earlier, and now only half of one remained. There were surely some beautiful places in Sonora, he told himself, and the temperatures would drop twenty or thirty degrees when darkness came. All he needed do was to focus on the narrow road and drive carefully. Only a fool would pit his eyes against that ball of fire in the sky.

Logan looked up—automatically.

It was a habit he had acquired with the Bloody 100th.

Bandits—German fighters—struck from above, knifing out of the glare to kill Allied bombers. Any B-17 pilot who wanted to live learned to look up regularly and frequently, in all directions. The gunners did the same thing. Even with the sunglasses, his eyes felt the impact of the fiery star. He quickly glanced down at the road.

Half a minute later he looked up again and his eyes swept the crests of the rocky hills ahead. Something metallic glinted. Could be a water pipe or a galvanized iron roof. Could be anything. Could be dangerous. This was unfamiliar terrain, and suddenly the queasiness yielded to tension. There it was again—ten o'clock. The adrenaline flowed, he recognized the old excitement. For a moment he wondered whether Van Bokkelen might be right about man being a hunter, then he refocused on the mystery ahead.

If it was an ambush, why here?

Was it because the turnoff to the plateau was only a mile away, according to the car's odometer? Whatever-whoever it was, Harry Logan meant to get to that plateau, and nothing would stop him. The Ford was rolling along at thirty-five miles an hour. There wasn't another car in sight, hadn't been for six or eight minutes. If anything happened, there'd be no help. He slowed the sedan to just under thirty as he searched for the turnoff the gas station attendant in Guaycora had promised. The Spanish that Logan had learned in high school and his tour in Costa Verde was helpful—but it wouldn't stop a bullet. He drove cautiously.

Nothing.

His eyes searched the crests again, but the glinting thing was gone. Had it been there at all? Was it a product of the sun and the fatigue, a creation of his fantasy? There was the fork—a hundred yards away. He didn't relax. He was thirty-five years and thousands of miles from those Kraut fighters and flak batteries, but the conditioning was still there.

The side road wasn't as good, so he reduced his speed to twenty-five and peered ahead. Nothing but boulders and cactus. He yawned. That was when—from somewhere off to the left—somebody fired two rounds from an M-14 rifle and blew one of the front tires into scrap rubber. Logan fought for control, lost. The Ford careened, leaping and bucking, until it slammed into the roadside rocks. . . .

The hidden marksman squinted through his scope, studied the car warily. The front was wedged between two boulders. The driver was unconscious. He lay sprawled across the steering wheel, perhaps dead. The orders hadn't been to kill him, merely to keep strangers away from the machine. The sniper told himself that he'd only been doing his job, and God had been doing *his*. If it was God's will to take this snooper, who might well be a police spy, so be it.

"Vaya con Dios," said the pious shooter, who had not been inside a church in nine years.

He scanned the whole car, stared at the body again. The driver might be wearing a good watch or carrying a gun, maybe one worth $60 or $80. In any case, the prudent course was to check the car and the corpse. If the dead man's wallet or personal property were accessible, well—what did a corpse need with such things? The sniper walked slowly toward the Ford, circled it slowly with the .30-caliber rifle at the alert. No, the driver was either dead or halfway there. It was going to be gory. They always were when their faces smashed into the windshield.

The marksman lowered his weapon, leaned forward to look in the open window. Which was when Logan sat up, swinging the door open and knocking the sniper reeling. The flier jumped from the car, bounding toward the dazed Mexican and lunging for the M-14. He grabbed the rifle, jammed the muzzle into the man's stomach. The sniper doubled up, gasped, clutching his middle. Logan swung the gun, first opening a two-inch gash in the man's right cheek, then shattering both his wrists. It would, he thought, be some time before this sniper pointed an M-14 at anyone else.

Breathing hard, Logan looked down at the man. There was blood trickling from the sniper's mouth and the gash in his cheek. There'd be a scar. Logan searched him to make certain he carried no other weapons, took a knife from the man's boot and returned to the Ford to put on the spare tire. It was exhausting in the heat, but his body was still charged with the fear and the anger, and the adrenaline helped too. He was soaked with perspiration by the time he was done, and he nearly burned his left hand on the metal of the trunk lid when he put away the jack.

What should he do with the sniper, who lay moaning and bleeding four yards away? He wouldn't waste a bullet on him, he might need every round left in the clip. There was no way to know what lay ahead, or even how far it might be to that place. Maybe the machine wouldn't be there when he arrived. Perhaps the whole story was a lie, a tissue, a deception. If it was true, there would be more armed men on the way. Logan stood there, panting, in the awful heat.

The easiest thing would be to drag the shooter a few yards through the sand and cactus and abandon him behind a cluster of rocks. Maybe he'd crawl to the road before the jackals ripped his flesh, or maybe some snake, a tarantula, scorpion or gila monster would finish the job. Logan shook his head. No, he couldn't afford the luxury of vengeance. The sniper might be able to tell him something, or at least serve as a hostage or bargaining chip when Logan got to the plateau. If this thug wasn't merely a free-lance *bandido,* his friends or employers might pay something to get him back alive.

The shooter's black eyes were open now, with hate and fear. He had every reason to be terrified—he would have cut Logan's throat —right now—if their positions were reversed. Unlike all the good friendly people of Mexico, this man was a special animal—species assassin. He killed as casually as he urinated, and did either whenever convenient. He looked up at Logan, expecting more violence.

"I ought to break your ankles," Logan told him. "You understand? You speak English? I ought to bust you up in ten more places —but I won't. I'm taking you along, in case I need you. Now you just pray that this car starts, *senor.* If it doesn't, there's a real good chance you could die out here. I can make it back to the main road, but I can't drag your ass too."

The sniper glared, and when Logan pulled him up he screamed. He took two steps toward the Ford, crumpled a few feet from the vehicle. Logan opened the left rear door, lifted and deposited him on the floor of the back section of the sedan. The man groaned again.

"Shut up, or I'll put you in the trunk. You'll fry there." The sniper became silent. Logan recalled the rifle and turned to get it. He got something else, across the back of the head.

An explosion. Blinding pain.

Total blackness.

26

ROGER PEDERSON did not work for IBM, which thought made him grin as he gunned the Kawasaki north from Chiang Mai. He had been a junior executive in the huge corporation's San Francisco office for nearly three years after he received his degree in business administration, but then he had quit. It was not that IBM was worse than other conglomerates in Britain, Germany, elsewhere. Rog Pederson had simply awakened on the morning of his twenty-fifth birthday with an overwhelming revulsion for suits, ties, memoranda, meetings and all the other rubbish.

"Routines bore the crap out of me," he confided to Laurie Obstler. She was the big-hipped lady he lived with during the next two years, highly intelligent and almost as passionate about natural foods as about his body. She'd taught him the candle-making business, and they'd earned a decent living in one of those noble valleys in northern California until the magic went out of their relationship.

In 1972 Pederson met a woman named Barbara, which was hardly surprising. He was amiable, good looking with longish blond hair, against Richard Nixon and industrial pollution and was a superior and considerate lover. With those qualifications, anyone could meet a woman named Barbara in 1972—and set up light housekeeping in Colorado. Barbara taught Pederson about rocks, astrology and nudism before she split to join a feminist bookbinding collective. He began buying and selling rocks and mineral chunks, studied Buddhism and went back to California, where he took up waterskiing and started a small business dealing in shells and stones. Only semiliberated from the vile profit ethic, he moved on to selling gems and semiprecious stones and ran his stake up to $19,000. That was when he made his first trip to Asia to buy rubies and sapphires cheaply at the source.

It was on his third overseas jaunt that he was arrested in Thailand with the smuggled stones, and he would have gone to prison if T. Robert MacBride had not intervened. MacBride should never have left the seminary in his second year—he was still, at heart, a Jesuit. He was extremely intelligent, analytical and moral. He was so smart that he had figured out a way to reconcile his religious principles with his work. He ran the Orient Arts Export Co. Ltd., and since he was unmarried and forty-two, most of Bangkok's foreign community assumed that he was either impotent or awfully blasé and some sort of spy. They were half right. He was a senior case officer for the CIA, and very good at his job.

Code name: Saint.

Whoever said there was no humor in the cloak-and-dagger world? MacBride himself was not that amusing, but he did manage to "fix" somebody so that Rog Pederson was released. Then he told the gem dealer that he could go right on with his shady business if he'd cooperate and do occasional favors, keep his eyes and ears open and carry messages now and again. The fugitive from IBM surmised that MacBride represented an intelligence apparatus, but told himself that going to jail would be a drag and a loose sort of now-and-then association of a free-lance nature would be tolerable.

He'd still be independent, and that was crucial. Now—two years and five buying trips after accepting MacBride's offer—Pederson was on his way north again to meet a Burmese smuggler who was always late—but also had the best prices on rubies. The American had taken the overnight sleeper from Bangkok to Chiang Mai, rented the motorcycle as he usually did. Cars were much more likely to be noticed by police or the network of informers paid by the American D.E.A. supervisor in Chiang Mai. The U.S. narcotics agents were curious about foreigners moving into the Golden Triangle, and Pederson did not want to be tracked by them—even for the wrong reasons. . . .

The Kawasaki roared noisily up the narrow road through the rich farm country, past the "royal" place where employees of the king were growing strawberries to show the peasants it could be done. Crop substitution was one of the monarch's efforts to demonstrate that raising poppies was not the only way to make a living. The Thai government—with foreign help—was also pushing coffee and tobacco, but these did not pay as well as opium and it was too early to predict whether the agricultural traditions of a century could be altered.

The cold wind tore at Pederson's face. Northern Thailand was no tropical paradise in the winter, with December temperatures often dropping into the forties and fifties in these highlands. It was worse for a man on a cycle, especially this early in the morning. By midday it would be warmer.

It could easily be too warm in the territory controlled by the Chinese Irregular Forces' Sixth Army, for General Wong wasn't going to like the message Pederson carried. The Sixth wasn't the biggest of the Chinese Nationalist units up here. The aged one—General Tuan Shi Wen—led the Fifth's two thousand soldiers from his mountain headquarters in Mae Saelong, and there were fifteen hundred in General Li Wen Huan's Third Army in the wild country around Tam Ngop. There were only one thousand—perhaps eleven hundred—still on the duty roster of the Sixth. Seven or eight years ago the Sixth had numbered more than two thousand, but after the Viet Nam warfare ended U.S. military aid began to slow down—bit by bit. The secret airlift of men and weapons from Taiwan had ended several years before that under international political pressure, and now even cash to pay the troops' wages was often late. The Sixth Army was in trouble. It had "understandings" with the Thai police and the few token military units Bangkok had scattered up here. Most of the Thai troops were fighting Red guerrillas down south or braced along the eastern frontiers facing Viet Nam, Laos and Cambodia. The Red Vietnamese were busy in an unofficial but bloody little war with the equally Marxist Cambodians, and there were rumors of fighting inside Laos. The giant to the north—China, traditional adversary of all these turbulent young countries—was flexing its muscles as it denounced its own ancient foe, Russia, and Moscow's Asian allies. The whole region was flickering with violence and threats of major conflagration, dangers that made the little Sixth Army seem insignificant and irrelevant.

It was midafternoon when Pederson rode into the village, a tiny trading center of three or four hundred people in the foothills. He respectfully slowed the cycle as he passed the local police sergeant, a heavy man whose force of two constables represented the token presence of the Thai government here. The real rulers and defenders of this place were the Sixth's infantry bivouacked in camps up on the nearby heights, and the trim sixty-four-year-old Nationalist general who commanded them. Unlike some of leaders of the various "armies" on the Burmese side of the frontier, Chu Ching Wong was a real general. He had graduated from China's military academy, won his promotions in the long war against the Japanese invaders in the 1930s and '40s and earned the command of the Kuomintang division that was now designated the Sixth Army. He was a professional.

He was doomed, of course.

He knew it, but he could not give up. He had given his oath and his life to a cause most people had forgotten, and he was too much of a soldier to betray that trust. His military skills were still remembered by Peking generals who had been lieutenants when he fought them a quarter of a century earlier, and he was proud of that. He had never cheated his men, never stolen their ration money like some other Kuomintang commanders. He had no fortune in Paris or New York, and when so many abandoned their troops as the Red armies grew, Wong stayed with his division. Fighting every step of the way, his force crossed the border by foot, and Wong walked with them.

Some twelve thousand men had followed him out of China—a long time ago. Some died, some fell ill and some decided that they did not want to wait any longer. Year by year, men drifted away to marry Meo girls or Shan beauties, to work farms and raise families. Many of them were the sons of generations of Chinese peasants, so returning to the land seemed logical. There were raids into Red China to gather intelligence for clever men on Formosa and in Washington, and casualties. Other troopers perished during the shadowy Indochina war on missions no journalist ever reported, operations planned by tough U.S. colonels and CIA executives who had several false names. It had all been too real to the Sixth Army's burial details, and to the man who sat drinking tea in the low wooden house on the hill overlooking Ban Sop Sa. Even if there had not been sentries outside, it was easy to recognize this trim erect man as a general—as Pederson had when they'd first met the previous year.

"Welcome. Would you like some . . . Pepsi-Cola, Mr. Pederson?"

"Tea'll be okay, general."

"It would be no problem," Wong assured him. "The merchants in town sell my men your national drinks. I am too set in my ways to change, but the troops are becoming quite Americanized. Your jeeps and your rifles, your radios and your uniforms—so why not your cola?"

There was a tinge of sadness in this commentary, as if the foreign soft drink was eroding what little was left of what had been a fierce Kuomintang division—a *Chinese* fighting force. They had no war to wage anymore, and only dimming memories of the China that had been. Other civilizations had been washed away by floods, earthquakes and invading barbarians in the past, and now artificially flavored beverages and chewing gum were the scourge—the low-calorie Visigoths of the atomic age.

"If you don't mind, I'd prefer the tea. It's cold on the road," the gem dealer said.

They drank tea, and Pederson told him about the new restaurant that had opened in Chiang Mai—next door to the brothel which called itself a Turkish bath and serviced visiting German tourists. The king had left his winter residence in Chiang Mai last month, and newspapers in the Thai capital carried official denials that another military coup was imminent. Between the rock and roll records that had dominated the London and Los Angeles airwaves last summer, Bangkok radio carried news of a mortar attack by Communist guerrillas over in Chiang Rai—even closer to the Chinese border.

"So they are up north now too," Wong said.

"It's still worse down south of the capital. They say it's nothing at all serious.

"Yet."

"Perfectly safe for businessmen and foreign visitors, except for maybe ten percent of the frontier areas. Hey, I sound like the government travel office. Sorry, general."

Wong waited for him to deliver the message. It would be rude and un-Chinese to ask. Pederson was in no rush to tell him; he liked this aged warrior and the news was not good. He delayed as long as possible, then took a deep breath and tried to say it as kindly as possible.

"Finest tea I ever had. Can't beat Chinese tea, or Chinese cooking either. One of the great cuisines, maybe the greatest. Oh, I ran into our friend a couple of days ago. Sends you his *very* best."

"In good health, I trust?"

"First class. Been on a diet. Lost twelve or thirteen pounds. Looking fine. Awfully busy—buying, selling. You know what those merchants are like," Pederson said with a counterfeit show of cheery humor.

The general still waited politely for the message.

"He asked me to tell you he can't put his hands on that merchandise—not right away. He's trying, but there's a problem."

The general's face showed no emotion.

There was always a problem, especially when dealing with these naive-complex Americans. Their ideas of morality were as unrealistic as their notions of toughness, and it was invariably someone else who suffered. It was not easy being an ally of the Americans.

"Did he mention what the problem might be?" Wong asked softly and refilled his guest's cup.

"No, sir. I'm afraid not . . ."

"Our need for this merchandise is urgent."

Shan rebel troops were crowding into this small domain from the west, equipped with modern arms captured or stolen from the Burmese Army. To the east, Communist guerrillas using excellent Red bloc weapons provided by Laos or China were growing bolder. The supplies of cannon, machine guns, mortars, radios, ammunition —almost everything—that the U.S. had been providing were running low, and the capacity of the remaining Chinese Nationalist units to defend themselves was shrinking every month. "Urgent" was an understatement. "Critical" would be more accurate.

"I'll tell him, sir."

"He must know this. He has a number of sales representatives in this area," Wong pointed out.

There were several networks of CIA operatives—some thirty Caucasians and ten times that number of Thai and tribesmen— covering this region, and Pederson was not going to be foolish enough to deny it. What the hell—he wasn't supposed to know about these clandestine teams anyway. MacBride was a fool if he figured these Nationalists were dummies . . . they hadn't survived all these years by being stupid . . . "I'm only a . . . I don't actually work for him, general. You see, I just do him a favor now and them and pass along messages. A sort of free-lance postman, you might say."

"We have been faithful clients for a long time." The corpses of thousands of dead Nationalist soldiers who had perished serving the interests of Formosa and Washington during three decades of secret war were proof of that. General Wong could not bring himself to be that blunt. He was Chinese, and a gentleman.

"Maybe a shipment will arrive soon."

"How soon?"

"I don't know. I don't have any idea. I'll tell him what you said

147

—next week when I'm back in Bangkok."

Wong paused, phrased his message carefully. "Say that we are close to bankruptcy. Fresh supplies—in quantity—are essential. If he cannot get this merchandise to us soon, perhaps he can advance the funds so that we may acquire them ourselves. That might be quicker and simpler."

There were arms dealers in Bangkok, Singapore and Hong Kong who could supply almost anything—including U.S. military hardware being sold off privately by men in Laos, Cambodia and Viet Nam. Huge quantities of American weapons had been captured or found abandoned, and certain Red commanders were quietly peddling this "capitalist-imperialist" war matériel which their own armies did not use. Some of the sellers were Communist regimes themselves, acquiring foreign currency and dealing surreptitiously through European or Eurasian intermediaries. Despite all the moralistic Marxist oratory in the shrilly virtuous Red capitals, this part of Asia had not changed *that* much yet.

"I'll give him the message, general."

"Thank you. I will be listening for his answer . . . Excuse me, I have been such a poor host. Have you eaten? The food our cooks serve may not match that of the great chefs of Shanghai, but it is not entirely unworthy."

"Thanks, but I had a bite on the road. Appreciate your invitation, general. Can I take a rain check?" He saw that Wong did not quite understand the idiom. "I mean can I accept your gracious invitation some other time, sir? I have an appointment. It would be a genuine privilege and an honor to eat with you when I come by again."

"The honor would be mine. Thank you for your visit, Mr. Pederson. Please come soon."

The sentries snapped to attention as the American left the house, but they were not quite as . . . as sharp . . . as they had been a year earlier. The cutting edge of this outfit was the slightest bit duller, and Pederson noticed one middle-aged trooper with a patch on his knee. As he guided the Kawasaki toward the road, he saw three other soldiers straining to remove a motor from an old jeep—cannibalizing because they lacked new spare parts.

The Sixth Army—or what was left of it—was hurting. Did anybody care, Pederson wondered as he speeded up and headed toward the village. Whatever the CIA decided, Wong was not going to give up without a fight. This skin-and-bones force was all he had left, and he was too much of a soldier to let it perish with a sigh or a whimper. He would do something. Hell, it was a mess. The gem dealer who loathed big organizations reminded himself that it was someone else's mess—not free and easy Rog Pederson's. The rich and the powerful had vast treasuries and arsenals, big government agencies to deal with political problems such as this. Who gave a damn about a gang of leftover Chinese Nationalists anyway? Even the new regime on Taiwan had more pressing concerns—including its own survival. Every man for himself, right? Everybody said the Nationalists were right wing bastards, typical of America's neo-fascist allies. Screw the Sixth Army!

Shit. Rog Pederson was as progressive and anti-reactionary as anybody, but he couldn't help feeling sorry for the old general and the hungry soldiers nobody needed anymore. It was ridiculous. His politically hip friends in the States would laugh at him, and they were probably right. Intellectually and ideologically, they were surely right. Even from the hard-boiled military point of view of those dumb Pentagon thugs who'd wasted America's youth and honor in the jungles of Viet Nam, carrying Wong any longer was a sucker move . . . Let MacBride sweat it out. He had all kinds of connections in Bangkok and Washington, and access to millions. He probably had enough cash in his own secret funds here to buy the stuff the Sixth needed. MacBride wasn't going to like it when he was warned that Wong would do something violent if the U.S. didn't keep its commitments . . . the CIA case officer would turn nasty and tell Pederson to mind his own goddam business.

Made sense. Take care of Number One. I'm all right, Jack—like that British flick. There was a sweet and healthy red-haired girl with a great talent for raising organically grown vegetables and Pederson's lusts waiting in San Bernadino, and a nice piece of change to be made on those rubies in the village ninety-five miles west. Sure, those were what counted—

Jeezus!

Pederson swerved sharply to avoid being pulped by some idiot driving a Toyota pickup, and it wasn't until his heart stopped pounding that he noticed the flowers along the road. Red—maybe poppies. He'd never been a horticultural ace. Whatever they were, they made him think of that fine folk-singing woman with the garden back in California. That red was the same color as her hip-length hair.

Too bad about General Wong, old soldiers were supposed to fade away . . . Why wouldn't he? No, he wasn't going to do it. He was going to make trouble, and a lot of people were going to get killed. The only questions were where and when. It would be soon, and Pederson hoped that it would happen when he was far away. After all, Rog Pederson was a pacifist . . . Now he accelerated abruptly, hoping that the damn ruby smuggler would be on time for once.

27

STARK NAKED, Alison Gordon faced the muscular chairman of the Joint Chiefs of Staff. General John P. Maxwell had four stars, a reputation for toughness even the Russians respected and the craggy good looks of a mature cowboy star. Air armadas, naval strike forces, armored legions and nuclear missile crews around the world awaited his coded commands. Despite all this, she was wholly unimpressed.

"You a man or a mouse?" she challenged as she wriggled her hips and shoulders.

". . . I know my job, and I'll do it," Maxwell was saying earnestly.

"Take a look at *this* job, soldier."

Confident that his new soft-lens contacts were the finest money could buy, the general was facing her squarely. "I've never shirked my duty," he announced, but he remained seated.

Another *talker.* Hollywood was full of them, and so many frustrated women. Licking her lips, she swung her lush breasts. "Let's do it—*now . . .*"

Any healthy male would have grabbed her, swept her onto the bed only two yards away. John P. Maxwell didn't move. Neither his face nor his eyes showed the slightest flicker of desire. Well, she realized her body wasn't quite that of a twenty-year-old anymore, but it was still firm, attractive. Within the past ten days she'd been propositioned by a TV network vice president, a famed British director not a day over twenty-eight and the wife of the head of a major record company. Nonetheless, the chairman of the Joint Chiefs of Staff merely looked wary and thoughtful for several moments.

And then the clean-cut host of the "Today" show asked him

another question, and A. B. Gordon broke into giggles. She was laughing by the time she reached the television set, and she never did get to hear General Maxwell's official position on the latest SALT talks . . . "You had your chance and you blew it, or rather you didn't, so to speak," she told the distant military mastermind, then flicked off the set and turned to inspect herself in the full-length mirror.

"General, you're truly a schmuck," and the laughter swept over her again. Logan wouldn't have minded the craziness of it. He liked her odd sense of humor, and the fact that she liked herself. There were too many men who weren't that comfortable with women who were frankly proud of their minds and their bodies, as well as their achievements. Logan wasn't one of those threatened by genuinely strong women, though he wasn't fooled by the arrogant or vulgar ones either. He was, she thought with pleasure, strong enough himself to enjoy all of Alison B. Gordon—except perhaps the smoking. She'd cut down from two packs a day to one a day since she'd fallen in love with him . . . "I'm in *love* with Harry Logan," she sang out exuberantly to the mirror, "and Harry Logan's in *love* with me, better be . . ."

She studied her figure, decided she could lose a couple of pounds. No more, though. Logan didn't mind the tiny bulge. He liked all of her—the slightly mashed little toe of her left foot, the small but still visible abdominal scar that memorialized a knife wound received in Africa, even the flamboyantly large tuft of pubic hair that had startled some other men in the past.

Before Harry Logan, whenever that was.

Where the hell was he?

Why wasn't he here to hold her, to admire and tease and take his pleasure in her—to allow her to do the same with him . . . ?

He was all right, of course. He *had* to be. He was—for her—the ablest, wisest, bravest—*and* the nicest. He'd be in touch with her at any hour . . . When she took her shower she washed every inch of skin and every strand of hair carefully, for her lover. He might arrive at any moment . . .

The thick, terrycloth cotton towel felt luxurious, and she didn't start wondering about him until she had the hair dryer in hand. The noise and the caress of the hot air were soothing, blotting out the room, allowing her to roam through her inner thoughts, and worries. There was something semi-hypnotic about this soothing droning sound, and the warmth that was reassuringly amniotic . . .

It was in this state that the questions floated up into her conscious-
ness. Why hadn't he called for nearly four days? Was he in trouble
or sick or—? Did he need her—right now?

No, she wouldn't panic. She forced herself to concentrate on
dressing and preparing to go to work, finishing with two quick
strokes of lipstick. She was about to put the .357 in her shoulder bag
when she heard the knock on the bedroom door. The heavy gun
was in her hand when she opened it and saw Hovde.

"Man wants to talk to you," he announced hoarsely.

She had last seen this visitor in coveralls at the San Paloma airfield. It was the almost hairless mechanic-philosopher who serviced
her lover's planes.

"He's okay, Don. I know him."

Hovde shrugged, pointed out that it was half past nine and
walked out of the house to resume his guard duty.

The balding visitor looked at her cautiously. "My name is Latourette. Ralph Latourette. Work with Logan."

"I met you at the flying school. Would you like some coffee?"

"Bad for my gut. I'll watch."

He accompanied her to the sunny kitchen, standing and looking
as she put down the .357, prepared her orange juice and morning
mug of Colombian caffeine.

It wasn't until she sat down to drink that Latourette spoke again.
"What's goin' on here?"

"Breakfast."

"That iron you were holding and the guy who brought me in? He
was hiding in the bushes with a grease gun, ready to cut me in half.
What's that all about?"

"It's a long story, Ralph. May I call you Ralph?"

He nodded. "Lady, I don't like that kind of crap—that bit with
the grease guns."

"I don't either. Sure you won't have coffee?"

"Got any . . . don't laugh . . . any Ovaltine?"

She found the half-can left over from her niece's stay, and the
mechanic told her why he had come.

"Harry and I been together since '43. I used to take care of Dirty
Dora. He ever mention her?"

"No. A girl?"

Latourette's seamed face rearranged itself in a grin. "Bird. His
bird—17. He used to fly 17s, you know. He tell you that?"

"Several times," she said, and put the steaming mug of chocolate-colored milk drink in front of him.

He blew on the surface, sipped tentatively. "Good."

"Pretty hard to screw up Ovaltine. What's up?"

"I met people who loused up Ovaltine. Cajun girl near Shreveport. Hot as a pistol, but awful Ovaltine. Almost killed me. You know—"

"I don't want to hurt your feelings, Ralph, but this isn't the script department. Why don't you peddle your life story to TV for a mini-series?"

He sipped more of the Ovaltine. "You got a temper, miss."

"Third shortest fuse in town. Ralph, why are you here? Is something wrong?"

"Maybe," he replied, and drank some more.

"Ralph, don't mess with me. I can get that man with the grease gun back here—"

"*Some* temper. Harry wired me a load of cash and told me to buy a 54. C-54, old cargo plane. Four-engine job, World War Two. You know about the deal?"

"All about it. I'm handling security."

"That's what the guy with the grease gun's all about?"

"None of your business. What about the 54?"

"Bought it. Parts too. Got a pilot, and another guy who navigates and handles the radio. Ready to go you-know-where."

She finished her coffee. "So?"

"Where's Harry?"

"He was in Tucson on Thursday. Is something wrong . . . ?"

Latourette evaded the direct impact of the question. "He was supposed to call me two days ago. Harry's always on time. You heard from him?"

"Not since Thursday. You think he's in trouble?"

"He told me you'd know where to reach him, and you don't. Yeah, he could be in trouble. He's got a lot of money, and he's dealing with some funny people. Greedy people. You know what I'd do? I'd wait another day or so, then I'd get on that 54 and haul-ass down to Costa Verde. He'll show up there."

The rest of the thought was written in his eyes.

"If he isn't dead," she said.

"Yeah. He said you were smart. Yeah, if he isn't dead."

She jammed one of the black cigarettes into the long holder, lit the Sobranie and inhaled. "He'll call," she told Latourette—and herself.

"And if he doesn't?"

"I'll meet you at the San Paloma field day after tomorrow. Noon okay?"

"I suppose. You bringin' that guy with the grease gun?"

"Maybe a couple of others. They've got grease guns too."

There was no telephone message from Logan, and she showed up at the flying school with three men—one tall and black and named Mercer. Mercer Davis came in a panel truck with five wooden crates, heavy mothers that made the others grunt as they manhandled the boxes into the fuselage of the C-54. There were already a dozen crates and two airplane engines lashed down in the cargo department. The mechanic showed them where to stow their suitcases, introduced Alison Gordon and her team to the flying crew. Then he invited her to sit up front near the pilot as they prepared for takeoff.

The first motor roared. "Suppose he doesn't show?" Latourette asked abruptly.

"He isn't dead."

"What if he is?"

She shook her head. It was inconceivable to her. Unacceptable. "He may be there already," she said.

There was no point in arguing with her. The second engine spluttered, coughed and thundered. Numbers three and four joined in, and then they were taxiing down the runway. The aged cargo plane lifted off only 150 yards before the concrete ended, climbed slowly to 6,800 feet and leveled off half a minute later. The pilots talked shop, exchanged jokes and checked their charts as the 54 bored south through the afternoon at 230 miles an hour. The sturdy Pratt & Whitney's could deliver enough rpm's to move the vintage craft 40 miles an hour faster, but these were reconditioned engines and the pilot saw no point in pushing his luck. He turned, saw the look in Alison Gordon's eyes and misunderstood.

"Don't worry. These old birds used to fly the Atlantic as regular airliners in '46 and '47. Slow but steady."

She shrugged, stared out the window hour after hour as they chugged south over Mexico. They refueled at the airport outside Merida in Yucatan, after which she fell asleep. It was half past seven in the morning when Latourette awakened her. Bleary-eyed and feeling unwashed in her rumpled clothes, she blinked and yawned before she reached for the carton of steaming coffee he held out toward her.

"Costa Verde," he said, and pointed.

Mountains ridged the middle like a spinal column, with foothills sloping down swiftly to coastal plain. Tropical green, cut here and there by twisting snakes that had to be rivers. That great mass of lighter color puzzled her for several seconds until she realized it was the Caribbean. Yes, she could make out a couple of small harbors. It wasn't easy from this altitude when she wasn't fully awake, but they looked like ports—maybe fishing villages . . . She made her way back through the crates to the toilet at the rear, found small comfort in the fact that her kidneys were still working. She was groggy and fretful. The sight of her puffy face and tousled hair added to her depression. She opened her shoulder bag, irritably pushed aside the Magnum and somehow found her compact and comb. A couple of passes at her hair hardly helped. She squinted at herself in the compact's mirror. "What a mess!" The hell with the lipstick. A "liberated" woman didn't need makeup or a bra or a lot of other crap, they'd told her. Which was garbage. What she wore or didn't had nothing to do with being independent. It was as dumb as all those ads that told her her life would be a horror if she didn't buy the right eye shadow and "delicately scented" douche. A. B. Gordon's future would be glorious if she could put together clean clothes and six hours of sleep in a bed—preferably with Harry Logan. She closed her tired eyes, shivered. It had to be fatigue. Why else would she even think about the idiotic sociological implications of lipstick, for God's sake . . . ?

"You okay?" Hovde asked as she walked stiff-legged back toward the nose.

She peered at him, nodded. "You look terrible, Don."

He smiled, flashed her a thumb's-up salute and stroked his unshaven face before he returned to the card game. She got back to her seat as the pilot was talking to the air traffic control tower at Garcia International Airport—named, of course, to honor the father of the president. There was the usual mumbo jumbo chatter about thirty degrees left and use that runway. And then the cargo plane was swooping down and on the ground before she could think of anything clever to say. It didn't matter, there was only one thing on her mind.

"Where's Logan?" she demanded as the plane taxied to the two-

156

story stucco terminal . . . "He's here," she said before the mechanic could reply.

"Always answer your own questions?"

She refused to be embarrassed. She told Ralph Latourette that his coffee was atrocious, his airplane uncomfortable and those lousy sandwiches unfit for human consumption. When the C-54 stopped, she was the first to the ground. It was hot and the sun hurt her eyes, and . . . Harry Logan was nowhere in sight. Every bone in her body ached. God, what a way to go.

The mechanic was pointing to the left, and up. She could just make out a small plane—painted oddly in a variety of swirls and blobs—descending to land. There didn't appear to be anything exciting about this aircraft, a four-engine plane with a high tail. It took her a moment to hear the noisy growl that said it wasn't a jet. For some reason she couldn't guess, Latourette was radiating joy.

"Beautiful, isn't she?" he said as if he'd built this craft himself.

She squinted into the glare, trying to figure the cause for his schoolboy elation. Something told her that she shouldn't say this was just another old airplane . . . "Splendid," she fenced.

The mechanic wasn't fooled. "Don't you recognize that bird? Hell, woman, that's it, that's a *B-17.*"

He said it reverently, as if he were calling this historical curiosity a Rembrandt or a Titian. Realistically, this plane was a joke compared to modern bombers, which were more than twice as fast, three times as big and one thousand times more destructive. It had been like this, she guessed, for centuries, men sentimentalizing some remembered glory or object—a battle-ax, a musket, a uniform that no longer fit or perhaps a helmet from some high school football game. Middle-aged Romans had probably done it, she thought.

"The best there was, they say," she recited.

"The best. This one's extra special. Look at the way he handles her. Smooth as silk. That's got to be Harry . . ."

The landing was perfect. She felt her heart pumping faster. When the props stopped spinning, she ran out to the plane. As she reached it, a man in his fifties slid out and a younger blond man followed moments later. They looked at her, and the older man spoke first. "Where's Logan?" he asked in a pleasantly ripe southern accent.

She choked, then grabbed control.

"Gordon. A. B. Gordon. I'm handling security for the movie company," she said firmly, and stuck out her hand. The southerner shook it, introduced himself.

157

"Beau Mayberry, ma'am. This here's my copilot, Ot-to Kopf."

The German didn't exactly shake her hand. He pumped it—twice, *correctly*. "You didn't answer the question, Miss Gordon."

One of those—the kind who kept score.

"What question?"

"Where is Logan?" Kopf demanded.

"He's coming," she answered, and started to turn.

"Are you cer-tain?" the German pressed.

She reminded herself that no single country had a monopoly on male arrogance, so she forced out a tired smile and nodded. "Sure."

She saw Kopf did not believe her. She didn't care. She started walking back toward the terminal slowly, wondering where Harry Logan was. If he was dead, she'd have to face—No, dammit, she couldn't, she wouldn't consider it.

28

SOLDIERS.

At each hangar, on the roof of the terminal, in the customs area and near the bank and the souvenir shop. Everywhere.

There were pairs of infantrymen in full combat gear all over Hernan Garcia International Airport—chunky little men with M-16 rifles and broad faces that spoke of Mayan ancestors. Half an hour after the B-17 touched down, thirty more troopers arrived by truck with the young officer who had burst into the president's office after the attempted assassination. He had good manners, an excellent memory and the whitest set of teeth she had seen in years.

"Capitan Delgado—at your service," he announced and tossed her a Number One salute. It fairly whistled. "Welcome back, Senorita Gordon. El Presidente has ordered me to escort your party to Puerto Linda. Two platoons are already guarding the field down there. A small problem with smugglers in the area."

She scanned the soldiers in their U.S. uniforms and steel pots. They wouldn't suffer the discomfort of those metal helmets in this steamy climate unless they expected to go into battle.

"And I have good news," Delgado continued briskly. "The cargo vessel bringing much of your equipment has radioed that it will arrive in one and a half or two days. Isn't that good?"

"Peachy."

"Peachy?"

"A folk expression. Left over from the twenties and thirties."

As the C-54 and the B-17 were refueled, Delgado told her that the dining facilities, offices and a dozen other air-conditioned buildings formerly used by the fruit company had been cleaned and were at full ready for the motion picture unit. He reported that his

159

aunt had just returned from Miami, where she had read a gossip column item alleging that George Roy Hill would direct the film and John Travolta might star.

"George Roy Hill would be good. He likes old airplanes," the captain said—obviously a disciple of his aunt.

"He's a wonderful director. I hear they're talking with him," she picked up. Good ol' Bernie Peshkin was earning his salary.

"And Travolta?"

"No way," she said. "His tits are too small."

She was right. Delgado had never thought about it, but now he thought back and realized Travolta was almost totally flat-chested. Good feet and hair, but no chest at all. In a big budget film such as this, those wily Hollywood moguls would not take any chances.

"I suppose that eliminates Warren Beatty too," the captain speculated as a sergeant walked up and said something in Spanish. Delgado responded curtly. "I must get my men into our plane, Miss Gordon. We will be ready to show you the way in fifteen minutes. Your cameraman might find our machine rather appropriate. It is the baby brother of your C-54."

The reference didn't mean a thing to A. B. Gordon, but Latourette seemed delighted when he saw the old twin-engine transport. Perched on the runway with its nose stuck in the air, it was just another small airplane to her. The mechanic told her that it was the historic C-47, a Douglas workhorse which many airlines flew as the DC-3 "as recently as a quarter-century ago." And then she remembered seeing them in Viet Nam, rigged with batteries of rapid-fire mini-guns to pulverize ground targets. She listened politely as Latourette lauded the sturdiness and mechanical reliability of the primitive craft—and she thought about Harry Logan.

At 9:20, the three sturdy relics rumbled down the concrete, and the C-47 led them in a wide arc southeast toward Puerto Linda. The flight lasted fifty minutes, and she saw the harbor and miles of banana plantations as they descended to land. Puerto Linda was even hotter and more humid than Costa Verde's capital. The airport complex was ringed by two barbed-wire fences, with a sand-bagged guard post at the gate. Armed troopers drove four jeeps and a truck out to the planes, and Delgado immediately set the soldiers to helping them unload their gear.

"Hot," Kopf observed.

"Mombasa was hotter," Beau Mayberry judged professionally.

As the boxes were being carried to the vehicles, Agajanian stud-

160

ied the base with the objectivity of a military tactician. "Don't like it. Damn jungle creeps up too close to the perimeter—*there.* And *there* too. Cong could come out of that shrubbery some night, chop the fence with wire cutters and *wham . . .* you like it?"

"Love it," Alison Gordon answered, and mopped her brow with a handkerchief. "Tropical paradise."

The accountant's eyes roved on, searching for weak points. "Runs right down to the water. Cong could come in from the sea."

"*What* Cong? This is Costa Verde," she reminded him.

"Goddam Costa Verde Cong."

The terminology was debatable, but the logic unquestionable.

"If there's no Cong," Agajanian challenged, "then why all these troopers with the M-16s and the .50 dug in at the gate?"

"Captain Delgado says smugglers," she replied deadpan.

"You believe that?"

"No. Tell the others. We're carrying weapons at all times—even in the john. Go. . . ."

There were sheets on the beds, soap and towels in the bathrooms, even a typewriter and three file cabinets in an office in the main building. Delgado introduced her to a pair of barefoot young maids, a potbellied cook and his adolescent helper and a pretty woman in her mid-twenties. She was better dressed and clearly more educated than the others, with a figure that could get her a part in lots of movies.

"Senorita Gordon, this is Clara Velez. She speaks English, can help as a translator. Knows the area and the stores, where to buy what and how much to pay. El Presidente would not want you to get . . . what is the expression . . . *sí,* ripped off."

"I type a little too, Senorita, and I worked at my uncle's company last summer at the *centrallila*—the switchboard. I am wild about movies."

"I mentioned Travolta," the captain said.

"Is Juan coming?" Clara Velez asked eagerly.

A. B. Gordon explained that the film wasn't quite cast yet, promised to let her know as soon as the producer in Hollywood decided. Delgado continued the tour, escorting her through the radio room, the control tower and a small theater filled with more than one hundred seats. The projector had been removed when the fruit company left, but a new one would arrive soon so that films could be shown again.

161

"All the comforts of home," she said as they stepped out into the sunlight.

There was a shout, and one of the soldiers pointed. This time she recognized the type of aircraft. It was another B-17, painted a dull black. She watched as it came in for a smooth landing, so graceful that Latourette would surely say Harry Logan was at the stick. The plane rolled to a halt some sixty yards from where she stood. Walking toward it, she noticed something strange. There was no number, no designation of any kind on the entire craft. With no flag or national emblem, it seemed like a pirate ship—black and mysterious.

One by one, four men emerged. The first three were strangers but there was something familiar about the last.

It was Logan.

He wasn't dead. He was here, waving at her and moving across the concrete. She began to run, and it wasn't until she was almost in his arms that she saw the bandage at the back of his head. They kissed, and kissed, and she held him tight as she burrowed into his neck and shoulder. She almost cried, but she didn't. She gasped and clung, and he kissed her again—on the face and eyes.

Then she stepped back, looked up at him intently. "Where the *hell* have you been?"

"I've been kidnapped, hon. Beat up and held prisoner by bandits in Mexico. They gave me this," and pointed to the bandage.

"Oh, my God. Are you all right?"

"Sure. Hon, like you to meet them. This here rotten thug is Pinball Baranovitch."

A barrel-chested man in a battered leather flying jacket and cotton work pants stepped forward, showing two gold teeth as he smiled. He seemed embarrassed.

"Was a mistake, miss. Thought Harry was a cop. Whole gang of *federales* and narcs—some 'Mericans—hunting for our black bird."

"What is this—*The Maltese Falcon?*"

Logan put his arm around her reassuringly, winked. "Pinball used to fly with the 100th. Good man. Went into business for himself a couple of years ago running in grass. Hauled it up at night in the black bird—down on the deck at two hundred feet, under the radar. Then our government put in new low-level radar a few months ago, and the game was over."

"Had to find a new gig," the younger man in peasant shirt, jeans and huaraches said.

162

"Hon, this is Pinball's partner. Flies, navigates, fixes radios—versatile. Crockett Duckworth, pride of Texas."

"San Antone. At your service, Ma'am." He had hair almost shoulder length, and a sweatband to hold it out of his large gray eyes.

The third man was the tallest—perhaps six feet. He zipped open his jacket and took off his rakish cap, and he wasn't a man anymore. A yard of yellow hair tumbled out, and two *Playboy*-sized breasts blossomed dramatically.

"Las Vegas," judged Alison Gordon.

"Very good, hon."

"Is she yours?" Alison's temperature was rising.

The blond stepped back defensively, sensing that she was in danger.

"She's my baby sister, ma'am," the Texan said. "She was down visiting our place when the *federales* came out into the hills lookin' for us. We just about got the bird off before they showed—shootin' up a storm. Marlene's a proper married lady, or was till last month. Been married several times—in church."

"Just three times, brother," she said sweetly. "Pleased to meet you, ma'am . . . I'm a Leo, on the cusp." The distant buzz of an airplane sounded, but there was no machine in sight . . . "I'll bet you're a Capricorn," Marlene Duckworth suggested.

"I'm a private detective and a registered Democrat. That's all I can handle."

The noise was louder.

"What about me?" Logan asked. "These fellows tried to knock my brains out. Don't I get any sympathy?"

"Harry, what you get is . . ."

The rest of her reply was drowned out in the thunder of 1,680 horsepower. A single-engine fighter whistled in low out of the glare, not a jet but a prehistoric propeller craft. At all of three hundred twenty miles an hour, the World War Two long-range escort charged in from the sea, skimming the Caribbean waves.

"51!" Logan shouted.

Now the P-51 was right down on the deck, coming toward them at no more than thirty feet. They threw themselves to the concrete as it blasted by overhead—no more than twenty feet above the ground. Logan was the first to his feet, and helped Alison up before he said, "Goddam you, Van!"

The P-51 was doing aerobatics, looping and rolling expertly.

Logan raised his right hand, gave the uni-digit salute of angry defiance.

"I don't believe any of this, Harry. First you show up with this wild story and three people you *had* to get from central casting, and then this other idiot practically kills us. I suppose he's one of Our Crowd too?"

He nodded. "Geoffrey Van Bokkelen, rich and crazy," and reached back to touch his bandage. He was in pain. She stepped forward, much more tender now than annoyed.

"It's okay . . . listen, you'll meet Van in a few minutes—after I kick his ass."

"Harry, tell me the truth. How bad is this Van, how crazy? Is he as strange as these three?"

Logan considered the question as the P-51 began to dive again. "I wouldn't say that."

"Thank God."

"He's *worse.*" He kissed her again, and they held hands as they walked to the black bomber together. It was nice to find a grown-up lover who didn't mind holding hands, she thought. It was good to have Harry Logan back, and near her. Touching her.

The interpreter watched them from the office window. Which was her assignment—to watch and wait and keep "El Stalin" informed. When the time was right, he would lead the attack. The planes and the foreign mercenaries would all be destroyed. "El Stalin" had said so. He had given his word.

29

"Captain Van Bokkelen reporting for duty, sir."

Snappy salute, orange coveralls, white silk scarf of the sort no pilot had worn in twenty years—and a sly grin.

"I'm going to break his face," Logan announced, and pulled back a balled fist.

"Harry, you might break his arm too, and we aren't that deep in pilots—or planes."

"Listen to the lady, Blue Leader."

Logan looked at the nearby P-51, and lowered his fist. "It's over, Van," he said.

"What's over, *sir?*"

"The baby stuff. One more dumb stunt and you won't have enough jaw left to shave."

Van Bokkelen turned to A. B. Gordon, shrugged.

"You'll love the intensive care unit," she said. "It's quiet. You'll hear your bones mending."

"I told you in New York. It's a real war. We aren't joking."

"Well, it seems this is the only war in town . . . Okay, let's start all over again. Captain Van Bokkelen, reporting for duty."

No campy flourish in his salute, and Logan returned it correctly.

"Alison, this is Geoffrey Van Bokkelen. He used to be a damn fine pilot. Van, she's running Security."

"I feel safe already. Who's your friend?" He gestured toward the trio entering the headquarters building twenty-five yards away.

"That's Baranovitch—used to be pinball champ of the whole Eighth Air Force. Remember him?"

"Not *him.* The other one."

"Oh, the kid. Crockett Duckworth—his partner."

165

"I *mean* the ample blond, Harry. Who is she, Miss Gordon—please?"

"Mr. Duckworth said she was his baby sister. The Duckworths are a very close family, I gather."

Van Bokkelen's eyes were large with admiration.

"She's *something*. What's she doing here?"

"She's our staff astrologer . . . and modern dance instructor, and I think she gives yoga lessons too."

"Gonna be some war, Harry."

"We've also got a Kraut pilot who hates 17s, two guys who used to fly in grass from Mexico, a high-born southern gun runner and—"

"A very difficult security situation," Alison interrupted. "Most of these people don't know exactly what's coming, and there's no reason for any member of this strike force to have the background or even the real name of any other. Need to know—that's the rule. When we split up and run, the less anyone knows about the rest, the better—"

"All I want to know is when the modern dance lessons start," Van Bokkelen said.

"Miss Duckworth will post the schedule later," Alison promised him.

While Logan was supervising the unloading and storage of the equipment, the other fliers and the rest of the mercenaries were finding quarters and unpacking. The detective made her way up the stairs to the control tower, where she found Don Hovde looking thoughtfully down at the field and the jungle. After a while, he pointed the index finger of his right hand toward the green mass—stabbing the air twice for emphasis. "That's where they'll come from," he predicted hoarsely.

"Sure, the whole Sioux nation could charge out of that jungle some afternoon."

Hovde ignored the sarcastic tone. *"Night,"* he corrected.

She felt the fatigue again, muffled a yawn. The depressing part of it was that he might well be right.

"You think I'm paranoid?" he asked suddenly.

"I hope so. Lord, I'm tired. Okay, put out some Claymores on that perimeter."

"I gave you the Claymore."

This time she didn't try to stop the yawn. "But you've got more. You're not the sort to stock one lousy mine. If you didn't have eleven or thirty-two more, you wouldn't have turned in that one so politely."

"Maybe they won't come at all," he said, trying for the moment to temporize.

"Sure. But if they do, you think it'll be from the east?"

"The east."

Some eleven thousand miles east, seven troop-carrying helicopters that had once belonged to the U.S. Army chugged north from a military airfield near Papun. There was a platoon of Burmese soldiers in each craft, small, silent men carrying 9-millimeter submachine guns made in their own land. They were proud of these weapons—no one had told them that the BA52 was merely a modification of the Italian TZ45 designed in 1944. The choppers were armed with pods of 30-millimeter machine guns too, and had been given to Burma to use against opium factories in remote areas where roads were few and poor. The dope lords and their bandit allies had spies everywhere, so the only hope for success was to surprise them from the skies. With these Yankee helicopters, the drug laboratories of the Golden Triangle would be destroyed—

But not today.

The enlisted men, like most enlisted men everywhere, had not been told about their target, and, of course, the fewer individuals who knew the better. Military wages were low, and many things were sold on Burma's booming black market—including information. Some trooper might have a girlfriend who was half Shan. The target was a camp of the elusive Shan United Army, the aggravating association of northern tribesmen waging guerrilla warfare to split their region from socialist Burma. The press and the Americans would be told that a major dope center had been hit. You could tell the journalists and those foolish Yankees *anything*. . . .

This was a perfectly routine operation. Only seven machines were airborne because two others scheduled for the attack lacked spare parts, which were either lost in some warehouse down in Rangoon or sold by some larcenous supply sergeant. There was no way to predict whether the four aging fighter planes would show up on time to strafe the Shan before the whirlybirds touched down. Burma's pilots were competent, but the maintenance wasn't that reliable. Captain Phaung looked at his watch, an excellent Japanese timepiece that a cousin in the customs service had confiscated from a smuggler.

6:35 A.M.—twenty-five minutes to H hour. He glanced down at the river a mile below, wondered whether the Shan would still be there. *They* had good intelligence too, and they shifted from one jungle hideout to another at unpredictable intervals. Now his eyes wandered east toward the Thai frontier, and his brow furrowed. Those Thai still harbored a national grudge because Burmese troops had invaded and sacked their cities—all right, *burned* their miserable capital—nearly two centuries earlier. The Americans had given the Thai much more and better arms, and that was vexing. Captain Phaung didn't understand too much about socialism, but he sensed that the border with capitalist Thailand had to be watched.

"Pagoda Three to Pagoda One."

Some idiot was breaking radio silence.

"Pagoda Three to Pagoda One, we're having rotor trouble."

Phaung grabbed the microphone. "Quiet! Radio silence!"

"We're going down—sir."

The captain watched the helicopter on his right slowly flutter in an emergency landing, drifting toward a patchwork of rice paddies. The Shan had radios too. If any of their agents or outlying scout units were monitoring this frequency, the whole element of surprise was gone. There was nothing to do but wait. It was in the hands of the Lord Buddha.

Finding the camouflaged camp was not that easy, but only twelve minutes behind schedule Phaung spotted the cluster of huts. Now he looked around for the fighters, saw nothing. He told himself they would be along any moment, and he ordered the pilot of his craft to circle away from the Shan base—hoping that his little armada had not been spotted. The helicopters followed the command craft obediently; every flier had the sense to stay off the radio. Some ninety seconds later, the captain saw the jets approaching.

Two, not four.

Better than nothing.

They made three strafing runs over the camp before they exhausted their ammo and rockets, and then the helicopter force dropped swiftly into the valley. The Shan should be battered and disorganized. They were not. They had hidden heavy machine guns on the ridges, poured fire at the choppers as they descended to unload the troops. One helicopter burst into flames, crashed. The pilots of the others flew erratic patterns to slip through the barrage. They handled their machines well, Phaung thought proudly. The Burmese soldiers swarmed from the helicopters, fanned out to engage the rebels. Men on both sides were wounded, some killed, but casualties were not heavy—this was merely a rear-guard force. Most of the Shan had escaped into the hills, probably warned by that fool who had broken radio silence. The firefight lasted less than fifteen minutes, ended when the soldiers could find no more rebels to fight.

"They're gone, sir," a five-foot lieutenant reported.

"The men did well," Phaung said.

"Shall we pursue, sir?"

The captain scanned the slopes, realized that half a dozen mini-ambushes were waiting in those green forests the enemy knew so intimately. He shook his head. "Casualties, lieutenant?"

"Three dead, ten wounded—only one seriously. We killed at least two, and there's one prisoner."

"Intelligence will like that."

The junior officer squirmed.

"He's hurt badly. I don't know how long he'll live."

Nothing unusual about that. It was rare to take a healthy Shan prisoner. They were tough adversaries. They'd been fighting for an independent Shan state for nearly thirty years. One had to respect their stubborness. "They're good soldiers. Not as good as our men," Phaung added hastily, "but quite determined. You find any American or Chinese weapons?"

The politicians in Rangoon were convinced that the CIA and Peking's own intelligence service were supplying the Shan and other rebels. Any officer who provided evidence would be commended, perhaps promoted.

"Two rifles, one submachine gun. American, but they could have bought them anywhere. Thousands of them were captured when South Viet Nam and Laos fell to the Communists."

The lieutenant was right, and bright—perhaps too bright. Volunteering such analytical comments was not going to advance *his* career, and Phaung would have to explain that to him some time.

"Yes, our men fought very well," the captain declared.

"Shall we burn the camp, sir?"

Maybe he wasn't that smart. They *always* burned Shan bases.

"Of course. Which way do you think they went, lieutenant?"

The junior officer pointed eastward. "Toward the border, sir. That's what they usually do."

Phaung smiled. "That's Chinese Sixth Army. Old Wong won't like that at all."

"You think they'll fight, sir?"

"They have before. It will be interesting to see what happens when the old general hears they're coming."

General Wong was listening. It was time. The CIA had set a specific schedule for coded messages, and he had been at his radio at the appointed times for five days. MacBride had to reply soon—perhaps today. The young gem dealer on the motorbike had surely given him the message, and MacBride must appreciate the urgency. The truth was MacBride had probably been aware of the deteriorating situation for months; there could be no doubt that the Americans had a network of agents in the Triangle reporting to that "anthropologist," who was pretending to write a book in Chiang Mai.

Where was the message?

It was twenty minutes past the time, and MacBride was a man who respected schedules. The young radio operator coughed politely. He was an able technician and a good soldier, like his father who had marched out of China with Wong so many years ago.

"Yes?"

"Excuse me, general, but perhaps there's atmospheric trouble."

Unlikely—but possible.

The command responsibility brought the obligation to be realistic, but it was no longer that easy to determine reality. Those dead infantry buried in the gullies of southern China—men such as the radio operator's parent who had perished on secret missions for the Americans ten and fifteen years ago, *they* were reality. MacBride's predecessor had been real enough, and so had MacBride until eight months ago. There'd been no "atmospheric trouble" until then. Of course, it might be the equipment. The radio gear of the Sixth Army was as old and tired as its weapons. Perhaps the general should send a courier to Bangkok, maybe even to Taiwan. There were still a few senior men in the army of Chiang Kai-shek's son who knew Wong, who understood what it was like for a military unit isolated far from home.

Where was home?

It was not Taiwan, not to the Sixth Army. None of them had ever seen that distant island, which had serious defense problems of its own. Those one or two old officers there who remembered Wong —was Fu Soong still on active duty?—might appeal on behalf of the Sixth to the president, whom Wong had never met. There had not been anyone here from Taiwan in almost two years, only the newspapers that came nine weeks late . . . no, there had been a letter from that colonel in the defense ministry last July . . . "Yes, it could be atmospheric trouble," General Wong replied, and walked from the radio hut to his headquarters, where he summoned Captain Chen and told him to prepare for an immediate journey to Bangkok in civilian clothes. Chen's mother had been Thai, and he spoke the language so well he might pass for a native. Chen would speak to MacBride face-to-face, and then General Wong would know what to expect and do.

There were very few options left.

If no one would help the Sixth Army, it would help itself. The Sixth was not finished yet. It was still a combat force. The Sixth would fight.

30

MORE MEN AND EQUIPMENT reached the airfield at Puerto Linda each day, some by truck and more in the Costa Verdan C-47. One morning a coastal freighter dropped anchor half a mile off shore, and launches brought in dozens of crates that sweating sailors hauled onto the beach. Then another four-engine C-54 arrived with more boxes and a dozen passengers. Two were black, three of Latin ancestry and one clearly American Indian.

"He looks like Geronimo," Logan observed.

"Don't say that, Harry," Latourette advised. "Thomas is Navaho. They don't appreciate the Apaches that much." The mechanic waved to the Indian, who walked over to shake hands.

"Thomas, meet Colonel Harry Logan. He's in charge. Harry, this here's Thomas Arroyo—a real good man, knows his business."

The Navaho did not appear to notice the glare at all. He did not even blink in the dazzling sun as Logan stuck out his hand and they shook—firmly.

"Bombs," Arroyo said.

"What?"

"That's my business."

"Fine. Thanks for coming. Plenty of work here. Get your gear and Ralph'll find you quarters."

Arroyo hesitated, scanned the base appraisingly.

"Where are the bombs?"

"Tom doesn't like to waste time," Latourette explained.

"Anything else I ought to know?"

"No jokes," the Navaho said bluntly.

"He means, no wise-ass remarks about Indians."

"You have got my word, Mr. Arroyo," Logan said . . . "Bombs are coming in tomorrow. See you later, Mr. Arroyo."

The man nodded almost imperceptibly. *"You* can call me Thomas," he said, and walked off with the mechanic. . . .

Logan heard the sound of an auto engine, turned to see a jeep pull up beside the C-54. Elroy Evans and A. B. Gordon climbed out, and Logan watched them greet the pair of newly arrived black men. The warmth in the exchange said that they knew Evans well. They put their fold-up suit bags in the back of the vehicle, and were about to climb in when Evans pointed at Logan. The recruits nodded, followed across the runway.

"This is The Man," A. B. Gordon said in a parody of Hollywood-style black argot.

"What man, man?" asked the shorter stranger amiably.

"My man," she answered.

Logan didn't mind her games. He loved her. Period.

The taller recruit—in silvered "aviator" glasses—looked at Elroy to explain.

"Colonel Logan's in command. Meet my cousin, Mercer Davis. He's my Aunt Martha's boy. Schoolteacher."

"Unemployed schoolteacher," Davis noted. "Last hired, first fired. God bless America."

"Mercer's very patriotic, and he's fantastic with automatic weapons," Alison said.

"God bless," Logan said.

"What makes *him* number one?" the shorter recruit asked.

"He's the best B-17 pilot in the world."

"No shit?"

"No shit," Alison Gordon assured him.

"Cool," the shorter man said, and reached out to slap Logan's palm in acceptance. "He fixes 'em, and I shoot 'em. We used to be a team."

"Jones is an excellent machine gunner," Mercer Davis said crisply. His speech was meticulous. "We were colleagues for several years at Air America in the Far East."

Air America had been the CIA's private airline for covert operations. Logan recalled rumors that some of its crews had made private fortunes moving opium during the Indochina war . . .

"That was a great gig, man," Jones reminisced. "Could still be goin' right now if we'd had the right management."

"That was Jones' favorite war," Davis added.

"Mine was better," Logan said.

"What war was that?" Jones asked.

"The big one—thirty-five years ago. If you like wars, that one was hard to beat. It had everything—even a good reason. Now all we've got is a movie war."

"A good war's hard to find," agreed the unemployed school-teacher, "especially at these wages. That's what Bobby says."

"Who?"

"The pilot," Leroy Evans answered, and jerked his thumb toward the cargo plane. They all turned to the C-54, saw a stocky man in flier's coveralls descending the ladder. He stepped to the concrete, gave them a cheerful thumb's-up greeting.

The shock on her face was stark, unconcealed. "Boti," she said harshly.

"Right, Bobby Boti."

Logan held back the question until after the three men had driven off in the jeep.

"What's wrong, love?"

"Bobby Boti. He's a Cuban, started flying for The Company before the Bay of Pigs. Worked for them all over the world. Africa, Far East, wherever they had some action."

"Not nice, hon?"

"He'd sell his baby sister for a quarter, and give you five cents change. He's not just a pilot. Informer, spy—you name it, Harry."

Logan stared at the Cuban. "Well, this one's yours. You're the security pro. Do we have to kill him—?"

"What?"

"I'd rather not. As you pointed out the other day, we aren't exactly hip deep in pilots."

"That's B-movie stuff, Harry. Nobody said anything about killing him. No, we'll watch him. Maybe we'll have to *neutralize* him somehow—later."

Now Boti recognized her, advanced with a broad Latin grin. There had been scores of decent, dedicated, trustworthy Cubans on the CIA payroll over the years—but Roberto Boti was not one of them. She had lied to Logan. No matter what she'd said, there was a very strong possibility that Agajanian or one of the others would indeed have to neutralize tricky Bobby Boti permanently. If and when the time came, she'd keep Logan out of it. A bomber pilot of his generation dealt best with death from four miles away, dropping oblivion on strangers he'd never seen. Western civilization had progressed since then. Today a female civilian could order the assassination of—or kill herself—someone she knew at point-blank range . . . there was probably some irony there about women's liberation, not to mention contemporary morality.

She couldn't get it in focus.

Boti was dangerous, and right now that was what mattered.

31

DECEMBER 3. Escorted by two armored cars of the Costa Verdan Army, six big tank trucks delivered thousands of gallons of aviation fuel. Other vehicles in the convoy brought canned food, crates of beer and soft drinks, a crane for lifting engines and assorted tools for the ground crews charged with the well-being of the planes.

December 4. The sturdy C-47 returned with drums of hydraulic fluid, eleven thousand rounds of .50-caliber ammo for the bombers' machine guns, cartons of cigarettes, four gross of condoms, mosquito repellent, two hundred .45-caliber automatic pistols with thirty clips and a holster for each—and fifty copies of the *Reader's Digest, Time* and *Hustler.* There were some complaints because the *Time* issues were of mid-November vintage.

December 5. Another fuel truck convoy in the morning. A. B. Gordon, Agajanian and Elroy Evans flew up to the capital. Just before sunset, they drove back in a green van, a bright red fire-pumper and a gleaming white ambulance. Evans, the man who had infiltrated the heroin ring, was at the wheel of the pumper, while Agajanian drove the van filled with his Claymores. Seated beside Alison in the ambulance was Dr. Noah Fishman, sixty-five years old and fed to the incisors with the *yentas* of North Miami Beach. In the rear of the vehicle were $29,000 worth of medical supplies and instruments and a nurse with a terrific ass. She was twenty-nine, competent and Haitian. Her name was Francoise Metier.

December 6. Both the bombers and the cargo planes were painted with the camouflage patterns and battle insignia of the 100th. Weapons expert Davis, Jones and a toothy Scot named Fergus were test-firing the heavy machine guns just uncrated. One of the M-3s blew up, costing the Scot the little finger on his left hand.

Dr. Fishman and the nurse coped. That night, one of the younger cleaning women was caught behind the hangar dispensing oral sex at $10 a job, and was fired. After examinations, four men received antibiotic injections for VD.

December 7. Logan and Van Bokkelen selected their crews, made first flights out over jungle seeking a bombing range. Radio specialists George Daifuku of Honolulu and Grover Holcomb of Butte, Montana, were checking a transmitter when Holcomb noted to his partner that it was the anniversary of the day "you yellow Japs jumped us at Pearl." Daifuku told Holcomb to blow it out his ass. The temperature was ninety-two.

Holcomb threw one punch before Daifuku dropped him with a jab that drew blood. Then Daifuku walked out, unaware the Montanan was pursuing him with a raised wrench. The dispute ended when a pistol barrel broke Holcomb's wrist and a kick in the testes left him rolling and screaming in agony. Daifuku turned, thanked the accountant who'd saved his life.

"Nothin'," Agajanian told him.

"You hear what he said?"

"Most of it."

"My father . . . my father was *blinded* fighting for the U.S. in World War Two—the 442nd."

The 442nd had been a fierce Japanese-American infantry battalion with a ton of Purple Hearts and other medals, perhaps the toughest unit in the Italian theater of operations.

"Sure, I heard of the 442nd. Nobody better."

The man on the concrete whimpered. After several days under sedation in the hospital bungalow, Holcomb was flown to the capital with a $2,000 check and an airplane ticket to Butte.

December 12. Thomas Arroyo completed inspection of 210 light practice bombs. Captain Delgado came by with the mayor of nearby Puerto Linda and a U.S. Embassy agricultural attaché named Zimmerman inspecting an experimental farm in the neighborhood. The captain warned that the bombing range Logan had chosen might be dangerous because some Indians were farming there, suggested another valley and gave Logan the name of the best brothel in town. The mayor confirmed this choice. When the visitors left, A. B. Gordon's alert that these whores were informers for Costa Verdan Intelligence was quietly circulated.

December 14. Keith Ashley flew in the third B-17 from Thorpe Abbotts. Logan was delighted to see it was equipped with gun turrets, surprised that the managing director of Norfolk Aircraft Ltd. had come himself.

"She's a nice kite. Brought back the old days. Could you use a vintage RAF relic in your film?" Ashley asked.

"It's more than a film . . ."

"I rather thought so. You really aren't the sort for make-believe, Logan. I've handled these machines before, old chap. We ran a few squadrons in '43 ourselves."

"We don't have any tea or pipe tobacco," Logan hedged.

"Brought my own. If it's my age, colonel?"

That did it. Logan nodded in acceptance.

"Thank you, colonel. I say . . . don't mean to be *pushy* . . . could you use my copilot? *Decent* fellow. Did some bombing for one of those lively African generals last year. Lovely voice. Welsh, you know . . ."

Ashley gave his solemn word as a gentleman that his crew would be told only that this was a movie project, and his sincere assurance that they would stay until the end if the operation was not "something vile." Logan and Alison Gordon interviewed them separately. The Welshman, Williams, and one Pierre Molyneux were on the payroll the next morning.

December 16. Arms dealer in Paris reported prospects poor for purchasing additional Flying Forts. Unidentified competitive buyer was in the market seeking B-17s. Logan sent a coded message to M. E. Steele requesting immediate transfer of $1.5 million more to the numbered Swiss account. The fat weapons merchant was instructed to double the price offered for any 17s available anywhere. . . .

First bombing runs began that afternoon, with initial flights at 4,500 and 3,500 feet. When Logan got back, he found his love in the security office drinking Danish beer with her three aides from her detective agency. She kissed him, poured him a Carlsberg.

"How'd it go?" she asked.

"Not too good. Rusty. Need a lot of practice. What're you folks up to?"

Hovde, Elroy Evans and Agajanian looked at her intently.

"Gambling, Harry. We've got up a little pool. Five bucks each—winner take all. Wanna play?"

"What's the game, hon?"

"*Our* game. Security. We've all got this silly-crazy idea somebody might try to attack the base, and we're betting on when."

Logan scanned the row of empty bottles.

"I'm stone sober, Harry. It's a big perimeter and Delgado left a small defense unit. It could happen. We've been going over what we know about guerrillas in general, and the local outfits in particular."

"*Bad* people, colonel," Hovde said in his hoarse voice.

"It's a question of trying to think the way they do," Elroy Evans explained, "and that means looking at their patterns, weapons, everything."

"Makes sense," Logan agreed, and pulled out a cigar. Then he remembered, offered another petit corona to Evans, who thanked him. The two men lit up, puffed.

"May I see the pool slips?" Logan asked.

She unlocked the middle drawer in her desk, took out a green envelope and dropped it beside his ashtray.

"We've got to figure that they know as much about us as we know about them," she said, and sipped her beer.

"Maybe more," Agajanian put in.

"You think we've been infiltrated?"

"I do, lover. Couple of dozen locals working on the base—bound to be somebody's agents in there. Delgado's don't worry me. It's the others. Nothing to fret about, Harry. We'll cope."

Logan nodded, extracted the four slips of white paper. He recognized her writing on the first he unfolded.

"December 24th? Christmas Eve?"

"When we'll be least defense-minded. Like the Arabs and the Yom Kippur War."

"Read the others, colonel," Evans suggested.

"Christmas Eve."

The accountant blinked assent.

"Christmas Eve . . . and Christmas Eve. It's unanimous. What're you going to do?"

She stood up. "We're working on it . . . Come on, Harry. Just time for a nap and a shower before dinner."

She took his hand, led him to their quarters, where they made love, fully and tenderly and exuberantly. Afterward they joked and laughed and kissed in the shower, enjoying the soap, the water, their bodies, the delicious intimacy . . .

Halfway across the world, the orderly awakened Wong.

"Sir . . . a thousand apologies, general, but the radio officer said that this might be very urgent . . . You asked him to let you know as soon as there was any word, he said."

The commander of the Sixth Army sat up, swung his bony legs over the side of the cot and forced himself to alertness. This simple bed was identical to those of his troopers. He took the message slip, found his steel-rimmed glasses and read the words carefully—twice.

MacBride was still *trying* to secure the merchandise. Captain Chen had just died in a Bangkok hospital, victim of an unidentified hit-and-run driver. Was it an accident, or had someone silenced him? Who?

"Anything else?" Wong asked mechanically.

"Major Lo asked if he might see you as soon as possible, sir. It's the Shan again, sir."

"What about the Shan?"

"They're at our outposts, general. They're coming this way—in force . . ."

32

"WHAT A GREAT Christmas party—could you lend me a couple of Tampax?" Marlene Duckworth, blurted as she checked her ripe lips in the women's room mirror.

"I'll get them."

"I'll pick 'em up later Al, thanks a fat bunch. Like my outfit?"

"Dynamite," Alison assured her solemnly. "Gold lamé hot pants and a skin-tight green T-shirt! Really catches the yuletide spirit. Piece on earth and good will to men."

"Piece on earth—that's cute." She adjusted her remarkable breasts, frowned as she renewed her lipstick.

"You look charming, Marlene."

Crockett Duckworth's baby sister nodded, ran a comb through her hip-length hair. "My hair and my boobs are my best features, Al. Girl's got to emphasize her strong points. Say, you've got good tits too. You exercise them?"

"Not too often."

"You *should,* sweetie. Take care of your boobs and your boobs will take care of you."

Infantry instructors and the CIA teachers who'd trained A. B. Gordon had said the same things about firearms. She shrugged, picked up the new straw purse she'd just received.

"Nice bag, Al."

"Christmas present from my accountant. How're you doing with Van Bokkelen?"

Miss Duckworth started for the door. "No problem. I'm used to rich guys. Funny, none of them want it face-to-face. What's wrong with the missionary position?"

"I never discuss religion or politics," A. B. Gordon replied, dead-

181

pan, and they rejoined the party in the dining hall.

It was a palm instead of a pine, but the tree was covered with tinsel and decorations and nobody cared about the incongruity. Bottles of rum, cans of beer, bowls of ice cubes and plates heaped high with taco-flavored potato chips adorned each table. There was plenty of whiskey, gin and mixers at the bar. Logan saw Mercer Davis and Charlie Clarkson speaking in a corner, guessed they were sharing teaching experiences.

"Shop talk?"

"No harm in it, Harry," Clarkson answered. The glass in his hand held bourbon, not sherry.

"Pleasure to speak with a real educator," Davis said, and walked to get another handful of chips.

"You seem to have a fan, Charlie," Logan told him, thinking it couldn't be easy for Clarkson in this roistering group of macho mercenaries . . . sooner or later somebody was sure to start mocking homosexuals.

"Bright fellow. There might be a job for him at my school . . . When's the mail coming in, Harry?"

He tried to make it sound casual, but Logan knew that he hadn't received a letter from his lover in eight or nine days, and he wrote every night.

"Can't tell. I think there's something screwed up with the post office in town. Couple of things I've been expecting are way overdue," he lied. "Mail service is lousy all over the world, you know . . ." He saw her nodding to him from across the room and started through the noisy crowd, exchanging greetings with Crockett Duckworth and Thomas Arroyo, smiling even at Van Bokkelen and almost bumping into Elroy Evans and wishing him a Merry Christmas.

Evans was upset. "That TV guy, the one who used to be so big? He's ridiculous. You know what that schmuck just said to me—to be *nice?*"

"Let's see. Uh . . . some of my best friends are colored folks?"

"Close. That *he* was one of the first to interview Martin Luther King on *network* TV. Ain't that terrific? I ought to bust his chops, Harry."

"You'd ruin his face-lift. Got to be patient with the liberals, Elroy," and Logan moved on, finally reaching Alison.

"It's going down," she announced softly.

"The way you said? The phone lines first?"

"Cut two minutes ago," she confirmed, and gestured to Evans. He saw her fingers moving in a scissors signal, left at once with Jones and the Scottish machine gunner whose injured hand still carried a bandage.

"And half of Delgado's men left for the local cathouse more than an hour ago. Which side do you think he's on?" Logan wondered.

"We'll find out. I'm going to my post."

"Be out in a minute . . . too bad this had to happen on Christmas Eve."

She opened the purse, showed him the interior.

"I got my first present early. See you, lover."

Moments after she departed, Van Bokkelen approached Harry. "Want to tell me what's happening?"

"Big boozy party, Van. Enjoy yourself, even if there isn't any champagne."

"Don't bullshit me, Harry. I saw the hard hats splitting. Have we got trouble?"

"Not unless the rum runs out," Logan said, and glanced at his wristwatch.

"Trust me. I'm your ole buddy, remember? And I am very good with guns. Remember those heads on my wall? This is Van Bokkelen, the decadent amoral killer speaking."

Logan hesitated, nodded. "Okay, the bad guys are coming—any time now. Guerrillas. Slip out quietly and get yourself a weapon. All clear, Van?"

Without waiting for confirmation, Logan headed for the men's room. When he was certain there was no one else in the room, he opened the window and dropped out into the humid night. Staying in the shadows, he made his way to his room and retrieved the M-16 and musette bag of extra clips from under the bed. No lights, just the way Alison had said.

Across the base, the sentry at the gate saw the Costa Verdan Army truck round the curve and slow down for the formalities. The guard put down his pint, straightened his shirt and stepped out for the routine inspection. Before he could challenge, the driver burst out in raucous laughter. "Up yours . . . that's the password for tonight—"

The other troopers roared a chorus of obscenities. The driver and the sergeant beside him were obviously drunk, and the bellows of the others confirmed that they were equally soused.

"Lucky the lieutenant isn't here to see this," the sentry said.

"He's back with a couple of Indian girls—little angels. That's what he called them—*angels,*" the sergeant chuckled.

"What kind of hole is this?" demanded the driver.

"Oh, you're replacements, knew I hadn't seen you. Not bad duty. Where's Pamplona's platoon?"

"Pussy patrol in town. Lucky bastards got three days, and we're stuck here over Christmas. Where's the barracks?"

The sentry pointed, the sergeant belched, and two in the back of the truck commenced singing a bawdy song as the vehicle rolled into the base. Shaking his head, the sentry took another pull at his own bottle and envied the troops at the brothel in town. . . .

A mile away, Elroy Evans peered down from his firing position in the blacked-out control tower. Squinting through the infrared night scope on his sniper rifle, he slowly scanned the waters just off the beach. A. B. Gordon had warned that some of them might come from the sea. A pincer attack was among the favorite tactics of guerrillas who used the Cuban handbook. The sole light in the control tower was the phosphorescent dial of Evans' watch. Ten minutes to midnight, and not a sign of them. He mopped the perspiration from his face—

There—something.

Another dark dot, now two more. He counted carefully, raised the walkie-talkie to his lips. "Elroy to everybody . . . Elroy to everybody. Shark alert. Shark alert. Eight, maybe ten. Just like you said, Momma. Shark alert, Blue Sector. You read me, Momma?"

"Momma reads you. Coming your way, Don."

"How many?" Hovde said.

"Two up front. Others hanging back. Yes, two scouts on the sand. Looking all around . . . moving toward Hangar One."

· "Andy to Momma. Andy to Momma. Army truck just dumped a load of troopers two hundred yards from the big birds. They're fanning out. Could be twenty-five or thirty. Ready, Jonesy?"

"Ay-fir-mative. Jones is on the case. You figure they're hostiles, Momma?"

"Ay-fir-mative," she parroted.

Evans in the tower broke in. "You've got company, Don. Point man's just around the bend."

Hovde didn't reply. He crouched in the bushes, knife in hand.

The scout moved cautiously, taking a step or two and then pausing to look and listen. He even sniffed like a hunting dog. A full thirty seconds passed before he leaned back around the corner of

184

the large hangar, gestured to his partner that it was safe, then stepped back to the front of the hangar.

He died quietly, Hovde's hand over his mouth, stifling the first scream, the three swift thrusts choking off any others.

Now the second scout slid confidently around the corner. He pressed his back against the corrugated metal wall, peered into the blackness for his comrade. He whispered a name, twice, strained to hear an acknowledgment. Nothing. Perhaps Julio had gone inside. The second guerrilla risked a few small steps, again listened intently, and skittered forward. Yes, Julio would be inside.

Hovde cut his throat, dodged the spurt of blood, stabbed him twice through the heart.

After he dragged the bodies inside, he collected their guns and reported by radio. "Scratch two. Uncle Don to Momma. Scratch two. Any more coming?"

Jones interrupted from his machine gun position across the field.

"They're closing fast, Momma. One hundred, maybe a hundred and fifty yards at most."

No more time. "Do it," she ordered.

Hovde's sniper gun in the control tower sounded twice, then again. A pair of the swimmers on the beach were hit, one fatally. Jones and Davis opened up with their machine guns, chopping up the disguised guerrillas in a cross fire. The first bursts took down five. The rest hit the runway, began firing back blindly into the night. They heard El Stalin shout, and they began shooting at the flashes. Agajanian opened up from off to the right, firing short bursts and moving five or six yards after each.

The invaders on the beach charged. Two more fell, one with a bullet in his stomach, the other with a red hole in his forehead. The swimmers sprayed bullets in all directions. Three of the control tower windows shattered, hurling a wave of broken glass that sliced Elroy Jones' chin and left ear. He shifted to another firing position, took careful aim through the scope, shut Chico Duarte's mouth forever.

More firing from the right. Some of the Christmas revelers had by now come out of the dining hall and were shooting their .45s at the rebel machine gun hammering from the back of the stolen truck. The fliers fell back when the guerrillas hosed them with bullets, but they kept shooting cautiously. Three of the attackers wriggled toward a cargo plane, rose and rushed forward with explosive charges. Logan stopped one with his M-16, wounded another, who shot back until Van Bokkelen killed him.

"There's another one, where is he?" Logan shouted.

"I'll find him," Van Bokkelen said, ran off.

Too late. Van Bokkelen found and cut him down, but only as he was hurling his charge. The blast was followed almost instantly by a gout of flame. One of the C-54s was burning. Moments later a second explosion, Van Bokkelen's old P-51. Fires danced along the fuselage and one wing, making the fighter look like some Christmas ornament.

Another truck filled with guerrillas in stolen uniforms roared past the gate. The sentry was raising his rifle when four bullets ended his military career. A dozen of the invaders got out, scattered swiftly into the action.

The army regulars assigned to guard the perimeter were courageous, but confused, uncertain as to whether they should leave their posts along the outer fence . . . "Jesus, they're in our uniforms," one baffled private called out to a fellow soldier—who nodded and killed him. El Stalin's ruse was not a total failure.

Alison Gordon prevented one guerrilla from reaching the main fuel tank by puncturing his intestines with four bullets, then ran toward the beach to help Hovde and Elroy Evans deal with the other swimmers. Agajanian fired a grenade that blew up the machine gun in the first truck, setting it ablaze. The second truck slowed to drop off another team of guerrillas, then accelerated swiftly toward the B-17s. . . .

Thomas Arroyo was waiting patiently. He squatted in the blackness, ready to defend his bombs. In due course, a guerrilla with a satchel charge crawled into sight. He wriggled along the ground in approved infantry-manual fashion. When he was near enough, the Navaho shot him in the face. Another of El Stalin's demolition men appeared shortly thereafter, and Arroyo let him run past, then hurled his throwing knife. The man fell on his own charge and blew chunks of flesh in a thirty-yard arc. Arroyo squatted again, waiting. . . .

Somebody shot Crockett Duckworth through the shoulder, and somebody put a bullet through the skull of a mechanic from Aliquippa, Pennsylvania—Henry Mancini's hometown, the mechanic used to tell people. It might have been the same somebody. Difficult to tell in all the frenzy. Perhaps it was also the same somebody Charlie Clarkson's .45 now dropped behind the dining hall. . . .

The truck raced at the bombers. Jones blew out a rear tire with a burst, but it did not even slow down. Logan stood up to protect his planes. It was not just a show of bravery. It was not necessity. He ran, silhouetted in the light of the burning P-51, and he fired again and again point-blank into the windshield of the truck rolling directly at him. The driver was killed but the vehicle didn't stop. With a dead man at the wheel, it hurtled on and tore off the tail of the Fort that Mayberry and Kopf had flown in from England. Still moving at high speed, it hurtled past Hovde down the sandy slope into the sea.

A star shell blossomed over the jungle.

Four more followed swiftly, and then flares lit up the base itself. Heavy firing sounded from somewhere in the distant darkness, and more shooting echoed from another direction. El Stalin shouted orders, blew his whistle. The guerrillas began to retreat toward the perimeter, pausing every few yards to shoot off more bullets. Now Claymores took their toll. The battle sounds from the jungle were louder, with the noises of machine guns tearing up the night. Alison Gordon turned from the beach, hurried toward Hangar Two, where the black B-17 was in for an engine change. She saw the straw purse she'd dropped there at the start of the fighting, swung it under her arm and put down the empty M-16. She'd fired all ten clips. It was useless now. She peered into the hangar, just in case.

"They're gone."

She looked over her shoulder at Clara Velez and three men in military uniforms.

"It's over, Miss Gordon. Our men and the soldiers have beaten them off. We can leave these troopers here to protect the plane and to clean up . . . we're all a mess."

She sighed and nodded. "You're right . . . I'll bet my hair's a snake farm. Just a second, Clara, I'll need a comb . . ." She opened the purse, spun around. Her hands held a strange little weapon—an Ingraham was less than a foot long, looking like a toy submachine gun. Actually it fired seven hundred rounds a minute. Clara Velez and her three comrades scarcely had time to be surprised before the Ingraham ripped them open.

"Now it's over," A. B. Gordon said over them.

Logan ran in moment later, stared at the corpses.

"You knew as well as I she was going to get it, Harry. From the minute we heard her talking to her buddies on the phone last week."

He nodded, ". . . not pretty, is it?"

"Nine millimeter at point-blank range never is. She was going to blow up your black bird, Harry. You're damn lucky I was here."

"Damn lucky."

"And you can thank the Lord that Agajanian has weird taste in Christmas presents."

"Very weird, and I do. Let's go check the damage."

It was bad. One B-17 crippled, perhaps permanently. Three dead, eight wounded—one critically. . . .

The sniper rifle in the control tower cracked twice, then once more.

"That Elroy never quits," Agajanian, who had come up to them, said admiringly. Logan sent three men down to the beach, and Alison borrowed her accountant's walkie-talkie.

"Momma to Elroy. What's the scene?"

"The shore has been pacified, Momma. Two, maybe three, swimmers paddling away. Out of sight now. Last seen heading south."

"Anything else?"

"Could use some body bags, and a coupla Band-Aids for me. I've been cut some, Momma."

"Bad?"

"Nothing awful. I'll hold the position till friendlies arrive."

"Andy's on his way."

The sound of the jungle fighting built. Logan recognized the engines of a helicopter, heard the screech of a jet closing swiftly at low altitude. Hovde ignored all this, concentrating on his addition.

"Fifteen, sixteen . . . and the two the Indian got over by the bomb bunker. Yes, sir, he was *outstanding.*"

Arroyo stood quietly, scanning the carnage in the light of the burning planes.

"Of course," Logan said, "what else?" Arroyo's large brown eyes acknowledged the approval.

"Fine job, Tom. Good work!" the ex-newscaster complimented him enthusiastically.

"Mr. Arroyo," he corrected, and walked away.

Hovde finished his computation. "I get twenty-six or twenty-seven dead and a bunch of wounded they dragged out there with them. We beat 'em up pretty good, colonel."

Logan shook his head. "But they can recruit more guerrillas, steal more guns next month. How are we going to replace *our* men— specialists—and our planes? We're down to two bombers—*two.* The mission was impossible with *three.* Two 17s and one cargo plane. What kind of a war can we fight with that?"

The ambulance pulled up, and Logan immediately went over to speak with Dr. Fishman and the nurse. The war would have to wait until tomorrow. Logan had to provide for his wounded first.

"You think it's finished, boss?" Hovde asked her hoarsely.

She shook her head . . . "Where the hell is that fire engine?" she demanded.

It was coming across the runway now, red lights flashing. Hovde pointed with his weapon. When she turned, she saw Bobby Boti standing only a few yards away. How much had the Cuban heard?

Where had he been during the attack?

33

"OKAY," THE MAN in the sunglasses said, and that was it.

The meeting was over.

He was the senior executive in the room, and he had the authority to terminate conferences, bridges or lives. Known as The Man With the Shades, he was the fourth most powerful official in the CIA hierarchy. He had been in the trade for a long time. He was good at his job, and professionals on all sides respected him.

He pushed back his chair, and the four men and two women in conference room D on the fifth floor of that drab bulky building near Langley, Virginia, ground out their cigarettes and collected their classified documents. They rose, waited for him to exit first. All of them had known him for at least three years, and none had ever seen him without sunglasses. Legend was that the opposition had done something to his eyes in Berlin during the hottest part of the Cold War. Whatever the truth was, these dark lenses had been his trademark for more than two decades.

"Tuesday," he said as he left the room. He walked down the long corridor, turned and made his way to his corner office.

"Mr. Castillo is here to see you," Ms. Kraft said crisply. She said everything that way to emphasize that she was *executive* secretary to a deputy director. When she pointed at the younger man waiting in the armchair, she did that crisply too.

"Arthur Castillo, Central American desk—sir," the visitor blurted.

The Man With the Shades remembered, led Castillo into his private office. When they were seated, the older man looked across his desk at Castillo and coughed. "Yes?" he asked a moment later.

"You asked to be informed about any developments concerning

190

those old U.S. bombers down in Costa Verde—sir."

"Yes?"

"Leftist guerrillas attacked the field the night before last, were beaten off with very heavy casualties."

"The aircraft?"

"C-54 and a P-51 destroyed, one 17 badly damaged. They're trying to replace them, sir. She called Atlas headquarters on that satellite frequency we've been monitoring, asked for another million dollars . . . I didn't know Atlas was in the movie game, sir."

"It's no game." He swiveled his chair to stare at the rain falling on the Virginia countryside. Castillo waited politely for several moments before he cleared his throat. The senior executive turned back to face him, showing no reaction.

"Sir?"

"Is there anything else, Mr. Castillo?"

"No, sir. I'll let you know the minute we hear more . . . Sir?"

"Yes?"

"I don't mean to . . . well, I'm just a desk analyst . . . Do you think we ought to watch this situation more closely? A field agent, sir?"

"That won't be necessary. Good-bye, Mr. Castillo."

After Arthur Castillo left, the deputy director buzzed and his executive secretary entered the private office with a steno pad and an air of alert curiosity.

"Since you were good friends, Doris," he said, "you might want to know what she's up to. Guerrillas hit the field on Christmas Eve, wrecked three planes. The Reds took very heavy casualties."

"She was expecting them. She's no dummy."

He nodded. "No dummy. One of the best we had. Now she's shopping for more bombers. Don't worry, Doris. There aren't any."

He glanced down at the fourth cable from MacBride, pushed it to one side of his desk.

"She'll find them," Ms. Kraft predicted briskly.

All of a sudden he felt old, tired. "Doris, loyalty is admirable—in principle. I'm a man of principle. I have so many principles I can't keep them straight. I respect your loyalty to her, Doris, but you're losing your perspective."

She glared at him. A short, fat, furious woman who was obviously considering biting him. They were an odd couple, he reflected. Sixteen years of working together—a cool man who hid his feelings behind dark lenses and an outspoken woman—mature, intelligent, forty-two years old—who had never learned to bury a single one of her emotions. It was preposterous for a woman her age to let it all hang out this way . . . His mind wandered. He thought about Arthur Castillo. "He called me *sir*. Kept calling me *sir*. Is that his good manners, Doris, or am I really that old?"

She hunched forward, like a bulldog about to leap.

"You're fifty-eight, October 17th. Don't try these tricks on me. Why don't you answer the question?"

"What question?"

"That's another one of your favorites, answering questions with questions. You're a clever man, smartest man I ever met. All right, I'll go along. That's my job, right?"

"Right. Now about this cable from MacBride—"

It didn't work.

"After all she's done for the agency . . . for the country," Doris Kraft challenged, "why the hell don't you leave Alison Gordon alone?"

"Goddammit, you've got it ass-backward. That's not the question."

"Don't curse at me," she replied righteously.

"You want to know what the question is, dammit?"

She pursed her mouth, nodded. "Certainly."

"The *real* question is . . . beyond any doubt . . . plain and not so simple at all . . . is why the hell *she* won't leave *me* alone. That's the question, dammit."

The executive secretary lifted her pencil to indicate that she was ready to take dictation. When he was in one of those moods, the only thing to do was to humor him. He was basically a decent, sensible man. He'd probably see it differently later, she thought.

She was wrong.

34

THE THREE CHINOOKS landed simultaneously. Troops charged from two of the helicopters, fanned out in a wide cordon to ring the third, the rotor of which was still twirling. The Costa Verdan infantry faced away from the VIP chopper, their U.S.-made automatic weapons at the ready. After surveying the area—a complete 360-degree check—a brawny lieutenant waved and the door of the third machine opened. Two more soldiers with submachine guns emerged, followed by the president of Costa Verde and Captain Delgado.

"I didn't know you traveled with the 102nd Airborne," Logan said.

"Got to, Harry. I'm the chief of state. Lots of Commie bastards out there would love to blow me away. Heard you had some excitement night before last. Came as soon as I could."

"I'll bet," she said.

"Hi, Alison, you're lookin' good. Base's one helluva mess, I see."

"Take a good look, Mr. President," she said angrily.

"I told you to call me Joe. What's she sore about, Harry?"

Logan pointed at the shells of the three ruined aircraft, reached into his pocket for a cigar. José Fabrega Enrique O'Brien Garcia snapped his fingers, and Captain Delgado instantly produced two Cuban coronas. The president nodded toward the B-17 pilot, and Delgado handed one of the fine cigars to Logan.

"My friends smoke the best," Garcia announced, and bit the end off his cigar.

"Are we your friends?" she said.

Garcia looked pained as he lit his corona.

"She got a temper, Harry."

193

"She's got a *reason,* Joe—your security."

"You're security, in a word, sucks," she told him.

"Hey, let's not argue. I got a nice surprise for you kids." He glanced at his gold Omega.

"Three minutes, Mr. President," Delgado said.

"He's never wrong," the chief of state boasted, and mopped his brow.

She took a step forward, but Logan stopped her.

"You don't hit your host."

"Not him, that creep Delgado."

"Let's talk nice in the shade," Garcia suggested. Without waiting for a reply, he began walking toward Hangar Two. The captain blew his whistle, and the whole cordon moved with them. When they reached the relative cool of the hangar, Delgado spoke. "This is where she shot four of them, Mr. President."

Garcia answered her question before she could ask it.

"Sí, the captain has agents here."

"Like Clara Velez?"

Delgado's grin was smug. "No, she was with the *bandidos.* I helped her get the job myself."

El Presidente laughed delightedly. "The capitan was with the *bandidos* too. He was their informer, their spy in the palace. *Magnifico!"*

"Double agent?" Logan said.

"You got it, Harry. He told you not to bomb that valley because they were moving up that way, and he sent half the guards off to get laid to make it easier for those lice to attack. We had most of a battalion out there to cut off their escape. Shot the crap out of them. If El Stalin got away with six or eight men he's lucky."

Delgado held up a single finger.

"Yeah, one minute. Your surprise is almost here, Harry. Like the cigar? I got two boxes for you in the chopper."

"Cigar is fine, Joe. What about this El Stalin?"

"Commissar of MPO-13—the Popular Movement of October 13th. Remember what Al called me—a prick? This guy's a prick and a half. We've been after him for a year, a cutie."

Agajanian walked quickly toward them.

"Tower says three planes coming in . . . You, Delgado, your security sucks."

"She already told him," President Garcia announced. "Okay, you're going to like this, Harry."

"I didn't like being set up, Joe."

Garcia waved airily.

"That's what pals are for—to help each other. You helped me, so I'm helping you. Who is this guy?"

"Andy Agajanian—my accountant," Alison said.

"An Armenian accountant? Ought to be dynamite. You know, Al, I could use some help with my taxes."

"Five sets of books can't be easy."

"Six," he said, and pointed up above the jungle.

Three glorious old aircraft.

B-17s, flying in a wedge formation.

"Look at 'em, Harry. *Look* at 'em. They got turrets and everything. They even got extra turrets and spare parts in the bomb bays."

"And they are beautiful . . . no question," Logan had to admit, almost willing to forgive the president for using him and his people.

"You had three, and now you got five and a half. From Joe to Harry, Merry Christmas!"

"Where'd you get them?" Alison asked.

"Argentina. General down there had them out at some base in the boondocks. Using them for training. He needed a little cash so he wrote them off as junk and sold them to me. Nice old tubs, huh? What do ya say?"

"I say how much will they cost us?"

José Fabrega Enrique O'Brien Garcia pouted. "She's a real pistol, Harry. Cost you? *Nada.* Nothing. Not a *peso.* It's my treat."

Agajanian studied the Forts as they swooped in to land. "What did they cost you?" he asked.

"Don't look a gift bomber in the mouth, sonny. Only an accountant would ask a question like that. They were cheap. He had the shorts. He's always got the shorts. Got this nooky hang-up. Keeps two, three broads all the time. It's like an obsession with him. Fancy broads, each one with furs and Paris threads and her own pad. His rent tab alone must go two grand a month."

Logan was still staring at the 17s.

Garcia said, "With some guys it's broads, other guys it's bombers."

"And with some, both," Logan said as he put his arm around A. B. Gordon.

The pilots were excellent. The three planes touched down in perfect formation, and Logan nodded in silent approval.

"Where's the can, Harry?" El Presidente asked. "You tell 'em about that tap, captain."

Delgado reported that his counterespionage technicians had found a tap on the base's telephone lines. They'd tried to capture the listener, but he'd escaped. Alison Gordon discussed the eavesdropper's equipment with the captain, was disappointed to hear it was "that Jap stuff everybody's using these days." Delgado apologized that he could not pinpoint the tapper's employer.

"Maybe it was Zimmerman," the captain offered.

"What Zimmerman?" she asked as Logan left them and walked out to the newly arrived planes.

"The one who was here with the mayor. Dr. Lawrence Zimmerman, the phony agricultural attaché our Big Uncle sent us last year. We had him pegged as the new station chief three days after he came to town. I was telling the president, Miss Gordon, CIA used to have better people."

"Hard to get good help these days."

When Garcia and Logan returned, they all made their way to the dining hall for cold beer. Then the president and his security aide rose, and the chief of state shook hands with his old friend, who thanked him for the 17s, and under his breath reminded him that real friends didn't risk each other's lives, or those of people close to them . . . even free Forts didn't change that. The president beamed and nodded, as though he'd just been awarded another stuffed ballot box.

"My pleasure, Harry. Nice place you got here. Air-conditioned and all the comforts of home."

"Almost. You wouldn't know where we could buy a jukebox and a pinball machine, Joe?"

"Got that, Delgado? I want them down here in three days. Find 'em in Miami if you have to. Anyone need a lift up to the capital?"

Logan looked at her, shrugged. They'd talked the plan out, and now it was time for her to go. She packed her bags swiftly. Two soldiers carried them to the helicopter, where Harry Logan kissed her, and she kissed him back—hard.

"She's a pistol, Harry," the president of Costa Verde reiterated admiringly.

The three choppers lifted off a few minutes later. At two that afternoon, Alison Gordon boarded the Pan Am jet north to Los Angeles. It was love all right, it had to be. The big transport was scarcely off the runway when she began to miss Harry Logan. It would be weeks before she slept in his arms again. The hunger was still with her and growing when the trim stewardess came by offering "beverages." Alison Gordon, who infrequently drank hard liquor, ordered a very dry martini—straight up. Then she had another. They didn't help that much. They were the usual sturdy drinks Pan Am served, but they didn't numb her a bit. She still hurt when she finally dozed off, and she dreamed of Logan and the strange little war that waited for them both, and what might happen to him. She awoke and asked for black coffee.

She didn't want to risk dreaming of Harry Logan and a burning B-17 anymore.

35

TO SOME it is Camelot, to others Smog City. The airlines' acronym for this up-to-date urban fantasy is LAX, which may be something of an overstatement, though exaggeration is legal tender in many parts of sprawling Los Angeles and quite a few residents are laid back so far as to be almost out of sight. Relaxed would be both more fair and more accurate.

Not all Angelenos, however, are *that* relaxed, and hype-heads such as Bernie Peshkin aren't relaxed at all.

"Fan-tas-tic," he called out over the bustle of the crowded air terminal.

What the hell was the press agent doing here?

"Did you see the coverage? Did you hear it, doll? It was—I hate to boast—*smashing*. Both wire services, Rona and Earl Wilson and Jim Bacon, all *three* networks, even Reuters grabbed it. I hate to boast, but it was ter-rific . . ."

A. B. Gordon stepped aside to avoid being trampled by a throng of squealing pubescents. "Please just tell me what this is all about."

"Mick Jagger," Peshkin explained cheerily. "He's supposed to be flying in now with that blond girl—the basketball player. Great cheekbones."

Another horde of hysterical adolescents charged past.

"Second wave—they're often the most dangerous," Peshkin warned, with authority born of experience.

"*What's* terrific, Bernie?"

"You didn't *hear?* Don't you read the papers? Even the New York *Times* grabbed this. Even the London *Times,* not to mention the *Hollywood Reporter.* Here."

She accepted the rolled up final edition of the Los Angeles *Times,* saw it was open to the entertainment-arts section. Everything seemed pretty normal. There was a film critique by Charles Champlin, a concert review by hard-to-please Martin Bernheimer and a rock "think-piece" on Bruce Springsteen by thoughtful Robert Hilburn. Then she saw the big three-column headline and the photo. Sheik Baroodi was holding up a model of a B-17G, which was being rapturously contemplated by a sensitive young woman in half a crepe de chine blouse with a neckline that plunged to *there*, and beyond.

"Is this a dairy ad?" Alison snapped.

The dateline on the first part of the story was the Costa Verdan capital, and the subject was the guerrilla attack on the American movie company unit and its aircraft. Sheik Baroodi, "dynamic head of Golden Crescent Productions," was quoted as vowing, "Nothing will stop the completion of this picture. This is a film whose time has come, a saga of patriotism, courage, violence and just enough sex to make it interesting. It's an old-fashioned people-picture."

"Terrific," A. B. Gordon agreed.

"I wrote that bit for him."

"Figured you did. Tasteful of you not to call it 'a film critics may mock but audiences will enjoy,' Bernie."

"I'm saving that for next month. Things are going great, you know. He's about to announce signing Wilber Greenstreet to direct. George Roy Hill's booked solid for a year."

Fifty additional teenagers bulldozed past.

"Just stragglers," Peshkin explained . . . "This Greenstreet kid's hot. Only four years out of film school. Got his start emptying chemical toilets on a Fellini set, then did a fab ciné-vérité thing on eczema—top honors at the Eskimo Film Festival. His big one was *Disco Trucker*—very allegorical. Made six-three for Metro, *and* copped the Silver Corkscrew at the Bordeaux competition. Wonderful copy. Both parents are in the nuthouse, and his older sisters are Siamese twins."

The enthusiastic press agent paused—but only to catch his breath. "Creative, that's Wilber. Strictly natural food, and does he hate that lousy Viet Nam War—"

"Bernie, there hasn't been a Viet Nam War in more than six years."

The publicist popped a breath mint, then another before he tapped the photo.

"Lovely, isn't she? Melody Angst, our new executive story editor.

They're due in from Palm Springs in ten minutes."

"Another natural-food fan?"

"She'll eat anything. Smart as hell. Reads Camus, Thackeray, Mario Puzo. You think Mario'd be right to do the script—? Look *out!*"

Concealed in a phalanx of private bodyguards, two nonchalant celebrities trotted by with a mini-army of lust-crazed children hurling themselves at the burly defenders. Flash guns and strobes glittered in blinding chorus, and the spectacles of a ladies sportswear buyer from St. Louis were dashed to the ground. Through it all, a pair of smiling young devotees of an ascetic Asian faith doggedly sold religious pamphlets and faded flowers.

"No TV," Peshkin scorned. "If I was handling Jagger, we'd have five crews here. He's a superstar!"

"So are you, Bernie."

The press agent thanked her again for sending the affluent sheik to him, legged it up the passage to his rendezvous. She saw him hop on the moving conveyor, the horizontal "escalator" that carried him out of sight. With the airline bag over her shoulder, she zigzagged through the swirling-intersecting flow of inbound and outbound travelers. It was like being adrift in a sea of amoebas, all moving without predictable pattern. She reached a telephone booth, dialed her secretary's home number.

"Ruth?"

"Love to talk to you, boss, but I can't. On my way out."

Alert—the phone may be tapped.

"No important messages. Teddy called."

Warning—your house is under surveillance.

"Did he say what it was about?"

"Sorry, boss."

No idea about who's watching or why.

"I'm leaving for the peninsula. Drop you a line. Bye." She hung up and hurried for a cab. Ruth would understand. Ruth had stayed at that splendid Hong Kong hotel several times.

Alison spent the night as Wendy Sherman in a nearby motel, returned to the LAX terminal in time to catch Pan American's flight 3 at 8:45 the next morning. Minutes after the 747-SP lifted off for the nonstop journey across the Pacific, the man who had been watching her since she stepped off the jet from Costa Verde phoned his superiors.

"It's Ken. Hope she likes sliced beef with scallions, Japanese style, duckling Cointreau, roast beef or filet of sole in lemon butter."

"A mixed green salad goes with that."

"Absolutely."

"What the hell are you trying to say, Ken?"

"Up, up and away. She's on Pan Am's flight 3—arriving in Tokyo in about eleven hours and thirty-one minutes."

"That's all very clever . . . Ken, did anyone ever tell you you're real clever?"

"Lots of people."

"They lied," the other man said, and hung up.

36

WHO WAS WATCHING her house?

The seats in the 747-SP were roomy and comfortable, twenty-two red and twenty-two blue alternating throughout the first-class section. Flying first class was expensive, but she told herself that it was part of her "cover"; film company executives always went that way. The blue-haired dowager across the aisle was plainly terrified, perhaps on her first journey by air. It was not the flight that scared A. B. Gordon, but the prospect of airline food—usually the culinary equivalent of the music one heard in elevators. Lunch turned out to be surprisingly good, with the only disappointment when she requested espresso coffee.

"We don't serve espresso," the well-dressed man in the next seat volunteered before the stewardess could reply, "but try the Japanese green tea."

"It's nifty," the stewardess said, and she was right.

Now there was a new threat. The helpful man in the next seat might be one of those compulsive-boring-murderous gabbers, the dread terrors of the skies. He was not. He was a worldly Pan Am vice-president named Gewirtz, who appreciated good-looking women, wanted her to like his airline, said so and returned to his latest Graham Greene novel.

She tried to read *The New Yorker*. It was no use.

Who was watching her house?

She did no better during the film. At Woody Allen's most antic moment, she found herself wondering where she—anyone—could find another P-51. She switched off the sound on her headset, sat brooding in the silence of the dark cabin.

Maybe it was the dope baron's assassins.

She switched to the earphone channel offering symphonic music, was suddenly immersed in the richness of Copland's "Appalachian Spring." Copland in her ears, Woody Allen in her eyes and *something* in the pit of her stomach. The film ended, the lights came on, and the attentive cabin personnel offered drinks for the fourth time. Her husband had often joked about the weirdly stilted language used by airlines, she recalled. Mark was dead, of course—years ago. Even his memory was fading. It was difficult to say whether it was time, or Logan, but in fact Mark was almost a wraith. . . .

The whole thing was blurred, and she forced herself to think about how to replace the burned fighter plane that her lover needed for his war and the general's war. It was difficult to maintain the focus in the echo of her secretary's conversation. When she'd worked for the Agency, it was easy to identify and destroy hostile surveillance teams. There were trained units for these jobs. The Man With the Shades had called them "wrecking crews," and he had several on each continent. He was very orderly, very clever. It wasn't that he was a bad person, but she was glad that she wasn't working for him anymore. He was too practical. He had probably never dreamed of either love or war, so all those dead people never troubled his sleep. Not like Harry Logan who dreamt and still dared, a rare and splendid lover—

It happened without warning at 36,000 feet.

"Ham, turkey, corned beef, whitefish, smoked salmon, sliced sable," the stewardess invited.

Manhattan deli time—one of Pan Am's secret weapons in the global air war for passengers.

"Norman Chow," Alison seemed to be saying in reply. Actually, she was merely thinking out loud. Chow had worked for the biggest movie company in Hong Kong, the multi-stage Run Run Shaw studios that turned out enough love-action-costume dramas to be called the MGM of the Far East. She did not explain this to the stewardess. She simply selected and enjoyed slices of the three kinds of cold smoked fish, and wondered what had been her mistake. If she'd done it all exactly right, would anyone be watching her house? It could be bad luck. It could be anything. Maybe it was the woman thing, the nasty self-doubt that led so many females to blame themselves. No, it had to be something else. She knew she wasn't *that* kind of woman. . . .

There were more hot towels before flight 3 reached Tokyo's new and controversial Narita Airport, where the security was intense and the coffee better than she'd expected. The connecting flight 1 south was on time, and she slept through much of the four-hour-and-thirty-five minute journey to the 11,300-foot runway at Kai Tak —the modern airport that juts dramatically out into the harbor of Hong Kong. The sight of that incredible city still thrilled her—a metropolis of eye-catching office buildings and lofty hills ringing one of the great ports of the world.

It was impossible to resist this splendid panorama of British tankers and Norwegian freighters, U.S. cargo ships and junks flying the flag of Red China, double-decker Star ferries with green and white funnels linking the Kowloon area and Hong Kong Island and low craft carrying tourists through Victoria Harbor to the massed fishing boats at Aberdeen. This wide harbor was alive, vital—a phenomenon that should have separated but somehow joined the parts of the extraordinary city. She saw a hydrofoil leaving on the seventy-five-minute swoop across the Pearl River estuary to Macao, and she remembered a CIA colleague who had acquired a particularly virulent social disease in that exotic Portuguese colony.

"Hong Kong means fragrant harbor in Chinese," offered another pretty stewardess who looked Chinese herself but spoke Californian, "and Kowloon means nine dragons. You know the story about the boy emperor and the eight hills?"

"Yes, and I enjoyed the flight."

She was in a taxi en route to the majestic Peninsula Hotel twenty minutes later. The customs search had been swift and cursory; it was the passengers arriving from Thailand and Burma who got the keen attention. Hong Kong was on another rampage to stop the flow of heroin, stung by another series of scandals about police corruption in the endless battle against drugs. The clerk at the airport bank who changed her one-hundred-dollar traveler's check into five hundred Hong Kong dollars told her this, and recommended his aunt's shop for the best camera buys.

It was only sixty-five degrees, the awful humidity of summer still five months away. The city was bustling, seething, working. The Peninsula was serene, dignified and perhaps just a bit old-fashioned. It did not have a swimming pool like the Hilton on Queen's Road or 922 rooms such as the new 18-floor Sheraton, but there was something very appealing about this elegant and classic "small" hotel—only nine floors and a mere 340 rooms. Who could resist the stone lions, so stately and Chinese, that flanked the front door?

Plan of battle.

That was the first thing she had to devise after the bellboy left her room. It was midafternoon and the harbor beneath her window—just across Salisbury Road from the hotel—drew her eyes inexorably. Staring down at the ships as she stripped off the journey-rumpled clothes and underwear, she abstractly stroked her body to rub away the elastic marks and bra strap indentations. And she planned.

They must not find out about Norman Chow.

If she moved swiftly before *they* could mobilize a full surveillance, she might beat them at the game she knew so well. Speed was the key. Ruefully rejecting the luxury of a hot bath, she took a quick shower and put on clean clothes. She wadded a light blue kerchief into her purse, dropped the .357 in beside it and left the hotel by the side door onto Nathan Road. Aching for a nap or at least a coffee at one of the tables in the high-ceilinged lobby, she hurried out without looking back. Her role was "lady shopping," not "female agent checking for tails." She thought of the Peninsula's fine pastries, mourned and turned away from the harbor into the pulsing action of Nathan Road.

Jewelry, souvenirs, cameras, clothes, little TV and radio sets, curios, tape recorders and mass-produced carvings, watches and watches and gold chains and watches—endless window displays and nonstop human and auto traffic. Ninety-five percent of Hong Kong's population is Chinese, but this street was alive with tourists from a dozen countries. Weaving through the bargain hunters, she slipped into the Lane Crawford department store and did what women under pressure used to do before Valium, grass and IUDs. She bought a hat—a large one. She put it on as she left the store, wandered on to investigate the duty-free wonders of other shops.

She was, of course, establishing an identity—an image in the eyes of any watchers. Alison Gordon was the woman in the large straw hat. Now she found a phone booth, and after three calls she found Chow too. They set the rendezvous, and she strolled on through four more stores buying a flacon of Cabochard *parfum* in one, pricing a Swiss watch in another. Then she hailed a taxi, told the driver to take her through the tunnel under the harbor to the Mandarin Hotel on Connaught Road across the bay. There were dozens of taxis exactly like this one. The easiest way to follow her was to watch for the woman in the large hat.

Which was the plan.

As the cab neared the Kowloon side, she took off the hat and slouched down as she tied on the kerchief. Long shot. Old hat trick. Unlikely to fool alert professionals, but it was all she had. Just before the taxi emerged from the tunnel, she instructed the driver to drop her at the Star Ferry terminal instead. Was *that* them? Some sixteen minutes and thirty Hong Kong cents later, she stepped ashore and found another cab to take her to the observatory atop the Peak —a popular place for visitors to look down at the panorama of a great city and port. She bought some postcards, enjoyed the view via telescope as tourists were supposed to do—and checked her watch.

5:50 P.M.—and Norman Chow was there. He was plump, expensively attired in a fine Y. William Yu suit and a tailor-made ascot, Chang shirt, and careful to respect her instructions . . . "casually sit beside me in the seventy-two-passenger gondola of the Peak tram and strike up a conversation as the cable car slowly descends."

He wasn't working for the Run Run Shaw studio anymore.

He could supply the machine and a trained man to operate it. They agreed on the price, time and place of delivery. She memorized the number of the post office box to which to mail the $6,500 "good will" down payment. They left the tram separately, and when she flagged a taxi she asked to be let out six blocks from the Peninsula. They'd be watching for her return, and they'd ask the driver where the ride had begun. They would wonder what had happened to the hat. . . .

Now she sank into the hot tub, and at eight enjoyed a first-class French dinner in Gaddi's, the gourmet restaurant on the ground floor. With care, she scanned the room several times and later checked for watchers when she strolled past the windows of the hotel's many shops. She did not spot anyone, but that was hardly conclusive.

At eleven the next morning she was on the Cathay Pacific jet lifting off from Kai Tak. The stewardesses were among the most beautiful she had ever seen, but her mind was far away. Had she really seen *them* in Hong Kong? Paranoia was so easy. The sleek airliner rose over the harbor, offering another magnificent view that she could not enjoy. The questions ran through her mind like a tape loop, over and over again.

What had gone wrong?

Who was watching the house?

37

THE THAI are a religious people, and more than ninety-two percent of the 40 million citizens of the kingdom are conscientious Buddhists. Bangkok, which has 4 million residents and an average temperature of eighty-two degrees Fahrenheit, is graced by three hundred monasteries. Many are of startling beauty, both in their soaring architecture and interior shrines. Orange slate and gold leaf adorn their roofs and spires, while magnificent and varied images of Lord Buddha inspire all visitors.

The name for these temple-monasteries is *wat*. On the grounds of the Grand Palace on Na Phra Larn Road is the Wat Phra Kaeo, with the Emerald Buddha no one may photograph. It is actually a fine work of jade, carved from one massive piece some time before 1464. It is sacred; admission is fifteen *baht*. A *baht* is, of course, one hundred *satangs*. The Wat Pho on Maharaj Road may be the biggest in town, with a colossal Reclining Buddha dominating the largest collection of Buddha images in the country and dramatic panels depicting scenes from the Ramayana. Admission five *baht*. Same charge at the Wat Arun, the eye-catching Temple of the Dawn, whose five towers seem ablaze as the first rays of the sun strike the tens of thousands of bits of glass inlay and Chinese porcelain that coat the roofs.

And then there is the Wat Traimit—monastery of the Golden Buddha. Admission is free, and the story that goes with this multi-million-dollar image is both romantic and incredible. Thailand had a great culture as far back as 1350, when King Rama Thibodi founded a new dynasty and set up his capital at Ayutthaya. Some thirty-three kings later the Burmese battered their way in and just about destroyed the capital in 1767. More than two hundred years after that, a crane lifting a huge ceramic Buddha snapped and the effigy fell. The pottery shell cracked. Inside—hidden centuries earlier from Burmese invaders—was a ten-foot-high Buddha of solid gold. Five and one half *tons* of pure gold—at least $20 million to anyone base enough to think in such terms, as many of the tourists most assuredly do.

Appalled by this vulgarity, MacBride never set his meetings there. The monastery of the Reclining Buddha not only offered that fascinating assembly of so many different styles of Buddha, but it was also the shrine where many of the better temple rubbings were sold. The peddlers outside the temple competed energetically, bargained cannily and drew enough of a crowd so that MacBride's rendezvous with Gannett might not draw attention.

Todd Gannett was an assistant to the CIA station officer who ran the Agency's operations in Thailand. His "cover" was a junior attaché at the U.S. Embassy over on Wireless Road, a place clandestine agents such as MacBride rarely visited. Gannett was here among the rubbing vendors with a message that MacBride was certain to despise. They pretended to meet by accident, spoke about the prices of one or two rubbings of dancers, and got to business.

"Congressman Edelstein arrives tonight," the messenger said, "and he's scheduled a press conference at the airport."

"What about Friendly?" MacBride asked, using the code name for General Wong.

"Let me finish, dammit. We've got a problem. Don't blame State this time. Blame Jack Bressler."

"You smoking opium? Who's Jack Bressler?"

"Father of Assemblyperson Gloria Bressler. He wanted a son, a doctor or maybe a rabbi. That's probably why Gloria grew up feeling rejected. I'll tell you, she's one hell of an overachiever."

MacBride shook his head.

"You haven't told me anything. What about our merchandise, Todd?"

"Please, it makes some kind of sense if you hear it all. Gloria's making a run for Edelstein's seat in the House, and he's grabbing for headlines. Blasting the heroin traffic is perfect. He's been the White Knight, ripping both our government and the Thais and

Burmese for not shutting down the trade. He hasn't got any other good issues, Mac."

Two women from San Francisco were bargaining ineptly with a vendor, while a British surgeon and his wife watched with scorn.

"What's the message?" MacBride demanded.

"No merchandise—not now. Delicate situation. He used that other stuff we supplied to ride shotgun for those opium convoys."

"And to do jobs for us, and fight off the Shan. Friendly's been a loyal client for years, Todd. We can't just dump him."

Gannett shrugged. It was true what they said. MacBride's Jesuitical preoccupation with principles and morality was retarding his career.

"Might be possible later. Couple of months—after Edelstein's found another issue or the election's over."

"That's six months. Friendly's desperate. Can't wait that long. We *owe* him. Tell The Man With the Shades we owe Friendly *plenty*."

The younger man nodded. "He *knows*, Mac."

A shaved-head monk in orange robes stopped beside them to admire one of the rubbings, ignoring the German tourist shooting his photo.

"Our client for thirty years, and we cut him off because of some idiot politician and a foolish man who messed up his daughter? I've got to give him something better than that," the agent insisted.

"Don't get involved emotionally. That's suicide. You've been authorized to send $16,000 U.S. for rations and medical supplies, and tell him to hang in there."

"$16,000 won't last his force two weeks. He needs merchandise to *survive*. Tell *that* to Jack Bressler—"

"When I see him. Don't sweat it. Things with Friendly probably aren't that bad," Gannett said smoothly and walked off to another stand.

MacBride received two messages within fifteen minutes after he returned to his office. The Shan were mortaring the Chinese Sixth Army outposts again, and a former Agency employee named A. B. Gordon had checked into the splendid Oriental Hotel on the edge of the river. MacBride was fond of the hotel and the twisting Chao Phraya with its boats and barges, but he did not like the Gordon woman. She was clever and arrogant and beautiful. Beautiful women always made MacBride uncomfortable. It was their sexuality, their animal appeal that defied logic which troubled him. He recalled Alison Gordon clearly now. She was powerfully sexual, and that made her dangerous to a man with a logical mind.

Logical? A bitter joke.

What was logical about what they were doing to Wong?

What would *he* do about Wong?

38

"DO YOU LIKE Thai *prik?*" the waiter asked.

"*Chai,*" Alison Gordon replied.

Thai food is not very hot. It is very, very hot, and terrific. *Prik* is the word for chili pepper, of which there are many types. The yellow-orange *prik kee nu lueng* is the flamethrower of the species and the *prik kee nu* will merely scar intestines for life, and there is a lesser Thai *prik* that goes into almost everything. So does coriander leaf, and there are lots of dishes—especially in the southern regions—flavored with turmeric, ginger and *takrai* lemon grass.

It helps to know Thai and something of Thai cooking when visiting Bangkok. A. B. Gordon knew both, so she could decline both the Parisian pleasures of the Oriental's Normandie Grille and the "tourist" cooking of the mammoth restaurants designed to impress foreign visitors. Dining at a little-known restaurant run by an Anglo-Burmese woman with the grandeur of a duchess, she feasted on *tom-yam* prawn soup, waterfall beef, fried crab with curry—and a lot of rice and good local beer. Government officials, journalists and diplomats weren't likely to eat in this steamy garden so far from the beaten path, and the fewer people who were aware that she was back in town the better. She finished her fruit and tea, asked for the bill.

Ninety *baht*—four and one-half dollars. She asked the waiter to call a taxi, and before she had smoked half a gold-tipped Sobranie she was on her way to the last address anyone had for Johnny Phranghit. The driver seemed startled when she told him her destination. But he recovered quickly. He pointed out that his meter was broken. All meters in Bangkok cabs are out of order—it's a form of folk art. She negotiated a price, and then he took off like that proverbial bat out of hell. She was not at all surprised by his cowboy technique at the wheel, for driving the streets of the Thai capital had never been for the meek. It was safer at night, of course, when so many trucks and *tuk-tuk* taxis were out of the fray. When she stepped out of the taxi, it raced off wildly, and she then turned to the chunky man who stood outside the door of number 36 Sukhothai Road.

"Johnny Phranghit?"

The man—perhaps a guard—opened the door for her.

There were fifty or sixty people seated at the score of tables in the dimly lit room. Two-thirds of them were foreigners, four-fifths male. Bottles of Singha beer rested on every table, but many of the group were sipping the local *mekhong* rice whiskey. There was an air of expectancy.

"Neung roi baht," someone said behind her.

She turned to the young Thai in the colorful sport shirt, who thrust out his open hand.

"Hunred *baht.* Twenny bucks U.S.A.," he translated instantly."

Phranghit skittered out of the darkness, at least fifteen pounds heavier than when he had worked for the Agency, but still smiling.

"Johnny?"

"Hey, boss. She's on the cuff. No charge. Sit down, boss. Can't talk now 'cause the show's about to start."

And he was gone. She had a fairly good idea of what was coming, but she also had to talk to Johnny Phranghit. They had called him Johnny Deal, and they were right. The lamps dimmed further, a sigh of anticipation washed the large room and a trio of yellow, pink and blue spotlights stabbed at the raised stage at the far end of the chamber. Three pretty dancers—girl-women between seventeen and twenty—moved onto the stage as overhead speakers came alive with music. The costumes and the songs were traditional Thai creations, and for two minutes the performance looked like those regularly offered tourists on those Bangkok nightlife packages. The dancing was poor, but the audience showed no sign of disappointment.

Then the young women began to disrobe. One by one, they stripped to the waist. Two by two, breasts larger than those of most Oriental women, blossomed in the strange light. There was another sound—a communal hiss as dozens of customers sucked in their breath simultaneously. The show was getting *better* now. The patrons gulped at their drinks, tensed for *the good stuff*. The teenagers on stage were still doing approximations of classic native dance, but now they were touching and stroking their nipples to make them hard and prominent.

They licked their lips, thrust out their pink petal tongues. The audience responded. Men and women squirmed in their chairs, and a Memphis real estate broker uttered a loud grunt of approval. The dancers were rubbing their breasts against each other. The music grew louder, and the wife of a Dutch dentist stood up to see better. The rhythm slowed as the dancers separated, caressed their bellies and let their hands roam suggestively down their thighs. Their hips were wriggling and their tongues licked their lips to signal, to promise.

The message was not lost on the customers, male and female. The performers slowly, slowly slipped their delicate fingers over their pubic mounds, and after several moments of circular massage began to rub the metallic cloth that covered their lower hips. The tempo of the taped music changed again as they bumped and writhed, building till they dropped their skirts.

This was not like striptease in Western nations. No underpants, no black garters or other saucy touches. Aside from their head-dresses and golden shoes, they were naked. They rubbed their thighs and flanks, teased their pubic hair and—slowly, slowly— probed their labia. Their mouths were open in arousal—probably a sham—but the viewers did not care. They were truly stimulated, even if the dancers were not. The music reached a crescendo as the performers did, ended dramatically at the precise moment of apparent shuddering, gasping climax.

Blackout.

Next routine, with new music. It was the cheery rock of The Beatles. The three naked Thai were joined by a large nude peroxide blond, with massive buttocks, breasts and feet. The pretense of traditional national dance was gone. All four did the hustle briefly to offer good views of all their working parts, after which the three smaller women used their hands and tongues on the shaking blond's various parts. She groaned and called out as if for mercy as they finished her off—and curtsied to the audience.

It was not over. Four men in bulging jockstraps bounded onto the stage enthusiastically, fondled and licked and penetrated the faces, loins and rumps of the women—first in individual pairings and then in complex and changing groupings. From time to time, one male would show the audience his dripping phallus to prove that the sex was not being faked. People were shouting, one couple shrilling instructions. They appeared to have a proprietary interest in anal intercourse, and the performers complied. Now three men—two Oriental and one a muscled African—addressed themselves simultaneously to the body openings of the blond woman, whose arms, legs and hips thrashed expressively. Either she was a superior actress or she was having multiple orgasms. Several of the customers were climaxing, but most stared in silent fascination, as if they were afraid or embarrassed to show that they were involved by or in such a spectacle.

The speakers boomed out the driving hard rock of Black Sabbath, and the sex grew wilder, almost frantic. The colored spots were flashing on and off, jabbing here and then there like tinted fists. The audience was being whipped into a frenzy. One woman was moaning and twitching, while her auto dealer husband chanted, "Yeah, yeah, yeah," as though at a home-team football game. A blank-faced Japanese stood in the aisle, taking flash photos with his fine Nikon. Two of the Thai females on stage beckoned invitingly to the customers.

"Suck? Screw? Fun-Fun?"

A. B. Gordon sighed as two members of a Scandinavian aircrew joined the performers on stage, and she closed her eyes for a minute as she thought about the Johnny Phranghit she had known. He had always been an operator, always had a little something profitable going on the side. A touch of watch smuggling, an odd and illegal gold or currency transaction, some fencing of stolen radios or hot cars—he had barely bothered to conceal such deals. She heard the voyeurs yelling encouragement as the Scandinavians plunged into the melee of sweating bodies, and she listened to the heavy-metal music to gauge when it would be over.

The music stopped, and there was a strange hush.

None of the babble or applause of an audience, none of the chat or other audible reaction. The Scandinavians—one tipsy—were pulling on their trousers, and the professionals were waving like a Broadway or West End cast taking curtain calls. The big blond girl was massaging one nipple that someone had pinched or bitten— and she was gesturing grandly. The exhibition was finished.

The customers did not look at each other as they began to file out. Most of them were gone before she saw Phranghit coming toward her. Yes, he had always been a grinning son of a bitch—pleasant but utterly devoted to Number One. Now it was a question of priorities.

She would have to be courteous and pleasant, for Johnny Phranghit knew where to reach Santee.

He asked her whether she had enjoyed the show. She said it was the best of its kind that she had ever seen. This was true, for she had never watched another. He told her how difficult it was to do a "class production," invited her to have a beer. She begged off with a lie about a business appointment related to the film company she'd been retained to help—and she asked about Santee.

"Up in Chiang Mai, last I heard. Went up there to study to be a monk or something, but dropped out before he finished. Got a little travel agency somewhere up there. *I* was a monk, you know."

"All young Thai males spend a few years as Buddhist monks, Johnny," she answered.

"Was that a put-down? You mad about something?"

"Not at all. Lively show, surprised there was no act with dogs," she said sarcastically.

"Only on Wednesday nights, business is slow then. You got a funny look, boss."

She lit a cigarette, shrugged.

"You were never an angel, Johnny, but I didn't expect to find you running a live sex show."

She could see his feelings were hurt.

"It's honest work. Our wages are union, prices fair and the acts are for real—mostly. I'm a businessman now. I even pay some taxes —sort of. You know, boss, this is a step up for Johnny—a kid who never finished high school. It's an improvement."

She nodded, visibly unimpressed.

"It's better, boss," he insisted.

"Than what?"

"Than what we used to do. It's better than killing people, isn't it?"

The son of a bitch was right. She thought about it all the way back to the hotel. The son of a bitch was absolutely right. She forced herself to ignore the implications of that reality, but she needed three drinks before she could fall asleep. There had been a lot of killing—by both sides, enough of death to haunt the least sensitive. She was fortunate. She did not dream at all. Except of Harry Logan . . .

After breakfast on the veranda overlooking the river, she did not take the tour to the crocodile farm, the boat trip up the *klongs* to the floating market or the popular "one-day Bridge-Over-River-Kwai tour with packed lunch included" by train. Instead, she boarded a jet for Chiang Mai—a cool and less hectic city that calls itself the Rose of the North although it is better known for orchids. She had always enjoyed the pace, weather and landscapes of this city—Thailand's second largest with a population of almost 1.2 million and still basically a large rural town. Situated in a rice-growing plain surrounded by most of Thailand's tallest peaks, Chiang Mai had a zoo, parts of massive thirteenth-century walls that once protected this place from Chinese invaders, the winter palace of the royal family and—on a mountain near the palace—the revered Wat Phra Dhat Doy Sutep built in 1383.

Which was where she went to find Frank Santee. The petite and helpful secretary at his travel agency said he was up there at the monastery. Alison Gordon rented a Datsun, drove up the endless curves of the mountain to the base of the *wat.* There were two empty minibuses and a larger one signaling the presence of tourists, and there were those 300 steps—*300*—up, up, up to the spired pagoda which contains "partial relics of Lord Buddha." Even for a healthy, fit and determined person such as herself, the ascent required several pauses. The snake helped too—the right one. The railings on either side of the steep, wide stone stair were carved in the form of ancient serpents. Thai devout of all ages were everywhere.

She showed knowledgeable respect, removing and parking her shoes before entering, then buying a small piece of ultra-thin gold leaf to place on one of the statues of Lord Buddha as a gift to support the shrine. In the big *chedi* containing the relics, she found Santee.

He was meditating, and praying. She did not disturb him. She waited until he seemed to refocus on the temporal world, then greeted him quietly. Unlike Johnny Phranghit, Santee was thinner —almost gaunt. His head was still shaven from his days as a student-monk, and he spoke slowly in short simple sentences.

She remembered that Santee was totally trustworthy, but she found herself speaking cautiously. A person could change after all these years.

"Yes, I know the air base you speak of," he admitted. "The B-52s bombed Viet Nam from there . . . a long time ago."

He told her that no airplanes used that former U.S. Air Force field, that he discussed orchids every Sunday at lunch with the young lieutenant who commanded the $100 million base's twenty-six guards. She told him about the motion picture, offered him $400 a week for ten weeks to help get the base back into working order.

"We have the permits from the embassy in Washington and the ministry of defense in Bangkok—a written lease. Five thousand a week for eight weeks, with an option to extend for up to eight more. It's all in order."

Santee peered into her eyes as if he were trying to inspect her soul. "I think . . . I don't think you're telling me the truth, not all of it. If you cannot trust me, I cannot trust you. Are we no longer friends?"

She assured him that they were, reasoned and cajoled and spoke of how refreshing and interesting it might be to work with a film company. She was logical, warm, charming. She needed him. It would be impossible to have the field ready without him. He listened, and it seemed clear that he was considering her skillful presentation. "Excuse me," he said, "but I want to pray again."

"Of course. When will I hear from you?"

"About what?"

"About your answer, Frank."

The tall thin man looked benignly down into her face.

"The answer is *no,*" he announced and settled down in the lotus position to pray. . . .

When she reached the rented car below, she recalled something else about Santee. He never changed his mind. He'd been an expert in getting clandestine air bases swiftly into service for the CIA, a specialist on whom she'd counted heavily. As Logan was counting on her. His strange armada of aerial antiques would arrive in four or five weeks to touch down at a ghost of a base, a shell of tired buildings and facilities no one had used for more than six years. No one could fight a war from this costly memorial to long and bloody battles the whole world wanted to forget. There was no time to find a substitute. She began to consider how she might buy, seduce, blackmail or trick Santee into helping. But what if she failed? Corruption was not, after all, really her specialty.

These thoughts were running through her mind the next morning at ten as she drove away from the hotel to keep her appointment with the police chief of Chiang Mai province—a courtesy call that would doubtless require tact, political savvy and a sense of what the correct under-the-table contribution would be. Too much, and she would be a foreign fool to be repeatedly ripped off. Too little, and she would be a stupid American woman who had insulted the chief with a gift fit only for a junior officer.

Her car was leaving the parking lot as a 1976 Ford station wagon passed. There were forty ceramic pots in the rear compartment, and the natty man behind the wheel was Mr. K. Lopburi—owner of one of Bangkok's most successful flower shops and orchid export firms. He was also one of Thailand's major dealers in illicit arms, and he was on his way to meet General Wong.

39

CUBAN PILOTS in Soviet aircraft were busy bombing Eritreans as a favor to Ethiopia, Britons were finishing the last bits of their fruity-boozy Christmas cake and a group of sincere Arab nationalists slaughtered another team of equally virtuous Arabs. Many Scots were still roaring drunk from the previous evening, an Indian ferry sank with fearful loss of life and good poems were written in Dublin and Tokyo. Millions of devout Americans were entrenched in their living rooms before electronic shrines, ready to watch four consecutive football games.

It was New Year's Day, gray and bleak. On this day one considered the triumphs and follies of the previous year, made resolutions to lose weight or give up smoking or spend more time with the children. January 1st was traditionally the time of vows and promises, but The Man With the Shades looked out his window and saw, felt no promise at all. Years ago he had gone to a college in New England where it often snowed between November and March, but this place was too far south. It would be nice to have snow on New Year's Day—cozy, but it was unreasonable to expect a blanket of winter white to cover his half acre on the southern edge of the District of Columbia. He sat in his favorite rocker, alone. His wife had gone out to visit her sick sister—one whiner who had been annoying him for almost twenty-four years. He despised everything about her—the fake illness, the self-pity, the cheap-shot criticism of the Agency. What did such people know about the pressure and responsibilities, the fear of wasting lives and the dread of being wrong? They were crazy. They read those exposés, and they decided the Agency was staffed with homicidal thugs. The whole nation was crazy. What other country would set rules barring the use of certain cover occupations for agents? The Sovs and the Brits must be laughing themselves sick. He was not supposed to drink brandy. His physician had told him that it was bad for an incipient ulcer. In irrational defiance of this advice, he poured two fingers of Courvoisier and glared out the picture window at the front garden. Why couldn't there be some snow—just a *little?*

He saw the car come over the low hill, recognized the vehicle immediately. What was *he* doing here? It wasn't likely to be a social call. The director of Central Intelligence did not often fraternize with his staff. Oh yes, the chairman of the Joint Chiefs was giving his annual New Year's Day reception just a mile and a half down the road and the D.C.I. never missed that prestigious event. The deputy director put down his brandy snifter, opened the front door and walked out to meet the D.C.I. at the gate. The director stepped out of the car, looking bright-eyed, tanned and very fit in his fur-collared coat.

"Afternoon, admiral. Come in for a drink?"

"No thanks. Just passing by on my way to General Cartright's wingding. Good day to stay in port, eh?"

The admiral had spent thirty-one years on active service aboard cruisers and aircraft carriers, and he retained a little of that lingo —with pride. Some people said it was an affectation, but they underestimated the D.C.I. He was clever and a good politician, an effective infighter in those weighty budget battles and jurisdictional wars. The D.C.I. suddenly clapped his arms across his chest, came to the point. A blast of his breath condensed as he spoke swiftly. "On this B-17 affair, it's insane, isn't it?"

"Yes."

"We're all agreed on that. They can't possibly pull it off, can they?"

"Odds are maybe a million to one against them."

"That's what I told Fairweather. Not a chance in hell. Damned embarrassing, though—the whole situation. That's what he said."

Like all senior diplomats, Arthur Fairweather embarrassed easily. He was quite senior in the U.S. hierarchy, being the secretary of state.

"He had a suggestion, a plan," the D.C.I. continued, and immediately explained the proposal . . .

"The secretary of state urged *that?* I thought *we* were supposed to be the gangsters, admiral."

The D.C.I. smiled. "What do *you* say? Will it work?"

220

"It'll be bloody. Goddam bloody. I thought we were finished with those games."

"Will it *work?*"

"It could. Anyway, what the hell have we got to lose? It's not as if any questions of principle were involved, is it?"

Was he being sarcastic? The D.C.I. had no patience for wise guys.

"You'll keep an eye—and an ear—on it," he ordered as he swung his arms across his chest again. "This is your baby. I want all the files —all copies of everything on this operation—in your office in locked destruct-boxes. If we go with Fairweather's scheme, you'll know what to do."

"And MacBride, sir?"

The admiral grimaced in annoyance. "You know what's necessary. Do it, dammit . . . Lord, what a dreary day." Then his face brightened suddenly. "Well, it's off to Cartright's bash. His wife makes a great honeyed ham, and she always knows the latest dirty jokes. See you on the bridge tomorrow."

"Aye, aye, sir." He watched the admiral climb into the rear of the limousine. He did not wave or wait for the large Chevvy to pull out of sight, but turned at once and walked back inside the house. His wife joined him there moments later.

"That was the director, wasn't it? I saw the car."

"It certainly was. How's your sister?"

She threw her coat on a chair, stared at him. "What's wrong?"

"Wrong?"

"Darling, you don't give a fart about my sister. You haven't for years. I can barely put up with her myself, but that's not the question. What did he want?"

He picked up the snifter. "I'm going to make a speech."

"That bad?"

"That bad. Over the years I've generally done what I want to do and I'm not ashamed of that. I've also done some things I'm not too proud of—'operational necessity.' That's the expression," he said, and gulped half the brandy.

"With your stomach, that's a dumb thing to do."

"A dumb thing to do," he agreed. "Over the years, you have been a warm and understanding wife—a patient mate. Even back in '59 and '60, you were patient."

She poured herself a large slug of brandy. "You aren't the first man to have a temporary problem with impotency. You've been a fine lover for years."

"The glasses don't bother you?"

"Here we go again. No. I love you, and I don't care about sunglasses or vests or bow ties. You're my husband, idiot—the father of my three children. Christ, why are you feeling so sorry today?"

He pointed at the picture window. "No snow. Why can't we have snow?"

"I think you're getting senile—and only fifty-eight. You were saying something about over the years."

He finished the brandy, coughed. The pain flashed on his face. "Over the years, you haven't asked many questions. You can't chat with the other women about your husband's job or the office politics. You don't know what the hell I do, Ann."

"You do whatever deputy directors do. Don't drink any more, will you? I just had the rug cleaned."

He began to pace. "Among the things that I have done out of operational necessity—none of which I can discuss, this is one of those that you wouldn't even want to hear about."

"If you say so. You want to take a nap, dear? You look ragged— stop that, keep your fist away from that brandy. Go sit in your rocker. If you can't sleep, watch football like all the other middle-aged adolescents."

He settled in the old chair, sighed. "Tell me all about your sister."

40

IT WAS EXCITING.

Every day, every week they were getting better.

They did the same thing over and over again, and Logan never let up for a moment. Some men grumbled about the six-day week, but not in his hearing. He'd explained that at these wages he expected them to be perfect. At three things: Bombing from 3,000 feet with high explosives and antipersonnel fragmentation weapons; strafing and hitting small ground targets from three hundred feet; following a preset strike plan with total precision and in complete radio silence.

"What kind of a movie is this?" Boti asked.

"The kind that pays a thousand bucks a week," replied Baranovitch, who'd been in excellent spirits since the pinball machine had arrived a month earlier.

"But it's funny, B-17s weren't made to fight from three hundred feet," the Cuban noted.

"Shit, man," said Crockett Duckworth who still wore a sling, "Ol' Pinball and me flew a lot lower'n that to beat the Yankee radar. Came across right down on the deck—maybe hunred feet. We was scraping burro shit from the belly after every damn run. Three hunred's eee-zy."

"Piece of cake," Ashley concurred.

"You believe that, *amigo?*"

The RAF veteran nodded solemnly to the Cuban, refilled his pipe. He was about to light it when the claxon on the control tower sounded Harry Logan's summons to another mission. The crews walked to the four 17s that were operational. The fifth was having hydraulic problems again, and the damaged one was still far from airworthy.

Dr. Fishman drove over in the jeep with Logan from headquarters. "You sure Crockett's okay?" Logan asked as they left the vehicle.

"Well enough to help a bit. He'll be out of the sling in two or three days. Young Texans heal fast. Must be that great chili . . . Colonel, I'd like to come out with you today."

"What for?"

"To see what it's like. Maybe try my hand with the .50s. Jones has been giving me lessons on the range. Not the same thing as shooting from a moving plane, of course."

"Listen, doc—"

"You think I'm too old?"

"Jesus—"

"Let's leave religion out of this. Harry, if you think sixty-six is too—"

"Get in the plane."

They started toward the cluster of bombers, with Dr. Fishman explaining that Jones had also checked him out inside one of the 17s on how the waist guns operated.

"So you won't shoot down one of our own birds?"

The physician looked indignant. "Harry, these are the trained hands that have circumcised five hundred babies, delivered hundreds more. These are the eyes of a scientist. This is the mind of—"

"Get in the goddam plane, con man," Logan broke in, and pointed.

"Yours?"

"That way at least you can't shoot me down, doc." Logan laughed and climbed up into his aircraft.

Nine minutes later, Dirty Dora led the procession of bombers down the runway. The roar of the engines, the vibration, the novelty and the brand-new danger all excited the doctor. He'd seen those old movies, but this was different. Now they were rolling, picking up speed quickly. He held on, enjoying every moment. Up front, Logan automatically rescanned the pilot's control panel.

The passing and running light switches.

Ammeters and voltmeter.

Generator and battery switches, the switches for the inverter,

Pitot heater, alarm bell, hydraulic pump and landing gear warning horn . . .

He again glanced at the important controls at his left.

Propeller anti-icer rheostats.

Aileron trim tab indicator, filter selector switch, oxygen regulator, vacuum selector valve, cabin air control, the emergency bomb release. Charlie Clarkson was working smoothly beside him, having completed the checklist and now watching the manifold pressure, rpm indicators and engine temperature and pressure gauges. With his left hand poised to adjust for manifold pressure variation, he leaned forward intently.

"100 . . . stand by . . . 110 . . . let's go, baby . . . 115, airborne," Logan sing-songed.

The old bomber rose, picked up speed and climbed slowly into the tropical morning. The others followed one by one, and when all were at 3,500 feet they swung into the wedge formation Logan had ordered. This was low-altitude-strafing day. After a dozen minutes of flying to the target area that the Costa Verdan president had set aside for them, Logan waggled the wings of his aircraft and the four planes shifted to a single column. He spoke to his crew via his throat microphone.

"Pilot to tail-gunner, pilot to tail gunner, are they lined up for strafing run?"

"Roger. All birds set like ducks in a row."

"Pilot to all gunners. You have one minute to test-fire."

The gunners each squeezed off three or four short bursts, reported back they were battle ready.

"We're going down," Logan said.

His 17 swooped in a 60-degree descent, moving at just over 200 miles an hour. Fishman would be unnerved by this, Logan thought, but he had better get used to it. He leveled off at 350 feet, bored in over the target area. He was down to 300 half a minute before the nose gunner spotted the initial markers and shouted over the intercom.

"Dead ahead, skipper. Nice navigating."

The Forts thundered ahead. They were going only 175 mph now, the shooting would be more accurate at this lower speed. One after the other, they roared over the targets and the gunners blasted. Dr. Fishman remembered everything, even how to unjam his heavy machine gun when an ammo belt stuck. The jungle was so close below, the mass of green so bright, the firing so loud and the smell of the shooting—it was dazzling and intoxicating, and a bit over-whelming—wild and frightening simultaneously.

Four passes, and they turned back toward their base. They'd done it more than three dozen times in recent weeks and they were professionals—most of them with many hours of combat experience. This was supposedly another training exercise, a drill. Despite that, every man's heart was pounding: blood pressures raised, histamines coursing through their systems. From Logan to the last navigator and gunner, every one of them was still *up*, still *high* on the speed and hazard and promise of battle when they climbed down from the planes at the home field. Their eyes gleamed and their faces were set in satisfied half smiles—the look of world-class athletes who know they've done it *right*.

"What do you say, Harry?" Clarkson asked.

"Not bad."

"Bloody good!" the Briton declared. "No disrespect to the squadron leader intended, colonel, but we were bloody good."

"The *Englander* is correct," Kopf agreed. "It is a credit to your command, colonel."

"Ot-to's raht, suh, and he don't give compliments cheap," Mayberry put in.

It was true. The German had high standards for judging everything and everyone, including himself.

"Not bad at all. You're getting better," Logan admitted. He was actually very pleased, but it showed only in the brightness of his eyes.

"What do you think, Charlie?" he asked to evade their demand for approval.

"We're ready, Harry."

"Almost," Logan acknowledged, and walked on to talk with the flush-faced physician. "How'd you like it, doc?"

"Fantastic. Beats the hell out of varicose veins."

"And proctoscopies?"

The doctor grinned, wiggled one hand in the mezzo-mezzo gesture. "Mighty close. Frankly, I was never too crazy about backsides. Colonel, this was terrific. I think a whole new career may be opening for me. It was—please don't laugh—*thrilling.*"

"I'm not laughing, Noah. I know what you mean, but I got hooked when I was nineteen."

They strolled back toward the hangar together.

"You think I'm a foolish old man, don't you, colonel?"

"What do you think? That's what counts."

"Aha, a lay analyst too . . . I think you just might need an extra machine gunner some day, even a sixty-six-year-old one."

Did he know? Had he guessed, or had somebody talked . . . ?

"You're okay, doc. Well, we've only got another ten days here. Plenty of work to do before we head east."

"I'll be a lot better with that gun in ten days," Fishman vowed.

"You'll be fine . . . you really liked it out there today, huh?"

Something glowed in the white-haired physician's face. "I've been a good doctor, and when this is finished I'll probably go back to that. It's important—but this is different. After all those years doing the same things, the same kinds of patients and problems—this is . . . you know . . . ."

"What?"

"Exciting," Dr. Fishman blurted, and hurried away.

After the debriefing and the discussion of what hadn't been done quite perfectly and why, the crews showered and changed to fresh clothes before gathering in the "rec" room for a predinner beer. Some of the men insisted that this 6:30 P.M. meal should be designated "supper," but whatever they called it Logan only allowed two drinks each. Neither the air nor ground crews enjoyed this limitation, but all knew better than to say so. They sipped their beer, played pinball for twenty-five cents a game—except with Baranovitch, the superstar—and listened to the newly installed but vintage jukebox.

The choice of records on the machine was unusual.

"Bizarre," judged Crockett Duckworth who longed for the talents of Willie Nelson, Waylon Jennings or Dolly Parton.

"Short on soul," Jones observed.

"You like it, honey?"

The tall showgirl considered Van Bokkelen's question and shrugged. "I never *heard* of this stuff. 'Coming In On a Wing and a Prayer'? 'They're Either Too Young or Too Old'? And this 'Do Nothing Till You Hear From Me'—that's far out. Somebody find these in a cellar?"

Clarkson wondered how much to tell them. "That 'Wing and a Prayer' was a big hit for Jimmy McHugh and Harold Adamson—a nice lyricist. Eighteen weeks on the 'Hit Parade.' 'Too Young or Too Old'—Frank Loesser and Arthur Schwartz, twelve weeks . . . Duke Ellington wrote the music for the third one. It was on the 'Hit Parade' too."

She looked to the millionaire for help. "What's the 'Hit Parade'?" she asked.

Van Bokkelen punched one of the buttons on the garish machine, moved toward her. "R-a-d-i-o . . . you know, TV without pictures . . . care to dance?"

"No love, no nothin'" cooed some prehistoric voice from the machine.

"Touch dancing—people in body contact?" Van Bokkelen invited.

"I've seen that in the movies," she recalled, and moved promptly into his arms.

The others watched them dance. They made a graceful couple, even though she was an inch taller.

Clarkson realized that none of the crews understood what Logan was doing, or why. Last week the records had been 1942 hits, and now 1943 was dominant. It was more than setting a mood. It was keeping a promise—in a strangely ritualistic way. If Clarkson was correct, 1944 disks would be added on arrival in Asia. Maybe Logan was right in not telling them . . . they might not share his personal fantasy. They might not care at all.

They might even laugh.

Descending to land, the old plane filled the television screen.

"A bit of history came back to Hawaii," that strong and famous voice boomed confidently in the dramatic singsong so many millions adored and trusted. "B-17s, the remarkable Flying Fortresses of World War Two, returned to the Pacific paradise. Once the masters of the skies, these rugged four-engine bombers defied the massed fighters and antiaircraft guns of Hitler's Reich and Imperial Japan in some of the greatest air battles of all time."

One was on the runway, a second about to touch down.

"Scores of U.S. airmen and a crowd of aviation buffs turned out to view, and cheer, these once-mighty war planes. Representatives of Boeing were there too, for the company that now thrives on selling the world's airlines huge 747 jet transports of peace is still proud of the B-17s it turned out by the thousands to help defeat fascism . . ."

The camera began to push in steadily.

"Only a few dozen of these amazing battlewagons remain," the veteran newsman said with more than usual concern. He had been a war correspondent himself. He remembered. This was his youth, when he was still a reporter and not yet a celebrity. "It was with great difficulty that a movie company managed to find, buy, and reequip a modest handful for a picture about World War Two in the Pacific."

Zoom.

Tight shot of fuselage beneath pilot's left window.

"Named the way they were when the freedom of the world depended on who ruled the skies . . . Able Mabel!"

Jump cut to tight shot of nose of second plane.

"Grable's Legs, celebrating the dancing film queen of that era . . ."

Jump cut to third plane.

"Hirohito's Headache—a challenge to Nippon's emperor . . ."

Fourth aircraft.

"Dirty Dora—naming bombers for girls was all the rage. Yes, it was unabashed nostalgia at Honolulu's main airport this morning as the old birds landed and their crews—many of them graying veterans of those bloody battles more than thir-tee years ago, stepped down in authentic, World War Two, U.S. Army Air Force uniforms . . ."

Medium shot of a trim, ramrod Air Force colonel—not a day over forty—plus five straw-skirted Hawaiian women with the inevitable leis leading a crowd of newspersons, civilians and tourists to greet Logan and his mercenaries. In the background, tall blond Marlene Duckworth waved at the camera.

"One of the young actresses flew with them to relive those glorious days, and perhaps to generate a bit of publicity. After Viet Nam, selling a war film to the pub-lic may not be that easy. Tomorrow, they fly off into the wild blue yonder, the last survivors of the plane that was a legend. . . . And that's the way it was, Friday, February 23rd, 1979 . . . This is Walter Cronkite saying good-night for CBS News."

41

IT WAS TIME.

The headman walked slowly through the field, studying the plants for the signs. The Meo had been raising poppies in these hills for generations, and even the children recognized the signs that announced it was time to harvest the sap. Now the greenish plants stood almost four feet tall, each with one main stem and five or six smaller ones. A few still bore the bright red flowers. The petals of many others carpeted the earth.

Three of the small village's elders—watched as the headman studied the now-naked pods. The seed pods were green, no larger than a bird's egg. The headman knew that these plants were ready for harvest, but he respected the traditions of the tribe. He turned to the oldest of his companions.

"What do you think, grandfather?"

The gnarled man with the wispy white beard nodded. "Yes, it is the time."

Still the headman did not draw his knife. He looked at the other two elders, waited until they had signaled their agreement. It did not matter that one was half blind and the other had never been among the smartest. Customs could not be brushed aside, for without them how could the Meo survive in this mindless, heartless world of constant change?

The headman pulled his curved knife from its wooden sheath, took hold of a pod, then carefully sliced a series of parallel incisions —not too deep—and watched intently as white sap oozed to the surface. It required a trained hand to make these cuts, for a hasty or clumsy one could destroy the pod. There were more than sufficient plants, but the Meo were not rich enough to be wasteful. The four farmers stared at the sap, waited.

"Aaah," the headman sighed, and the others nodded in approval. The white sap was congealing, altering to a brownish black as it should. Yes, it would be of good quality, and the Haw trader would be content. There would be no dispute. The merchant would pass them the goods without wrangling or acrimony. The headman would summon the other farmers of the community, who the next morning would scrape the dark gummy substance from the pods. All that afternoon the Meo worked in the field, cutting the incisions in the manner of their ancestors. Shortly after sunrise, most of the village returned to scratch free the gum. Each pod's oozing yielded enough opium to form into a small globe the size of a pea, and the peas were deposited in wooden boxes the harvesters wore on leather cords around their necks. They toiled for some two hours until the boxes were filled. Later in the day the contents of all the boxes were combined and the headman shaped the sticky opium into larger balls—two and a half or three pounds each.

Then the Meo waited.

The Haw merchant would come soon on his horse. He had learned well from his father about weather and time and opium. He would know—many miles away in that distant valley—when the pods were ripe, and he would ride in soon with the trade goods the Meo needed. It was as certain as the morning sun. As far back as anyone in these hills could remember, it had always been this way in the Golden Triangle. National frontiers, flags and technological advances meant nothing up here. There were tales that there had been a time when the tribes did not grow poppies to provide opium for strangers in lands whose very names were unknown even to the headman but no one could be certain. The Chinese merchant would come in a few days, return again for two more crops before this land was exhausted. The village would move on to another place, and the trader would find them to barter again. These were the things that were definite. These were the truths of the Meo. . . . He arrived in the early afternoon two days later, made the exchange and rode off slowly to the next village on his circuit. Some thirty other Haw merchants were doing precisely the same thing, picking up opium in *their* villages, completing their appointed rounds. Some of them managed to buy only thirty-five or forty pounds. A few of the more affluent rode with bodyguards and several pack animals to bring out as much as one hundred forty pounds.

They traveled slowly through the difficult country, but they did not tarry. The wholesalers were waiting. . . .

Logan was not. The fifth bomber with the hydraulic problems would have to catch up with the main force. His four B-17s flew on from Manila to the Thai capital, where photographers for the Bangkok *Post* and two other dailies took pictures before the refueling was complete and the four-engined curiosities took off for the final leg of their long journey. Everything was going well. The trip had been tiring, but everyone was in good spirits, looking forward to a promised day of rest before the next phase of the "film project." Some sixty miles south of Chiang Mai, they were joking over the intercoms—until they saw it. The keen, young eyes of Crockett Duckworth were the first to spot it.

"What the hell is it?" he demanded, and pointed up and directly overhead.

Baranovitch reacted immediately. He'd been through this before. "Bandit, twelve o'clock high!"

It was thirty feet long, a single-engine fighter with wings that spread more than thirty-six feet. They all stared at the strange insignia it carried—a large red ball. A veteran of the Pacific campaigns, Beau Mayberry automatically identified it. After all, that silhouette and emblem were still burned into his unconscious. "Zeke! Hot damn, it's a Zeke, model 32. Look at him come . . ."

The Briton's voice sounded in Logan's headset. "What is it, colonel?"

"A Japanese Zero. Their best World War Two interceptor, max speed 335 at 19,000."

"Nasty buggers," Mayberry chimed in. "Machine guns firing through the prop and 20-millimeter fucking cannon in the wings."

The Zero was accelerating.

"There *aren't* any more Zeroes, gentlemen," Van Bokkelen reminded them sullenly.

"And there aren't any B-17s either. This is Blue Leader. Tighten formation, and prepare to go down on the deck."

They had no other defense. Not one of the bombers' .50 caliber machine guns was loaded.

"What the hell is he doing?" Crockett asked.

"He's getting ready to attack," Harry Logan said, and pushed Dirty Dora into a steep dive.

It was all insane.

It couldn't happen, but the Zero was there, coming in for the kill.

42

"DIVE, DIVE," Logan repeated, and the other 17s followed Dirty Dora in abrupt descent.

More than one pilot wondered whether the wings could take the strain.

4,600 feet—and the Zero was closing fast.

3,500 . . . 2,500 . . . 2,400 . . .

A wing rivet popped on the black bird. Baranovitch was too busy fighting to maintain control to curse . . .

Something was rattling ominously in Mayberry's and Kopf's plane . . .

1,200 . . . 700. The Zero would surely cut loose any moment.

People were cursing, hanging on to avoid broken limbs and teeth. Some of the finest obscenities were chanted by the sometime show-girl who had acquired the complete glossary of a Mafia chief during a 1976 affair.

500 . . . 300 . . . and the bombers leveled off. Somehow all the Forts were still intact. Not one had lost an engine or busted a fuel line. The crews started to relax—

"On the deck! I said the deck, down to 100," Logan commanded.

B-17s were not made to operate at one hundred feet. There were stories about some low-level operations in which U.S. bombers went under German radar to surprise Balkan oil fields, but those were B-24s and the casualties were high. There was also a legend about a Fort damaged during a strike against Berlin limping all the way home to East Anglia on two engines at a preposterous seventy-five feet. True or not, those aircraft were fresh from the factories. History, in any case, did not matter now. The other pilots set their teeth, carefully . . . very carefully . . . eased down to one hundred feet.

There were hills ahead.

"Trouble up front. Watch your ass and follow the leader."

"Roger, Blue Leader."

Somebody had set them up.

Someone had planned this weird ambush, someone with a sick mind, a grotesque sense of history and precise information on when the old Forts would arrive. There was no time to think about it. Logan raised Dirty Dora's nose to clear a small hill, saw the ones ahead were taller.

The Zero was on them.

A mere hundred and fifty yards to the right, the attacking plane swerved and thundered on—parallel to the bombers. It could outrun them easily, but it did not. It could savage them with those 7.7-millimeter nose guns and the 20-millimeter wing cannon, but the pilot did not fire. He was an excellent flier, maneuvering the Japanese fighter with agility and that special extra flair that made what they used to call a "hot" pilot.

The Zero flew past the whole column of bombers, sped up to the circle across Dirty Dora's nose, then charged down the other side, the pilot waving jauntily as he passed them, almost as if in friendly greeting.

The sadistic son of a bitch was playing cat and mouse. He'd let them sweat before his guns chewed them out of the sky. The fields and homes below were flashing by as if in a speeded-up movie. Trucks pulled off the road, people jumped from bicycles and farmers threw themselves flat as the ear-shattering armada thundered by overhead. The crews of the Forts felt the hot sweat that coated their bodies.

Still the Zero did not open fire. He swooped around the Forts, turned sharply and charged directly at the nose of Dirty Dora.

"This is it, Harry," Clarkson said.

Logan swung the 17 off to the right, ordered, "Evasive action."

The Japanese interceptor did not shift with Dirty Dora. It climbed suddenly, and Logan caught a flash of the pilot tossing a thumb's up salute. Was the Japanese—or whoever was handling that Zeke—totally nuts? The Zero kept climbing—away and out of range, and within seconds out of sight.

Gone. Was this only a threat, some kind of stagy warning?

The 17s flew on at low level for half a minute before Logan

ordered them up to 3,000 feet. As soon as the planes reached that cruising altitude, a babble of questions and comments clogged the command frequency.

"This is Blue Leader. Okay, the party's over so let's concentrate on flying. We're about nine minutes from base. Here comes a course adjustment."

They listened, and they got off the radio, though they were undoubtedly still chattering to each other over the intercoms. Who wouldn't after such an experience?

Logan looked over at his copilot, Clarkson, who asked, "What do you think, Harry?"

"Still thinking. I don't believe it was a nut or a prank, Charlie . . . You were cool as ice back there."

Clarkson shrugged, moved his head from side to side. "Not exactly, Harry. Maybe I'm trying to prove I'm no sissy, or something."

Logan adjusted a control on the main panel.

"You're no sissy, Charlie. Maybe that notion bothered you in 1943, but you've proved exactly what you are. A *smart* brave man who knows how to teach and how to fly B-17s—"

"Blue Leader, Blue Leader, this is Na Krang tower," the radio interrupted. "Visibility ten miles, northeast crosswind at five miles per hour. You are cleared to land on Runway Two. Please confirm. Runway Two."

Who the hell was it? How did this stranger at Na Krang even know that the bombers were so near?

"Please confirm, Blue Leader."

The voice was American, male.

"Runway Two . . . I can see the field now."

It was big, not as large as some of the other bases the U.S. had built in Thailand to bomb the North Vietnamese, but still a major installation that had cost the American taxpayers $100 million or more. Those were the sturdy old dollars, which the whole world saluted before the desert princes jumped oil prices and wrought nine kinds of havoc. There were three strips long enough to handle jet bombers, a dozen hangars and enough food, housing, medical and recreational facilities for 3,900 "personnel." The U.S. Air Force was always a trend setter, having had "personnel" some thirty years ago when less progressive organizations still signed up *men* and *women*.

There were two aircraft already on the ground.

One was the C-54 cargo plane that had left Costa Verde eleven days before the bombers.

The other was a Zero, emblazoned with the World War Two insignia of Imperial Japan.

"Model 32," Mayberry identified.

What the hell was it doing here?

The four bombers landed, and it was Alison Gordon who answered the question. She walked to Dirty Dora with a Japanese flier, an erect middle-aged man who stood taller than most Japanese. She opened her arms to embrace Harry Logan, but Blue Leader had something other than love on his mind. He pointed at the fighter. "Whose Zeke is that?"

"It's ours, Harry. I bought it from a man in Hong Kong to replace the P-51. Honey, I'm so glad—"

Logan didn't let her finish the tender greeting. "Is *he* the pilot?"

"Sure. Hiroshi Nakamura, major in the Japanese Air Force in the war. Very good pilot. Major, this is our commander—Colonel Logan."

The other members of the bomber crews were approaching with Marlene Duckworth, staring at the Zero and muttering. They saw Logan speaking to the Oriental in flying gear, and they guessed. Nakamura's face was blank—an unfinished Noh mask—as he snapped to attention and saluted.

"Was that you? Did you pull that fake attack, major?"

"It was not meant as attack—not even fake attack, colonel. It was friendly greeting—"

"My ass . . . We've got a German with a wild hair up his butt because 17s may have wiped out his daddy. Now you—"

"I regret to say you are in error, colonel. A friendly welcome," Nakamura insisted.

"From whom?"

"From Imperial Air Force. No, sir, B-17s did my family no hurt. B-29s caused vast damage, many deaths—but not 17s. I know 17s well."

Logan thought he understood . . . "How many 17s did you shoot down, major?"

The Japanese could not quite suppress his prideful smile. "Three, and three your B-24 also. And two U.S. naval fighters."

The bastard was boasting . . . well, no, it wasn't exactly that. He was saying that Japan may have surrendered in '45, but the Imperial Air Force and Major Hiroshi Nakamura still had their professional honor—

"I would not engage in private vendetta. Personal revenge is not

236

suitable for warrior, I am of warrior family, back to fourteenth century. My code is warrior's—"

"I don't believe this shit," Logan told her in exasperation. "This guy's doing samurai movie numbers to show the Jap air force can still scare people."

"Everyone wants to be taken seriously, Harry . . . especially old soldiers." She looked at him closely as she said it.

Two small trucks were approaching.

"Do you know what you almost did, major?" Logan demanded, not getting her point. "Your honor and friendly welcome gag could have cost us a 17, maybe two. These buckets are more than thirty years old. People could have been hurt, maybe fatally—"

"I meant nothing such as that, colonel—"

"If I didn't need you and your Zeke I'd disembowel you with a rusty beer opener—"

"Sir . . ." Van Bokkelen interrupted. "If you don't hit him, I will —"

"Come off it," Logan told him irritably. "You're the guy who distinguished yourself when you flew in with the 51—remember? Take a walk, Van." He focused on the Zero pilot again. "Okay, major, you made your point, now I'm making mine. As of now you're confined to the base. You'll get your pay and you can eat with whomever you please, but keep out of my sight. You fly well, major, but your head is a mess. Dismissed."

Nakamura saluted and turned on his heel and walked off—as ordered. Still the soldier. Only then did Alison and Logan embrace, kiss, caress each other . . . until one of the trucks pulled up beside them and the driver spoke out of his left window.

" 'Scuse me, Al."

Logan recognized the voice.

"You were the guy in the control tower who gave us the runway, right?"

"Santee," said the thin, earnest-looking man behind the wheel. "Going into town for vegetables. Need anything else?"

She hooked her arm through Logan's. "Not now . . ." She squeezed his forearm affectionately—and Logan remembered.

"Santee? You're the guy I heard didn't want to help us."

Didn't he know it was time to make love?

"She talked me into it," Santee said.

"I told him the truth. It's okay, Harry," she quickly added. "He hates heroin traffickers."

Well, her judgment was excellent, he thought, especially about people. He thanked Santee and they shook hands briefly before the truck moved away to pick up the food. Then he put his arm around her shoulder, and she put hers around his waist as they walked off to her quarters to try to make up for too much time. . . .

News of the arrival of the American bombers was carried across the Chinese border the next day by a Lahu tribesman who was paid three kilos of salt and four boxes of shotgun shells by Lieutenant Teh of the intelligence service of the People's Liberation Army. After being evaluated and encoded, it was telegraphed to Peking for further analysis at a higher level. Careful men, not less obsessive than their counterparts in Washington and Moscow, considered the report and the photos from the Bangkok papers. Perhaps the Americans were making another of their silly films, but these *were* bombers and the CIA was extremely devious. MIG-23 squadrons and frontier radar of the Southern Defense Command were alerted, and the Chinese espionage apparatus in Chiang Mai province was instructed to look into the matter.

The agents would find out whether this was merely a motion picture company's second unit, filming scenes to be integrated with those to be shot in Hollywood. If that was the case, the old aircraft could be tolerated.

If it was not, they would be destroyed.

43

"New weapons?" Gannett asked.

"That's what I hear," MacBride answered.

There was a shout from the crowd of enthusiastic Thais watching the fighting kites. Throngs gathered regularly here at Pramane Grounds in front of the dazzling architectural splendors of the Grand Palace to enjoy this sport—gloriously exotic kites in the forms of birds, dragons and other mythological creatures battling to destroy each other symbolically. The goal was to maneuver one's kite so its string cut that of the adversary, which then floated away out of control. The kites were marvelous in color and design, and this national sport was almost as popular as the unique fists-knees-elbows-feet Thai boxing which filled Lumpini Stadium on Rama IV Road four times a week.

"How many?"

"Quite a few."

The gem dealer-smuggler had reported that half of Wong's force was sporting new M-16s, that he'd personally seen eight mortars that looked "fresh out of the box" when he delivered the money. Pederson was no military expert, but he'd spent two years in the U.S. Army and he knew better than to lie to MacBride.

"Can't you be specific? Give us hard numbers?"

These bright young desk commandos always wanted "hard numbers." It made them look good to their superiors back at CIA headquarters. MacBride remembered how they had thrived on "body count" figures during the Viet Nam fighting, and he despised them for their arrogant naïveté.

"Approximately half the infantry were carrying real clean M-16s, and at least eight mortars—mediums—were observed. My agent said these appeared to be quote, fresh out of the box, unquote."

"Goddam. Is this confirmed?"

MacBride nodded as another roar of approval swept the crowd. He looked up, watched the big red and gold kite drift up and off over the elegant spires and pagodas of the palace grounds. This was a place for a chief of state, MacBride thought. Beside its grandeur, the White House and even Buckingham Palace were second-class hotels—but he wouldn't tell that to Gannett. Gannett's idea of beauty was a well-typed report, with lots of "hard numbers." He'd consider such a thought unpatriotic.

"Two of my other people in the area—reliable people—say just about the same thing. Wong's got the hardware, Todd."

"From whom? Don't say Taiwan. We know hardly anything has moved out of there in at least a year." He eyed MacBride appraisingly. "Did you—"

"I gave him the *money,* the exact sum The Man With the Shades authorized. That hardware was already at Wong's camp when my courier arrived. How's Congressman Edelstein?"

"Don't change the subject, Mac. We've got to find out about those guns. Any thoughts?"

MacBride didn't even consider telling him about the weapons dealer who'd been seen with Wong at the Chiang Mai zoo. The remains of the Sixth Army needed those guns to defend itself, deserved them. The intriguing question was how had Wong paid for the hardware, and why had he done business with this arms merchant who was notorious for high prices, opium smuggling and a fondness for twelve-year-old girls.

"Nothing very *hard.* We're working on it. Lots of action up north. Chicom agents filtering down, the tribes say. Couple not far from Na Krang, where that movie outfit is. Alison Gordon's with them. You know her?"

Gannett shook his head as another kite soared skyward. "Starlet?" he asked.

"Used to be a full-fledged star, for us. Those old planes flew in mighty low, got a lot of farmers mad. Local police chief used that as an excuse to check out the airfield scene. It looks legit."

Half the police chiefs up north were selling information to somebody or other, so Gannett was not surprised that this one was picking up a few thousand extra *baht* a year scouting for MacBride.

"Let's not waste time on grade-B movies, dammit. You find out about that hardware, Mac."

The older man nodded. "Those B-17s look battle ready," he thought aloud, "and got some real bombs. Old stuff, but real. I never liked that woman."

People were shouting encouragement as two kites resembling crocodiles maneuvered for attack position.

"What the hell are you talking about?"

"Could there be a connection?"

"Not unless Wong's got enough cash to buy himself an air force, Mac. Listen, he didn't get that hardware from Santa Claus. Tell your people to get us facts—*hard* information. That's what you pay them for, isn't it?"

"Maybe I'd better go up there myself?" MacBride suggested.

"Not a chance. That's a flat order, a standing order. No Agency or other U.S. government personnel may be seen in contact with the C.I.F.—ever. State would go crazy, and you'd lose your job."

It was a definite threat.

"You're serious," MacBride said.

"And I'm going. See you Saturday afternoon at the boxing stadium—half past two. Ought to be more fun than this jerky kite fighting."

MacBride sighed, looked up at the beauty as Gannett left. There could be no doubt about it, and it was depressing. The man was not only brutal and ignorant. The man was a barbarian. MacBride spent another hour watching the wood-paper-string war, enjoying every moment. It wasn't until the last fight was over that he let himself think about Wong's new weapons. There was one person in Bangkok who might be persuaded to shed light on the matter, an unpleasant individual who frequently lied. Persuading him was certain to be ugly, MacBride brooded as he left the grounds with the homebound crowd. He only smiled as he looked at families, the graceful women and delightful children.

The Thai were a beautiful and cultured people.

It was a pleasure to live among them, and one had to pay for one's pleasures—sometimes by doing things that were ugly. He would try to persuade the dreadful man tomorrow, with a minimum of pain.

"Did we order a 130?" Hovde croaked.

"No."

"Well, we got one. It's Herky Bird time."

A big C-130 turboprop—the Lockheed Hercules that normally hauled freight in Korea and Viet Nam before somebody rigged

241

them with seven multi-barrel Vulcan cannon to "suppress" hostile ground forces—was rolling to a halt on Runway One.

"Cover me," Alison Gordon ordered, and picked up her Ingraham.

Hovde was manning a .50-caliber on the roof by the time she reached the plane. The large cargo doors opened. Six men and two women walked down the ramp. She stared at them incredulously.

"It looks terrific," Peshkin announced.

"What the hell are you doing here?"

"The whole setup, real military. Nice and authentic, wouldn't you say, Omar?"

"Great, great."

The sheik was sporting jodhpurs and riding boots, and the dramatic woman with him, named Melody Angst, had a pair of 40-D cups that could break store windows. Oh yes, the executive story editor. The skinny young man with them had bad skin, ragged long hair and a viewfinder on a gold chain around his neck. He appeared to be twenty-two or twenty-three, sleepy-eyed and in need of a bath. He'd certainly been wearing the rumpled Gary Cooper T-shirt and baggy jeans for too long.

"Wilber Greenstreet—our director," the press agent said proudly.

"I . . . I like it," the director managed to get out.

"It feels . . . right," Omar Baroodi agreed.

No doubt about it. The Arab had become a genuine movie producer.

"Has a nice smell of violence," the endowed story editor solemnly judged.

"The garbage truck is late today," A. B. Gordon explained. The other woman with the three cameras turned out to be Peshkin's publicity "unit photographer," and the chubby swarthy man was Pepe Madrigal, cinematographer. He seemed very professional, very affable as he told two of his fellow travelers how to unload a pair of crated 35-millimeter movie cameras and other gear. His voice sounded New York-Latin, and he obviously knew what he was doing.

"Pepe's Puerto Rican," Peshkin said.

"Isn't everybody?" the pudgy cameraman joked.

Baroodi told her that the director wanted to see the second unit in action, to *experience* Asia so it would motivate him when he started filming the rest of the picture at the Burbank Studio in April.

242

"We got one hell of a script," the sheik confided.

"Not bad for a first draft," agreed the executive story editor. "My analyst's sister is working on the rewrite."

Greenstreet was peering through his viewfinder, studying the base intently. "Something's missing!" he declared.

"The bombers. They're out on a practice run,"

The young director nodded sagely. "I knew there was something missing."

"Smart as a whip," said Peshkin. "Only twenty-five, but loaded with talent. He'll do the final draft himself. Say, I guess we should have cabled ahead. Omar tried to phone, but we didn't have your number."

They all heard the noise of the fighter's 875-horsepower engine, saw it descending.

"That's not a B-17." Melody Angst said it like an accusation.

"Jap Zero. We're using it for combat sequences. It attacks the bombers."

Wilber Greenstreet smiled, delighted by the poetry of it all. Alison Gordon took Baroodi aside. "Let's get something straight, sheik. Your uncle *told* you, didn't he? We're only going through the motions. Our purpose isn't to make an actual movie."

Baroodi nodded.

"You know it can be dangerous here?"

"I want to learn. I've learned a lot already. Below the line costs, distribution deals, points, natural food—it's wonderful. I can learn more here. Don't worry about the others," he said, "they don't know what you're doing. I don't either, by the way. Not really."

"Better that way," she assured him. "It's going to get messy when it hits the fan. You'd be surprised, indignant, and give *furious* interviews . . . if the press ever hears about it. Scream about your money and your picture, like all the other virtuous producers. Offer to take lie detector tests. Bernie can handle it. He'll make you at worst a victim and at best a saint."

The sheik reflected. "But I'm a Moslem."

"A Moslem saint. Bernie's very good. He'll get you on the 'Today' show. Carson will call *you.*"

Baroodi's face showed misery. "We came here to make my first movie. Can't we stay for just awhile? Long enough to shoot some action sequences and footage of the planes in battle?"

"Why not? It would lend credibility to the whole operation. Omar, I don't want, as they say, to pee on your parade. Sure, crank up your cameras and do your number. But when I say it's time to split—"

He beamed. "We'll split."

"No questions or arguments?"

"You've my word."

"Good enough for me," she said, and shifted the Ingraham to her left hand so they could shake hands to seal their understanding.

They started back toward the others.

"That little gun? What is it?" the young sheik asked.

"Ingraham. I got it as a Christmas present."

They trudged along several more steps.

"Can I buy one? It's . . . cute."

"It isn't cute at all, but you can buy a gross. My country loves yours. $120 a piece, maybe cheaper by the dozen."

She told him the name of the manufacturer, and the city near which the factory was located. The Zero had come to a halt now, and a mechanic was removing the camera magazine as Nakamura dropped to the concrete.

"Major Nakamura, Sheik Omar Baroodi—our producer. How did it go?"

For an inscrutable Oriental, the Imperial Air Force alumnus was not doing too subtle a job of concealing his curiosity about the Arab stranger.

"Did you see anything?" she pressed.

"One sees little at 8,000 feet. Colonel Logan specified that as the minimum altitude. I made my run, took my pictures, *as ordered.*"

Baroodi and the others who had arrived with him in the C-130 were eyeing the Japanese as if he were an exotic character actor. His World War Two flying attire fascinated Greenstreet, who whipped out his monocular to study it closely.

"Good. He likes people who follow his instructions as ordered. Thank you, major."

Nakamura was of the old generation of Japanese, which saw women as inferior, but he was no fool. He was a highly intelligent man, much too well informed to treat *this* woman discourteously. He still had little doubt that females were lesser creatures, foreigners coarse and Caucasians devoid of spiritual values, culture or a sense of beauty—but she *had* hired him. He could not be rude to an employer, especially one who gave him the rare opportunity to fly a beloved Zero again . . . "Thank you, Miss Gordon. An honor

244

to meet you, Sheik Baroodi," Nakamura replied, bowed stiffly, and headed for the photo laboratory.

"I love it!" Peshkin said. "Sessue Hayakawa, right? *Right?* Saw all his flicks. Star quality! I hear he was a great stud, too. Banged everything that moved, know what I mean?"

The director was still staring at Nakamura through his lens. "We can use him. He's cold. The critics will go ape, and college kids will grab him as a swell new anti-hero. We'll play him off against our hero-hero. Who's his agent?"

She explained that Major Nakamura was a flier hired to pilot the interceptor for scenes in which the Zero would attack the American bombers, and could be filmed only in his plane—for the moment. After the battle sequences had been completed, Greenstreet could explore, negotiate other arrangements. The massed roars of four B-17s landing ended the conversation.

Some ninety minutes later the fast-process film had been developed and Agajanian had strung it up on the 16-millimeter projector. Logan turned out the lights. Moving pictures—a bit grainy and a trifle garish in harsh color—flickered on the screen. No one spoke for more than a minute.

"That's it!" Logan said.

They were looking at the place they'd seen only as squiggles on a map at Steele's headquarters in the Caribbean—the Burmese pass where they'd ambush the opium convoy.

"Not much detail, isn't that clear, is it?" Alison said.

"No, he'll have to go in lower. Meanwhile we'll get blowups of individual frames for our plot table, try to build a rough model of the valley."

The hum of the projector was the only sound now. More film, more infrequent comments.

Finally Agajanian spoke. "This place? What did you say they call it, boss?"

"Dead Moon Valley. Don't mention it to anyone, *anyone.* Not even to our own team. There could be bugs."

Less than one hundred yards away, Bobby Boti sat down and placed his coffee cup on the cafeteria table where Nakamura was finishing his tea. It was something of a surprise, for the other bomber crewmen were still shunning the Japanese out of anger at his aerial "greeting." The conversation was desultory, general in nature. Boti spoke about the housing, heat and the 17s' morning training mission. The fighter pilot mentioned that he had been out on a photo-reconnaissance sweep over some uninhabited area and Boti sipped his coffee, glanced at Ashley and the Navaho playing chess two tables away, and stifled a yawn. "Really? Where was that?" the Cuban asked casually as he offered Nakamura a filter-tipped Kent.

44

THE ARMS DEALER screamed.

As loudly as he could, but MacBride could barely hear the sounds of pain. The radio in Lopburi's office filled the room with Elton John's joyous version of "Don't Go Breaking My Heart", the 1976 hit that at least one of Bangkok's stations had not forgotten. The building that housed the flower shop was large and sturdily constructed. Sitting in the owner's big chair, MacBride looked at the splendid collection of exotic plants and blossoms. The noise from the cellar was hardly audible.

MacBride looked at his watch. How could anyone stand that agony this long? Sighing, he put down the book on the flora and fauna of Thailand and made his way to the door at the far end of the office. It was almost seven P.M., and Dr. Kee had been inserting the long steel needles for nearly an hour. The principle was simple and logical. An expert acupuncturist knew the human body and nervous system as well as a first-class neurologist. This was an ancient form of Chinese medicine, still practiced in the People's Republic and other nations. Elder specialists spent years training younger practitioners in the how and where to insert the needles to help treat certain illnesses, and they regularly achieved the apparently impossible by doing this without inflicting pain.

They knew where the metal probes would cause no suffering. They also knew where the needles would inflict the most terrible agony.

MacBride started down the stairs, stopped and closed the door behind him. As he descended, he thought about the logic of torture by acupuncture. It would be entirely scientific, with maximum suffering and almost no marks. Most violent interrogations left the subject bloody, disfigured and permanently marked with scars or ugly stumps of fingers and toes. Other forms made grotesqueries of breasts or genitalia, or even left people deaf or blind. Only a few inconspicuous needle holes, which would heal swiftly, came with acupuncture. The problem had been to find an acupuncture doctor who would use his healing arts for suffering. The vast majority were men and women of high principle, but Dr. Kee was a heroin addict who desperately needed money for his degrading habit.

The screams were much louder now. MacBride opened the door to the cellar, absorbed the impact. The arms merchant was stripped to his silken, orchid-colored shorts. He hung by his bound wrists from a beam so that he barely touched the floor with his toes, thereby stretching his entire body and making it altogether accessible to the needles.

There were many of them sticking out of his flesh. He looked like a huge pincushion, a lunatic's doll made human size: Metal protruded from his shoulders and elbows. Wrists and knees and ankles. Stomach, chest and neck. Cheeks, skull, buttocks, thighs—at least thirty needles, inches deep into his flesh.

Dr. Kee tapped one of the needles in the gun dealer's back, and the man convulsed in suffering as his body twitched.

MacBride was in a no-win situation: he hated the arms merchant, and he hated the torture . . .

Dr. Kee heard the sound behind him, turned. "He is ready now, sir. I believe that he is properly tuned."

Lopburi was drooling, glaring his exhaustion and anguish at the two strangers. "Why . . . who . . . are you?"

MacBride ignored him.

"Tuned? Like a piano?"

"Exactly. High note?" Kee flicked a needle, and the shrill made MacBride sick.

"Low sound?" The acupuncturist tapped another piece of steel, and a throat-tearing growl accompanied the body's flailing.

"Chopin? Mozart? Any favorites?"

MacBride shook his head, stepped closer. "Lopburi, you heard what he said—and you know he can do it. You are not a man anymore, just an instrument. He'll play rock and roll on your nervous system until you're broken—physically and mentally. People will pity you. A lot of them will get sick when they see you—even those twelve-year-old girls you rent."

The arms merchant made some incomprehensible noises, and

Kee touched two needles simultaneously. Lopburi twisted, jack-knifed, began to cry.

"You can't take much more. We don't want to put you in prison, or even to steal your money or dope. We're not the police, and we don't work for your competitors. All we want to know is how did Wong pay for those guns?"

Lopburi gasped and finally squeezed out a few words. Wong was paying with services, not money. His Sixth Army would provide armed escort for a very large opium caravan, protecting it from Shan or other hijackers. Half the weapons had been advanced, and the rest—with much more ammunition—would be delivered to the Chinese when the opium reached the frontier lab where it would be converted into much less bulky morphine.

The pragmatists at the State Department wanted to write off the Sixth Army as obsolete, embarrassing and politically expendable. The moralists at State insisted that no weapons or supplies go to Wong's forces because they had ridden shotgun for dope shipments in the past—and thereby pushed Wong into taking on another opium assignment as his only way to survive. MacBride did not say anything about this irony to the arms and drug merchant. He simply warned him that they would come back and do much worse things if Lopburi said a word of this night to anyone, and then he gave the addict the promised 1,200 *baht* and told him to cut the man loose in a few minutes.

It was all terrible—the plight of the Sixth Army, the policies of the bright young toughies at State, the depraved acupuncturist, the gross and evil Lopburi . . . and MacBride's own role in this horror piece. He felt very depressed, utterly alone as he walked up the stairs slowly and opened the door to the office. The radio was now offering Carole King's pretty-sincere rendition of her lovely "You've Got a Friend." He picked it up and hurled it against the wall, shattering a big mirror and smashing the set. The release did not help at all. He was still burning with frustration and bitterness as he started his car and drove off into the night.

His report reached the deputy director at CIA headquarters thirty-two hours later. It got to the communications center somewhat earlier, but the decoding and other procedures added half a day to the interval between transmission from Bangkok and the time Doris Kraft carried it—and three other messages—into the office of The Man with the Shades.

"She's got a Zero!" the executive secretary announced.

"You sound like a proud mother, Doris."

"A Zero!" she repeated, and dropped the cable from Hong Kong onto his desk.

He shook his head. "I know, Doris. It's right here in the damn pictures."

He opened a large manila envelope stamped TOP SECRET—NATL. SURVEILLANCE OFFICE, removed a sheaf of twelve- by fifteen-inch photos. He shuffled through four, found what he wanted and pushed it at her. Handing her a magnifying glass with built-in light source, he pointed at the print. "Zero—right *there.*"

She knew how to use the magnifier, and she had learned about aerial photos when she'd worked in Air Force Intelligence during the Korean "police action," just before joining the Agency. She bent low, peered at the picture. "Zero," she confirmed crisply. "I didn't see *these.*"

"Forgive me, Doris. I believe they came in yesterday afternoon when you were at your gynecologist."

"Spying on people *every* minute? What business is it of yours what kind of physician I see?"

"Doris, *you* told me. *Please,* what else have you got there?"

She handed him three more message forms, wondered about the other photos shot by the U.S. spy-in-the-sky satellite.

The Man with the Shades read her mind. "Nine small mule trains —presumably carrying opium because this is the harvest season and nothing else is worth hauling up in those goddam hills—are moving toward an assembly point between Samka and Mawmai in northeastern Burma. Shan troops are building up north and south of that area, and good old General Wong's Sixth Army is rolling that way on a goddam collision course," he said.

"You're swearing a lot these days. I'm used to it, but I don't like it. Just thought you'd want to know."

He studied the dispatch from the CIA station officer in Bangkok.

"I don't want to know. I'm in a terrible mood. My daughter's getting divorced again, and one of my best friends was shot three times yesterday by a mugger in downtown Washington. Not Berlin or Tokyo or Cairo—downtown goddam Washington . . . Shit, you read this thing from Satchmo?"

Satchmo was the code name for the head of the CIA in Thailand, a nation whose king loved jazz. The late great Louis Armstrong's nickname had been Satchmo, so some clown had pinned that designation on the Bangkok station officer.

"I saw it. MacBride's very . . . conscientious, isn't he?"

The Man With the Shades made a noncommittal comment somewhere between a hum and a grunt, picked up the report again. "Priority One signal to Satchmo."

She raised her steno pencil.

"Highest authority instructs you take all measures necessary . . . repeat . . . all measures necessary to insure completion of Clean Slate . . . stop . . . Kettle coming to boil any day . . . Maximum vigilance on your part essential . . . Holding you personally responsible."

He began stuffing the satellite pictures back into the envelope.

"Is that all?" she asked.

"Add this: Happy birthday."

"Is this Satchmo's birthday?"

"I have no idea," he answered, "but it never hurts to wish someone a happy birthday. It shows the men that you care."

"What about the women?"

"I apologize. Thank you, Doris."

She rose and guessed. "Are your eyes hurting again?"

"Among other things. Thank you, Doris. You're a very decent . . . person. Thanks."

She dashed from the room, glowing, and he direct-dialed the director on the private line. "It's moving fast, admiral. Picking up speed . . . soon . . . maybe three or four days, ten at the most . . . Yes, I've sent those orders. All measures necessary . . . Yes, Cyclops is on line. Manned around the clock . . . Right, we can patch through to your set, if you like."

The director of Central Intelligence declined the offer. He did not have to explain why, the reason was obvious. If something went wrong . . . if everything did not go right . . . if the whole thing blew up, neither the secretary of state nor the D.C.I. would have anything to do with it. This was an administration of blinding virtue, of pious populist, biblical morality. No members of the cabinet of that devout President could risk being tainted, having any link with those things the press, the hypocritical politicians and the clergy found so abhorrent.

The Man with the Shades thought about Clean Slate, and he smiled wanly. Whether it worked or not, what counted most was that the Agency have no provable link or role. The *semblance* of virtue—like those two-dimensional Hollywood sets—was what mattered, was what would be far more important to the holier-than-thou legislators, TV pinup commentators and Monday morning philosopher-quarterbacks than all those dead men who would be rotting in the hills of the Golden Triangle.

There would be many.

Soon.

45

EVERYTHING SEEMED to be proceeding normally at the air base Tuesday night. Baranovitch was teaching the attractive unit photographer the fine points of pinball, which was only fair since she had taught him her favorite game until after four that morning. The jukebox flown in on the C-54 was blaring Dinah Shore's rendition of "I'll Walk Alone," and when that ended it came to life again with a group named the Pied Pipers chorusing "Ding-Ding-Ding Went the Trolley."

"Judy Garland sang that in a film titled *Meet Me in St. Louis,*" Mayberry recalled.

"She's dead, isn't she?" Crockett Duckworth said.

"Yeah, but she was fan-fuckin'-tastic. She was like Logan—a genuine superstar."

"Ridiculous," said the ex-television newsman. "The whole world celebrated her—especially the fags. Nobody outside his squadron ever heard of Logan."

Marton and Dexter—the pilots of the cargo plane—had been talking about baseball, about the prehistoric times when the San Francisco Giants and Los Angeles Dodgers were both New York teams and cities such as Atlanta, Houston, Oakland and Seattle had no big league teams at all. A navigator mentioned the batting exploits of Joe DiMaggio and Ted Williams, and somebody recalled the 1944 World Series in which both the National and American Leagues were represented by St. Louis teams.

Clarkson thought about the records. It was happening. Every disk in the machine had been a hit in November or December of *1944.*

"Maybe Garland was bigger," Mayberry answered, "but combat pilots all over the world—especially 17 jockeys—knew about Harry

Logan. He was the Joe Namath, the Pele, the M.V.P., most valuable pilot."

"Garbage. You're just kissing ass. I could have kept my job if I'd been willing to kiss ass," the tipsy network reject jeered.

"I thought it was the young blond with the jugs who took your job, Bart," Duckworth reminded him as he drained an Amarit beer.

"Her and the guys with the little mustaches. They's infiltrated the whole business, the limp-wristed bastards," Kendall said.

Alison Gordon watched as Logan stood up, and she understood that he was going to stop this—now. He was crossing the room when Clarkson spoke.

"What do you mean—*limp-wristed bastards?*"

"The queens, they could never stand me. I'd be right up there with Cronkite today if—"

The teacher was blunt. "You're a bad drinker and a worse fool. I'd bet that it was liquor and age that wiped you out—another victim of ad agency research. Too old to pull the younger viewers, or some other idiocy. No, it was the trendies and the demographics that stole your job—not *us.*"

The boozy newsman grinned nastily. " 'Us?' "

Logan stopped. He couldn't intervene now. This was Clarkson's moment.

"So you're one of those dirty . . . those *degenerates?* Out of the closet, eh? Here's something for *you,* fruit . . ." He scooped up two beer bottles, rushed toward Clarkson. Dexter and Marton jumped up to stop him, but they never made it. The ex-television celebrity didn't either. Duckworth stuck out a leg, tripped him. He fell on his face, screamed in pain and with hatred as the cargo plane pilots picked him up and carried him out of the room.

A new record started, Otto Kopf began dancing with the lady from Las Vegas, and Van Bokkelen offered the Haitian nurse another glass of his private supply of champagne. He brought the bottle over to Clarkson a few moments later.

"Bit of the bubbly, Charles?"

Clarkson realized that this was no mere liberal gesture of paternalistic acceptance, and he felt good about what he had just done himself. He drank some champagne, returned to his conversation with Wilber Greenstreet about the classic Bogart films.

When Logan went to refill their drinks, Alison Gordon hurried outside, where she found the groggy television alumnus seated on the ground, leaning against the building and holding his injured nose. She leaned over, spoke confidentially. "Bart, don't do that again. We can't afford fights. You've got a constitutional right to dislike anyone you please, but do it when you're alone, in the toilet or someplace. If you make any more trouble in the ranks—*any,* I'll ask Logan to fire you on the spot."

"You're with *them?*"

"I'm with Logan. If it's any consolation, there are people I loathe too. You're one of them, so watch it."

She returned to the table, told Logan how fortunate Bart Kendall had been.

"I don't get it."

"He could have—easily. Dexter and Marton could have kicked the hell out of him."

"They're strong bulls all right."

"Harry, they're lovers."

Logan's eyes showed his surprise. "Didn't know that."

"Harry, this outfit's got more than a hundred and twenty men. Did you think there'd be only one gay?"

"Didn't think about it. C'mon. This is one of my favorite records. Let's dance."

Some 268 miles west, General Wong was baiting his trap.

The Shan had more troops and greater stocks of modern arms, more ammunition and younger soldiers too. The Sixth Army had its pride, some new guns but not nearly enough and the cunning of Wong. The old general had a plan for the destruction of the Shan forces. His scout teams had located them north and south of the jungle village where the opium-laden mules were assembling, waiting for the entire convoy to be gathered before attacking. The Shan had to be wiped out before they got near the opium, and Lieutenant Tzu would help. His wife was Shan, so he spoke the tongue.

Tzu spoke it into the powerful radio that the Americans had given the Sixth Army four years earlier, discussed the new orders for the rendezvous fifty-one miles west of Mong Mau on the riverbank.

Phase Two of the plan was to complete the arrangements with the wholesalers, organize the 712 mules into ten units and assign his troops to their defensive positions. This took a full day and a half. Every detail had to be handled correctly if the plan were to have any chance of success. An armed Chinese trooper would accompany each pack animal, with two mobile forces of 150 soldiers each as roving reserves. No fires, no smoke, no hot food until they reached the frontier laboratory where the chemist from Hong Kong and his three helpers waited with the oil drums, lime fertilizer, flannel cloth and ammonia to convert the raw opium *choys* to chunky white kernels of morphine. The ten small mule trains started east toward the Thai frontier, one leading the rest by two miles as a safety measure. After two days of slow progress through the hills, Lieutenant Tzu was on the radio again, speaking Shan, to reschedule the delivery of the opium to the processors in Dead Moon Valley on Sunday afternoon. As he spoke, the advance unit was peeling off and heading for Dead Moon Valley on its own. The Shan scouts saw its fires that night, alerted their commander that the convoy was following the traditional route to and through the valley. Phase Three—completed.

The main body of mules swung north, moving only at night. After covering some thirty miles, Wong ordered a complete halt and had all the animals and men take cover under tall trees. There was to be a minimum of movement or talk—with a bayonet in the stomach for any violator. The lone advance unit reached the valley Saturday night, lit their cooking fires and settled in for sleep. At quarter past two in the morning the Chinese soldiers and the tribal muleteers removed their shoes and made their way to the rafts hidden in the brush along the riverbank. Quietly they slipped onto these crude craft and floated downstream—out of the valley—in the darkness. Phase Four—on schedule.

The Shan were too. At ten minutes before seven in the morning they opened fire on the encampment from both ends of the valley. First they pounded it with mortar fire—killing nearly a score of mules and sending the others in panicky flight. Mortar fragments left one maimed mule tottering on three legs, another spouting blood from the place an ear had been. Now Shan squads began sweeping the camp with .30- and .50-caliber machine guns, murdering more of the terrific pack animals. Convinced that their surprise ambush had destroyed Sixth Army resistance, the Shan infantry charged, spraying bullets as they came. When they got to the encampment, they found thirteen dead and twenty-seven wounded—all four-legged. Not one human was anywhere in sight. The attackers collected some sacks of opium, wondered where the surviving Chinese Nationalists might be—

The Burmese artillery raked the valley.

Maintenance crews had worked hard when Intelligence reported that the Shan would be in Dead Moon Valley on Sunday morning, and five cargo planes had been, somehow, readied to airlift the paratroops and their cannon. This was an elite unit, tough and hungry for the promotions, honors and other benefits that would come to those who killed many rebels. They had jumped into another valley at dusk the night before, manhandled the pieces of the howitzers to positions dominating this valley and assembled the artillery pieces just before dawn.

The cannon pounded the Shan. The clever ambushers had been ambushed. A dozen shells a minute rained from the heavens. Out in the open with no defenses against artillery, the Shan could do nothing but perish. More than one hundred died within six minutes, and three times as many were wounded. Broken by the cannon's barrage, the tribal forces fled out of both ends of the valley, abandoning their dead to the birds and the animals that would pick the bones before nightfall.

It was a great victory for the armed forces of Burma. . . .

The Shan were not beaten, of course. They had lost men and matériel, but not their dream. They would train new suppliers, buy or capture fresh stocks of weapons. They had lost skirmishes and battles before, and they were ready to fight on for another century for a free, independent Shan state . . . During World War Two, American O.S.S. agents had spoken of how long it took Ireland to become a proud nation—many *hundreds* of years. The Shan were just as proud and determined. Angry but undefeated, they trudged away from Dead Moon Valley in small detachments that would regroup sixty miles to the south in three days. Still, for now . . .

Phase Five—total success.

Even Logan was impressed. Looking at Nakamura's latest photos the next afternoon, he pointed out to Alison the carnage in Dead Moon Valley.

"Somebody did one hell of a job on them, Hon. Just look at all those corpses! "

"Awful, who are they?"

"The blowups say they're Shan. As to who hit 'em, had to be a big outfit with lots of firepower."

"What about the opium convoy? We had some excellent pictures of these mule columns two days ago. Where are they now?"

They looked at the rest of the pictures three times, checked the map with the Zero pilot to make certain he had flown over the correct sectors. Not a trace.

"It's impossible," Agajanian declared. "According to the pictures, it was Chinese Nationalists riding shotgun for the opium, and according to Santee that's probably old Wong. We always knew he was foxy, but making more than six hundred mules disappear? That's no parlor trick."

"Six hundred mules can't simply disappear," she agreed. "They must be up there *somewhere*, and we're not bright enough to see them."

"My uncle ran a Sunday school," Logan said, "and he'd probably consider everything we're doing a sin. He'd say we're being punished for our sins."

She patted his hand. "Harry, we're Americans, and there are only two sins in the U.S. today. For men, it's being out of work. For women, V.U.L."

" 'V.U.L.?' "

"Visible Undie Line, wearing your slacks so tight your darling little panties show. Honey, we haven't committed either of those sins, so let's figure out where that shrewd old son of a bitch is hiding the caravan. If the pictures don't help, forget them."

He stared at the wall for several seconds before he spoke. "Long border, a dozen places he could cross. He knows the country a lot better than we do . . . It's a race now. Got to bomb him on the other side of the border . . . that's wilder, less populated and safer for us . . . He'll make his move within three or four days. He has to . . . About plan B, is *Bolivar* in position?"

"Has been since yesterday. Let's get back to Wong. The way I see it, darling, the only way to find this tricky old Chinese party is to—"

"Think the way he does—like a 'tricky old Chinese party.' "

It was wonderful loving such a warm *and* intelligent man.

Now, where in the world was that caravan?

"*Live* bombs?" the Red Chinese major asked.

"Yes, hundreds of them."

"I don't like it. As an intelligence officer, as *the* assistant chief of intelligence for the Southern Air Defense Sector of the People's Republic, I do not like it at all."

The solemn young lieutenant nodded.

"Not just practice bombs?"

"No, major. Our information is quite specific. High explosive and antipersonnel ordnance—in quantity."

The senior officer meshed, unmeshed and remeshed the fingers of his fat hands. "And one of their spy satellites has recently altered course to monitor that area, the nearby sector of Burma and our frontier defenses . . . No, I do not like it. The Americans are surely up to something, lieutenant." More interlocking of fingers. "And what's more, that Fascist Wong and his gangster force are on the move. How do the bombers at Na Krang fit into the plan?"

The junior officer wondered *what* plan, wisely decided not to ask.

"I would feel better if those B-17s were . . . neutralized," the major brooded.

"You don't mean an air strike?"

"Of course not. That would create all sorts of diplomatic complications . . . at a time we are seeking the good will of the whole region. Can't have neighbors believing the lies those Vietnamese are spreading about us. *No* air attack."

"A fire?" asked the lieutenant.

"What kind of fire?"

"Fuel tanks, comrade major."

The senior officer actually smiled. "A nice little accidental fire that destroys all the petrol they need to fly? That would be most convenient."

The lieutenant waited for the compliment, did not get it.

"Take care of it," ordered the major, "and don't delay. I've noticed some of you younger fellows have a tendency to put things off. Generational problem, they say. Don't have the kind of revolutionary discipline we had . . . aah, dismissed."

The intensely Leninist junior officer controlled his temper, sent off the message ten minutes later. The aviation gasoline supply at Na Krang was to be destroyed as soon as possible, and the fire must look like accident—not arson. Incendiary devices made in the People's Republic were not to be utilized, but the fuel tanks must burn. Within seventy-two hours.

The men and the mules were tiring.

Traveling at night at this speed was exhausting, but Wong sensed that he had no choice. Animals stumbled and troopers fell in the darkness, but the Chinese general insisted that each unit of the caravan maintain the grueling pace. When a mule broke its leg, it was killed with knives. Gunfire sounds would carry far in these hills.

They slogged on relentlessly until dawn, when Wong gave the order to halt. Sweaty, red-eyed soldiers dropped to the ground, bone weary.

The commander of the Sixth Army checked his map again. "Good."

The captain did not reply.

"It's going well. This is a difficult operation, captain, but the worst is over. The Shan are scattered, and I believe we have a clear path to the laboratory."

"Yes, sir."

"You do not have to tell me the men are tired. I am proud of them. In less than forty-eight hours we'll make delivery, and within a fortnight after that we will have enough weapons and supplies for a full year. Tell them that I am proud of them—*very* proud. We may not be the youngest force in the world, but we are still one of the toughest."

"Yes, sir."

The old man rubbed his arthritic legs, nodded.

"Sir?"

"Yes, captain?"

"Will the forced marches at night continue?"

"One more night, and we will be safe. Tell them that," Wong said, and returned to study his map.

When the sun rose, Nakamura took the Zero out for another flight.

"I regret to inform you that I saw nothing, colonel," he reported on his return to Na Krang. He pointed to the large map on the wall, explained exactly where he had flown. Logan stared at the chart, and suddenly smiled. "The old fox," he said happily.

It did not make sense. There was no trace of disappointment in his face or voice.

"Brilliant, brilliant."

"I don't understand, colonel."

Logan pulled out two cigars, offered one to the puzzled Japanese.

"I smoke cigarettes, sir."

"Try a cigar. Bet you've never smoked one with an American bomber pilot."

Nakamura shifted stiffly on his booted feet. "I have never met one *socially,* until recently, colonel. The previous relationship was somewhat different . . ."

260

Logan laughed. "Nobody's too old to learn new tricks—from any-one. I just picked up a good one from a damned clever old Chinese general. The old fox . . . what a stunt . . ." The American pointed at the map, shook his head. "Maybe you'd prefer a drink, major. These are fine Canary Island coronas, but if you'd enjoy a whiskey or a glass of Van Bokkelen's champagne, say the word. I'll even join you in a toast to the Imperial Air Force."

Nakamura hesitated.

"It's okay, major. Time to forget about that messy day we met. Time to put aside past differences. Time for new and bigger things, okay?"

Major Hiroshi Nakamura was astounded to find himself shaking hands with a B-17 pilot. A moment later, he was even more sur-prised to find himself puffing on a Don Diego.

"Fine cigar," he agreed politely—and coughed. "Thank you, colo-nel. I don't mean to be rude, but I must tell you that Americans are an . . . extraordinary people." He puffed again.

"Where are you from, major?"

"Osaka, sir."

"You met George Daifuku, our radioman from Hawaii? I think his parents were from Osaka."

The uneasy Japanese flier welcomed the arrival of Alison Gordon as an excuse to leave, and as soon as he was gone Logan embraced and kissed her enthusiastically.

"You've got it," she guessed.

"I think so. What can we absolutely positively expect Wong to do?"

"The unexpected."

"Give the smart sexy lady a cigar." He offered her a puff on his corona. She took two and returned it.

"And what would nobody in his right mind expect him to do after that shoot-out in the valley?"

She grasped the thought immediately. "You're kidding . . . no, you're right, Harry. *Has* to be."

"Right . . . doesn't matter where he is. What counts is where he's going, where he'll be in thirty-six or forty-eight hours. He'll have to come out for his final run, and I figure it'll be about then. *That's* the area Nakamura will scan from now on—and that's where we'll hit 'em."

She eyed the map. "It's a big border, Harry. If we're wrong, we won't get a second shot."

"You believe we're wrong, hon?"

"No. I believe you're thinking like a tricky old Chinese party."

They went to work. There was a great deal to do, for on the day after tomorrow Hacksaw Two would reach its climax. The bombers would smash the opium convoy—*there,* in that place.

Dead Moon Valley.

46

WHILE ALISON GORDON was at the Chiang Mai telegraph office the next afternoon sending the cable to Miami, ordnance teams and maintenance crews at the airfield argued about the batting of Willie Mays and Pete Rose, the breasts of Raquel Welch versus those of Dolly Parton, and the comparative merits of Thai, British and U.S. beer as they began to arm the B-17s for battle. Every machine gun had to be checked, every explosive and antipersonnel bomb examined before the loading could start. Trucks and jeeps rolled back and forth in a steady stream with weapons and other equipment. . . .

On the ridge a mile and a half away, the man with the binoculars watched and waited patiently. His orders were clear, and his replacement was not due until dusk. The job was boring, but the relatively cool February weather of northern Thailand made it bearable. Peering through his glasses, he saw her car return from town and observed her entering the headquarters building. . . .

Baroodi and the press agent were seated in her office.

"I was just going to call you," she said.

"We'd like to talk to you about the picture," the sheik replied.

"Remember our deal, Omar? When I say it's time to split, you split. The make-believe is over, I'm afraid. Take a look at what's going on out there. That's no Hollywood pretend."

"I told Bernie."

"Listen to your executive producer, Bernie. He's always right. Time to pack up and bug out, boys."

"And Bernie had a great idea," Baroodi continued.

"Full of great ideas. That's why I recommended him. With that imagination, Bernie could even write terrific science fiction." She slid into her chair.

"Not writer, producer." There was a wild look in his eyes.

"Omar's the producer, Bernie."

"Executive producer. I've always wanted to be a *line* producer," Peshkin confessed.

"Of what?"

The press agent and the sheik exchanged canny glances.

"Of this movie. We can do it. Bernie says we can do it, Wilber says we can do it and I say we can do it! "

She looked exasperated.

"There is no movie. There never was," she reminded them.

"There will be," Peshkin declared firmly. "A terrific war movie —World War Two is *in* again. We've got a million bucks' worth of great footage. Pepe Madrigal is one of the best young cameramen around, and he swears on his mother's *arroz con pollo* that we've got some fabulous stuff. We'll take it back to Burbank and get a script written around it. Brave aviators, nurses with great asses, topless native girls—you can do that and only pull a PG if you make it cultural."

Maybe they could do it; crazier schemes had succeeded in the film industry . . . "Okay, I won't stand in your way. It's your footage anyway. Good luck. Sorry I had to lie to you fellows about what we were doing."

"What *are* you doing?" asked the sheik.

"Don't ask, Omar. You said she told you not to ask, so don't. Two things, Alison. First, I'm used to people lying to me. After all, twenty years a Hollywood press agent . . . I've done some pretty fancy fabricating myself, you know. Old Bernie is one of the top crap artists in show biz."

"You're sweet, Bernie. You sure you're rough enough to be a producer?"

He threw two mock jabs like a boxer. "If the price is right, I'll be a monster. Now the second thing . . . you ask her, Omar, it's your production."

"Will you come to the premiere, please?"

She promised she would, kissed them both and shooed them out with instructions to have their C-130 airborne with all their footage and gear by midnight. Then she went to tell Harry Logan about their scheme, and what she'd seen in town.

"Boti?"

"Leaving the post office as I arrived. I checked. He made a phone call to Bangkok. I don't like it. Who does he know in Thailand?"

"At least one or two of the local hookers. Boti and Otto Kopf have been hitting the local massage parlors every couple or three days—"

"Harry, this isn't funny."

He was exhilarated by the nearness of the mission, feeling much too buoyant to worry.

"And I think now that Machine Gun Jones is scoring with our lovely Haitian nurse. War makes strange bedfellows . . . like you and me."

She reached forward, stroked his cheek. "Harry, you and me is not strange, it's wonderful. But Boti and a phone is dangerous."

"Nobody can stop us now, hon. We'll take off right after Nakamura's dawn run over the valley. It's nearly dark, so there's only tonight before we go."

"This night is serious," she quoted from a favorite poem.

"Louis Simpson," Logan identified. "Wrote a lot of good stuff about my war. He was with an airborne infantry outfit, I think."

It was nice to have a man who read poetry, but frustrating to have one who did not realize what sort of forces the intelligence organization of any major power could mobilize in hours . . . "Harry, I want to seal the base and cut off phone calls out of here. Okay?"

"You're the security chief." He excused himself to check on the combat-readiness of the bombers, especially the fifth B-17 named Raunchy Rita, which had arrived only six days earlier. She found Agajanian, gave him orders to isolate the airfield and establish additional defenses.

"Who're we expecting?" the accountant asked.

"Does it matter?"

"Hell, no. All those different Cong're same to me."

Five years from now—if he was alive—he'd be referring to armed burglars in Burbank and violent cycle gangs in Denver as "Cong." It was a category now. While Agajanian summoned Hovde and Evans and Arroyo—he'd gotten tight with the Navaho—she went to find Santee.

"Time for me to go," he said simply.

"That's what I came to tell you. You wouldn't want to be here tomorrow. After dinner, collect most of the Thai staff and tell them we're giving everybody a day off because it's . . . an American holiday. Washington's birthday ought to do."

"Ought to do fine."

"Frank, explain that to celebrate we'll pay wages up to the end of the week—tonight."

He nodded gravely.

"All we'll need tomorrow morning are a couple of cooks," she explained, "and we'll send them into town right after breakfast. I don't want any innocents to get burned on this."

They shook hands.

"Back to the travel agency?"

"I must think . . ."

"Thank you for helping us."

"It was probably a mistake. We make so many. Say good-bye to Logan." He smiled. ". . . and may peace and happiness, new bride, be yours." He was reciting from the Buddhist wedding ritual.

There was suppressed excitement in the air at the base that night. All but a few of the men believed that one of the important scenes in the movie was to be filmed, and this time their bombing and strafing would be immortalized for movie-theater and later television audiences around the world. As they finished eating, the crews joked and boasted and teased.

"Now you pay 'tenshun, son," Mayberry told Crockett Duckworth, " 'cause we got to get it right first time. Making movies costs a ton, so we can't afford any SNAFUs."

"What's a SNAFU?"

"You're a baby, boy. Standard military term back when men were men—the Big Shoot-Out. Means . . . lessee . . . Situation Normal, All Fucked Up. Some kind of a goof. We blamed 'em on gremlins."

"That's a car," the young Texan said, pleased with himself.

Somebody guffawed.

"Didn't used to be in '44," Baranovitch said gently. "Was some kind of nasty little spirit or spook."

"Spook is CIA," Kopf declared with confidence.

"Only recently," Mayberry said . . . "Crockett, we got a generation problem, but we're both southern gentlemen and we'll solve it together. You gotta learn these expressions. My brother is a distinguished professor of drama at Vanderbilt University, and *he* knows SNAFU. He knows ruptured duck—that's the discharge pin. Son, not being familiar with this kinda talk is like not knowing Rita Hayworth—"

"Who's Rita Hayworth?"

That was when Van Bokkelen tossed the champagne at him. They all laughed and shouted epithets, and wandered to the "club" to down the maximum allowance of two drinks Logan had imposed earlier in the week.

"I don't believe this," the gray-haired United Airlines retiree said as he punched the button on the jukebox. What came out hadn't been on the machine three days earlier . . . Bing Crosby singing "White Christmas."

Clarkson understood. That record meant the second week of December 1944—the time of the bloody raid on Düsseldorf. Now another bombing attack led by Logan, this time to devastate a drug convoy, was about to happen. The teacher looked around, saw Van Bokkelen grinning, and guessed that he understood too.

"It's going down, Charlie," Van Bokkelen said, nodding.

"I suppose."

"Be honest. Did you ever really think he'd do it?"

"Logan always does it, if he wants it seriously. Remember?"

Von Bokkelen thought back, shrugged.

"By the way, I'm glad you're with us, Van."

"Me? Why? Even Harry will tell you I'm bad news. You must have received some good mail today."

Clarkson touched the breast pocket of his shirt, thought of the three letters that had come in a clump from Alex. He had worried that Alex might have gotten restless, found some other person, though that wasn't really likely. Alex wasn't terribly strong, but he was loyal. No, their relationship was firm and the letters made Clarkson feel a lot better.

"You're not bad news, Van. You're flashy, but you're not half as bad as you pretend. I've met some rotten people, and I know.

"On a rotten scale of one to ten, where would you rate me, Charlie?"

"I don't like to rate people. I don't even rate Harry."

Van Bokkelen jerked his thumb toward the jukebox. "Harry's easy. He's like Irving Berlin—number one. Plenty of other fine songwriters, lots of people who don't realize Berlin created all those terrific songs—but the composers and the lyricists know he's the champ. Well, lots of fliers since our war, but the old pros—including guys with three stars in big offices in the Pentagon—know there was never anyone better than Logan."

"You admire Harry the way I do."

"Charlie, I'm burning up with jealousy. I hate his guts," Van Bokkelen announced, and returned to his table. . . .

There was the usual grumbling when the bar was closed at ten, but everyone wandered off to bed without too much argument because tomorrow's briefing would be half an hour earlier. Nobody explained why the schedule was being changed, but that wasn't surprising. After all, it was established protocol that commanders never told fighting men what was going on, and Logan was running this whole deal in a highly military manner.

Blue Leader did not go to sleep, and neither did Alison Gordon. He was over in the hangars and on the flight line, going over every detail with the armorers and maintenance chiefs. She drove a jeep from defense post to defense post, checking the perimeter. The front and rear gate positions were secure, but there were a dozen other places to check this cool clear night. She looked up at the perfect yellow orb hanging in the sky, wondered about tomorrow's weather.

What would it be like over Dead Moon Valley?

What if Logan were wrong, and the old Chinese outfoxed him?

At 11:20 she was driving slowly toward the four large fuel tanks when she saw something moving. She swung her night binoculars to her eyes, stopped the vehicle for a better look. It was a man, crouched low and running in spurts toward the outer fence. She let the glasses fall, rammed the jeep into gear and gunned the motor to top speed.

An intruder?

Her instincts had been right—her female instinct and that other one she'd developed during those years with the Agency. The intruder heard the noise of the approaching vehicle, rose to his feet and ran. Suddenly she saw another one scuttling along twenty or thirty yards off to the left. Driving with her right hand, she pulled the .357 from its holster and took aim.

The first bullet missed, but the second spun him like a top. The third shot merely grazed him, made him break stride, but he stumbled on. The fourth drilled a one-inch hole in the middle of his back. He fell forward like a sack of sand. She spun the wheel, pointed the Magnum at the second intruder, squeezed the trigger.

The gun jammed.

The invader's gun did not. A slug shattered the jeep's windshield, another hit the engine. She jerked the wheel back and forth, zigzagging toward the man, constantly shifting her body to offer less of a target. His third and fourth bullets missed completely. He was panicking. He saw her moving nearer and nearer, closing the gap. He dropped his pistol and bolted.

She ran him down, the jeep smashing him into the air, a tangle of shattered bones. Seizing the walkie-talkie on the seat beside her, she sounded the alarm.

"Armed intruders. Red alert. Armed intruders near the fuel dump. Red alert. Send up flares. Security team to the gas tanks. Let's go!"

She sounded the siren on the jeep. Men responded swiftly on foot and in vehicles. Three flares hung in the night, illuminating the entire east side of the base. It was not only the regular security force that responded. A dozen fliers not yet asleep grabbed their sidearms and ran to help. They fanned out to search the whole area around the dump. Some moved to the tanks to search for delayed-action bombs. Minutes ticked by.

"Looks okay," Hovde's scratchy voice reported over the radio. "We've checked the bases of three tanks and—"

A ball of fire interrupted. The fourth tank went up like a giant blowtorch. Hovde was saying they'd successfully removed incendiary devices from three tanks, but nobody was listening. The ambulance and fire engine charged through the night, and now teams were battling the blaze and searching for casualties. They were still pouring foam on the conflagration and pumping water on adjacent tanks when Dr. Fishman gave Logan the score.

"One dead, Harry. Guerrero, the Argentinian who brought up one of the planes right after Christmas—burned almost beyond recognition. Drucker has a broken leg. He fell. Our Navaho friend got quite a scorching, might have died if Otto here hadn't dragged him out. Went right into the burning gasoline to save him."

Logan looked at the German. "Otto, how's your arm?"

"The bandage is nothing, colonel. This doctor treats me as an infant. A minor burn, I assure you. I give my word I'm fit to fly."

Logan turned to Fishman. "What do you say, doc?"

"It's nasty, but more painful than serious. I wouldn't *recommend* that a patient in that shape use the arm for a week. However, I bet he'd kill somebody if we ground him now. I think I know what he's feeling. I'll give him anesthetic ointment. Let him fly."

Logan stared off at the burning tank. "It's a question of the safety of the bird and the success of the mission. Honor has nothing to do with it—"

"The hell it doesn't," Alison Gordon said.

"My conscience? Okay, it has something to do with it. Otto, if you find that it hurts too much—"

"Thank you, colonel. Thank you," Kopf said, pleased, and climbed into the back of the ambulance.

"That Kraut still suspects I killed his poppa," Logan told her.

"You're all crazy. I just happen to love you, Harry, but every one of you is stark raving. We aren't out of the woods yet, you know. There could be more time fuses, or more saboteurs out there."

"Who the hell are they?"

"Can't tell. All I can say is time is our worst enemy, and we'd better get out of here as soon as possible."

Logan gave orders that all personnel not attached to a bomber crew or serving a critical maintenance or refueling role be flown out within three hours on the old C-54 or the large C-130 chartered by Baroodi. Twenty-six men were paid off and airborne in the C-54 by one A.M., none of them quite sure what was happening.

"I'm not going on any cargo plane," Dr. Fishman insisted.

"You've got to go with Drucker and Arroyo. They need care, and doctors don't abandon patients. Pack your sack, Noah, and don't argue," she said.

"Harry," he appealed. "You promised me I'd fly with you as a waist gunner."

She shook her head. "I said it before. You men are all adolescent loonies. Give it to him straight, Harry. Tell him where to shove this gray-haired hero act."

"Next war," Logan promised. "My solemn oath, Noah. Next war I find, you're in."

The physician glared at her. "If I didn't like you, Alison, I'd tell you what a bitch you are."

"I'm glad you like me, Noah. I like you too. Pack."

Dr. Fishman, Arroyo, the Haitian nurse, the corpse and the entire movie group were all prepared to board the transport at a quarter to three. They didn't. There was an electrical problem somewhere in the left inboard engine. The C-130 couldn't take off before seven at the earliest. Maintenance crews worked on the engine all night, and Alison Gordon checked and rechecked the perimeter.

The next attack would be coming soon.

The only question—the crucial question—was when.

47

AT TEN MINUTES to six, Nakamura took off in the Zero, heading due east. His course was direct for Dead Moon Valley. The Red Chinese frontier radar stations tracked him every inch of the way. The bombs were in the racks on the B-17s, the machine guns loaded and extra ammo stacked. A team of electricians was completing the installation of the minicamera in the nose of Dirty Dora, and the aircrews were dressing in flying gear. Some thirty-five minutes later they began to wander toward the mess hall, when Elroy Evans reached them with Logan's unexpected instructions.

Pack all clothes and personal gear for immediate departure.

The fliers and maintenance crews were surprised. Veterans such as Ashley and Baranovitch asked no questions, but Crockett Duckworth wanted to know what was going on and where they were going.

"Going to work," Van Bokkelen predicted.

"What's he talking about, Elroy?" the young Texan asked.

"I'm just the messenger boy. Colonel Logan will give it to you at the briefing after breakfast. Truck's coming by in fifteen minutes to pick up your stuff."

The truck arrived, and while the men ate and speculated the baggage was loaded into the C-130 beside the cameras and the precious cans of combat-flying footage. Several of the fliers wanted to query Logan about this unexpected development, but he was nowhere in sight. He was in the radio room with Alison Gordon, waiting. They smoked, sipped coffee and hoped.

At one minute after seven they heard the voice of the Japanese fighter pilot. It was barely audible at first, but suddenly it broke through the crackling static.

271

"Zeke to Harry. Zeke to Harry. Weather forecast correct. Weather forecast correct. Rain two miles from farm. Should reach farm in about an hour. Moving slowly. Much rain. Exactly as you predicted, Harry. Visibility not good, scattered clouds at 3,000. Going down. Do you read me, Harry?"

The convoy was about to enter the valley.

Logan took the microphone.

"Read you loud and clear. Do not descend. Repeat, do not descend. Weather too dangerous. Return to base immediately."

Nakamura acknowledged the order, and obeyed.

Logan embraced Alison, squeezed her tightly. "We're going to do it, and after we finish here we'll take care of that other business."

"What other business?"

"The love, honor and obey business . . . simple gold bands okay?"

She was joyous, and very afraid. "Harry, about Mark—"

"You'll have to think about me now. Your days as a sexy widow are just about over."

Should she tell him they'd never found the body of her first husband, that there was a chance in a thousand he might be alive somewhere—perhaps not far from here in a Viet Nam prison or mental institution? Why did she still torment—or was it indulge—herself with these anxieties? Mark was legally dead, and Logan was alive, in every way . . . Why should the idea of marrying the man she loved so completely make her want to tell him her uncertainties and imperfections . . .?

"Simple gold bands will be fine," she replied.

They kissed again, and Logan left for the briefing room.

In Bangkok, MacBride was anxious too. He had been up most of the night because the pieces just did not fit. He sorted and resorted, shuffled and reshuffled all the bits of information and wondered why he could not assemble them properly. One fragment of the jigsaw was missing. What was it that was troubling him? Wong's force was across the frontier convoying another large opium caravan, and when the Sixth Army returned it would be well enough rearmed and supplied to defend itself for a full year. In that period, the ungrateful bureaucrats and diplomatic planners might change their minds and come to their senses. They had to see what America *owed* the aged general and his remaining soldiers.

Those pieces fit, but there was something else.

It was up there in the northwest, but what was it? That disturbing woman was up there with those sentimental fools making the World War Two movie. No problem there. The film company had proper permits to rent the abandoned base and import the old planes, valid licenses to bring in all their equipment, vehicles, antique arms and even the live bombs.

That was it.

He telephoned the police headquarters in Chiang Mai, asked for the chief.

"He is not in right now, sir," the sergeant on duty told him.

"When is he due?"

"Soon. May I take your name and number, sir?"

"MacBride. He has my number. Maybe you can answer a question for me."

These foreigners were pushy. This one spoke superior Thai, much better than most, but he was just as aggressive as the others . . . "I'll try," the irritated sergeant mumbled.

"That movie company? Where do their planes fly?"

"East, sir. They fly east toward the border, every day. Must be boring. I suppose they film the same scenes over and over until they get exactly what they want."

"Do they have all the required permits, sergeant?"

"Yes, and all countersigned by senior officers in the capital." . . . It was never easy to get these garrulous Westerners off the phone.

"Including the permit for bombing?"

This American was an idiot. "We do *not* license people to drop bombs on Thai territory," the sergeant pointed out.

Then where and what would they bomb? "Sergeant, this is important. Please tell the chief that these foreigners are not here to make a movie. They are criminals, agents for some other power. Maybe they're Russians. He's got to go out to the field immediately—at once—and arrest them all. It's *urgent.*"

"I'll give him the message, Mr. Maglide."

"MacBride, you fool—sorry, sergeant, didn't mean to be rude. Please accept my apology and give the message to the chief. He can phone me, collect. This is very important—"

"I'll tell him the moment he returns. Any time now, sir."

MacBride hung up the phone. This was, he decided, obviously a Peking operation. He'd repeatedly warned those smug desk jockeys that the Chinese Reds were not to be trusted, but they'd brushed him off as an hysterical "old line" anti-Communist obsessive. They hadn't said it to his face, not quite. Still, he'd known for a long time that the glib advocates of détente—the trendies of the chic Georgetown cocktail party set—thought of him as paranoid. They hadn't battled Communist subversion and aggression in Asia, and they couldn't even imagine how tricky and violent the Reds could be. They had broken Angleton and the others, hadn't they?

Yes, it had to be the Red Chinese—but why now?

Because Peking had learned that the little Sixth Army was about to get stronger, and wanted to deliver a knockout blow first. Perhaps there was unrest in the southern provinces. Maybe the Communists feared that Wong could recruit new soldiers, light a spark that might set the whole frontier on fire . . . and as these thoughts tumbled through his mind he realized what he had to do.

He could hardly risk everything by counting on that dull sergeant to get the message to the police chief swiftly enough. He could just catch the 8:40 flight to Chiang Mai if he hurried. He picked up his car keys, walked quickly to the '76 Ford in the alley and started the engine for the nine-mile trip to the airport. The damn morning traffic was heavy, but he drove boldly, cutting in and out, sometimes riding up on the shoulder to circle slow-moving columns of vehicles. He had to make that plane, and concentrating as he was, he did not notice the blue Pontiac that was following . . .

Thank God, there was the field less than a mile ahead. He glanced at his watch, heart pounding. Yes, he'd done it, he'd catch the plane with a few minutes to spare.

As he swung the Ford into the airport parking lot, the police chief was sauntering into his office at Chiang Mai provincial headquarters. He listened to the message, nodded.

"Urgent?"

"He said *immediately,* sir."

The chief hesitated for a few moments. "He isn't the sort to panic. Get my car and a dozen men. No, twenty. Let's go."

The C-130 was ready, and the last of the passengers were boarding. Alison Gordon was surprised to see Ashley escorting Marlene Duckworth to the plane, even more startled to observe the graying Englishman kiss her good-bye.

"I had no idea," Alison said.

Marlene smiled almost demurely. "We've been . . . I know I fooled around with some other—it happened kind of fast, and slow too. He's the nicest guy I've met in years, Al. Not just after my ass, if you know what I mean."

"I know what you mean."

Ashley was stowing her bag in the plane.

"These English guys are kind of classy. This one is, and he's even a gentleman. He wants to do the whole number, church wedding and everything.

"You'll make a lovely bride."

"I always did," she chuckled. "You think he's too old for me?"

"Hell, no. He's perfect."

"Al, I don't expect *perfect* anymore. I think I'm growing up."

"It's not easy. Congratulations."

She bit her lower lip. "What kind of place is Norfolk?"

Alison thought of the countryside and the English weather, the rains and the rotten winters that often lasted seven or eight months. Could a young woman used to the sun and heat of Las Vegas survive? "It's beautiful, Marlene. Pretty country, lots of flowers and charm."

"I like flowers. Bye, Al."

Marlene Duckworth kissed her future husband, boarded the C-130.

"Thank you, Miss Gordon," Ashley said. "She's marvelous, isn't she?

"Terrific. Congratulations . . . best wishes."

The cargo plane's engines sounded, and it began to taxi as the Englishman and Alison Gordon walked quickly away. There was Jones, waving farewell to the Haitian nurse. Maybe something would work out for them too. Maybe life really could be one of those good old movies where LoveConqueredAll. Probably not. After all, they didn't make those films anymore. . . .

She was in the briefing room with Logan when Nakamura entered.

"Fine work, major. You'd better get your plane refueled immediately.

"Another mission?"

"No, we're pulling out. Miss Gordon has your final paycheck, and a going away present."

She handed him two envelopes. He opened both.

"I don't understand, colonel . . ."

"As they say in Beverly Hills, wear it in good health. It's a good fit, isn't it?"

"Miss Gordon?" Nakamura appealed to her.

"That's what they say—especially on Rodeo Drive. You'll look splendid in it, don't you think?"

"These are the ownership papers for the Zero!"

"All yours. We don't need it anymore, and you're certainly the right guy to have it."

Japanese officers were not supposed to have emotions, certainly not to show them. Nakamura fought to contain his.

"This is . . . I never . . . you are very generous, colonel."

"Crazy Americans. They always overtip. I have one final order for you, major."

"Yes, sir?"

"I want that bird out of here in thirty minutes, and out of the country as soon as possible. If you don't, the Thai government may seize it. Oh, and stay out of Burma. Go south or east—fast. Goodbye, major, and give my regards to the Imperial Air Force."

Nakamura went out of the room, about three inches off the floor. As he left, the bomber crews poured in and found seats in the first five rows of the folding chairs.

"*Sawadee Krap,* that's what she said," a bombardier told his friend.

"Means *welcome,*" Mercer Davis translated from the next row.

"*Krap* or *clap?* Just pray you didn't pick up a dose," a machine gunner advised.

Logan walked to the podium.

"Settle down. Okay, this is a classified briefing. Clear? Anything you hear in the next ten minutes is secret—top secret. Permanently. You will never speak of it to anyone."

The men stirred in their seats.

"Anyone who can't accept this should leave right now. You'll get your money, and no flak. Just pick up your marbles and go."

Crockett Duckworth turned to Baranovitch. "Sounds better'n pinball, don't it?"

"Those who stay and go with us will each receive a bonus of $5,000 and a ticket home. You've got thirty seconds to decide."

One man stood up as if to leave, hesitated and sat down.

Logan leaned over to speak softly to Alison Gordon. "Have you alerted *Bolivar?*"

She nodded.

"Okay, let's get down to business," he continued. "A few of you signed on just to help make a war movie. Most of you took the job

276

with the understanding that after we finished filming in Thailand we'd fly on to Africa to do some real bombing. Well, as they say in the movies—this is it. We're going to do that bombing—only it's today."

A low murmur swept the room.

"This isn't a political thing. No government is involved. Our target is across the border in Burma, in a place called Dead Moon Valley. It's a caravan of mules hauling opium to a lab where some people will first turn it into morphine, and then into heroin."

More sounds of excitement, surprise.

"Big caravan. More than six hundred mules, with maybe eight hundred or a thousand armed mercenaries riding shotgun. Could be two hundred fifty kilos of heroin if they get to that lab. Our job is to blast them first."

"Right on," Jones shouted. "Sorry, colonel . . ."

"Don't be sorry. Just be good with that .50. We're going to bomb them first, then go in to finish the job strafing at low altitude."

"Three hundred feet," Boti said.

"You got it. They've got plenty of machine guns, light and heavy. No antiaircraft stuff as far as we know. We don't know everything. I wouldn't want to kid you. Before we get to the pictures and the model of the place, are there any questions?"

"How fast will this caravan be moving?"

"At the speed of mules carrying eighteen or twenty kilos each—about two or three miles an hour."

"Those automatic weapons? Are they set up for antiaircraft fire?" Ashley asked.

"I don't think so, but I'm told the men carrying them are experienced combat veterans. They've got good officers, so don't expect a picnic. We will have—I think—one major advantage. Tactical surprise."

He looked directly at Boti.

In a fourth floor office many thousands of miles away, two intelligence specialists were discussing a freshly decoded radio message from Bangkok.

"Should we tell the Burmese, Vincent?" the senior officer wondered.

"They'd only be rude, sir."

"The Burmese are a terribly polite people with a fine and ancient civilization."

"Who are rude to us at every opportunity. Elegantly rude, insufferably rude and endlessly rude. Is that proper socialism?"

The older man shrugged, wondered why this government building *still* wasn't adequately heated.

"Let's not discuss isms, Vincent."

"Very well, the Burmese could be snotty. How about sharing this bizarre morsel with the CIA boys?"

"They're not much better than the bloody Burmese."

It was sad, but true. "Of course, we can't be one hundred percent sure this is accurate. What do we pay this fellow?"

"A lot less than the CIA did, sir. £200 a month, and a bonus for important bits. Perhaps we could trade this to the CIA for an electric typewriter. Our machine's a ruin."

The senior officer stood up wearily. "Or a decent heater. I've a date with Ostrander over at their embassy. I'll try it on him."

It was probably rubbish, Group Commander Sanderson thought as he reached for his raincoat and umbrella. The whole affair was as depressing as the London weather. After all, how much stock could anyone—even those information-mad Yanks—put in a report from a £200-a-month Cuban?

48

LOGAN FINISHED explaining the geography of Dead Moon Valley, repeated his warning about the dangerous peaks at either end . . . "And that's it. Any final questions?"

Van Bokkelen rose. "Colonel?"

"Yes, Van?"

"Aren't you going to say it? For General Steele's sake?"

"You always want the last word. You say it."

"But you're the CO, Harry."

Only a few men in the room, and the one woman, understood.

"You always wanted to be the CO too," Logan reminded him. "Be my guest."

Van Bokkelen faced the bomber crews. "Maximum effort!"

"Maximum effort!" all eighteen alumni of the Bloody 100th gave back to him.

"Maximum effort!" Van Bokkelen shouted again.

This time *everyone* in the room thundered back the slogan.

It was like a football team that had just had a rousing halftime Knut Rockne pep talk. Only more so. The aircrews ran out of the briefing room, some still shouting the contagious words. These were no longer just mercenaries. Now, as Logan had planned and hoped, they had taken on the spirit of this unique mission . . .

Alison walked to Dirty Dora with Logan.

"You really want to do this?" he asked.

"Whither thou goest . . ."

"Don't get mad, hon, but you know it could be dangerous—"

"Why else would I put on this ridiculous flak jacket?" she replied as she struggled with the catches of the flexible plastic body armor. "I must look awful in this thing."

"Let's hope you don't have to put on a chute," he said.

"I look like a teddy bear, Harry."

He smiled. "You're sure you know how to handle a .50?"

"Lover, I've been checked out on more types of machine guns than you have teeth—and you're short one gunner. Rest easy. I was working .50s when you were giving flying lessons to horny old ladies."

Before he could reply she started to climb up into the fuselage. He followed her, showed her her gun and checked on her oxygen and intercom lines.

Eight minutes later Dirty Dora led the small force of 17s up into the sky.

Fourteen minutes later the radio operator and five mechanics who would attend to refueling when the Forts returned—the only men left at the base—heard the sound of engines. Three. They looked up, saw the C-130 limp in for a landing. The defective engine had malfunctioned in flight. The mechanics rushed to repair it. They were still working when the truck and car loaded with Chiang Mai police arrived.

"Where are the bombers?" the police chief demanded. Like most Thais, he was usually extremely polite but the flat-tire-induced delay had frayed his composure.

"My name is Bernie Peshkin," the press agent volunteered. "I'm the publicist . . . and producer . . . line producer for a *major* motion picture being made by Golden Crescent Productions. This is our executive producer, Sheik Omar Baroodi."

The police chief nodded to the Arab and the pair of eye-catching women, both obviously starlets.

"The film will be called *Vengeance Squadron,*" Peshkin continued.

"Mr. Peshkin, that's very nice. Where are the bombers?"

"They're gone," the executive producer answered for him.

"When are they coming back?"

"I don't think they'll be back at all," Baroodi said quickly.

"They took their laundry and everything," added Peshkin.

The police chief of Chiang Mai—like his colleagues on other forces around the world—prided himself on being a great stud and a fine judge of character. These two men were lying. Obviously.

"We'll wait," he announced, and assigned men to take over the telephone switchboard and the radio room. Marksmen were sent to concealed positions, and the chief himself settled down behind

280

Logan's desk to make his call to Bangkok.

Thirty-one rings, but no answer at the home.

Thirty-four rings, and no one picked up at the shop.

It was obvious that MacBride was out—somewhere.

In point of fact—as Ashley would say—MacBride was in . . . trouble. He was also in a rage, and in a small room at Don Muang Airport outside the capital. There were four men with him, the quartet who had followed him here in the blue Pontiac. It didn't make sense. What the hell was Gannett doing here—now—with three armed agents?

"Todd, I don't think Satchmo understands. I've got to get up to Chiang Mai. Every second counts," MacBride was pleading.

"The Man With the Shades understands. He wants to see you in Manila. This afternoon."

"He's in Manila? Okay, but what about those bombers? Who's going to stop them?"

"I will. Tell me what has to be done and I'll attend to it personally. I'll fly up on the embassy plane."

MacBride spelled it all out, explained that he had alerted the police chief and diagrammed his reasoning and suspicions. It was encouraging that Gannett understood so quickly and clearly, and MacBride felt much better by the time he boarded the U.S. military jet for Clark Field near Manila. Gannett did not fly north to Chiang Mai on the embassy plane or any other aircraft. He drove back with the three armed men to CIA headquarters in the Thai capital to report to the station officer that the lies had worked and MacBride was no longer a problem. Of course there might be some unpleasantness when MacBride found that The Man With the Shades was not at Clark Field, but that was nothing for Satchmo to worry about. By then, the problem would belong to the station officer in Manila and the operation would be over in any case.

It was only a matter of hours.

"Navigator to pilot. Navigator to pilot. Frontier dead ahead."

"E.T.A. target area?" Logan asked.

"At current airspeed, sixteen minutes, colonel."

"Thanks. Did you get that, bombardier?"

"Roger, colonel."

Logan looked over at Clarkson, smiled.

"You're feeling good, Harry?"

"Great, like a twenty-five-year-old. You?"

Clarkson hesitated for just a second.

"Fine, Harry. Strange how it all came back so fast after all these years."

"For me I don't think it ever really left. They took away our 17s for a while, but now it's back in the saddle again." Unembarrassed, he broke into the last phrase of the Gene Autry classic with youthful gusto. Clarkson automatically registered 1940, the year the cowboy star wrote it and made it his theme song. Logan sang it, all of it, as if the intervening thirty-nine years had never been.

"Pilot to tail gunner. Pilot to tail gunner. Everybody in formation, Jonesy?"

"Bet your ass, colonel."

Logan laughed. "You're supposed to say 'Roger,' but who cares? Pilot to all gun positions. We're leaving Thai airspace in less than one minute. I'll let you know when you can test-fire. Turret gunners, set target dimension dials on K sights. Acknowledge."

They did.

"You okay, Alison?"

"Roger, colonel, but your airplane isn't that comfortable and I'm not too wild about your slipcovers."

"What slipcovers?"

"Fly the bird, Harry, and leave the shooting to us."

Three minutes later all the gunners squirted off bursts, reported the .50s were functioning properly. Two minutes after that, Logan told the radio operator to switch to the special frequency to alert the relay that the transmission was about to begin.

"Relay notified, colonel."

"Turn it on, Charlie," Logan ordered, and Clarkson closed a red switch that no other B-17 in history had ever carried.

The color was excellent, the image bright and sharp.

"That's some picture," Miss White exclaimed.

"We spent enough on that goddam satellite," General M. E. Steele, USAAF, Retired, replied.

It was cool in the air-conditioned command post, but Dr. Milton Steiner was starting to perspire. It was really happening, just the way he had planned it. He had given Steele many other ideas and proposals and possible solutions to complex problems, but so few of them were ever implemented. Despite their logic and solid statistical support, most of them fell away somewhere, somehow. It was almost shocking—sitting here in the Bahamas—to see this one move from briefing paper to hard fact on the television screen.

Suddenly the focus began to shift.

The jungle seemed clearer, nearer.

"He's going down to three or four hundred feet to dodge under the frontier radar," Steele explained.

The Chinese radar operators noticed the same swift descent—and then the blips were gone.

"They're off the screen," one sergeant told the major in command.

"Impossible."

"They're gone. It looked as if the entire flight lost altitude simultaneously."

"Then it's a maneuver, not an accident. Where are they?" the major demanded.

The two radar technicians exchanged embarrassed glances. "They *were* about twenty-five miles inside Burma, heading west," one said uneasily.

"And they could be flying north right this minute to attack us." The major took up the telephone, advised the commander of the nearby fighter base of the threat. Two flights of MIG-23s were ordered to scramble immediately. Yes, those thousand-mile-an-hour jets with their heat-seeking missiles could blow those aged prop-driven bombers right out of the skies. . . .

The B-17s droned on at two hundred miles an hour. Logan sneaked a glance at his wristwatch, calculated rapidly. If Wong hadn't changed his route again, two-thirds or perhaps three-quarters of the long line of mules should already be in the valley. It was make or break now. They'd know in four minutes.

It was time to climb to bombing altitude.

He waggled the 17's wings to signal the others, pulled back the control and pointed Dirty Dora's nose fifty degrees up. He could just make out the peaks at the entrance to the pass into the valley.

"You're not just blowing in my ear?" Major General Sanford Mendenhall asked as he entered the office.

"Sandy, this was your idea," The Man With the Shades reminded. "You said you'd flown with the Bloody 100th and you insisted you wanted to be here. I'm doing you a favor."

"Bullshit. I'm a deputy director just like you, and there's no way you could keep me out no matter how damn top secret this job is. I think you're full of crap, but I'm rooting for the boys anyway."

The skies over Virginia were leaden, but The Man With the Shades knew it wouldn't snow—not here. There was a foot on the ground in Cambridge, two up on the Dartmouth campus at Hanover. Not a millimeter in this lousy moderate climate, he silently mourned.

"Rooting? Are you sick, Sandy?"

"Yeah, rooting. What the fuck would you know? You've been a spook all your adult life. You never flew a 17. You never flew anything but the flag on the Fourth of July . . ."

The Man With the Shades drummed his fingers on the desk. He'd always believed that it was a mistake for the Agency to take in senior military and naval officers on three- or four-year loans. Even the smartest ones had that "blow 'em up" mentality, that visceral reaction to the promise of battle. The door opened, and Doris Kraft entered.

"Don't you knock anymore?"

She ignored his challenge, feeling compassion for his puffy eyes and painful stomach. The poor man was exhausted.

"Cyclops says come quickly," she reported.

He got to his feet, pointed at her. "You'll want to see this, Doris. Your friend Alison is giving a party and you shouldn't miss it."

Why was his voice so harsh and angry? She knew better than to ask . . . She followed him and Mendenhall up the corridor some twenty yards to a locked door. He produced a strange-looking key, opened the heavy metal barrier, led them inside, then locked the door from the inside and threw a steel bolt. There were five chairs in the room. A young woman sat in one, and Doris Kraft recognized her as someone called Pyle or Kyle. Yes, Peggy Kyle. She was staring at a twenty-five-inch television set on a table ten feet away: A sprawling aerial view of a mass of light green, with a wiggly worm that had to be a jungle river on the lower left side of the screen. Twin peaks at the mouth of a valley, with stumpy hills framing the sides beyond.

"Came on a couple of minutes ago, sir," Peggy Kyle noted.

Sir—just like that Arthur Castillo.

"Holy shit!"

"This is General Mendenhall. He always talks like that," Doris explained.

"Holy shit, it's *happening*," the Air Force officer repeated.

284

The secretary of state should be proud of himself. The sanctimonious son of a bitch had said, "*Let* them wipe out the Sixth Army, let them get rid of Wong's politically bothersome remnants for us and we'll come out of it clean." Clean? That was a laugh. ". . . three thousand, no more than four," Mendenhall estimated. "At that height he can't miss . . . what's the name of this place . . . ?"

"Dead Moon Valley—that's it, Charlie," Logan said.

He switched on his radio.

"Blue Leader to Blue Flight. Target dead ahead. Here we go . . ."

There they were.

Hundreds and hundreds of men and animals—long lines of dots in three parallel columns winding across the valley floor. The geography below looked just like the pictures, Logan thought, as the vision of that sand-table model jumped into his mind. . . .

"Dead Moon Valley," said Steiner, who also remembered the maps and photos.

"Don't miss, Harry," Steele urged, as if Logan could hear him. The people in that room in the Bahamas and the other one at CIA headquarters could hear Logan clearly. The satellite circuit was functioning perfectly.

"Cyclops . . . that's the name for the Atlas satellite monitoring operation, general," Doris Kraft volunteered.

Mendenhall paid no attention to her. He was totally focused on the television screen.

"It's all yours, bombardier," they heard Logan say over the intercom.

"Bomb bay doors open. Just hold her steady and fly her straight . . . steady . . . steady . . ."

The Chinese soldiers and the mule drivers heard the thunder of a score of 1,000-horsepower Wright engines, looked up and saw five relatively small aircraft—small by modern standards—drifting slowly across the cloud-stained sky. Wong studied them himself, sensing something familiar and trying to identify the craft.

"Cargo planes, general?" an aide asked.

"Five. Why five—here? Do the Burmese use such machines to drop paratroopers?" Wong wondered.

"Too small for that, general. They look harmless to me."

The column trudged on through the heat. The stench of sweating mules was strong. Tired men forced themselves ahead with the encouraging thought that the laboratory was less than nine miles beyond the far end of the valley.

Wong suddenly remembered.

B-17s . . . And he now saw the sun glint on the tiny metal things falling, and he *knew.*

"Air attack, sound the alarm to disperse—"

While the aide relayed the message by the field radio strapped on the communications mule, the young bugler who always accompanied Wong swung his polished instrument to his lips, played and replayed the call that warned of enemy aircraft. It echoed up and down the valley, shocking the troopers into swift action.

But the bombs fell even more quickly. Five-hundred-pounders that blasted soldiers and animals into the air as if they were miniature toys from Crackerjack boxes. Antipersonnel canisters that hurled out thousands of deadly metal balls, scything across the valley floor and ripping flesh with scientific efficiency. Stunned men stared at the stumps of fingers, groped at holes in stomachs and faces. A mule driver screamed, clutched at the ruins of his genitals and fell rolling on the ground. Animals with broken legs, others with blood spouting from where ears or eyes had been, tottered on crazily.

The bugle sang again and again, its brassy song mingling with the screams of the men, the brays of the terrified mules.

The fifth Fort salvoed its high explosives. When Dirty Dora reached the far end of the valley, Logan threw it into a sharp turn and led the bombers back to strike again. This time it was more of the canisters—and napalm. Sixth Army troopers busy taking cover, others setting up their .30- and .50-caliber machine guns, were splattered with globs of instant pain, the burning jelly affecting eyes, chins and necks. . . .

Mendenhall was impressed. "Look at that! Look at the job he's doing!" he said admiringly. It was purely a professional critique. After all, he had nothing against these little figures on the television screen. These electronic images certainly weren't related to the Chinese Nationalist troops and airmen he'd known during his two-year tour of Formosa, as it was then called, in the early sixties. Those were real people, good Joes.

"Finish 'em off," Steele shouted. . . .

Alison Gordon looked down from the waist gunner's post, tried to make out what was going on below. It was difficult to register or judge. Dirty Dora was moving almost too swiftly for her eyes to focus, and she had had little experience with aerial combat. There were many killed and shattered on the floor of the valley. Suddenly she thought of Camus' comment on the 1956 Hungarian uprising. "There are already too many dead in the stadium."

But it wasn't over.

Back at the eastern end of Dead Moon Valley, Logan swung his Fort into a wide circle and the other 17s followed as if linked by umbilical cords.

"Blue Leader to Blue Flight. Blue Leader to Blue Flight. Stand by all gunners. We're going in."

He put the Boeing into a steep dive as it moved in a 180-degree arc and raced back into the valley between the portal peaks. 1,400 . . . 700 . . . 300. . . .

"They're off the screen again," reported the Red Chinese radar operator.

"Our jets are on the way," the angry major replied. . . .

The bombers swept in for the kill.

The Sixth Army troops did not run. They stood their ground and fought. From a hundred knolls, gullies and clumps of underbrush, the infantry fired back with M-16s and submachine guns. Crews of heavier automatic weapons on tripods crouched, poured bullets at the 17s. The flying gun platforms chopped a swath through the Nationalists' ranks, raking them with fire. From the navigator guiding the chin turret in Dirty Dora to the tail gunner of Grable's Legs at the end of the column, Blue Flight came at them . . .

Alison Gordon handled her gun well, squeezing off short bursts whenever she saw a target or flash of defenders' fire. She shot the way she had been taught, without wasting a round. Ignoring the ear-shattering noise of her .50 and the other guns near her, she fired at the opium-bearing caravan, and silently cursed M. E. Steele.

The 17s also took hits. American-made ammo fired by longtime allies in the struggle against Communism ripped into the bowels of Bart Kendall, ruining his comeback chances in TV news.

Keith Ashley wasn't in a position to pay much attention. Too busy flying Raunchy Rita, he could do nothing to help his wounded copilot except summon the radioman over the intercom. "I think he's bought it," Ashley said, "but get up here with the medical kit."

Ashley was right. Sheet-white, Kendall was losing blood at an awful rate. The radioman shook his head after examining the gut wound, plunged a hypodermic of morphine into the arm of the dying man to ease the final moments, then returned to his gun and resumed firing. . . .

The Chinese kept shooting back, knowing that ground troops could not stand up to strafing but determined to take some of the attackers with them. Even General Wong was firing, emptying a submachine gun taken from a fallen lieutenant and then calmly reloading. It was preposterous, almost like the way Custer defied the Sioux hordes with pistol and saber until they hacked him to pieces. . . .

Logan wheeled Dirty Dora again for the final assault. "Blue Leader to Blue Flight. Well done. Repeat, well done. Everything goes this time . . ."

And the old planes charged. As he'd trained them, the pilots shifted from a single-file column to a five-abreast formation and thundered down the valley. . . .

At first The Man With the Shades thought it looked like something out of a World War Two film, then changed his mind. All they needed were the swords and lances and it was a classic cavalry charge. You could almost hear the bugle. . . .

The Sixth Army stood up in its positions, firing every weapon it had. Even the wounded were shooting. Men were triggering rifles, pistols and light mortars. It was hopeless to fire mortar shells at aircraft, but there was just that tiny chance one might strike a plane . . . General Wong was very proud, and he was not finished. Mules were running about in crazed efforts to escape the noise and the flying chunks of metal. Half the animals in the caravan were killed or wounded. The awful noise grew louder, more deafening.

And the mules stampeded. Hundreds of them ran down the valley, trampling and kicking and pounding over any humans in their path. The Forts swept right over them, inflaming the animals even further. General Wong raised a rocket launcher—an infantry weapon used to fight ground troops—to his shoulder. It was an act of pure defiance. He launched the missile a split second before the mules ran him down.

It hit Dirty Dora's left wing. It did not explode, but it lodged there like the banderilla of a bullfighter. Everyone on the plane felt the impact.

"Harry?" she asked.

"It's okay. Nothing to worry about. Just a sweet little rocket stuck in our wing. Stay cool."

"Mother," groaned Jones, who understood the threat.

The armada swept on toward the east end of the battlefield.

Clarkson shook his head. "It's close to the aileron, Harry." They both realized it could explode when Logan adjusted the controls to climb again.

"I think we've got a clean three inches to spare. Two, anyway," Logan said. Gently . . . very gently . . . he pulled back and Dirty Dora began to climb slowly. The peaks loomed ahead, and the navigator wondered whether his wife could cope with widowhood. It was going to be extremely close.

Dirty Dora cleared the rocky peak by no more than ten feet. The crew cheered.

We aren't out of the woods yet, Logan told himself, said nothing.

As the Forts swept over the valley rim, cheering broke out in every plane—even the ones with dead and wounded. They'd done it. They'd smashed the biggest opium caravan of the year, precisely as Logan had trained them to do. Proud of themselves, their skills and their victory, the crews exchanged congratulations. Logan gestured to Clarkson, who turned off the transmitter that had sent the pictures to the Atlas satellite. . . .

"Like I told you, best damn B-17 pilot in the world," Steele said. "You asked for him, Milton, and I got him. Didn't I?"

"Yes, general," the stunned scientist acknowledged.

"Blew the hell out of the bastards who killed my grandson, didn't he?"

"He certainly did."

"I knew he would. Wasn't it terrific?" he asked Miss White.

"I've never seen anything like it." It was an evasion he missed.

"You never will. Logan's the greatest. Let's have a drink."

Steiner explained he "had some things to clean up," and Miss White promised to join the general in his living room in a few minutes.

"Congratulations, Milton," she said after Steele left.

"Honestly, I never expected . . . I mean, on paper . . . God, did you see all those bodies? Didn't he see them?"

"You'll get a bonus," she predicted.

"You saw them, didn't you?"

She stood up, smoothed her skirt.

"Milton, I saw them the moment you proposed the idea," she replied, and walked out of the room.

"May I have the tape?" The Man With the Shades asked.

"We usually send these to central files."

"Give it to me," he insisted, and Peggy Kyle obeyed.

Without saying another word, he unlocked the door and started up the corridor. Doris Kraft and Mendenhall followed, and neither spoke until they entered her office. At the door to his private office, The Man With the Shades turned to face her.

She opened her mouth to speak, couldn't think of anything to say. She looked at him helplessly, blinking to keep back the tears. She tried to speak again, failed.

"It's all right, Doris. I think it's over now. Don't worry. I'm going to leave her alone."

Mendenhall trailed him into the private office, closed the door. "One of the finest demonstrations of tactical airpower I've ever seen," the two-star general said. "And with 17s, a strategic bomber. An *obsolete* strategic bomber. Christ, that Harry Logan's a genius. A *bloody* genius."

The Man With the Shades decided not to comment on the irony of Mendenhall's choice of words. He took out his key ring, unlocked the steel door to the walk-in vault for top secret materials.

"I knew Logan, you know," the general continued. "Knew Steele too. Maximum Effort Steele, tough bastard. Say, how did you guys stumble on this Clean Slate operation?"

"Hacksaw Two. Steele called it Hacksaw Two. Clean Slate was our name for it, and we didn't stumble on it at all. Steele and his conglomerate have been under surveillance for almost three years, Sandy. Rumors about selling advanced weapons to foreign powers. We've had his place wired for a long time."

It wasn't necessary to explain that Steele's security expert was getting $2,000 a month to help the Agency. That was none of Mendenhall's business. The Man With the Shades reached into the vault, pulled out a wheeled dolly containing four large destruct boxes equipped with incineration devices. He unlocked one, dropped in the videotape and relocked it as Mendenhall rambled on about the professional execution of the raid. "Whatever you say, you've got to admit that it was one hell of an operation," he concluded.

The Man with the Shades leaned over, released the safety latches on each container and threw the bright yellow switches. Every document, every photo and tape relating to the affair was reduced to ashes in seconds. The smoke sifting from the edges of the lid was all that was left.

"What operation?" he asked, then looked out the window and frowned in surprise.

Snow was falling.

Shortly after Mendenhall left, Doris Kraft brought in the message from Bangkok that Thai police had seized the movie people and the C-130 at Na Krang. "Cable Satchmo to ask the Thais to let them go," he instructed. "He should be able to fix that. And we'd better bring MacBride here for a while to cool down. He's been in Thailand too long anyway."

It was going to be messy.

MacBride was going to be very difficult, righteous and moralistic. The Man With the Shades sighed, turned to stare at the snow.

49

NINE MINUTES after the bombers crossed back into Thai airspace the Red Chinese radar operators pointed out that they were flying southeast *away* from the borders of the People's Republic and the MIGs were ordered to return to their field. The 17s bored through the skies at a comfortable 6,000 feet, low enough so that the crews would not need oxygen.

Alison Gordon made her way forward, ascended the steps to the cockpit. "Everything okay, Harry?"

"Just fine. Jonesy tells me you did a fine job with the .50, proud of you—"

"I don't think I want to do that again."

"Well, you won't have to. You're going to be the wife of a rich and proper member of the comm-u-ni-teee. $250,000 rich. We'll build up the flying school, make it a real solid business. No problems now."

She saw the clouded expression Clarkson wore. "Something wrong, Charlie?"

He pointed at the missile protruding from the wing.

"Don't let it spook you, hon. We're cruising home at a nice conservative 200 mph, and I can promise you a most delicate landing."

"Is that thing still *live*, Harry?"

He shrugged.

"Is it?"

"Hard to tell. Never know about those damn fuses. Probably a dud. Right, Charlie?"

"I don't know. Do you?"

She looked at it, recognized the 66-millimeter rocket as part of the M72 antitank system. The fin-stabilized rocket carried an M18 high explosive warhead and a sensitive M412 impact detonating fuse. "That thing could blow the wing right off, couldn't it, Harry?"

"Only if I screw up, and I won't. We'll radio ahead to have the fire truck ready, just as a precaution. You know the exits, don't you?"

"What are you talking about?"

"We may all have to roll out of this bird kind of fast once we kiss the runway. Tell the boys back there to prepare for a swift getaway."

She started for the steps, stopped. "Harry, you wouldn't do anything stupid like get yourself killed, would you? Not now?"

"And miss the wedding? Hell, no. Simple gold bands. Scout's honor."

She passed the word to the rest of the crew in the rear, and Logan alerted the navigator and radio operator to move back there—away from the rocket.

"Why don't you join them, Charlie?" he suggested casually as he saw the field on the horizon.

"That a suggestion or an order?"

"Does it matter?"

"No, I'm staying, Harry. Copilot's place is up beside the pilot. I'm not moving."

Logan adjusted the pitch on the right outboard engine. "For a teacher, Charlie, you never were too bright. Big on loyalty though, not to mention neatness."

Clarkson rechecked half a dozen gauges swiftly. "Are there points for neatness?" he asked.

"Points for everything . . ." Logan radioed the base to have the fire truck stand by, then instructed the other B-17s to stay back at least two miles behind Dirty Dora when she landed. If there was a wreck, they could avoid ramming into it in a devastating multiplane pileup. He guided his bomber down to one hundred feet, saw the runway below and started to ease it down to land.

Until he noticed two things: the nose of the C-130 poking out of Hangar Three; a Thai police car and an official looking truck. A moment later he also spotted the marksmen on the mess hall roof.

"Abort, abort, wheels up!" he called into his throat mike.

Dirty Dora was down to twenty feet. He poured on full power, fought the mushy controls to lift the plane from the danger. Clarkson added his muscle too, and the old bomber wallowed for several terrifying seconds.

The nose hesitated, fell.

They were going to crash.

"Plan B, plan B," Logan called out to the other planes.

It was a miracle. The sturdy Boeing shuddered, veered and picked up speed. The nose came up, and Harry Logan started to smile. "Up, baby, up . . . good girl, that's it, *up* . . ."

And then the miracle failed. The police opened fire from half a dozen positions, pouring bullets at the cockpit. A score of slugs shattered the glass, pierced the 24ST Alclad skin in many places. Logan and Clarkson struggled, finally saw the airspeed build. Straining, they managed to lift the 17 just over a large storage shed and up away from the police guns.

"Airspeed 140, manifold pressure 35," Clarkson said.

Logan didn't bother to answer, concentrating on climbing out of range. The shock of the ambush showed in his face. It was a look of pained outrage, one Clarkson hadn't witnessed before. The copilot waited until the altimeter showed 1,500 feet before he spoke.

"You did it again, Harry, but what was that all about?"

"Police. We must have made a mistake, or else that Boti sold us. Alison warned me about him but I wouldn't listen—"

"Don't blame yourself. You saved us, Harry . . . we'd all be arrested or dead in a wrecked plane if you hadn't seen them."

Logan would not be reassured. At 3,000 feet he told Clarkson to take over and instructed the navigator to set a course for *Bolivar*. It was only then that they remembered the explosive warhead in the rocket, still projecting from the wing.

"We're lucky those bullets didn't set it off," Alison's voice crackled over the intercom.

Even over this scratchy circuit, it was a lovely voice to him.

"This is my lucky plane," he answered. "Nothing's going to hurt Dora. She'll be at our wedding."

Clarkson pointed at the gasoline gauges.

"If our fuel holds out," Logan added. "Slow down a bit, Charlie, and look out for the potholes."

"You say those were Thai cops?" she asked.

"With bad tempers. Guess I should have paid those speeding tickets, hon."

His strained humor annoyed her.

"Be serious. If those cops shot at us, there may be Thai interceptors after us at any moment."

He ordered the 17s into a tight formation, one that would provide interlocking walls of fire if fighters struck. Every crewman on every Fort scanned the sky intently, waiting for the supersonic jets to attack. Thailand had good pilots and modern U.S. interceptors. The threat was real, acute. Logan faced it on the radio forty minutes south of Na Krang.

"This is Blue Leader. Blue Leader to Blue Flight. We may have bandits real soon. Probably isn't safe to fly Dora at more than 180 or 200, and it surely isn't safe for you guys to hang back here with us. Go on ahead at max speed and we'll catch you later."

"Blue One to Blue Leader. No way," Baranovitch said.

"This is Blue Two," Van Bokkelen reported. "We're hanging in with you, kid."

The other aircraft commanders rejected his proposal with equal vigor. They'd all decided to make it to *Bolivar* together, or not at all. Logan argued, threatened, ordered, insulted. Van Bokkelen answered with an obscene joke.

Baranovitch told Logan to stop bothering him because he was already in plenty of discomfort. "One of those people back there creased my arm—my *pinball* arm . . . so I'm in no mood for your noble hero act, Harry. Shut up and get us to *Bolivar,* will you?"

"He's a decent guy," Logan said softly.

"They love you, Harry. Can't you understand?"

"With me it's ladies, Charlie—especially lady detectives. Wake me when the fighters come."

Alison Gordon came forward with a thermos of coffee twenty minutes later, saw him dozing and shared some of the hot brew with the copilot. "You'd better stand by your gun until we're off the coast," Clarkson advised her, and she returned to her .50 to watch for the jets.

The minutes ticked away at half speed, or so it seemed to the tense crews.

"Bandits—three o'clock," Ashley sung out.

Two F-4s, coming at nine hundred miles an hour.

"Blue water ahead," Clarkson reported.

It would be a close race. The Thai fighters could not attack once the bombers were far enough out at sea. How far was far enough? Each country was setting its own limits on territorial waters these days, anywhere from twelve to two hundred miles. Clarkson jostled Logan awake, pointed at the jets.

"I warned you folks," Logan said. "You had to do your Four Musketeers number."

But the fighters did not open fire. They flew closer to inspect the exotic old bombers, and the Thai pilots gestured amiably before zooming off toward the capital. The Forts were merely curiosities to the young fighter pilots, who would speak about the antique craft at dinner that night. By then the Boeing crews would all be safely away. The 17s crossed the coast. . . .

"Ninety miles. Time to alert *Bolivar*," Logan announced. After he radioed that Blue Leader and four friends would arrive in twenty-five minutes, he smiled wearily at the copilot. It was almost over.

"Alison has some more coffee," Clarkson suggested.

"Good, I'd like to see her."

She brought the thermos, filled the cap-cup and handed it to him. Logan sipped, joked about the wind whistling through the bullet holes. She told him about the damage other planes had taken during the assault on Dead Moon Valley, gashes she'd seen from her waist gun position, while he stared straight ahead.

"That's the leader's job. I should have checked on damage. See, I'm only almost perfect. I'm no saint."

"I couldn't marry a saint, Harry."

"Right. Simple gold bands. I remember."

Something was wrong. She stepped forward, slipped and looked down. She saw two spent machine gun cartridges, and a pool of blood.

"Harry!"

"Take it easy."

"Charlie, he's hit. Look at the blood—"

Logan shook his head. "Stay where you are, Charlie. It's your job to fly the bird when the pilot can't—and he can't. How long to *Bolivar?*"

"Maybe eleven or twelve minutes. We've got a tail wind. Why didn't you say something? What the hell's the matter with you?"

"Harry! Harry!" She couldn't accept it.

"Don't sweat, it isn't catching. Good coffee, hon, you'll make a great wife . . ."

"Jonesy," Clarkson called over the intercom, "bring up the medic box and get us a tourniquet."

Logan sipped more of the dark bitter drink, thought what a dumb way to go . . . shot by the wrong people for the wrong reason . . .

He forced himself to speak. "Damn lucky that thing in the wing didn't kill us back in the valley. Got to hand it to them. Those Chinese fought well. Tell that to Vandal."

"That bastard, if he hadn't—"

"We'd never have met, hon. Don't blame him. He gave me my last chance, and I was happy to take it . . . Charlie, tell them to suit up . . ."

Clarkson radioed the orders for all crews to put on their parachutes, looked down and saw *Bolivar.* The freighter of that name was registered in Panama. Atlas owned the seven-thousand-ton vessel via a Luxembourg holding company. Plan B was for the fliers to chute down, be picked up by *Bolivar* and carried to an East African port.

Jones arrived, opened Logan's flying suit and saw the ugly pair of wounds. He shook his head.

You don't have to tell me, Logan thought. I'm half dead already, lost most of the feeling in my lower body, can't move my legs . . . Hey, been a pleasure to know you, Jonesy . . .

"That was one hell of a raid we pulled," Jones said, and went back for his chute, trying not to admit the truth to himself.

"There's a doctor down on that ship, plasma and equipment . . . for God's sake . . . and mine . . . please . . . you're not dead yet," she pleaded, convincing herself for the moment.

I will be damn soon. How to tell her I always wanted to die in a 17, this was my only shot at it, that it's right . . . all right . . .

She began to cry. No, dammit, she wouldn't allow it to happen, he was the right man, she was the woman for him . . .

"Help her with her chute, Charlie. Tell them all it's jump time. Set autopilots for attack V formation, course straight out to sea."

The thermos cap fell from Logan's hand as Clarkson radioed the orders, and as Logan made certain that her parachute was properly attached she shivered—for just a moment. It was impossible to know how badly Logan was hurt, but she told herself that the medical team on the freighter was highly skilled and well equipped to handle battle wounds. She looked out the window, saw the crew of "Raunchy Rita" abandon their aircraft.

"Everybody out," Logan ordered in a voice that sounded almost angry. Now the crew of "Dirty Dora" began to jump, with Clarkson counting carefully to make sure no one was left behind.

"They're all gone, Harry," he reported.

"You two go ahead, I'll be right along. I'll set her on autopilot to take her out of the area and be down in a minute . . ."

"Harry—" she began.

"See you in the ditch . . . now get the hell out of here . . ."

Clarkson opened the hatch, and she tried to get ready to jump. Something made her turn to Logan again.

"Harry—"

"I love you, hon."

She started toward him.

"Now, Charlie," he said, and Clarkson pushed her out. The shock of the chute opening jarred her, and she looked up to see Clarkson leaping from the plane. The sky was filled with parachutes, and moving away from them the bombers flying out to sea in perfect formation. Harry Logan was up there setting the controls of the lead B-17, the way he'd said. He'd jump in a minute. She stared up at "Dirty Dora," waiting for his parachute to blossom.

It didn't, and suddenly she was in the water. It was colder than she had anticipated. It took several moments to spring the release catches, swim free and spit out a mouthful of salty water. Where was Logan? She looked around, saw *The Bolivar* steaming toward her.

Logan . . . ? She looked up at the sky in time to catch one final glimpse of his B-17 before it disappeared into the clouds